Lincolnshire
COUNTY COUNCIL

Working for a better future

discover librar~~ies~~

This book should b~~e returned~~ ~~on or~~ before

~~the d~~~~ate~~

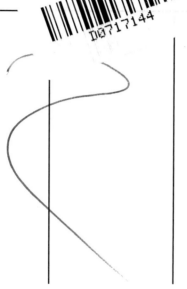

D0717144

ONLY A PAPER MOON

CRISTINA PISCO

First published 1998 by
Poolbeg Press Ltd,
123 Baldoyle Industrial Estate,
Dublin 13, Ireland

This edition published 1999

A catalogue record for this book is available from the British Library.

ISBN 1 85371 827 0

Cover design by Vivid
Set by Poolbeg Group Services Ltd in Garamond 10.75/14.5
Printed and bound in Great Britain by
Cox & Wyman Ltd, Reading, Berkshire.

About the Author

Cristina Pisco was born in Spain of a Spanish-Filipino mother and an Italian-American father. She was raised in seven different countries, speaking three languages. Her family eventually settled in Brussels where she married a Belgian, and built a career as a freelance journalist and television producer.

In 1992 she quit her job and moved to Ireland with her family. She is now separated and lives with her four daughters in a small village in West Cork.

Only a Paper Moon is her first novel. *Catch the Magpie,* her second novel, will be published shortly.

Acknowledgement

In the course of writing this book (usually when the end seemed nowhere in sight), I would sometimes sit back and think about the acknowledgement I would write when it was finished.

It is traditional to thank a vast quantity of people "without whom this book would not have seen the light of day". I toyed with ideas about whom I would thank and in what order. There were so many!

I would start by thanking my family. My parents for their unconditional love and support in a very difficult year. My sister, whose addiction to long-distance telephony is a great source of joy for both me and the phone companies of the world. My four daughters for putting up with a mother who locks herself away for hours on end and is the worst grouch to ever have crawled out of bed in the morning. And of course, Anne Crowley, for all her help.

I'd have to thank those wonderful people at Poolbeg, especially Kate Cruise O'Brien, my editor, who pulled me out of a short fiction workshop and forced me to write a novel, holding my hand most of the way.

I would have to put in a word about all those who helped with the research, especially the Irish Warplane Research Group, the staff of the Air Force Museum in Dayton Ohio, the B-17 Combat Crewmen and Wingmen Association, and of course the Travelling Community of Clonakilty, especially Bridget Williamson.

I'd also have to thank all those lovely people who shared their memories of the real landing of *T'Ain't a Bird* in Clonakilty back in 1943, especially Guy Tice, top-turret gunner. Guy was just 18 when he landed in Clon. He did not hesitate when I phoned him out of the blue, over fifty years later, and asked him to help me write a book. The days we spent together in Wisconsin were delightful. Guy Tice is one of the world's true gentlemen and I am proud to have become his friend.

Other friends, of course, deserved a mention. Martin Kelleher for always being there, Dave Edmund for reminding me to go into each of my mind's rooms every day, and Jenny Mac for the craic (yes, we will talk some day!). Elaine Walsh, for being the best friend-and-neighbour a blow-in in a small Irish village could ever want.

I would thank all those who repeatedly told me I could do it. Especially John Noonan who made me believe it.

Thinking about the acknowledgement always

gave me the hope that I would one day complete the task that Kate and I had set.

After a long winter's struggle, I finished the book on the morning of Thursday March 26th after an all-night writing session. I couldn't wait to phone Kate and tell her. Over the months she had become more than an editor. As they say in West Cork, I had all the time in the world for her. I was looking forward to spending the weekend with her and consuming "copious amounts of wine"!

Kate died that day at noon. I don't even want to try and write what that means to me. It's still too raw and I wouldn't want to presume to share the pain that her family must feel.

Merely thanking Kate does not reflect the profound effect that she had on the course of my life. An acknowledgement is much more fitting.

Kate Cruise O'Brien is the reason I wrote this novel, the reason I'm being published, the reason I am finally an author. Had she passed away a few months before, there would have been no book.

I could not have done it without her.

April 23, 1998, West Cork.

To my daughters,
Chloe, Amelia, Sasha and Francesca,
with all my love

ONLY A
PAPER MOON

Chapter One

❖

Mary walked carefully down the stairs. Her left side was very sore. It made creeping silently down the creaking wood difficult. Every time she shifted her weight off her right leg a bolt of hot pain shot up and down from her hip.

She must have hit it hard on something. Maybe the wall? No. She distinctly remembered her shoulder slam against the wall, the delph rattling in the press as she slid onto the floor. She touched her shoulder gingerly. It was stiff and bruised, but nothing was broken. Gerald always left her badly bruised but he'd never broken bones. Maybe she'd banged her hip as she landed.

On the landing she stopped to listen. She could hear someone moving around in the kitchen. Gerald had stormed out into the night, leaving her lying on the cold stone floor thankful that this time the pull of the pub was stronger than both his anger and his desires. He probably hadn't come home, but she couldn't be sure.

God knows where he went. He had always disappeared for days on end, coming and going with no warning, but furious if the dinner wasn't ready when he arrived. He was always away "on business", whatever that might be.

As the country settled into the Emergency he was gone more often and for longer periods, which suited her just fine. She suspected that he was involved in shadier deals than just a little off-track betting. She kept her mouth shut but she was no fool. She thought he must be involved in smuggling of some sort. Sure why else would he come home, his pockets bulging with notes, his case filled with things that you could no longer get for love or money, like tea and baccy?

He would tap his nose and say he got lucky. She hated that more than the nights when he came home dishevelled and dirty as if he had been sleeping outside in his clothes for days. When he got lucky he wanted to take her. When his luck was down he just wanted to beat her. And sometimes, for no apparent reason, he wanted both.

Mary strained to hear over the barking greyhounds outside. She was late this morning and they were howling for their breakfast. Sweet Jesus, she'd have to get on with baking the brown cakes right away. No time for a cup of tea to warm her. The hall was drafty and Mary shivered as she braced herself to walk down the last steps. Please God, let it be Imelda and not Gerald.

She silently opened the kitchen door and peered in. The warmth of the room came at her through the crack, carrying with it a smell of broth and baking. Mary smiled as she caught sight of Imelda's slight frame at the fire. The girl was carefully stirring a large pot hung over the fire, humming softly under her breath.

"You've made an early start to the day, Imelda Tanner," said Mary as she walked into the kitchen. The happy crackle of the fire and Imelda's bright smile lifted her spirits. She stood up straighter, the pain in her hip more bearable. She would have both help and company today.

"'Twas so cold I couldn't sleep, so I came in and started the fire early," said Imelda.

"You've started more than just the fire by the looks of it." Mary eased herself onto a chair at the big kitchen table. "Have you seen himself this morning?"

"No. Thanks be to God," answered Imelda, stifling

3

a giggle. "But Tommy's here. He's cleaning out the kennels. I've cooked up the bones and made the brown cakes for the dogs. We'll feed them their breakfast."

Mary started to rise and stopped as pain shot out from her left side. She tried to hide it with a smile, but she saw Imelda's bright blue eyes flash and then soften.

"Don't move. You just sit there. Everything is looked after," she said, laying her little hand on Mary's shoulder. "You've no tea left. Have a nice hot cup of broth. Just sit a while and have a cup of broth and a nice slice of bread."

Imelda busied herself at the fire. Mary was glad that her back was turned so she wouldn't see the tears brimming up in her eyes. She was becoming very fond of the girl and the girl was clearly fond of her. That little hand on her shoulder and soft words were more difficult to bear without crying than the beatings Gerald gave her.

In the first years of her marriage she had swung blindly from hope to despair, settling finally on hatred as the only way to face the new day. Joy, too, had made a brief appearance in her life. But when her darling boy had died, hate and joy went to the grave with him. She had become a dry desert, all feelings locked deep inside. This scrawny girl with the bright smile touched her in a way she hadn't felt for a long, long time.

"There you go," said Imelda sweetly as she placed a mug of steaming broth on the table. "Drink it before it gets cold."

Mary nodded her thanks and raised the mug to her lips. It smelled rich and inviting. She took a careful sip and smiled with her eyes over the rim of the mug as Imelda set a small plate with two slices of fresh brown bread in front of her.

"That's the last of the flour as well," said Imelda. "You'll be going into town this morning?"

"Yes. And I'm taking you with me," said Mary.

"Me?" asked Imelda, visibly surprised.

"Yes, you. You can help with the messages," answered Mary with a laugh. "As soon as we've finished with the hounds, I'll tell Tommy to get the pony and cart ready and we can all go in. And by the way – when you've finished here, look into the tea chest in the hall. In the bottom you'll find a blue blanket. I want you to have it."

She didn't wait for Imelda to protest but got up, and taking the mug and a slice of bread walked purposefully out into the courtyard leaving Imelda nervously wiping her hands on a tea towel.

As she crossed the yard she caught sight of Tommy Tanner's wiry frame inside the greyhound enclosure. He was almost two years older than his sister but he was even shorter, which caused him no end of embarrassment. His dark blonde hair was dirty and tousled and he wore a strange collection of torn and tattered clothing, all of it either too big or too small. It was a mystery to Mary how Imelda managed to keep herself looking so clean and tidy.

It was a brilliantly sunny day in late March. One of those days when West Cork decides to forget the season and pretends it is summer for a few glorious hours. Mary walked through the little flower garden her mother had planted and which she tended in her memory. She passed under the arbour of gnarled wisteria vines and walked up the hill, ignoring the pain in her hip. Yes, thought Mary, she really was getting very fond of the girl. She didn't know what had prompted her to take Imelda to town, but she felt good about it.

Mary knew very little about Imelda, apart from the fact that she was a Traveller and that she was spending most of the winter in Clonakilty before moving on again in the spring. Mary had grown up with Travellers around. As a child she was always delighted by their gaily painted pony-carts and wagons. The men mended all manner of tin and iron things and the women would come round begging or selling pins and needles at her door. She'd passed their tents and caravans on the side of the road, and never really thought twice about who might be living in them. They were as much a part of the landscape as the estuary that surrounded her.

Tommy had been in charge of the hounds over the winter, exchanging his labour for grazing for his pony and the odd pennies that Gerald threw his way. Though he never lost an opportunity to clown around he was diligent with the hounds. He walked them in rain or shine, rubbed them down with poitín, and carefully measured out each one's feed according to their training programme. He was quicker than Gerald himself to spot if a hound was doing poorly or had an injury. Try as he might, Gerald had never had occasion to criticise him. Imelda had started coming up to the house with her brother, from time to time. Shy at first, she was always eager to lend a hand in exchange for whatever Mary could give her. Mary felt a pang of guilt as she remembered how, at first, she had watched Imelda like a hawk, sure that she might steal something if her back was turned. The pair had brought laughter back into her home. The trip to town was an acknowledgement. What Gerald would think of it she didn't dare consider.

Mary reached the top of the hill and sat herself

down at the foot of an old Celtic cross. The cross itself lay on the grass as it had probably lain for hundreds of years. As a child she would often sit up here and wonder about who might have put the cross on the top of the hill. Whoever it was had a sense of setting. From where she sat, Mary could see all of Inchydoney Island, the sea, the estuary, and the green rolling hills stretching far away until they met the mountains many miles inland.

Facing her was Virgin Mary's Bank, jutting out to sea. Beyond was the vast expanse of the Atlantic. The sea was as still and silver as a mirror this morning and Mary had to shade her eyes as she looked out to the horizon where a long ridge of puffy white clouds hung like a mountain range in the sky.

Behind her, the green hill she had just climbed sloped gently below her, tucking the farmhouse and outbuildings into its curve, while to her left rose the sand dunes guarding the channel into the estuary. If she turned her back on the sea she would see the two causeways linking the island to the mainland, both built during the Famine. "Dying hands built those walls," her grandmother used to say as they drove into town. And she would cross herself and say a prayer for their poor souls. Over the hundred years or so since the causeways had been built, the trapped water had drained out and a marsh had been created between them, a slice of land that claimed the Island from the sea. Since childhood, Mary had always been delighted when the sea claimed the Island back, flooding the causeways and cutting it off from the mainland again, if only for a few hours.

Two miles beyond, you could just about make out the grey quays of Clonakilty. The tide was out and Mary spent a few minutes eating her breakfast and watching the flocks of birds feeding on the sandbanks. It would have been easy to sit there and forget, if only for an instant, that the last twelve years had happened.

Instead she rose and walked a few yards to her left where a fucshia grew. It was still small but sturdy. This year it would be in full bloom for the first time. In the summer its leaves would almost hide the small gravestone but today it was clearly visible, the short inscription easy to read even at a distance: *Gerald Séan Burke – 1938-1941*. Mary knelt beside the grave and said a short prayer. Though she knew his little soul had needed no assistance to go straight to heaven, it was a comfort to say the words. Her prayer finished, Mary rose, and softly touched the cold stone.

When she came back into the kitchen, Mary found

Tommy and Imelda leaning over the kitchen table, a newspaper spread out in front of them.

"Who bought the paper?" asked Mary, surprised at the extravagance.

"'Tis a week old, missus," said Tommy. "I found it and brought it home to Meldy. Can't read much myself, but you know she'll read anything she can get her hands on."

Imelda was oblivious to her brother's chatter as she eagerly scanned the page.

"Look, missus. Now wouldn't that be a fine suit for yerself?" Tommy asked, pointing to an advertisement. "And only 9/6d this week from Roches stores. In green only, but sure wouldn't that go well with yer eyes?"

"Cheeky brat," said Imelda, snatching the paper back. "What are you going on about?"

"You'd look like a duchess, missus," continued Tommy undeterred.

"And where would I be going looking like a duchess, Tommy Tanner? I've a right mind to knock some sense into your head, but I'll get you to rig up the cart instead." Mary gave him an imaginary whack over the head.

Tommy shrank back in an exaggerated posture of fear. "No missus – don't bate me. I'm not worth the effort."

"Go away with ya, ya eejit, and do as you're told," said Imelda.

"Yes, sir!" answered Tommy snapping smartly to attention. "On the double!"

"A clatter is what he'd be wanting," said Imelda, catching Mary's suppressed laughter as she watched Tommy march himself out of the house.

"Ah, the charm will get him off many a clatter," said Mary smiling.

"He's not a bad lad," said Imelda. "Cheeky, but not a bad lad. And he's right," she added turning back to the paper. "You would look well in the suit. I looked into Roches store in Cork once. 'Twas full of fine things. I couldn't believe it. To see so many fine things, and all the fine people shopping. I wish I could see the big stores in Dublin. And the tramway, and the cinema. I've never been to the cinema."

"And neither have I, Imelda Tanner. But for today we'll both have to be content with Rossa Street in Clonakilty."

It took another hour to get the morning chores done but then they were settled in the cart and on their way to town. Tommy stood holding the reins high as the pony trotted smartly down the curving road that hugged the contours of the island. Mary and Imelda sat on the back, each one to a side, Mary in her good black coat and Meldy wrapped in the bright blue blanket she had pinned across her breast.

As they turned onto the causeway, a flock of lapwings rose in a cloud from the marsh. Imelda pointed excitedly as Tommy waved his hat. They watched mesmerised as the flock of birds swooped through the air in one graceful arc, flashing black then silver as they all turned in perfect unison.

"How do they do that?" wondered Imelda out loud.

"They all went to pilot school, don't ya know?" answered Tommy. "They'll be flying formation soon," he added importantly.

"Must be British birds then," said Imelda with a smirk. "Sure, no Irish bird ever went to pilot school."

"I'll have you know that we have a fine air corps that you should be proud of, Imelda Tanner," said Tommy. "Seeing as I, your one and only brother, am going to be their best gunner."

"And why should they take you?" retorted Imelda. "Even on the odd chance that they might have one rickety old plane to fly?"

"And why shouldn't they take me? As fine a figure of a man as ever offered his life for his country," said Tommy, puffing out his chest. "You can't be too tall to be a gunner. You wouldn't fit in the turret."

"Ah, you'd fit all right. But they'd just as soon take

Sister Ailish in her habit before a tinker with his trousers held up with a bit of ould rope."

Mary sat back, enjoying the jaunty pace of the cart, and let herself get caught up in the merriment as Imelda and Tommy took turns describing the Flying Nun. She was having such a good time that they had almost reached the end of the causeway before she remembered to say a silent prayer for the wretched souls whose dying hands had allowed them to cross so merrily.

Tom slowed the pony to a walk as they came into town. It was market day and the streets were jammed with traps and carts of all shapes and sizes. Since all cars had been taken off the roads, except for those belonging to doctors and priests, the town had reverted to an earlier age when the horse and bicycle still ruled.

Tommy pulled up at the wheel pump and dropped Mary and Imelda off, arranging to wait for them at the back of the church. Mary could not help but notice the disapproving glances as she jumped off the cart.

Two biddies draped in black stared intently as she passed, and Mary overheard one say to the other, "Well, I'd never had believed it if I hadn't seen it with my own eyes. Mary Burke riding into town on a tinker's cart, proud as a peacock."

"Come along, Imelda," said Mary, holding her head high. "We've better things to do than stand around gossiping."

Imelda looked frightened but followed along behind her. "I should have stayed home," she whispered. "Those old crows will get you into trouble."

"Nonsense," said Mary as she strode purposefully into the first shop, but she thought to herself that the girl was probably right.

Going from one shop to the next, Mary arranged for their monthly ration of turf which Tommy would pick up, haggled for an extra ration of flour, exchanged some fresh eggs for bones at the butcher's, and bought the few items they needed at home: soda, sugar, salt, and the tiny ration of tea which was allotted per household. In each shop she carefully counted out the coupons and money, tucking her card and change back into the pocket of her coat.

Many nodded to her as she passed, with Imelda walking behind her carrying the basket full of small parcels, but no one stopped to chat. Mary could not help but notice that Imelda seemed to draw more into herself the further they went along. She hardly recognised the girl. Her usual bright smile was replaced with the sullen stare of those who are used to being rejected. Mary's heart went out to her and, on impulse, she decided then and there that it was time they both had some refreshment.

Imelda followed Mary dutifully up the street. She hesitated a moment when Mary walked into O'Donovan's Hotel. She'd never been inside the building, but she couldn't resist the chance to have a good look. As she stepped into the main hall she saw Mary disappear through a door marked *Tea Room*. She caught up with her just as Mary sat down at a small table in the corner of the room.

"Well, don't just stand there gawking, girleen. Sit yerself down." Mary took the basket from Imelda's arms and put it on the floor behind her chair.

"Oh, Mary. 'Tis so lovely here." Imelda's eyes widened as she surveyed the pretty tablecloth and sparkling cutlery.

"We'll have tea. And cakes if you have them," Mary said to the waitress who was openly staring at Imelda.

"Hello there," said Imelda, smiling at the waitress. "Remember me?"

"I knew 'twas you!" The waitress grinned. "Imelda Tanner! Fancy that. How're ya keeping?"

"Well, and yerself?" replied Imelda. Both girls giggled and turned to Mary who was looking confused.

"Mary Burke, I'd like you to meet Ruth Bennett,"

said Imelda grandly. "Ruth Bennett, meet Mary Burke."

"We used to play together when we were small," added Ruth. "Imelda's family camped on our land every summer. Where are you staying now?"

"I live with my brother and sisters down by the marsh. Da and Ma both passed away a few years back so we went to live near our aunties and uncles."

"That's terrible. I'm sorry for your troubles. I wondered why you never came back. Still, great to see you again, Imelda Tanner. Fancy that! Tea and cakes it is then!" Ruth was still giggling as she went off to the kitchen.

Mary sat silently watching Imelda who glowed with pleasure. In the last few moments she had learnt more about Imelda's life than in the past few months. It had just never occurred to her to ask.

"Your parents died?" she asked softly.

"Yes," answered Imelda simply. "Two and a half years ago. 'Twas an accident. What could you do? But we're grand now. We have our own barrel-top and the girls are coming along fine."

"A barrel-top? Is that a caravan?" asked Mary.

"That's right," said Imelda. "The ones with a roundy sort of horseshoe shape on top. Like a barrel. Ours is lovely, with fancy paintwork and all," she added proudly.

"I never knew my mother," said Mary, surprising herself. "She died when I was born."

"What about yer da?" asked Imelda.

"He was a weak man. Not bad. Just weak. I was raised by my grandmother. A fine strong woman. They've both passed on."

Ruth Bennett arrived with a pot of tea and a plate of sticky brown buns, cutting off their conversation. Mary sat back and sipped her tea, lost in thought, as the girls chattered happily.

She remembered her grandmother dishing out huge plates of spuds and bacon to the farm-hands who came in at dinner-time. The farm was hers and she always told Mary she must learn every bit about running it, for it would be hers one day. Many a night Mary had stayed up late by the fire, quiet as a mouse, watching her grandmother write down the day's accounts and the next day's chores in her black-bound notebook. Though she was only twenty when her grandmother died peacefully in her sleep, Mary felt ready to step into her shoes.

Her father had other plans. He said it was time they took a break. A bit of fun for her before she got married and settled down.

"How are you ever going to get a rich handsome husband if you're always stuck under a cow or a bale of hay?" he teased. And Mary was only too pleased to go along with the game.

He took her on a whirlwind tour of shops and race meetings, once even to Dublin to stay in a fine hotel. She often questioned him about the expense, but he'd laugh and say the Granny had squirrelled away so much by pinching and saving that they had more than enough. Weren't they entitled to a bit of happiness and luxury? He made it sound like a lark. A holiday they deserved before getting back to the business of running the farm.

It ended soon enough. One night she found her father crying alone in the kitchen. The fire had gone out and an empty bottle of whiskey lay on the table. He admitted that he was deep in debt. That was when he first mentioned Gerald Burke.

Mary had met Gerald Burke once at a greyhound race her father had taken her to in Cork. He said he came from Galway and was some kind of businessman. Mary was impressed by his fancy clothes and city manner. He treated Mary and her father like royalty, insisted on paying for drinks and a meal and drove them back to their hotel in his fine car.

On that bleak night in the cold kitchen, her father had broken down and said that he owed more than he could ever pay back. He owed money to bookies in Dublin and Cork, he owed money to shops and banks. Most of all, he owed Gerald Burke. The only thing he had left was the farm.

Gerald had agreed to strike a deal. A stroke of luck, said her father, brightly. Gerald Burke would clear all debts and take over the deeds of the farm in return. Mary was in shock. Too shocked to point out that the farm was not her father's to give.

"But where will we go?" was all she could manage to say.

And that was when her father explained the rest of the deal. He didn't put it like that. He said she needn't accept. He made it sound as if Gerald Burke was just another potential suitor who had asked for her hand.

Mary's head was reeling. She'd only met him once! She tried to remember what he looked like.

She didn't even notice when her father placed a large parcel on the table wrapped in layers of tissue paper.

"It's for you," he said. "A dress. A fine dress. From Gerald."

Silently Mary took the parcel up to her room. It *was* a fine dress, though too big around the waist. She couldn't sleep and so spent half the night altering it to fit. As she sewed, she thought about what her father had said. Stitch by stitch, she saw her future unfold and with every stitch she saw that this was indeed a stroke of luck. Gerald was a saviour who would come and woo her, pay off the debts and together they would make the farm prosper. He would be gentle and loving and she would learn to love him in return. They would have a lovely family, three boys and three girls. She could see them going to Sunday Mass in town, all sparkling and clean, occupying a whole pew between their proud Ma and Da.

Gerald arrived the next morning in his fine car. Mary watched from her bedroom window as her father greeted him warmly. He was a big man. A shock of grey hair flicked his temples which framed a large face with a florid complexion.

Gerald Burke was older and larger than she remembered and she shivered at the thought of having to speak to him. She sat in her fine new dress waiting for them to call her down. After two hours she finally plucked up the courage to go downstairs and softly knock at the front-room door.

It was Gerald who opened the door. His face was red from the roaring fire in the hearth and the bottle of brandy Mary spied half-empty on the small table between the two fireside chairs.

"Here she is," he said, grabbing her around the

waist and pulling her into the room. "Here's the fine filly that I got in the bargain!"

Mary was mortified. She tried to catch her father's eye as she pulled away from Gerald's embrace. But he just looked away.

"Mary, are you all right? You haven't touched your bun. Eat it! They're beautiful!"

Mary looked up to see Imelda smiling at her. She waved the plate away. Something was wrong. She didn't know why, but she had to leave. She felt she had to leave *now*.

"Why don't you ask your friend Ruth to wrap them up? You can take them home. I've never been one for cakes really," she said apologetically. "I'll leave some money for you to pay with. I've a few more errands to run. I'll meet you at the church with Tommy."

Imelda nodded, her mouth full of bun. Mary left the tea room and stopped dead in her tracks. The door to the pub burst open and there, standing in the doorway, was Gerald. His leering smile showed that many a pint of porter had already been consumed.

"Well, looky here. There she is," he said. "Mary, my angel. My life. My trouble and strife," he added laughing. "Come in an have a drink with the old man.

It's been too long since I had my lovely wife by my side." He took her by the wrist and pulled her into the dark pub.

"Here you go lads. Meet the missus. A fine figure of a woman, is she not?" he announced grandly as he signalled to the barman for a pint and a glass.

It took a few seconds for Mary's eyes to get used to the dark, smoky pub. The men lining the bar shuffled uncomfortably at this female arrival into their male domain. Some took their caps off to her and she nodded in return.

"What's this I hear? You're cavorting with tinkers now?" he hissed in her ear. "Don't you know they'll steal you blind? Murder ya in yer bed as soon as give ya the time of day?"

The barman put the drinks in front of them. "Tell me what's a man to do when the wife won't behave?" Gerald asked loudly.

He took a long pull from his pint as he watched her standing primly at the bar. He put down the pint and smiled broadly. It was just like Gerald to change moods at the drop of a hat.

"You're looking well, woman," he said politely, as if they were a happy couple. As if he hadn't just embarrassed her in public. As if he hadn't shoved her against a wall the night before and left her lying on the floor. As if he cared.

"I'm going away for a few days on business," he said, reaching into his pocket and handing her some money. "This should do you until I return. Mind yerself, now."

Gerald took up his pint again and turned his back on her. She had been dismissed. Her glass stood untouched at the bar.

Without a word, Mary quickly walked out the side door and into the brilliant sunshine.

Chapter Two

•—•

Imelda sat at the foot of the monument in Astna Square. Ruth was finishing her shift and had suggested meeting Imelda there. Imelda looked up at the statue of the pikeman standing proudly in the sunshine. He was a fine-looking man, she thought. She blushed and quickly turned away in case anybody had seen her and guessed what she was thinking.

She was pleased that Ruthie had asked her to wait. Ruth had no qualms about being seen with her. Most of the settled children Imelda had known as a child pretended they didn't recognise her as they got older. She didn't blame them. Sure why should they risk getting a clatter for messing with the tinkers when they went home? They would do as their parents

25

bade them until they were old enough to have children of their own to pass down warnings and stories about the dirty tinkers. And so they started to look right through her as she passed. Sometimes one of them would give her a sorry little nod as if apologising. Imelda learned to ignore those and go her way. Back to her own kind.

Imelda had never lived in a house. None of her people ever had. They were Travellers, living a few days here and a few days there, camping on one site for a few weeks, sometimes even for a month or two, if there was work to do and the locals were friendly, but always moving on. She'd probably seen more houses than any settled person, as she went door to door with her mother as a child, but she couldn't imagine what living in one would be like. While her parents were still alive she'd lived in a tent. Now she lived with her brother and sisters in the barrel-top wagon that her uncle had made them.

The barrel-top they had was lovely and snug and hardly leaked at all. Still, sometimes she missed the big shelter tent. Her da had never skimped, like some. He always built it carefully, putting the big rigging-pole and bar in first and bending the hazel wattles around it. Her mother made big ticks out of flour bags and they filled them with fresh straw and laid them down as beds for the night. The straw was always dry and smelled sweet as she snuggled under her blanket in the dark. She missed the warmth of it. Most of all she missed her parents.

They'd gone off together one afternoon in the cart to pick up some straw. No one really knew what had happened. It seemed the pony had bolted. The cart overturned in the ditch. They said her Ma died instantly. Da died on the way to town. Life had never been the same again.

Travellers had come to the funeral from every county. After they were laid in the ground, Imelda had stood next to her uncle all night as he burnt all her parents' belongings. All she had left was her mother's ring that her father had made out of a two-shilling piece.

Imelda felt a shadow pass over her and realised the clouds were starting to roll in over the town. She looked up and saw Ruthie striding down Pearse Street. Ruth saw her and waved. Yes, she was pleased about Ruth, she thought, as she waved back. Ruth was different. And so now was Mary Burke.

She was a queer bird that one. She could be cold and distant and yet generous and kind. Mary was the most beautiful woman Imelda had ever seen. Her hair was the colour of a copper penny. And her eyes changed from grey to green depending on the weather, like the sea. Red hair was meant to be unlucky. She knew people who would turn back for home if they met a red-haired woman when setting out on a journey. But the bad luck Mary attracted seemed on to fall on herself alone. To Imelda she had been a godsend.

"I hope I wasn't too long," said Ruth, as she sat down next to her.

"Not at all," answered Imelda. "So now. How's the family?"

"Very well. My sister got married last year and is going to have her first. I'm going to be an auntie! Fancy that! Auntie Ruth. And yerself?"

"We're all well. Thank God." Imelda crossed herself.

"I can't stay long," said Ruth. "The Local Defence Force is meeting tonight and I'm to help serve the teas when they get back. My brother and my da are both in it. And so is Dennis."

"Who's Dennis?" asked Imelda, raising an eyebrow.

"He's this wonderful fella," said Ruth grinning. "Are ya seeing anybody?"

"Ruth! Don't be daft," said Imelda blushing.

"How old are ya now? Sixteen, like me. Come to think of it – you'll be married off soon – isn't that how your people do it?"

"I'll be fifteen this summer but I'll not be matched yet. Not if I have any say," said Imelda emphatically. "I've told my aunt there'll be no matchmaking until I've reared my baby sister."

"But you'll be ancient by then! Nobody'll want ya!"

"I'm not bothered," said Imelda.

"But what will ya do if they set up a match?" asked Ruth.

"I won't go," said Imelda, surprised at her own resolve. "If they tell me to fetch my shawl and go down to the church – I won't go. They can't make me. Anyway, who's ever going to want me and four extra mouths to feed?"

"Look. Here come the LDF now," said Ruth, pointing at three men in green uniforms walking down the middle of the street. "I'd best be going soon."

"Don't they look well? Is that the uniform, so?"

"That's right. The green are the LDF. My da's got one. He fought in the Great War. My brother and Dennis haven't got theirs yet. But they have badges to wear. And Dennis has a rifle," Ruth answered proudly.

"Do ya really think they could fight off the Germans?" asked Imelda as two more men in uniform came around the corner of Rossa Street on bicycles and pedalled towards the hotel.

"What would the Germans want with the likes of us?" laughed Ruthie.

"Well, I heard stories of the bombs in Dublin two years ago. They said the Germans made a mistake. The bombs were meant for Belfast but it gave me a fright. God forbid," said Imelda solemnly.

"That's true enough. And last month, when I was serving in the hotel bar," said Ruth, whispering in her ear, "I heard a garda sergeant tell someone that three German spies were caught in Baltimore."

"German spies in Baltimore?" repeated Imelda, her eyes wide.

"Three of 'em. Walked straight up the main street off the beach with their suitcases in their hands."

"Go away!" said Imelda, grinning.

"I swear on my mother's head," said Ruth laughing. "There were two Germans and one blackie!"

"There were not!" exclaimed Imelda.

"The blackie was wearing a turban," added Ruth with a hoot of laughter. "And the best bit, the best bit, is that they couldn't figure out how they got found out so easy, like. They didn't even get as far as the end of the street!"

"Oh Ruthie, stop!" said Imelda, holding her sides with laughter.

"God's truth. Ya see there was this off-duty garda sitting having a pint when someone looks out the window and says 'There's two foreign fellas and a blackie walking up from the strand'. And the garda says, 'Oh, that'll be German spies'. And he watched them while he finished his pint and then walked out and arrested them!"

"I've a stitch now. You always did make me laugh, girl!"

"'Tis the truth! Anyway who cares about bombs and spies?" said Ruth, getting up. "So what if there's a war, or an Emergency, or whatever they want to call it. What I'd like to know is when we'll see the likes of stockings and bath-soap again?"

Imelda waved Ruth goodbye and started walking back to the church yard. She looked down at the tops of her Wellington boots and thought of the straw she had carefully stuffed in the feet that very morning. Emergency or not, she had never owned the likes of stockings nor bath-soap.

Men were milling around the entrance of the hotel, surrounded by a gaggle of little boys openly admiring the green uniforms some of them wore. The uniforms' charm was not lost on the ladies of the town who smiled as they passed, receiving sharp salutes in return. The main topic of conversation was the weather. The fine day seemed to be blowing away fast, replaced by slate-grey menacingly pendulous clouds. At the first drop of rain, it was decided that the wisest course of action was to wait for the rest of the squad while taking shelter in the hotel.

Gerald Burke looked up as the boisterous group burst into the main bar.

"Will ye look at the likes of ye?" said one of the men in uniform. "Ye should ashamed of yerselves. Have ye nothing better to do than sit in the pub, while the brave men of the LDF are defending the Nation?"

"Watch what ya say there, boyo," answered a thin man who was nursing a small whiskey. He pointed to the blue armband he wore. "LSF. Local Security Force. Too good for the likes of ye. Ye run around playing soldiers. We do the real work around here."

"LSF? What do ya do?"

"Look-out post. Coastwatch duty on Galley Head," the man answered importantly. "Now that's what I call defending the nation."

"So who's watching now? Herself?"

"That she is," he answered, laughing "And I can tell ya nothing gets past those eyes of hers!"

"Ah, but ya see," retorted the first man, "when your missus reports that a column of submarines and flock of aeroplanes is heading straight for Clonakilty

Bay it's the Local Defence Force they'll be calling out. Who'll be defending who, then?"

"Whom. Who'll be defending *whom*? Is that how you boys defend the nation? By calling for a pint?" said Con O'Leary, to the general amusement of the patrons in the bar. Cornelius O'Leary was a regular at the hotel bar. After ten years working in England he had returned to Clonakilty where he pursued a happy life as a confirmed bachelor and local character.

"Is that how we'll stop them if they try and invade?" he continued, "Ply them with porter? Drink 'em to death? Never mind my bad back – maybe I will join up after all!"

Gerald had sat quietly through the laughter. He finished his pint and left the bar with a nod.

"Now there goes one who ya wouldn't see in that uniform. Wrong colour," said Tony the barman under his breath. "I've a cousin who knew him back in Galway. Seems a black shirt was more to his liking back then. You should have heard him earlier with his missus. A pure disgrace."

"I don't think the colour matters to the likes of him," answered Con O'Leary. "His favourite colour is the one that pays most."

"That it is," Tony agreed, shaking his head. "He'd sell his own mother to the highest bidder."

The darkness deepened as the weather outside

took a turn for the worse. The barman left his post to pull down the blinds before turning on the lights.

"How do ya like the new blackout blinds?" he asked. "'Twas a terrible chore putting those bits a paper up and taking them down. The blinds were dear. Same ones they use in government offices. But they look well, don't ya think?" The men at the bar all nodded their appreciation.

"It's a serious business all the same," said Con O'Leary solemnly. "Isn't that so, Dr Moloney?"

"Absolutely," agreed the doctor, his large frame remarkably balanced on the next bar stool. "The government is taking all this very seriously. Just last week I received a circular about not using the car for any personal business at all. All the doctors and vets in the county got one too, and I believe the parish priests did as well."

"Damn. There goes our spin up to the All Ireland," joked the doctor's companion.

"Still, it's a funny old thing, this Emergency business," added Tony the barman. "I've less quarrel with the Germans than the Brits, and no quarrel at all with the Yanks, but didn't it break your heart to hear about the bombs in London?"

"I've family in England, God bless them," said the man on coastwatch duty.

"Don't we all? Sure didn't Dan Murphy's two boys

go off just last week. There's good money to be had in Liverpool these days."

"And now that the Yanks are in, seems like the only Irishmen not in the fighting are the ones left in Ireland," said Con O'Leary, raising his glass.

"Does it really matter who wins?" concluded the doctor. "As long as they get it over with and leave us be to get on with it."

The rain was lashing down, creating a river down Pearse Street. It looked like some of the squad wouldn't make it in. The general consensus was that the weather must have held them up. It was therefore decided to suspend that evening's LDF exercises and the barman pulled another round.

Chapter Three

◆━◆

Mary sat in the kitchen and listened to the wind roaring outside. The downpour had started just as they reached the house and Tom and Imelda had quickly dropped her off and headed for home. She thought about them out there and, for the first time, wondered if they were all right.

It was raging up from the south-west. Every gust winged through the house, sending a shrill screeching whistle through the rafters and a howl down the chimney. The rain was bucketing down and the branches of a bush kept up a ghostly knocking as they slapped the windowpane. It sounded as if the house would be torn apart.

But Mary wasn't scared. Wrapped up in a rug by the fire, she was as safe and as close to content as she'd ever felt. Gerald wasn't coming home. She needn't worry about him for a few days. The dog at her feet was soundly asleep. He also seemed happy that Gerald was gone. When the master was in the house the dog slunk in the shadows, keeping close to the walls.

Mary had built up the turf fire so that she could start it up quickly in the morning. Imelda wouldn't be in, but Mary looked forward to doing the chores on her own. The fire burnt brightly. Mary forced herself to blot out the memory of the pub that afternoon and the night before. She sat and dozed, thinking of the day ahead when she needn't worry about what mood Gerald would be in . . .

She was walking along the strand. She could feel the wet sand between her toes. The sea pounded on her left. She turned from the frothing water to the grey cliffs and green hills beyond. The sun beat down but a warm breeze rustled through the folds of her dress. Mary smiled down at the small boy by her side. His sandy hair was streaked with gold and his freckled nose scrunched up as he smiled back up at her, flashing the gap in his front teeth. She reached out to pat his head, but he skipped off, kicking up the sand as he went. Mary stopped and watched him. She was confused. It wasn't Séan. This boy was older than

Séan. Five or six years older at least. But he was her boy. She was sure of that. Mary became aware of a strong soft hand holding her own. She looked down and saw her left hand entwined in a large male hand. It was deeply tanned with soft black hairs. It was a lovely hand, clean and uncalloused. She looked up to see the hand's owner but the sun was too bright. She tried shading her eyes. Still, she could not see him. But she knew that she loved him. She loved him and their child more than anything she had ever loved before. She watched the boy running up and down the surf. Mary had never felt such happiness. Even as the gale rose up from the west and swept the beach away, she could still feel the touch of that gentle hand . . .

She woke up refreshed. She had been on the beach. She remembered the sunshine and a feeling that her heart would burst with joy. The gale still raged outside, but she had slept soundly. Mary looked at the clock and was surprised to find it was past midnight. She lit a small candle and quenched the lamp before going upstairs.

Sitting on her bed she watched herself undress in the mirror on the big oak dressing-table. The reflection flickered with the flame of the candle. Her skin was so white it seemed to glow, and her hair caught the light as she unpinned it and let it uncoil over her shoulders. She turned modestly away as she pulled off her underclothes and slipped on her nightdress. The dream still held her and she watched herself smile as she picked up a brush and started brushing her hair. Humming to herself, she wondered what it all meant. Her grandmother had been a great believer in dreams. She'd always listened intently and asked for details, debating out loud about what each bit of the dream meant, until she came to a conclusion and decided if any action needed to be taken. Mary only half-believed in her grandmother's interpretations, but she enjoyed the telling.

A sharp slam in the back of the house snapped her out of her thoughts. Could she have forgotten to bolt the door? She put the brush down and listened hard. She could not hear very clearly above the gale, but she thought she heard a noise again. She went to the door of her bedroom and looked down. She thought she saw the dog below in the hallway. She'd best go down and lock him in the kitchen.

Sure enough the dog was creeping around at the bottom of the stairs. Mary thought it strange that she had to coax him to come to her. A shiver went down her spine as she walked into the dark kitchen to call him in. The stone floor was cold under her bare feet. The fire had died down to a deep red glow. She put her candle down on the table and went to get some more turf. An arm shot out of the shadows. It grabbed her around the waist.

"Gerald!" she gasped. "You scared the life out of me."

"Why? Where you expecting someone else?"

His clothes were drenched and the peak of his cap was dripping. He pulled her closer and Mary could feel her nightdress getting wet. The smell of drink coming off him was powerful. His eyes were hooded under the shadow of his cap. Mary desperately tried to see his eyes.

"No. No, of course not," she said, gently trying to push him away. She needed to see his eyes. They would tell her more than anything else what was in store.

"You're soaked to the bone. Come dry yourself."

It was like trying to push a wall. Gerald held her around the waist with one arm. Though he staggered slightly his grip was firm. He pulled her tightly up to him until she was lifted up on her toes, her arms pinned against the rough wet wool of his suit. His left hand slithered up the back of her nightdress to the nape of her neck. When he ran his fingers through her hair, Mary couldn't stop herself from shuddering in disgust.

"Where's my dinner, woman?" he whispered in her

ear as he stroked her hair. His breath was foul and hot.

"I haven't it ready, but I'll get it right now," pleaded Mary, still tottering on her toes. Gerald coiled his fingers around a thick tress and yanked her head back.

"Where's my dinner?" he said, his voice rising with every syllable. Mary was reeling. The pain in her head blinded her and the stench off him made her swoon.

"You weren't meant to be home," she whispered.

"I changed my mind," he said, letting go of her hair and gently cupping her chin, pulling her face up to his. "A man's got a right to change his mind, hasn't he? Hasn't he?" His fingers tightened on her jaw and he lifted her off her feet. Mary looked into his eyes. She was terrified at what she saw.

"Leave me be," she hissed.

"Why should I?" he said, dropping her roughly against the table. He took a bottle from his pocket and took a long pull. "You're mine to do with as I please."

"I'll never be yours," whispered Mary. She wished instantly that she hadn't said it.

His hand moved too fast for her to avoid. It cracked like a whip as he slapped her hard across the cheek, sending her tumbling to the floor.

"Yes, ya are. Even if ya are a hoor. Sure didn't I buy ya? That makes ya both a hoor and my property."

She lay on the cold stone catching her breath. He stood looking down at her as he took another long deliberate pull from the bottle. The flickering candlelight made him look larger than life. He was a hateful shadow looming above her. His cap had fallen off and dark tendrils streaked with grey stuck to his forehead. Clumsily, he took off his jacket and tried to hang it on a chair, never once taking his eyes off her. He missed the chair by at least a foot and let the jacket lie where it fell. She watched in horror as a smile played across his face.

She could not bear to look at him. She closed her eyes and wished the black slate would open up and swallow her.

"Please God, no," she thought silently. She could hear Gerald snapping off his braces and fumbling with his belt. He hadn't wanted her in months. She'd hoped he had tired of her. She could not stand the thought of him touching her.

"Get up, woman," he barked, prodding her with his boot. "Get up, I said!"

Mary did not move. The prods became sharp little kicks as she curled up into a ball on the floor. He reached down and grabbed her shoulder, yanking her back on her feet. Her nightdress ripped and she tried to hold the bits of fabric together.

"Ho, what have we here then?" he said, laughing at her modesty. "A right hoor who needs to be taught a lesson. Just like that other little hoor you've been cavorting with."

Mary's eyes flashed open. She hardly felt his rough hand as he squeezed her breast. Who did he mean?

"Sure aren't they all hoors, them type of women. They're different." Gerald pulled at her nightdress, scratching her thighs, but Mary didn't feel it.

"Who? Who's different?" she whimpered.

"The tinkers. You know yer one. That Imelda. I've seen her flaunting herself around the place. She's all grown up. Sure, don't they grow up faster than normal people? Oh yeah, I've seen her all right. She's asking for it."

"You leave her alone!" Mary pounced at him, pummelling him blindly.

He shoved her away but she came back scratching and tearing at his hair. He staggered backwards, surprised. Then he slapped her hard again. The blow sent her crashing against the wall.

"I'll give ya a lesson," said Gerald, his voice ugly as he pulled off his belt. "I'll give ya a lesson, ya hoor."

The blows were clumsy but hard and sharp when

they hit the mark. Mary faced the wall and started to pray. Her back and legs felt as if they were on fire and her head was throbbing. She closed her eyes and sank to the floor. The blows stopped.

"You're a poor excuse for a wife," he said, dropping the belt to the floor. She lay very still and listened to the howling of the gale, the soft crackle of the fire, the branch slapping at the window, the dog whimpering in the hall. She tried to concentrate only on the sounds. To blot out the pain. To blot out the dread. To blot out Gerald's weight as he fell on her and yanked up her nightdress. Her stomach turned as he pushed his hips up against her and buried his face in her neck. His bulk crushed her. She could hardly breathe. Mary closed her eyes tightly and prayed that it would be over quickly.

Chapter Four

━◆◆━

Beauregard St Soucis looked out the window and watched the coast disappear below the clouds. The big B-17 bomber rattled and roared all around him as the four engines thrust them off the African continent and into the skies. No wonder they called it a flying fortress, he thought. With its gun turrets, its heavily armed gun positions and huge bomb bay, it was literally a flying war-machine. And like the fortresses of old, it was pretty rudimentary inside. Two long benches in the big middle-waist compartment were the only comfort offered. The other compartments were cramped, and the commode was a white enamelled bucket in full view, right in the middle of the plane.

The crew had christened her *T'Aint a Bird*. He guessed it had something to do with *Superman* on the radio. Where did they get these names from? He'd seen planes called *Shoo Shoo Baby*, *Roger the Lodger* and *Impatient Virgin*. Then again he supposed they weren't any sillier than some of the names of his father's racehorses.

T'Ain't a Bird it was, and her crew was headed for England. That suited Beau just fine, as it was exactly where he wanted to go.

The last time Beau had visited was before the war when he had accompanied his father through England, Scotland and Ireland. It had been a pleasant trip, combining his father's business interests with his passion for thoroughbred racehorses. Beau remembered a succession of beautiful stud-farms, of dinners in men's clubs, and of pretty girls introduced to him by their mamas. That and the rain. It had rained the entire time they were there. He remembered the bleak damp cold which had made him yearn for the hot muggy climate back home in Louisiana.

From where he sat Beau could look all the way down the waist compartment and through the radio room. His view of the cockpit was obscured by the gunner's long gangly legs standing on a ledge just outside the radio room. The gunner's head and shoulders disappeared into the plexiglass bubble of the top turret. That guy literally has his head in the clouds, thought Beau to himself as he settled in as comfortably as he could. It was going to be a long flight. He heard a crackle of static above the general din as the pilot's voice came over the intercom:

"OK, men. We're now at cruising altitude. We'll stay under 10,000 feet. High enough in case we come across any German subs, but you don't need to use the oxygen masks. However, we'll still check in every twenty minutes. I can see McKnight here is alive and well."

"Speak for yourself," said a voice Beau assumed was the co-pilot's.

"Bombardier?"

"Yeah."

"Navigator?"

"Gotcha."

"Engineer Tate?"

"OK."

"Radio. Russell?"

"OK." The guy manning the radio grunted his presence as the pilot continued his check.

"Ball turret?"

Beau could see the diminutive ball-turret gunner curled up against a door in the radio room. He had fallen asleep immediately after take-off. From the look of the crew, they had all had a good time out the night before.

49

"Chief's asleep, Captain," answered Russell, the radio man, curtly.

"He's fine, Captain. Why don't we let him sleep it off? Had to carry him home last night," said a swarthy stocky guy, speaking into the intercom. He winked at Beau. "Chief's a Cherokee Indian. He was a school-teacher back in Oklahoma. Drink and the Chief don't mix too well. If you know what I mean."

Beau nodded.

"Russo? Is that you?" asked the pilot.

"You got it," answered the airman in his nasal New York accent. He extended his hand to Beau. "Matt Russo."

Beau took his hand. "Beau St Soucis." His soft Southern drawl was a contrast to Russo's accent.

"OK, let him sleep," said the pilot. *"Top turret?"*

"Pilot to top turret?" repeated the pilot. *"Wagner? You asleep too?"*

"No, sir. I'm here, sir," a voice mumbled.

"Well, that's reassuring. Thought we left you behind. Tail turret?"

"OK. Just starting a little friendly card-game here with our engineer 'Lucky Bastard' Tate. See if I can win back some of the money he took off me between Dakar and Marrakesh," said one of two guys sitting together on the bench. They were settting up a makeshift card-table.

"Hope springs eternal," chuckled the other as he

shuffled the deck. "You hope you can win it back and I hope you've still got money left."

"*OK,*" said the pilot over the intercom, "*I'll check back in twenty minutes.*"

The top-turret gunner's long legs stepped off the ledge and the young man bent his tall frame into the radio room. He went over into the waist compartment and sat down next to Matt Russo. He had pale blond hair with light blue eyes and a dusting of freckles across the bridge of his nose. He shook his head sheepishly as he sat down.

"Hey kid," Matt Russo yelled over the din of the plane. "You feeling a little rough?"

"I swear I'm never going near red wine again," said the gunner, looking miserable. He was very young, and had all the classic signs of a really bad hangover. Beau couldn't imagine a worse place to have one than in this throbbing tin can, with its rattling body, and its screaming engines.

"Why so glum? In less than twelve hours you're gonna be in the 95th Bomb Group of the 8th Airforce, ready to bomb the hell out of Hitler's Germany. You better snap out of it," continued Matt.

The kid could only nod his head.

"Hell, we're all a little rough this morning. Tell ya what, Les – open the window and catch a blast of air. It'll clear your head."

The kid did as he was told and let out a gasp as the freezing cold slipstream hit him. Still breathing hard, he sat back down across from Beau. His face had taken on a healthier flush.

"This is Beau," said Matt, introducing him. He threw his arm around the kid. "And this guy is Les Wagner. It's his birthday today."

"Many happy returns," said Beau smiling. "How old are you?"

Les beamed back a goofy grin. "Eighteen."

Matt started rummaging through the knapsack at his feet. He sat up and held out a a hipflask. "There's what you need," he said triumphantly.

"You've gotta be kidding," said Les.

"Are you cold? Is it your birthday? Need I say more?" argued Matt, pushing the bottle up to his face.

"All right. All right." Les took the bottle and drank a large gulp. When the liquor hit his stomach he doubled over, coughing like crazy.

Matt thumped him hard on the back, laughing and shaking his head.

"Eighteen today, say what? Looks like it's time we learned a couple of things here. Need to learn how to drink and I suspect we need to get laid."

Matt took a long swig and let a shiver of pleasure run down the entire length of his spine. Les was still caught in the throes of his coughing.

"Salute Les Wagner," Matt said, raising the bottle high and passing it to him once again. "To your eighteenth birthday!"

Les shook his head, gasping, but Matt wouldn't take no for an answer.

"Take it like a man. It's the hair of the dog that bit you. You'll feel better – believe me. You don't want to do this too often, but it works. Looks like I'm going to have to take care of your education."

Les took a sip, bracing himself. Beau could tell that it went down a lot easier. He didn't even cough. Les wiped his mouth with the back of his hand and handed the bottle back to Matt.

"Good," said Matt. He held the flask out to Beau. "Have a drink for the kid's birthday." Beau accepted and took a small sip after lifting the flask to Les. It was bourbon. Beau tried to hide a look of disgust. If there was one drink he hated, it had to be bourbon. He thanked Matt and handed him back the flask.

"That was some night last night," said Matt, leaning back against the curved fuselage. "All those guys in turbans. And all those food stalls." Matt turned to Beau. "We tried to get the birthday boy here to eat some grilled sheep's head."

"What I liked best were the snake-charmers," said Les. He closed his eyes and smiled.

"What you smiling at, kid? Remembering the belly-dancers?" said Matt.

Les blushed and shook his head. "Nope. I was just thinking of you walking around with that monkey on your back."

"What monkey?" asked Beau, enjoying the men's easy banter.

"Matt is always buying things and dragging them back to the plane," explained Les. "Cases of rum in Puerto Rico. A parrot in British Guinea. He got us all handmade boots in Brazil. His latest is a black and white spider monkey."

"Come on, kid," urged Matt. "Any red-blooded American has to have women on his mind first thing in the morning. With a smile like that, you must be thinking about your girl."

"Haven't got one," said Les, looking pleased at being ribbed. "What about you?"

"God forbid. Nope. No girl. At least not just one. That's when the problems start, kid – when you've got just one. Better to have lots."

"Never a truer word was spoken," said a red-headed guy who had just stepped into the compartment. Beau nodded to him as he staked out a corner near the ball turret and grabbed an orange from a bag. Using a knapsack as a pillow the redhead settled down to eat and read a copy of *Life* magazine.

"That's Mahoney, our navigator," said Matt. Mahoney waved an orange segment in his direction.

"So, how many women have you got?" Les asked Matt.

"All the women in the world – theoretically speaking," he answered laughing.

"It's a wonderful thought. My grandfather, bless his soul, used to say a man was like a bee going from flower to flower."

"Does that mean a woman is like a flower – with lots of different bees?"

"If you're lucky she is, smartass," said Matt. "Unless she's your mother or your sister, of course."

"What about cousins?"

"Cousins don't count. Cousins are different. A great training-ground in large Italian families. As long as *their* brothers don't find out."

"It's the same in large Irish families. Must be a Catholic thing," joked Mahoney from behind his magazine. "Hey Russo, by the way, the Lieutenant said you'd better watch that monkey or he's gonna end up with the parrot."

As if on cue, a small black and white monkey with big eyes and a long tail walked in and headed for a bunch of bananas. He chose one carefully, strolled up to the commode, and sat on it while he delicately peeled and ate.

Beau laughed out loud as he watched the monkey eat.

"Well, will, you look at that? Looks just like a king on his throne," he drawled.

"He's no king," said Matt. "He's a politician. Named him Tojo, after the Japanese Prime Minister. See those big rings around his eyes? They look just like those thick glasses that Jap has."

"Tojo? Well, he sure is ugly enough. What happened to the parrot?"

The five men chuckled as Mahoney recounted the story.

"You see, Russo here bought this parrot. Beautiful bird, but a real pain in the neck. He was always flying around the plane crapping on everything."

"I can see how that could be vexatious," Beau grinned. "A highly contrary animal. And not house-broken it would seem."

"That bird was a regular guano factory," added Matt, joining in the laughter that was peppering the compartment.

"So one day, between South America and Africa, the parrot starts flapping around the cockpit. And he shits all over the instruments," continued Mahoney. "And the co-pilot, McKnight, he's trying to catch the damn thing. The parrot flies into my compartment squawking, shits over all the maps, and flies back into the cockpit. All hell breaks loose. Then the parrot lands and perches himself right in front of the pilot."

"And cool as a cucumber, Charles Hansen III grabs him by the neck, opens the side window and throws him out. 10,000 feet over South America!" concluded Matt as he mimed the parrot disappearing out the window. "*Finito bambino*. Gone."

The monkey was startled by the outburst of laughter. He waved his banana at them and chattered.

"So you watch it, Tojo my friend, or you know where you'll end up," said the navigator, putting away his magazine. "Well, I gotta get back to work. Make sure we don't end up in Berlin!"

Tojo continued to chatter as the men laughed at him. Then when he'd finished his banana, he jumped off the toilet, threw the peel at Matt, and strolled back into the radio room.

"I swear that monkey speaks English," mused Matt.

"I don't care if he speaks Chinese." Les stood up and followed Tojo. "I'm gonna go with him and try to catch me some sleep."

Beau sat back and watched the young airman go through the door to the radio room. They seemed like a nice bunch of guys. He knew they were all curious about him. But if they didn't ask, he wasn't going to say. The less they knew the better it was. So far, keeping a low profile had worked well for him. Except for that unfortunate business back in Libya. Still, after holding him for two weeks they had to let him go. Whether they believed his story about a fishing trip, or whether the French Embassy had put pressure on the authorities didn't really matter – they let him go.

He had enjoyed the last months roaming from one airbase to the other. Posing as a journalist here, an airman there, a photographer there until he lost his camera in Belem. He hitched his way from Puerto Rico to Casablanca. His letter of introduction gave him access to the top brass everywhere he went. The President's signature opened all official doors. And his father's long list of friends ensured that a decent dinner was always to be had. The President's Special Envoy: it sounded much more grand than it was. All he had to do was look around, check on morale and living conditions and report back to Washington. The President wanted to be sure he was getting the right information back from the bases. He needed someone he could trust.

It was a stroke of luck meeting Lieutenant Hansen at Monsieur and Madame Etienne's party last night. Hansen seemed a nice guy, only a couple of years older than himself – Harvard class of '39 and smart enough not to ask too many questions. He must remember to give his mother Madame's regards, she had insisted twice when saying goodbye.

Beau had enjoyed his little break in North Africa. The Mammounia Hotel in Marrakesh had been a delight. Fountains tinkled in shady courtyards full of giant palms. Huge baskets of fruit were placed alongside comfortable divans covered in soft rugs. No wonder it was Winston Churchill's favourite hotel. He would tell Father about it next time he wrote. Maybe after the war they could arrange a trip to Morocco. Soon he would see England's green and pleasant land again and his trip would nearly be over. By tomorrow night he should be in London, tucking into whatever they were serving at the Savoy Grill these days. Even with a war on, he had no doubt that it would be delicious and that the service would be impeccable.

It was ironic, he thought. Here he was at the end of his mission and he was travelling with ten men for whom things were only just beginning. Poor bastards. There but for the grace of God . . . or rather Papa's intervention. His father and the President went way back. They'd been in school together. Beau had wanted to join the war effort. A lot of his friends back home had. But Mother wouldn't hear of it and Father felt his only son would best serve his country by staying home and helping with the family's many business interests. Beau pushed the thought to the back of his mind and concentrated instead on the book he was reading.

Matt Russo sat back and lowered his eyes. He was good at getting a rest without actually sleeping. It also allowed him to watch people without them knowing it. It was a trick he had perfected while sitting on the stoop watching out for his sisters.

That passenger sure was a rare bird. He was tall, dark and handsome. Good-looking as a movie star. Matt bet that his deep tan had more to do with summer sailing than the couple of days he'd been in Africa. He knew that type all right. He'd delivered shopping from his grandfather's store to those fancy Upper East-side houses ever since he was twelve. Always at the back door and straight into the kitchen, but you got a feel for the places and the people who lived in them. Sometimes, when only the servants were home, you got to look around.

But this one, this Beauregard something or other, was really different. It wasn't just because he was southern. Rich kids all looked the same. There was something more than just his tailored uniform and fluid manners. Matt would bet his bottom dollar that he was no airman. Not that it mattered. After all it was none of his business. If it was all right by Charlie

Hansen, it was all right by him. The pilot was another of those Ivy League summer-sailing types, even lived in the Upper East side, but Matt would follow him anywhere.

Tate and Merdeza were still playing cards. They were both older than the rest of the crew and had wives back home, which was probably why they stuck together. That and the fact that they could both play poker for hours on end.

"Waist to radio?" said Matt, leaning into the intercom. *"How about you find us some music, Russell?"*

"Radio to pilot. Is that OK with you, Lieutenant?" the radio operator asked the pilot.

"Sure, Russell. I'll want you guys at your stations once we get past Spain and over the Atlantic. But you can relax for now."

Strains of Benny Goodman could be heard faintly through the rattle and roar of the giant plane as it sped towards England. Matt didn't like Russell much. Sometimes he could be a a real prick. But he was a great radio man and that's all that really mattered. Matt had been an army sergeant before transferring to the Air Corps after the war broke out. He knew that the important thing was that every man would do his job. That these were guys you could count on because, at the end of the day, your life depended on it. He was glad of the crew he'd gotten.

The Chief walked down the length of the plane, nodded to Matt, and went to relieve himself at the white enamelled bucket in the back. Now there was a guy that Matt really liked. John Wilson, but they called him Chief on account of the fact that he was a full-blooded Cherokee. He was the first Red Indian Matt had ever met. He was like a magnet for beautiful women even if he was only 5'5". The guys in the crew had quickly learnt that the Chief was a great guy to go out with if you wanted to pull the babes. They were forever getting his cast-offs.

Matt had become good friends with him over the last few months – even if he could drink him under the table every time and had to carry him back to the base. The kid, Les, was a good buddy too. Best gunner in his class. He said he had learnt to shoot in the woods back home in Wisconsin. Matt thought of the crew and his heart sank a little. They all looked like they were going off on some picnic in their own personal Flying Fortress. But the Air Corps hadn't trained them, equipped them and built them a B-17 so they could have their own little junket around the world. The B-17 was the biggest, heaviest bomber the US had ever built. And tomorrow they would have to face the fact that this was no picnic.

Scrunched up in the corner of the radio room, Les tried to sleep but only managed to drift off for a few moments at a time. The noise in the plane was deafening, and there was no place you could sit, stand, or lean where you wouldn't feel the vibrations. If you managed to nod off through it all, then something was sure to wake you up. They weren't using oxygen, but the pilot still wanted them to check in every twenty minutes. Les guessed he wanted them to get used to the drill for when they started to see some real action.

And if it wasn't the pilot it was the monkey. Well, not the monkey – it was that damn Russell teasing the monkey. Poor old Tojo had settled in to sleep over the radio man's head, using the curtain on the window as a hammock. Russell would wait until Tojo was fast asleep and then poke him with a pencil. This enraged the monkey, who then jumped all over the plane, screeching and chattering. Just a few minutes ago, Tojo had bounced off the top of Les's head and gone careening into the waist again. Les opened his eyes and decided to give up on the idea of sleeping. Surprisingly, he felt a lot better. Sitting up, he saw that their passenger, Beau, was asleep on the other side of the room.

The music over the intercom was interrupted by

Mahoney telling the pilot that the bad weather they had been warned of was coming up ahead.

Les sat staring at the rivets along the fuselage above him and thought of his bedroom ceiling back home. How many nights had he laid on his bed and looked at the little model aeroplanes hanging there, dreaming of planes and flying aces? Les rummaged around for a cigarette and thought about a cold December morning just over a year ago.

He had been out shooting squirrels early that Sunday. The snow was crisp on the ground and he walked carefully so as not to make it crunch and scare the game. He shot a brace of squirrel and was coming home when his path crossed a deer track. A big stag by the looks of it. Though his gun was far too small a calibre for deer, he stalked it, carefully following the tracks in the snow through the towering paper birch and giant white pines. The Potawatomi Indians said the woods were full of spirits, and Les had no doubt that they were right.

The land rose slightly above him. The deer tracks went straight up and then disappeared. Les knew there was a gully just below the ridge. He dropped on all fours and silently crawled up to the tree-line, sliding on his belly for the last few yards to peer over the edge. There, just twenty yards away, was the biggest stag he had ever seen. It stood there unperturbed and Les could have sworn it was looking straight at him.

Hunger finally got the better of him and he turned for home, looking forward to breakfast. As he walked he tracked the deer again in his mind, imagining himself telling it over the breakfast table as his father and brother sat entranced. His mother wouldn't say a word. She didn't much like killing, she said, and so would shuffle quietly from the stove to the table with plates of pancakes and pots of strong black coffee. He carefully constructed the story so as to avoid interruptions. His brother would want to know all the details of the stag, and would make believe he had seen that one before. While his father would want to know the exact location of the stag, where it had been, how he had tracked it. Les added a few embellishments for good measure as he walked up the short drive to the house. The smoke from the chimney hung straight out above the house in the cold winter air, carrying a delicious smell of warmth and breakfast.

"Howdy," said Les as he walked into the kitchen. "Wait till I tell you what I did this morning!"

But no one was listening. His father, brother and mother were all huddled around the radio.

"I tracked the biggest stag you ever did see," tried Les again. "Bigger than the one Mickey Schor brought down last Thanksgiving . . . " his voice trailed off as all three turned and waved at him to hush up.

The radio was turned up but Les couldn't make sense of it. It seemed to be about the War. Had there been another great battle in Britain? Whatever it was, he could tell it was bad news from their drawn faces. His mother was even dabbing her eyes with her small white handkerchief.

"The Japs bombed Pearl Harbour," said his brother, his voice trembling with excitement.

Les looked back puzzled.

"Pearl Harbour. The Japs bombed us in Pearl Harbour, Les. In Hawaii," added Mike, his voice rising further.

Les felt his heart start to race. "What do you mean?" he asked, his voice a whisper.

"They bombed our subs and ships."

The full brunt of that news was just starting to sink in as his father turned and put his arm around him. "It means we're going to war, son."

The stag was forgotten. His life had changed in that second and he didn't even know it. He never did get to tell that story, thought Les, as he pulled a pack of Lucky Strikes from his flight jacket. On the other side of the radio room, Beau stirred and opened his eyes. Les lay back and smoked. Tojo had calmed down after the latest pencil-poking incident and was back in his hammock above the radio operator. Every now and then he would peer over the top.

His dad had been right, of course. The very next day they had all sat around the radio again as President Roosevelt told Congress that December 7th 1941 was "a day that will live in infamy". And Congress voted war on the Axis powers – Germany, Italy and Japan.

Beau stretched, and tried to massage the crick in his neck. He had somehow managed to fall asleep despite the noise of the plane and the monkey's outbursts. That little critter sure could screech, thought Beau. He looked up and saw Tojo peering from behind the little curtain. He looked like he was up to no good. The kid, Les, was sitting on the other side of the room smoking a cigarette.

"Did you sleep well?" asked Les.

"As well as could be expected," answered Beau.

"So it's your birthday? I could think of better places to spend your eighteenth birthday than stuck in a B-17 with ten other guys and a monkey."

"It's OK. I've always been crazy about planes. I made models since I was six. I even had a big picture of Baron Von Rickhoffen on my wall. You know the World War I flying ace?"

Beau nodded.

"I had to take him down after we got into the war. It didn't seem right having him up there. But what I mean is, I couldn't think of a better place to spend my birthday."

"So how is it that you're only eighteen?" asked Beau. "I thought you had to be eighteen to enlist? You're already a gunner."

Les smiled. "It's kinda a long story."

"I'm not going anywhere," said Beau.

"Well, like I said, I always loved aircraft. When the war was declared my brother and I read every article. We listened to every news bulletin on the radio. We wanted to be a part of it. Hell, we were scared it would all be over before we had a chance to enlist. I was real jealous of Mike. I was still a high-school senior but Mike was working at Pete's garage learning to be a mechanic. He was waiting to turn eighteen so he could join up."

Beau lit a cigarette and relaxed. He enjoyed the kid's enthusiasm. Above him he saw Tojo peek out and hide again.

"Mike turned eighteen two days after my graduation. Dad drove him to the recruitment centre in Oskosh. I just went along for the ride," continued Les. "Mike went through the line with Dad while I hung back and looked at the posters. Then Dad called me over to the recruiting sergeant. He was a big Swedish guy.

68

And Dad says to him: 'I've got another son here if you want him.' The sergeant asked if I was eighteen. Dad kinda said yes and that was that – I joined up. I bet that was the only fib Dad ever told."

"That's some story," said Beau appreciatively. "You must be the youngest gunner in your bomb group."

"Hell, I'm probably the youngest man in the whole US Army Air Corps," corrected Les laughing.

The sharp slap of rain pattered on the fuselage as the light dimmed in the radio room. Russell snapped on the little lamp over his desk. He was intent on his work, and did not notice that he was being keenly observed by Tojo, who was peering slyly over the top of the curtain again. Beau watched as the monkey peeked, then hid, then peeked again. He seemed very busy behind his curtain, poking his head out every couple of seconds as if assessing the situation. Finally, after one long glance at Russell's head bent over his instruments, Tojo retreated into his hiding-place.

Beau couldn't believe what happened next. With perfect aim, a long thin stream of urine shot out from behind the curtain and landed a direct hit on Russell, showering his neck.

"What the heck?" Russell, jumped up and bumped his head as he tried to catch Tojo, who bounced onto his shoulder and then straight out of the room.

"That damn monkey peed on me!" Russell bellowed.

"Serves you right for teasing him," Les laughed. Beau could hear the commotion in the waist as Tojo swung from one end of the plane to the other, chattering loudly.

"Waist to top turret." Matt's voice came over the intercom. *"What the hell happened up there? Tojo's in here doing somersaults."*

"He's probably celebrating," Les answered. *"He just peed on Russell. Scored a perfect hit. We should send him up to Reisenbeck. He'd make a great bombardier."*

The laughter ringing through the intercom was cut short by the pilot.

"Cut it out, men. We have some ugly weather hitting us. Top turret, get to your post and tell me what you see."

Les jumped up and scrambled to his position just behind the pilot and the co-pilot. Standing on the small ledge, his head emerged in the plexiglass bubble of the top turret. Beau stood behind him and looked into the inky darkness. The rain was coming down so hard he could barely see past the swirling water. Through the pouring water Beau could just make it out. It was huge and dense.

"Top turret to pilot. Big black cloud up ahead," Les yelled.

"I see it, top turret," answered the pilot. *"Brace yourselves, we're going in."*

The plane bucked as it entered the cloud. The rain doubled in intensity, pounding the plexiglass bubble and drowning out the sound of the engines. Beau hung on to the sides of the turret as the giant plane shook in the storm. Sparks flew off the nose and snaked down the wings.

"Radio to pilot. The radio signal is breaking up. The static is real bad."

"Navigator to pilot. All instruments have gone haywire. Must be some heavy electrical activity out there."

"Pilot to crew. We're taking her up. Maybe we can get above this storm."

Hansen and McKnight were struggling to keep control of the plane. The laughter had stopped as each man in the crew became acutely aware that only a thin sheet of metal and the pilot's ability stood between them and a 10,000 foot drop into oblivion. Even Tojo seemed to sense the gravity of the situation as he slipped quietly into the radio room and huddled in the corner.

They rode the storm for over half an hour, climbing steadily upwards as they tried to get above it. At 12,000 feet they put on their oxygen masks. Beau took one of the portable units hanging in the radio room and slipped it on. One minute later they broke through the storm. Beau breathed a sigh of relief as he felt the bomber level out and steady itself. A round of applause rang through the plane. He leaned in past Les's legs and stuck his head into the cockpit.

"Nice work, Hansen," he drawled. "You had me worried back there." Lieutenant Hansen waved an acknowledgment without taking his eyes off the instruments.

"Don't thank me. We're not home and dry yet," he said. *"Pilot to navigator: Where the hell are we?"*

"Well, Charlie, I hate to say it, but I have no idea. The last time I looked we should have been coming into the Bay of Biscay. But that was before we hit the storm. We could be anywhere by now."

Chapter Five

◆━◆

Imelda sat near the campfire, cradling the hot jamjar of tea in her hands. The sun was just starting to rise and she heard the sounds of the others waking. In a few minutes she would drag the girls from their bed and get them washed and ready for the day. They'd all got back late the night before after travelling out west for a week and needed the extra sleep.

The camp by the marsh was down a small boreen that was seldom used. At the end of the lane was a little rise with a stone shed. Her Uncle Paddy had an arrangement with the farmer who owned the land so that he and his family could use the shed for weeks at a time when they were in the area. Uncle Paddy and Auntie Helen had fourteen children, with eight still living at home, so they were glad to have a bit of space. When they camped by the marsh the boys would sleep in the barrel-top, instead of under it like when they were on the road, and the girls would sleep in the shed with their parents and the baby. The farmer was a kind man, and did not mind that Imelda and her sisters camped alongside or that every now and then another family would pull up for a day or two. The ground was high and dry with good water only a half a mile away. Imelda heard the soft south-west breeze rustle in the trees above her bringing a sharp smell of the sea. Birdsong filled the air and she felt happy to be back after shifting camp every day. The weather had been foul and wet all week and it had been impossible to dry anything out. Today looked as if it would be fine, so they might get some of their washing done and hang it out to dry along the hedgerows.

Tommy had been up since five to go and tend to Gerald Burke's hounds. He should be back soon. Imelda wondered how Mary was doing. She'd dropped in before they'd left for Skibereen and Bantry, but Mary had been busy and rather brusque. She'd just about pushed her out the door with a loaf of bread and a dozen eggs before she could set foot in the house.

Imelda climbed into the barrel-top with a fresh jar of tea. The air was sweet and warm with the smell of straw and the girls' soft breathing. Imelda dug around where she herself had lain, and pulled out the grub box where she kept the food locked up. It was handy as a pillow and no child could try and steal a bit to eat during the night. In the box were two of the four loaves she'd baked the night before, a bit of bacon and a small onion. She'd fry the meat and onions for Tommy, and give the girls a cut of fried bread and tea each. Tom would be glad of a meal after walking the hounds.

"Get up, ye lazy heads," she said as she tickled the girls who were curled up together under their blankets. "Here's your tea. I want ye washed and brushed by the time I have your breakfast ready."

"Brigid, get the small ones ready," she called out to her ten-year-old sister as she carried the grub box outside.

Imelda went around to the back and rolled up her sleeves to comb her hair and have a good wash before she touched the food. The water in the bucket was icy cold and stung her face and arms. Her mother and father had taught her early how important it was to wash, and keep all the pots and pans, and buckets and basins, separate and clean. The only time she'd ever seen her father lose his temper was once when her mother's hair had come undone as she stood over the fire cooking a meal. He'd ranted and raved before sending her down the road to plait her hair again, and shake herself thoroughly to make sure no hairs had fallen on her clothes. He then yelled at her to take each of the children and comb and shake them out as well. And he had refused to eat, though she knew he was hungry. Sure weren't they always?

Tommy arrived back in by the time the girls had finished their breakfast. Imelda sent them off to play with their cousins for a while as she sat with him and watched him eat.

"Nellie's got a bit of a cough," she said. "I should have saved the onion for her. Would you be going into town today? I could go to the shops and buy one, maybe. I'd boil it in a bit of milk for her."

"Sure I have to go myself. We've still a fair bit a money left from the trading. We could buy some food while we're in. A bit a meat would be nice."

"That it would. I could send Margaret into school as well. She needs to learn some more if she's to make her First Holy Communion this year. And she could do with a bit more learning to read and write."

"Leave her be today. She'll help Brigid and Nora tidy up and mind Nellie. Mary Burke needs to go in today. We could call in for her."

Imelda didn't take long to decide. "That would be

grand," she said smiling. "I'll sort the girls out and we can go."

All week Mary had been fearful that Imelda might return while Gerald was still around. The thought of him even looking at the girl was more than she could bear. Then this morning he'd got up early, packed a bag and left, saying he'd be away on business for at least a week. The house had reverted to the comforting silence that Mary loved and she thought how strange it was that silence could be so many different things. They had barely spoken a word to each other while Gerald was home. Gerald spent his evenings in town, came home late and collapsed in the front room where he slept most of the day. He would awake late, wash and dress and leave again. He had not so much as looked at her, and for that Mary was thankful. But the silence was heavy and threatening, like a black suffocating cloud pressing down on her. While Gerald was home, Mary went quietly about her day, careful lest she drop a fork, or scrape a plate in the basin, or do anything that would echo through the quiet house and call attention to her presence. Still, she gained comfort as always from the routine of her chores. She knew that was the only way to retain whatever shred of herself she still had. The well-known gestures, repeated day after day, soothed her body and her mind so that by nightfall when she locked herself in her room she sank, tired and numb, into a sleep which released her from her troubles.

As soon as Gerald was out of sight the silence changed. It was as if someone had thrown open a window and let in the salt air to flush out the gloom. When he was gone she truly enjoyed her work and would often catch herself humming as she went about her day.

Mary smoothed her dress and stood up straight as she heard the cart pull into the courtyard. She knew that the angry red welt on her cheek was almost gone, and she hoped that Imelda's quick eyes would not notice it. What was she going to do? She wanted to push the evil thoughts that Gerald had planted out of her mind. The sight of Imelda's slight frame wrapped in the blue blanket made her determined to make sure that Imelda and Gerald would never meet again. She knew the easiest thing would be to close her door to Imelda. Just tell her to go away and never come back. But she could not do it. The thought of hurting Imelda was unbearable. She missed her and couldn't keep from smiling as Imelda waved.

"How's it going?" said Imelda as she came into the kitchen.

"Come in, come in," said Mary warmly. She would

enjoy Imelda's company for a little while yet. For today. Tomorrow she would find a way to make the girl go. She patted the chair by her side. "Sit down. Have a cup of tea. I've the kettle ready."

"We were going into town and we thought you might need some messages," said Imelda, sitting herself down at the long kitchen table.

"I'll come with you," said Mary. It cut her heart to see Imelda's eyes light up and her face break into a beaming smile.

Imelda reached beneath her apron and pulled out a small bundle of white cloth. "I brought you something. It's only a small thing but I thought you might like it. It's pretty."

Mary unfolded the border of lace and stared at it. "It's very pretty," she said, carefully turning the piece of cloth in her hand. "Very pretty. Thank you, Imelda." There was about a half a yard of it, snowy white with a pattern of roses and ivy trailing through it.

"It's nothing really," said Imelda shyly. "And 'tis only fair. You gave me a dozen eggs last week."

"It's the nicest thing anyone has ever given me," Mary softly replied. She did not add that it was the only present she had received since the dress which still hung, unworn for years, in her bedroom wardrobe.

"You could sew it on a petticoat. Or at the bottom of a curtain. That's what most of 'em do. I sold yards of it down around Skibereen," said Imelda, rattling on to cover her embarrassment. "We did very well altogether. Tommy and Uncle Paddy sold loads a pots and buckets they'd made, and got a few repairs in as well. The farmers were kind. One woman even gave me a pair of shoes that fit Nora. She's very proud of 'em."

"Nora? That's your youngest sister, right?" asked Mary as she poured out the tea.

"No. Nora is six, and the baby – that'll be Nellie – is two and a half. The eldest is Brigid, who's ten. Then Margaret. She's coming on eight."

"That's quite a family you've got."

"Oh, they're a right handful. Especially Nora. She a devil, that one. When we were walking up to yer woman's house – the one that gave me the shoes – I told her to wait down the lane and not touch anything. I could see her eyeing the flowers. So I said to her, 'I'm watching you going up this lane and if you touch this lady's flowers, I'll kill ya on the way down.' And wouldn't you know it? After we'd left I found she had a bunch hidden in her skirt!"

"So what did you do?" asked Mary, enjoying Imelda's story.

"I dragged her off to the priest in Skibereen and told him to sort her out," answered Imelda, shaking her head. "And ya know what he said? He said, 'There's some good in her if she's fond of flowers!'"

The laughter filling the kitchen was light and airy. Mary felt as if she had just taken a big gulp of fresh stream water.

"You know, sometimes I'm at my wit's end with them," said Imelda seriously. "I don't know if I'm doing right by them. I know I'm old enough to have a family of my own but sometimes I worry if I'm raising them right."

"But you're only a child yourself."

"I am not a child. I'll be fifteen this summer. My mother was married at fourteen, and so was my auntie. I'm old enough to have a family – only, one at a time might be easier."

"I would have loved a big family," said Mary surprising herself again. How easily she could talk to this girl. "I never could keep the babies though. I always lost them in the first months. Except for Séan and he was a sickly child from the start."

"I'm sorry for your troubles, Mary," said Imelda, her eyes soft with compassion. "You're young yet. And fit. Please God, you'll have another."

The moment was interrupted by Tommy who came noisily through the door.

"What's this then? Here I thought we were going to town and the pair of ye are having a tea party!"

"Just having a bit of a chat," said Mary. "Come in and have a cup of tea yerself."

"Thanks, Mary but I won't. We best be getting a move on."

Mary looked up at the old clock on the mantle that had been her grandmother's proudest possession. "Goodness, it's half past twelve! You're right. Go on and have a cup while I get my things."

Mary went into the front room and opened the bottom drawer of the big oak sideboard. She kept the money Gerald gave her in a cigar-box. As always there was more than she knew what to do with. Money never seemed to be a problem with Gerald. She knew he had his own box, that he kept locked in another drawer. God knows how much he might have in there. And what for? If she could, she knew what she would do with it all right. Save it up until she had enough to buy new stock and pay strong men, and get the farm working again. Gerald allowed her to keep a few hens and grow some vegetables to keep her busy. As long as it cost him little and bothered him less. Gerald was no farmer. As far as he was concerned the farm was an investment with Mary thrown into the bargain. It allowed him to indulge in his one passion: greyhound racing. That in turn let him indulge in his two favourite pastimes, drinking and making money.

Mary put some money in her pocket and looked out the window to see what the weather was like. It was bright at the moment but looked changeable. The roll of what sounded like distant thunder made her decide to take a coat and scarf, lest it should rain.

Imelda and Tommy were ready with the cart when she came out again.

"Did ya hear the thunder?" said Imelda.

"I heard it all right," said Mary. "'Tis coming in from the east. It could get colder. I thought I'd better take a scarf."

"It didn't sound like thunder to me," said Tommy. "'Twas out to sea, all right, but 'twas high above us and passed very quickly."

"'Twas thunder. Sure what else could it be?" said Imelda dismissively. "Here, Mary, hand me up the basket of eggs."

"Hush, Meldy," said Tommy suddenly, gesturing to them to listen, "Can ya hear it?"

Mary and Imelda listened. Far, far away they could hear a rumble.

"'Tis the thunder," said Mary.

"See, I told ya! Must be a storm out to sea," said Imelda.

"No, listen! 'Tis coming from the west now. 'Tis

over there," said Tommy standing very still as he pointed out above the rise of the hills to the west.

"What are ya going on about? There's a storm over Ardfield, ya eejit!"

"That's no storm. Listen!" The rumble was quite clear now, hanging over the hills across the estuary.

"What's up with you, Tommy Tanner, have ya gone demented?" teased Imelda.

"Here it comes. 'Tis coming our way. 'Tis a plane. 'Tis got to be a plane. A big plane," said Tommy excitedly.

"Will ya ever shut up, Tommy? You've planes on the brain," said Imelda sharply. Sometimes her brother could be a real cross to bear. Worse than the girls by far.

"'Tis a plane!" insisted Tommy. "There's loads of them fly by, don't ya know? Mick out on Galley Head said he's seen German planes go past."

Imelda had had enough of it. They should have been in town by now instead of wasting Mary's time watching the sky. She started to berate her brother but she didn't finish. The words froze in her throat. The roar over Ardfield came closer, getting horribly loud. It was the loudest noise Imelda had ever heard. She stared in the direction of the sound but the clouds were heavy and dark in that part of the sky. The noise grew louder still and Imelda bit her knuckles in fear.

Mary's heart was beating fast and her hands were trembling. The roar filled her entire being, shaking her from head to foot. Behind the clouds she made out a darker shape moving through the grey mass. It couldn't be. Nothing could be that big. Yet the shadow moved swiftly towards them. It passed over the house, blotting out the light and filling the air with its thunder. Instinctively Imelda and Mary crouched down. The pony whinnied and tossed its head nervously.

"'Tis a plane. 'Tis a plane. 'Tis a plane!" shouted Tommy. He stood on the cart waving his cap, jumping and hooting, as the large green mass passed directly over their heads and headed out towards Clonakility. Only when it had passed completely out of sight, its rumbling still vibrating the air, did Tommy look down at the pair crouching alongside the cart.

"I told ye 'twas a plane," he said, beaming.

Chapter Six

•—•

A deep rumble was rising in the east. Mick O'Sullivan was just getting ready to go home for his dinner when he first heard it. He took his binoculars back out of their case and listened. The rumble grew. He lifted the binoculars and followed the sound. He could see nothing behind the brilliant clouds. The rumble was too far out, but he knew it was a plane for sure. And a big one by the sound of it.

Mick lowered the binoculars and listened as it moved out west. Even after it was out of earshot he waited, his gaze searching the skies. He knew it would probably be back. Most of the planes came back – unless they crashed into Mount Brandon, God help 'em. After all there was nothing out west except for the sea. All the action was in the opposite direction. Out west the next parish was New York.

While he waited he took out his notebook. The sharpened nub of a pencil was tied to it with a bit of string. Earlier he had walked out to the look-out post at the edge of the lighthouse and thoroughly scanned the sky before checking his watch and carefully recording his entry: *April 7, 12:30. Clouds heavy. Coast clear.*

Now he leaned on the sea wall, licked the lead and carefully started to write again. He had only managed to note the time when he heard the plane returning. He had no need for the binoculars – he could see it. Sweet Jesus, but it was big.

He stood stock-still as he watched the plane. It was bigger than a house. How could it fly at all? The roar of the mighty engines filled the air as the huge plane approached. Trembling, he lifted his binoculars for a closer look. He counted four engines, but he couldn't make out any markings. It must have a one-hundred-foot wingspan at the very least.

The plane was just about level with Galley Head. He could see it quite clearly. Holy Mother of God! He could see a man in the nose. His heart was racing as he quickly jotted down the markings on the tail as it passed.

He struggled to keep sight of the plane as he leafed through his aircraft identification manual.

He checked his watch again. He licked the pencil

and carefully noted: *12:37. Large aircraft sighted flying Seven Heads to Galley Head in the direction of Mizen Head. Seen returning over Galley Head and heading back from whence it came to the east. The aircraft seems to be losing altitude and may attempt to land.*

Then he got on his bicycle and started pedalling furiously down the rutted lane. His stomach growled at the thought of his dinner waiting at home. Then again, he'd best tell herself what was up. He'd pop into the house quickly, talk to the Missus, and grab a bit of bread to eat on his way into town.

John Joe O'Mahoney walked along the muddy boreen relishing the day in a way that only those who have a legitimate reason to miss school can do. He had been given the day off to help his da drill potatoes in the high field. Bottles of tea clinked and sloshed in the basket he was carrying. His mam had wrapped the bottles in old socks "too far gone to darn". John Joe looked forward to eating with his da and the farm-hands. The sun was shining in patches where it broke through the grey clouds, spotlighting a patch of green here, a tree over there, or a hill across the bay on the Island.

John Joe stopped for a minute and leant against a low stone wall to catch his breath. He was rather on the plump side for a ten-year-old and often found he had trouble keeping up with the other boys at school. The bottles were heavy and he was glad of the rest. Dr Moloney said he might have a touch of the asthma and his ma said he shouldn't over-exert himself. Above him he could see the small figures of his father and the two farm-hands bent over as they moved up the drills. As he watched, they suddenly all stood up straight and started pointing.

Instantly he heard it. Distant thunder, only louder, bigger. John Joe turned to where the men were pointing.

And then he saw it.

It looked just like the pictures in the comic books and magazines his uncle sent him from America. An American Army Air Corps aeroplane! A B-17 Flying Fortress. Full of brave US airmen! A real aeroplane, right here in Ardfield! They didn't even have one car in the village and here was an American aeroplane right there in the skies above.

John Joe watched as the plane disappeared into the clouds above Inchydoney Island. The men in the field above him were all whooping and waving their caps. John Joe dropped the basket and ran like the wind.

Ruth Bennett came into the bar carrying a tray full of clean glasses from the kitchen.

"Here, pet. Let me give you a hand," said Tony the barman.

"Thanks, Tony. I'm grand," Ruth declined.

"Actually, could you mind the bar for a minute while I pop out?"

"Work away," said Ruth as she manoeuvred herself behind the bar. She nodded to her father who was deep in conversation with Con O'Leary and Dr Moloney. Ruth's face broke into her most appealing smile as the side door opened and Dennis walked in.

He nodded to the men on the bar stools and then seemed to notice Ruth.

"Hi there, Ruth Bennett. How's it going?" he said beaming.

"I'm well, Dennis," she said trying to sound natural. They had been meeting whenever they could manage it for about a month. Dennis would leave a note in with one of the other girls in the hotel, and Ruth would try and find an excuse to leave the house after dinner. She had developed a liking for long walks with the dog, which puzzled her mother but not sufficiently to require an investigation.

"Could I get a pint of Murphy's when you're ready?" asked Dennis.

"Of course ya can," said Ruth. The glasses tinkled as she looked around for a place to set the tray down. She steadied the tray on a side table, but the glasses tinkled even more. She watched, holding her breath, as a whole row toppled over and crashed to the ground. She was going for the dust-pan and brush when she realised that all the glasses in the bar were ringing in chorus. The bottles lining the back of the bar clanked along with them.

"What the hell is going on?" Con O'Leary asked aloud.

"The room's shaking," exclaimed Dr Moloney. He slipped off the bar stool and joined his companions who had gathered in the middle of the bar, carefully balancing their pints.

The main door burst open and Miss Aileen O'Donovan ran in, shrieking. She was a plump woman of advancing years and Ruth had to smother a giggle. Her hair was in disarray. Wispy grey curls framed her face which had gone beet-red around the open circle of her mouth.

"'Tis an earthquake. We're all going to die!" gasped Miss Aileen as she fumbled in her ample bodice for her scapulars. Her rosary beads were already in her hand and she kissed the cross several times.

"Calm down woman! It can't be an earthquake," said Con O'Leary.

"'Tis an earthquake, I tell ya," affirmed Miss Aileen, her breasts heaving as she sought to catch her breath.

"We don't get earthquakes in West Cork," argued Dr Moloney. The patrons all nodded in agreement.

Ruth looked to her da for reassurance and saw Dennis move towards the window. A roar filled the room, scaring the life out of her. Maybe it was an earthquake, after all.

Miss Aileen let out another shriek and crumpled her large frame onto one of the benches. *"Hail Mary full of grace, the Lord is with thee!* We're all going to die," she cried.

"Hang on 'Tis coming from outside," said Dennis, pulling back the heavy curtains. "Jaysus! 'Tis a plane!"

Ruth joined the others as they ran to look out. She could only see the street. People were running to and fro in front of the hotel. Ruth stood on tiptoe to try and see over the men's shoulders as they held their pints aloft. She could just about make out the rooftops across the road. As she struggled to see, the thin blue-grey line of sky was blotted out by the huge green body of a plane which passed quickly out of view. Pressing into Dennis's back, she slipped her hand into his.

"It looks like a bomber." Dennis gave her hand a squeeze.

"A bomber! Holy Mother save us, we're being bombed. We're all going to die," screeched Miss Aileen who stood up to get a better view.

"Would you ever get a hold of yerself. It's too low for a bombing raid," said Con O'Leary. "It looks like 'tis going to land."

"Land? Lord above! We're being invaded. We're all going to die," whispered Miss Aileen, panting, as she fell back on the bench. She sat staring straight ahead, her eyes glazed over, clutching her rosary.

"Nobody's going to die." Dr Moloney came around to feel her pulse. "Come now, Miss Aileen, calm yerself."

Miss Aileen still stared straight ahead, her mouth silently working its way through the *Our Father*.

"Ruth! Get Miss Aileen a shot of whiskey. She's taken a turn."

Miss Aileen raised her head and waved her rosary. "No. No whiskey."

"It'll calm yer nerves. Go on now."

"No. No whiskey," said Miss Aileen waving her rosary. "Brandy. Brandy would be better. With a drop of port."

"A brandy and port, so," said Dr Moloney smiling as he patted her free hand. "Ruth! A brandy for Miss Aileen, please."

But Ruth didn't hear the order. She was out the big front door and running down Pearse Street with Dennis hot on her heels.

Martin Kelleher was wrestling with a moral dilemma. Every midday he was let out five minutes early so that he could go and help his mother with the lunchtime rush in the sweet shop. This had only been arranged after devout promises of rectitude from Martin, further promises from his mother that he would cause the least possible disruption to the class, along with a little divine intervention in the shape of Father Collins who had had a word with the school-master, intervening once again on his behalf as he had when he agreed to take on the fatherless, and totally unsuitable, Martin as an altar boy. Mrs Kelleher was not only a formidable woman, but a regular provider of Father Collin's best cream teas.

Martin had sworn on his honour, and his dead father's memory, adding Our Lady and a few saints in for good measure. There would be no messing on his part. But today he was being put to the test. Martin's stomach twisted as he stood in the middle of the playground, unable to decide whether to go on home, or sneak around the back of the school building where he knew the Barry boys waited.

He had only a few minutes to make up his mind. Soon the bell would ring, the playground would be flooded with boys and the Master would want to know what he was doing there still. Martin's heart jumped as the school door banged open and Pat

Barry sauntered out towards the toilets. Before he reached them, he shot a wink at Martin and darted behind the building. Martin knew that Joe, Frank and James were already there. The brothers had stolen a cigar from their grandfather and were planning to smoke it during the break. Martin couldn't believe his luck when Pat asked him, casual like, if he wanted to come along.

In a world populated by his mother and sisters, the Barry boys seemed to Martin like a haven of maleness. It was almost too good to be true that they had asked him to share the cigar. Who knows what wonderful adventures he'd have if he didn't chicken out today? Surely that was worth risking his mother's wrath, or Father Collins' sad beagle eyes and inevitable lecture. It was even worth a good whack across the back with the Master's ruler.

The sun broke through the clouds throwing the shadow of the church steeple ominously across the playground. It seemed to be pointing straight at Martin. The shadow reminded him of the promises he'd made. How could he serve Mass next Sunday, knowing full well that he was impure in both deed and spirit?

Even if he found an excuse that his mother would believe (that woman could read minds). Even if the Master didn't catch them, even if he didn't turn green at the first puff and be sick all over Joe Barry, even if no one ever found out – God would know.

Martin looked over his shoulder towards the church and willed himself to look up at the steeple. He half expected to see a host of angels sitting up there pointing their heavenly fingers at him. But all the saints in heaven lined up in a row couldn't have surprised him as much as the roar that suddenly filled the air. He instinctively dropped onto the hard concrete. Peeking out above his crossed arms, he looked up.

A giant green plane was skimming over the rooftops. It was flying so low it looked as if it was going to be skewered on the steeple. Martin jumped up and craned his neck to see. Time stood still as he watched the monster bear down on the church. He nearly lost his balance as someone shoved him from behind. Two boys flashed past him. Martin caught sight of Pat Barry in hot pursuit of his brother Joe, who cleared the playground wall in one graceful leap. How did he do that? He was followed closely by his two younger brothers and a herd of little boys. Martin was running before he realised his legs were moving.

"Come on, Kelleher!" shouted Pat as Martin drew level with him. "Come on. Come on. Come on!"

"What's up?" yelled Martin. "Was that a plane?"

"Of course it was, ya fecking eejit! And 'tis coming down. 'Tis going to land. *Come on!*"

Kitty Kelleher was almost ready for the morning invasion. She had everything planned with military precision, down to the last detail.

First she locked the door at exactly ten to one. Most of her customers would be home making the dinner, but the little thieves that God had disguised as children wouldn't be out of school yet. Kitty took the chair from behind the counter and placed it solidly in the middle of the tiny shop. From this vantage point, her back to an untempting range of cleaning products, she could watch the more risky areas: the rows upon rows of big glass bottles filled with sweets which gave off a rosy glow and intoxicating smell that made the little beasts go wild. Martin should be in any minute now. His orders were to only let them in four at a time. Kitty had arrived at the perfect number after careful calculations. Four was enough to keep up a healthy turnover, but still not too many to keep an eye on.

Kitty sat on the chair and watched the door. Where was Martin?

The question went unanswered as all the glass bottles started shaking at once. Sweet Mother of Divinity – what was happening? An unholy row was going on outside. Kitty could hear people shouting. There must be an accident out on Pearse Street. A quick glance at the clock told her it was five to one. Martin should have been in by now. She hesitated an instant before unlocking the door – you could never be too careful with those little scoundrels.

Kitty put the cigar-box safely back behind the counter. She opened the door and peered out. The street was full of people pointing to the sky. Some were running. What in God's holy name was going on? A large group of boys was coming down the middle of the road, adding bodies as it advanced. And wouldn't you know it, leading the pack was that eejit son of hers!

Chapter Seven

❖

An hour earlier, Beau had been trying to read to quell his nerves as he sat in the waist compartment. He had to concentrate just to keep the book level. His eyes kept skimming over the page and he found himself reading the same sentence over and over again. He tried to forget the mounting anxiety he felt. He imagined a conversation in which he would charm his dinner companions with the absurd situation of being stuck in this huge rattling tin can, flying practically blind, over what could well be enemy territory. He was comforted somewhat by that thought until a particularly nasty jolt made him slide onto the floor and reminded him that he wasn't back in polite society yet. In fact he was scared shitless. Who were these guys anyway? Would they be his companions on his last voyage? He didn't even know them. Half of them were even younger than he was.

Beau put his book down and lit a cigarette. The crew all seemed relaxed but there was an air of intensity that had not been present that morning in Marrakesh. The pilot hadn't said anything yet – but Beau figured they would eventually be getting low on fuel.

T'Ain't a Bird had ridden above the storm for two hours. Though it seemed to have calmed down, the clouds were still dark and boiling below them. The front of the plane was a hive of activity as the pilots, navigator, and radio man tried to figure out where they were.

Mahoney worked furiously on his maps, setting a course that he hoped was south-west. But Beau knew that with the radio compass unsettled by the storm it would be hard to tell where they were. Beau heard the pilot tell Russell to break the imposed radio silence in an effort to get a bearing. He managed to get one, but whoever sent it refused to identify themselves. It was more than likely that the "helpful" transmission had come from a German sub.

"You got a light?" asked Matt as he sat down beside Beau.

"Sure. Would you like a cigarette?" said Beau, holding out the pack.

"Thanks. You from the South. Right?"

"That's right. Louisiana. New Orleans," said Beau grateful for the company.

"Good place for music. I love music. Used to play the clarinet," said Matt, lighting up. "Always thought I'd like to get down there and hear some New Orleans jazz."

"Jazz? I play jazz myself."

"No kidding? Wadya play?"

"Piano. Mostly jazz, ragtime. Anything that swings. My folks forced me to take lessons when I was a kid. But I kept running off to the French Quarter to play the devil's music."

"Sounds like fun," chuckled Matt.

"Oh, it's fun all right." Beau shook his head. "Damn sight better than bumping around in the middle of nowhere in this ol' plane."

"Don't worry, kid. Hansen's a great pilot. He'll get us home and dry. Isn't that right, Les?" Matt called out to the lanky gunner who was sitting up against the ball turret playing with Tojo.

"Remember that time in Gulfport, Mississippi? We were flying around for hours with a stuck aileron. But Hansen got us down safely."

"Yeah," said Les. "We were running pretty low on fuel then, too."

"How low are we?" Beau asked.

"Real low," Les answered calmly.

Beau lit another cigarette and tried not to think about what that meant. He was suddenly acutely aware that this plane, large as it might be, was just some sheet-metal held together by rivets hanging 10,000 feet high in the sky. He chuckled nervously as the words of a song popped into his mind. Beau began to sing, snapping his fingers to a slow swing beat:

I get no kicks in a plane –

Flying so high, like some bird in the sky, is my idea of nothing to do –

Cause I get a kick outta you!

Matt and Les listened appreciatively. Applause and catcalls rang out through the compartment. Beau took an exaggerated bow.

"Hey, New Ohleeans!" said Matt, imitating Beau's accent. "Don't worry. Everything's gonna be OK. Trust me."

"Do you know any barber-shop quartet?" asked Les. "I used to sing in one in high school."

"No kidding," said Matt. "Maybe we could get something going back here. Anybody else a singer?"

"Pilot to crew. The choral society is going to have to wait," Hansen's voice came over the intercom.

The men all stood in silence waiting to hear.

"We're gonna have to start thinking about ditching.

I'm going to take her down and see what's under those clouds."

"See, I told ya," said Matt patting Beau on the shoulder. "Everything's gonna be OK. You Southern boys know how to swim, don't you?"

As the drone of the engines changed their pitch, every man went to a window. Merdeza climbed into the tail turret and Les clambered back into his plexiglass dome. The lights flickered as the plane hit turbulence. They descended through the thick grey mass of clouds into a thick white mass of clouds.

Beau's anxiety was matched only by his feeling of uselessness. All he could do was sit and wait.

"New Orleans!" Matt called out, catching Beau's mood. "You're better off in the radio room. Could you look after Tojo for me?"

"My pleasure," said Beau, happy to have something to do. He settled himself on the floor of the radio room, having enticed the monkey with a banana. He really was a cute little guy.

"Tail turret to pilot. I think I can see water."

Beau tried looking out the tiny window behind the radio-operator. All he could see were clouds.

"There are a few breaks in the clouds up ahead," said Hansen. "I'm bringing her down some more." Beau sat back down, held Tojo on his lap and listened to the conversation over the intercom.

"Top turret to pilot. I see land. Twelve o'clock!" Les called out.

"I got it," answered Mc Knight, the co-pilot. *"Do you see it, Charlie? Straight ahead."*

A short burst of applause ran through the plane. Beau felt his spirits lift. He felt a lot better about landing on the ground than in ice-cold water in the middle of the ocean.

"OK. Let's get down a little lower. We'll follow the coastline and see if we can spot a place to land. We've only got a quick look-see. If we don't get a sure thing in the next ten minutes – we're taking her out to sea and ditching. We've only got twenty minutes of fuel left."

The plane was on full alert. Beau could only listen to the calls over the intercom and imagine what was going on. He stroked Tojo who seemed oblivious to the mounting tension.

"It looks real rocky."

"I can't see much. Just a glimpse every now and then."

"That looks like a beach."

"Yeah. But it's too short."

"Top turret to pilot. There was a longer-looking beach back a few miles."

"OK, kid. You've got the best eyes here. Let's turn her around and go check it out."

"Hey!" Matt gestured to Beau from his window at the waist-gun. "I see a little tower. I think it's a lighthouse."

Beau couldn't see.

"There's not much down there," said Matt. "It looks real green. Great cliffs. They've got cliffs in England, don't they?"

"They've got cliffs in Norway," answered the Chief looking out the same window. "They've got cliffs in France."

And both countries are occupied by Germany, thought Beau.

"Top turret to pilot. That's it there."

The plane banked to the right and Beau steadied himself on the radio room door. The plane dropped significantly lower and slowed down as the pilot searched for a place to land.

"Nine o'clock. There's a flat field! Looks as good as a runway!" exclaimed Les. The crew pointed out the windows excitedly.

"OK. We'll bring her around and give it a try," said the pilot. *"Wait a minute. That looks like a town straight ahead. Any idea where we are, Mahoney?"*

"I don't really know. But I figure we could be over Holland," answered the navigator.

Beau risked standing up and looking out the window again. He could just make out some low grey houses as they flew over the rooftops, turned around, and passed over the town again. Tojo clambered onto his shoulder and threw a dirty look at Russell.

"Was anybody down there?" asked Beau. "I could only make out some roofs. I thought I saw a church."

"I could see some people on the street," answered Russell. "And I sure as hell know they saw us. We'd be pretty hard to miss."

"Pilot to crew. Prepare for a forced landing. Assume we are in enemy territory."

Paper flew past the window and Beau realised the pilot and navigator had ripped up all the documents and thrown them out. A shot rang out up front and startled him. Tojo flew off his shoulder in a panic and went straight for Russell.

"Get the hell off me, you dirty ape," yelled Russell, swatting him out of the radio room.

"What was that?" asked Beau, shaken.

"Reisenbeck just shot out the bomb-sight. It's top secret," explained the irate radio-man. "Can't let it fall into the wrong hands. Would you go catch that monkey? Maybe we could shoot him too."

Tojo was bouncing off the walls, shrieking. Beau clambered out after him. Tojo scuttled in behind the commode and refused to come out. Beau bumped into Merdeza who was climbing out of the tail.

"Hey! What are you doing? Get in the radio room."

Beau tried prying the little monkey from his hiding-place but he was stuck like glue. Beau grabbed a banana and waved it slowly.

"Come on, Tojo. Come on, little critter."

Tojo slowly crept out and reached for the fruit. He happily allowed Beau to pick him up. Beau felt a tap on his shoulder.

"This is it, buddy," said Matt.

"Pilot to crew. Assume crash positions. We're bringing her in. Once we've landed I want Les to go out and have a look. If anything looks suspicious, I want you to give me a sign. If I sound the alarm – you all have four minutes to clear the plane before she blows. But I want to be sure we're not in England before throwing away Uncle Sam's $250,000 plane."

Beau looked around and realised the compartment was empty. Confused, he questioned Matt with his eyes.

"You're not an airman, are you?" whispered Matt, grinning. "That's OK. I didn't think you were. Come on. Get in the radio room."

Beau followed Matt, cradling Tojo in his arms. Matt stepped into the radio room where everyone except the pilot and co-pilot were stacked back-to-belly like dominoes. Matt sat himself down between Russell's outstretched legs.

"So this is Holland?" said Matt. "What's in Holland?

Big women – ain't I right? Blondes. Could be interesting."
He motioned to Beau to come in and sit down in
front of him. "What you reckon, New Orleans? Think
they've got jazz in Holland?"

But Beau was distracted. He'd caught sight of
green fields, low stone walls, and a tiny cottage
nestled on the side of a hill. It tripped something in
his memory. Beau loosened his grip on Tojo as he
leaned to get a better look.

"I don't know if they have jazz," said Russell. "But
if a band comes out to meet us – you can be sure it'll
be a German welcoming committee."

At the sound of Russell's voice, Tojo started
wriggling. That wasn't Holland, thought Beau. No
way was that Holland. He turned to tell the crew
when Tojo jumped away. Beau struggled to keep his
balance. He tripped and fell, knocking his head
painfully. He lay on the floor, his head reeling, feeling
the engines throb through his body, hearing voices
far away yelling. He felt himself being dragged and
tried to look up. He wanted to tell them not to worry.
There would be no Gerrys to welcome them. Then
he blacked out.

Chapter Eight

—•—

Mary's heart was still thumping. What was a plane doing here? And what sort of a plane was it? The war had seemed so far away. She'd heard all about the bombs in Dublin and the raids on Belfast, but they might as well be in London or Paris as far as Mary was concerned. Her world started and ended on Inchydoney Island. In West Cork, the Emergency just sounded like a fancy name for rationing. But now the war threatened to land on her doorstep. That felt more like an emergency than any ration-book or petrol ban did. She could no longer hear the drone of the engines but her body was still tingling. A sense of excitement hung in the air. The hounds were barking to beat the band, and the chickens and ducks were still squawking loudly. Tommy went on jumping and waving long after the plane had disappeared.

"Ah jaysus, but I wish I could follow it," he said finally, calming down enough to talk. "'Twas real low. Maybe 'tis going to land."

"Are ya sure 'twas a plane Tommy?" said Imelda still very shaken.

"Of course 'twas a plane. What else do ya know that's as big as a house, as loud as thunder and that flies? Ah, but I wish I could've seen it better!"

"I hope that doesn't put the hens off laying," said Mary, regaining her composure.

"Do ya think it was landing, Missus?" asked Tommy, still scanning the horizon from on top of the cart.

"Tell you what," Mary felt herself get caught up in Tommy's delight, "we'll go into town as we planned. They must have news of it. We'll go and find out what happened."

"Right so!" said Tommy. "On ye gets. We're off."

The pony trotted smartly under Tom's flicking reins. Sunlight poured down through breaks in the clouds in long straight rays. Imelda pointed at it.

"I always think that God is going to speak when the sky looks like that. It reminds me of when God spoke to Noah in the Bible."

"Why couldn't God have spoken when that plane

flew over us?" asked Tommy, shaking his head. "Then I might have seen more than a big green shadow."

The pony started across the causeway. Mary looked over the stone wall at the marsh. A large flock of curlews were feeding in a small pond. Their reflection was mirrored in the water. The sunlight made the marsh grasses glow like gold, in sharp contrast to the soft green hills of the mainland beyond. On the other bank Mary saw the figure of a man working. He was swinging a long scythe in regular wide sweeps. At the sound of the pony's hooves on the causeway, he looked up and wiped his brow.

"Who's yer man?" asked Tommy, returning the salute as the man waved his handkerchief in their direction.

"Barry Kingston. He's probably cutting reeds," answered Mary.

But Tommy wasn't listening. He reined in the pony.

"Wait up. I think I can hear the plane again," he whispered. This time Imelda did not berate her brother, but listened intently. Mary strained to hear. Barry Kingston had gone back to cutting his reeds and the swish of his scythe could be heard clear across the marsh. Tom shook his head and flicked the reins for the pony to move on.

When they reached the middle of the causeway Tommy stopped again. This time they all heard it.

Mary saw Barry Kingston stop and listen. They all turned to face the estuary.

"Oh, my God!" gasped Mary. It was heading straight for them. It was a plane all right. But it must be the biggest plane in the world.

The screeching of birds could faintly be heard through the rumble of the engine. Mary flinched and covered her head with her arms as thousands of birds lifted off the estuary and flew overhead in front of the oncoming plane.

She was jolted off the cart as the pony reared. Tom jumped down and grabbed the bridle. The pony reared again, its eyes wide with fear. The roar of the engines was matched only by the force of the wind. Mary held on to the side of the cart for dear life. She saw Imelda and Tommy struggle to keep the pony under control. Mary stood as if suspended in time as the great green giant passed only a few feet over them and landed in the Marsh.

Minutes passed and still none of them spoke. Mary's ears were ringing though the engines had been silenced. Out of the corner of her eye she saw Barry Kingston drop his scythe and start running towards the plane which was now directly in front of the causeway. Tommy let go of the pony and clambered down over the wall.

"Where are you going?" yelled Imelda, hanging on to the nervous pony.

"Tom, don't be a fool! Come back!"

"I'll be grand," said Tommy, pulling at the brambles that were holding him back. "Look, the door's opening!"

"You'll get yerself kil't," cried Imelda.

"I will not get myself kil't! Don't be stupid." Tommy slid down into marsh and ran towards the plane.

"Why wouldn't ya?" said Imelda. "Come back! They'll shoot ya!"

"No, they won't," yelled Tom over his shoulder. "They're Yanks!"

Les took a deep breath and reached out for the door. He paused a moment with his hand on the cold metal. His mind was racing. There was a town back there. It was only a few miles away. They must be getting a party together to come out and investigate. They wouldn't have more than five or ten minutes before the first people arrived. If Mahoney was right, and this was Holland, that could mean one of two things: either they'd been spotted by friendly Dutchmen – and they still had a chance, or the German forces would be there to greet them. What if Mahoney was wrong? What if they were in Germany itself? Or in England? Maybe they'd made it to England after all?

"We're right behind you, kid," said Matt.

Les turned and saw Matt and the Chief give him the thumbs-up. The rest of the crew were bunched up beside them except for Merdeza and Tate. They were tending to Beau who was lying outstretched on the floor. A small gash on his forehead was bleeding slightly.

"Is he going to be all right?" asked Les.

"I don't know," said Mahoney. "He's breathing fine. Nothing seems broken but he's out cold. We better get him some medical attention soon."

"Right," said Les and he opened the door.

A man was standing a few hundred feet away. Les jumped down and immediately sank into cold brackish water up to his shins. He could see McKnight watching out of the cockpit window ready to relay his signal to Hansen. Les could feel eight pairs of eyes behind him, willing him on. He pulled out his revolver slowly and faced the man. He was dressed in a jacket over a big bulky sweater. His face seemed flushed though Les couldn't see clearly under the man's cap. He tried to imagine what a Dutchman would look like.

Slowly the man raised his arms.

"Do you speak English?" yelled Les.

The man looked incredulous and confused. His hands remained in the air.

"Do you speak English? Do you understand?" Les repeated slowly. "Where are we?"

"Ye're in Paddy White's bog," said the man.

Slowly Les lowered his weapon. He could hear chuckling behind him as Matt leaned out the door.

"Paddy's what?" yelled Matt.

"Bog. Paddy White's bog," said the man as he lowered his arms. "And from the look of it ye're sinking in it. And so's yeer plane."

Les started to laugh. He gave a thumbs-up to McKnight. One by one the crew spilled out the door. The men swore as they sank into the cold marsh.

"So where are we?" said Mahoney, looking around.

"Hey, Mahoney?" chuckled Les. "Did it sound like he's speaking Dutch to you?"

"Mahoney? Did you say Mahoney?" asked the man, splashing through the marsh water to shake Mahoney's hand vigorously. "Of course ye're pronouncing it wrong. Americans always do for some reason. It's Maany, not Mahoney. You must be an O'Mahoney? That's a local name. Welcome home, man. Welcome home."

Mahoney shook his hand, laughing, as the rest of the crew slapped him on the back.

"You mean to say we're in Ireland?" Mahoney shook his head in disbelief.

"Of course ye're in Ireland. Ye're in neutral Ireland. Where did ye think ye were?"

"Mahoney here thought we were in Holland." Les pulled out a cigarette.

"Oh no, ye're in Ireland all right," repeated the man.

Les was offering the man a smoke when a boy about his own age came thrashing through the high grass. He was dressed like a beggar, in frayed and old clothes, but he was beaming from ear to ear.

"Are ye Yanks?" he asked gulping for breath. "What are ye doing in Ireland? Do ye need some help?"

"Hold on there now," said Barry Kingston, shooing the boy with his cigarette. "We've all had a terrible fright here. But we mustn't be rude to our visitors. I know you, boy. What's yer name?"

"Tommy Tanner."

"Fair enough." Barry Kingston pulled himself up and faced the smiling group.

"Tommy Tanner here, and myself, Barry Kingston – Squad Leader for the Local Defence Force – are honoured to be the first people to welcome you all to Clonakilty. And on behalf of – Holy Mother of God! What manner of a creature is that?"

Les looked around and saw Tojo peering out the door.

"That's Tojo. He's a monkey."

"A monkey? Fancy that, now!" said Barry Kingston.

Mary watched from afar. The big green wing was in the way but she could see that a man had come out. Fear gripped her stomach as she saw Barry Kingston raise his arms. Tom was still struggling through the bog. Then Barry Kingston lowered his arms and the sound of laughter could clearly be heard. Mary watched as a group of uniformed men jumped out of the plane. They were laughing and shaking hands with Barry Kingston as Tom reached them.

"I suppose Tom was right," said Mary.

"So you think they're Yanks?" said Imelda. "There seems to be a lot of 'em."

"I don't know what they are," answered Mary. "What would Yanks be doing here?"

Something was happening down there. Some decision had been made. Tommy waved and signalled to them and the men in uniform climbed back into the plane.

"What does that fool want?" said Imelda.

"I think he wants you to bring the cart around," said Mary.

Tommy walked to the edge of the marsh, still signalling.

"You're right," said Imelda. "He wants us to bring the cart over there, closer to the plane."

Imelda sat up in the front and grabbed the reins. As they trotted back over the causeway Mary could see the men in uniform unloading something. It took five of them to carry it. One fellow led the way through the tall grass. They all followed Barry Kingston across the marsh to the bank of the Island where Tom stood waiting on the road.

"What's that they're carrying?" asked Mary.

"I don't know. It looks like something wrapped in a blanket." Imelda stood up, still holding the reins, to get a better view.

Mary marvelled at how she could balance so solidly on the bouncing cart.

"I think they're carrying a man. He must be hurt. Hang on, Mary!" Imelda cracked the reins.

The pony broke into a canter. His hoofs made a terrible clatter on the road. Mary hung on to the side as the cart swerved down the bumpy road. Imelda drove the pony on, her feet firmly planted apart, her knees slightly bent. Her eyes sparkled as she concentrated on controlling the pony and her long plait bounced on her back. Mary was surprised to feel a laugh of pure delight rise in her throat. The men in the marsh stopped at the sound of hooves and watched as Imelda pulled up in front of Tommy.

"They've an injured man," said Tommy, grabbing

the bridle. "I told 'em we could bring him to the farm. Is that all right, Mary?"

Barry Kingston scrambled up the bank and nodded to Mary. "'Tis very good of you, Mary Burke, to be helping these here fellas. Very good indeed. They're Americans."

The six men in green reached the bank and stopped. Mary had never seen the likes of them before. They wore short-fitting leather jackets that zipped up the front. Some of them even wore fancy sunglasses. They were all fairly young. One of them, a tall very pale blond fella, was no more than a boy. He looked up at Mary and Imelda and smiled a big open smile. Next to him were two shorter, darker men. The shorter of the two was very dark indeed. His skin was the colour of burnished copper.

The man being carried didn't seem to be moving. The Yanks hoisted him up the bank as Barry Kingston stood on the road above and advised them on the best path to take.

"Mind you keep him straight now. He has a nasty bump on the head – though I say he'll be fine. This here is Mary Burke, who will gladly take him in."

The Yanks all nodded in her direction. Imelda was still standing on the cart staring openly at them. Mary realised she must be staring too and she felt a blush creep across her face. She slid off the cart and came around to the pony's head as one of the Americans came up to greet her. He was the tall one who'd been leading the way. Unlike the rest, he was wearing a cap. On the brim was a shiny gold crest with an eagle on it. The man extended his hand to Mary. His grip was firm and friendly.

"Lieutenant Charles Hansen, ma'am. I'm the pilot. We're very grateful for your help. We need to get this man somewhere warm and quiet."

Mary nodded. Behind him stood the five men carrying the injured man.

"He's Sergeant Beauregard St Soucis. He fell and hit his head as we were landing. He's in need of medical attention."

The young man lay there, his knees slightly bent, as if he were sleeping. He had a strong nose above a full mouth, which reminded Mary of a picture of a Roman soldier that she had seen as a child. His hair was a rich brown and unruly waves framed his face. A small gash on his forehead had bled down over his sharp cheekbones. Though his eyes were closed, Mary could see he had long black lashes. He stirred and groaned softly. His eyes opened for a second and Mary was surprised by a dark flash. The men struggled to keep the blanket steady as he tried to lift himself up. The blanket rocked and he groaned again and vomited down the front of his uniform. Mary was aware that they were all looking at her expectantly. She pointed to the roof of the farm just visible above the hedge of hawthorns down the road.

"You can bring him up to my house," she said. "Tom will go into town and fetch Dr Moloney."

"Sergeant Russo and Sergeant Wilson will accompany him, if that's all right with you, ma'am," said the pilot pointing to the two dark men Mary had noticed earlier. They both greeted her as they climbed on the cart.

"We'll hoist him up on the cart, lads," said Barry Kingston. "Mary, you sit up there and make sure he doesn't bump his head." The one called Russo took off his jacket and folded it.

"Here, Ma'am, you can use this as a pillow," he said giving it to her. With the help of Barry Kingston, the men on the road lifted the injured man up to those on the cart. Together they carefully laid him out along the wooden slats. Mary gently lifted his head and slipped the folded jacket under it.

"The rest of us will wait here for the cart to come back," the pilot said to Tom. "Some of us will go in to town with you. The rest will stay and guard the plane."

"Are we right, so?" asked Tommy as he took the

reins. One of the Americans held the man across the shoulders as the other held his legs.

"You'd better take it nice and slow. There's no hurry and we don't want to jolt him," the one with copper-coloured skin said to Tommy. He then turned to Mary with a warm smile. "Would you mind holding his head, ma'am?"

"Not at all," she answered. "As long as ye all stop calling me 'ma'am'. It makes me nervous. Call me Mary." Cradling the man's head carefully she nodded to Tommy to move out. The pony started up the road at the slowest pace Tommy had ever driven it.

"Well, Mary," said the dark short Yank, "My name's Mateo. It's Italian – but everyone calls me Matt. This is John Wilson – but we call him Chief. He's a full-blooded Cherokee Indian. And that poor guy there is Beau."

"Bo?" repeated Mary, puzzled.

"Means 'handsome' in French. His name's Beauregard. That's French for good-looking," offered the Chief. "He's from Louisiana. They speak French there."

She looked down at the man called Beau. Though he was ashen under his dark tan, Mary thought that the name was certainly right for him. She couldn't help but notice how the dark curls seemed to wrap themselves around her fingers, how soft his hair was as she held his head on her lap.

"Do you speak French?" asked Mary, quite amused at the sudden barrage of information.

"Yes, ma'am. I mean Mary," answered the Chief with a wicked grin. "In fact before I joined the Air Corps I was a French teacher. High School History too."

"Go away! You're not serious?" said Mary shaking her head and laughing. "I'll tell ya, if anybody had told me when I woke up this morning that I'd be driving home with a French-speaking Indian, an Italian, and a Yank called 'handsome' – I'd have never believed it."

As the cart pulled out slowly down the road, Imelda sat herself on the low stone wall. Everyone seemed to have forgotten about her. She didn't mind. Her head was reeling with the excitement of it all, and she felt quite shy with all these strangers. She stared at the plane. She couldn't believe the size of it. It was bigger than a house. And there it was, like a giant insect, just sitting there in the marsh. The birds had started to settle back into feeding. A few gulls had even landed on top of the plane and were inspecting it. Three Yanks stood around smoking while four more crossed the marsh to join them.

Barry Kingston was still chatting away to the pilot.

"Do ya think you can fly her out?" Imelda overheard him ask.

"No reason why not," answered the pilot. "As long as we can get some gasoline."

"Gasoline? You mean petrol?"

"That's right. In fact there's nothing we'd like more than to get that man seen to, tank up, and leave. We've got a war to fight."

"Aye. Don't I know it. I've a brother in Seattle," said Barry Kingston. "His boy's gone off and joined the Marines."

"Have you got a depot?"

"We've a depot," said Barry Kingston, shaking his head as if to say no. "Ye've got a war to fight and we've got an Emergency. So we've a depot all right but the petrol is rationed. To get as much as what you'd be looking for now, would require the consent of the proper authority. But if we alert the proper authority, chances are ye'll be spending the rest of the war in neutral Ireland."

"Do you have to alert them?" asked the pilot.

"Well now. We would have to tell the army that a plane had landed. Of course we would. The question is not if we tell 'em, it's when we tell 'em. If ye were to fly off again – we mightn't have the time to alert them until after ye've gone."

"So don't inform them."

"Ah, but you need the petrol," sighed Barry Kingston. "Still, it seems an awful waste to have come this far and not make it."

Imelda was enthralled with the conversation though she couldn't understand the half of it. She was startled by a voice at her side. The tall young fella she'd noticed earlier was sitting down along the wall. He must have come up without her hearing him.

"You really know how to handle a pony," he said. "My name's Les Wagner. I'm from Wisconsin. Do you know Wisconsin?"

Imelda was too shy to answer and just shook her head.

"It's up near the Canadian border. In the Midwest," he added stammering slightly.

Imelda sneaked a sideways glance at the him. Les Wagner. What a lovely-sounding name, she thought. He was very fair, and at least a head taller than she was. He looked as shy as she felt.

"My name's Imelda Tanner," she said bravely. The Yank called Les Wagner smiled and Imelda felt as if the sun had suddenly come out after a fortnight of rain.

"Pleased to meet you, Imelda." He pointed at the plane. "That's a B-17. A flying fortress. We call her *T'Ain't a Bird*. You know, Superman: *Is it a bird? Is it*

a plane? It's Superman! On the radio. I'm the top-
turret gunner. See that little kinda tower on the top.
That's the top turret."

Imelda didn't know what he was going on about,
but she was fascinated. She wished she had a nicer
dress on, and wondered how to keep this conversation
going when she didn't have a clue what it was about.
Their attention was caught by four Yanks climbing up
the bank.

"That there's the rest of the crew," he said. "The
one with the cap is the co-pilot McKnight. And the
next one's the navigator. He's the one that got us lost,
I guess," he added with an embarrassed laugh.

Imelda tried to look interested so he would keep
talking. She couldn't think of a thing to say. She felt
a right eejit. Thankfully he kept on describing the men
as they climbed onto the road.

"The last two guys are Russell the radio man, and
Riesenbeck, our bombardier. He sits in that little
glassed-in compartment in the nose. It's not glass
though. It's plexiglass. Do you have plexiglass over
here?"

Imelda could only nod and hope for the best.
What in God's name was plexiglass? To hide her
embarrassment she looked intently at the crew on the
road. Two of the men were carrying bottles. The last
one seemed to be struggling with something small

and wriggly. Whatever it was jumped out of his arms and came running along the wall down to where Imelda and Les were sitting. Imelda let out a shriek as a small furry animal jumped on Les's shoulder.

"Don't be scared," said Les. "This is Tojo. He's a spider monkey. Say 'hi' to Imelda, Tojo."

Imelda reached out her hand and the little monkey jumped over and settled on her lap.

"He likes you," said Les.

"Oh, he's a dote!" said Imelda, delighted with the little animal. She wished her sisters could see him. Tojo sat quietly as Imelda stroked his head while she thought of what to say next. She stole another glance at Les. He was listening with interest to the conversation that was still going on between Barry Kingston and the pilot.

"So now. There's ten of ye in the crew and yer man who is injured," said Barry Kingston.

"That's right," said the pilot, "and we'd like to try and get some gasoline as soon as possible."

"Take yer time," said Barry Kingston. "We'll sort all that out later. First I reckon ye could all do with a bit of refreshment. I know I'm missing my dinner. And ye'll need a place to stay. I suppose we should wait for the cart to come back, and then we can go into town."

"Looks like the town is coming out to us," said Les, turning back to Imelda.

Imelda looked up and saw a large group walking fast over the causeway. In front was a gaggle of little boys. She could hear them shouting and whooping loudly as they pointed at the plane in the marsh. Behind them she recognised Ruth Bennett walking with some fella. Imelda waved. The whole group waved back and broke into a run. People were walking all along the road on the mainland as well. About a half a mile down, but gaining fast, was a motor-car. Imelda knew it well.

"Well now," said Barry Kingston pointing across the marsh. "We won't have to call for the doctor. That's his car now. And it looks like 'tis full up. That'll be the welcoming party. You must have caused quite a stir in town. They'll all be out to see what's up."

"Maybe this will help to break the ice," said the pilot, holding up a bottle that one of the men had passed to him.

Barry Kingston read the label and smiled. "Rum. We haven't seen rum for a while. I'd say this will come in handy."

The first of the boys reached them with Ruth Bennett and her companion right behind. They were all out of breath. Ruth nodded to Imelda.

"A monkey!" she exclaimed. "I've never seen a real monkey." She walked straight up to Les and held out her hand. "Hello. My name's Ruth Bennett. Is that your monkey?"

Les smiled broadly as he took her hand. "Les Wagner. Pleased to meet you." He gestured to the monkey who jumped off Imelda's lap and back onto Les's shoulder. "This is Tojo. He's our crew's mascot."

Imelda watched them chatting away happily as the little boys all gathered to marvel at the Yanks and their monkey. People were running up in groups, crowding her out. They were chatting and laughing, and patting the Yanks and each other on the back. She could barely make out the top of Les's head as he stood talking. Why couldn't she have thought of anything to say? She hadn't even shaken his hand. She'd sat there gawking while Ruth just walked right up and introduced herself. Fair play to her, thought Imelda. At least Ruth didn't just sit there speechless. All the same, she had some cheek.

The crowd moved aside as Dr Moloney's motorcar drove up. Barry Kingston opened the door, brandished the bottle of rum and started making the introductions. The first one out of the car was the garda sergeant, followed by Ruth's da and a few men Imelda recognised from town, including Tony the barman from the hotel.

"Don't they all look like film stars?" said Ruth, standing next to her again.

"Who? Yer da and Dr Moloney?" asked Imelda annoyed.

"Don't be silly," laughed Ruth. "The Americans. They all look like film stars."

"What would you know about film stars, Ruth Bennett?"

"Sure, you know what I mean," Ruth replied, unperturbed. "And what do you make of yer man? I think he's lovely. How old do you think he is?"

"How should I know?" answered Imelda. "Who was that you were walking up with?"

"That's just Dennis." Ruth craned her neck to see what was going on.

"Just Dennis?" mimicked Imelda raising an eyebrow. "Last week he was 'Wonderful Dennis'. Now he's 'Just Dennis'."

Ruth ignored her.

The open bottle was raised and the crowd applauded. A second one followed immediately and Imelda could see that the bottles of rum were being passed around as everyone toasted the Yanks. She saw the garda sergeant moving off to one side with the pilot and Barry Kingston. After a short discussion he motioned for Ruth's da and Dennis to follow. The five men huddled together talking.

"What's yer da and Just Dennis got to do with all this?" asked Imelda.

"Dunno," answered Ruth, still busy trying to catch Les's eye. He was in the middle of a large group who were having a great time as Tojo jumped from one shoulder to another. Every time he leapt, a yell of appreciation went up from the group. "I suppose it would have to do with the Local Defence Force, seeing as they're all in it. Sure isn't that what they're for?"

The five men all shook hands and returned to the main crowd. The pilot called over the rest of the Yanks. After a quick word with them, they all handed over their guns to Garda Coughlan, who put them carefully into the boot of the car. Ruth's da and Barry Kingston tried to move people away down the road back to town. Nobody paid the least bit of attention to them.

Dennis strode over to Ruth and Imelda. He was proud as a peacock and flushed with excitement.

"Garda Couglan is taking the Yanks up to the barracks," he announced. "And I'm to stay with your da to guard the plane!"

"Up to the barracks?" exclaimed Ruth. "What for? He's not arresting the Yanks, is he?"

"Well, technically they'd be under arrest I suppose,"

said Dennis scratching his head, "seeing as they have no choice in the matter."

"That's terrible." Ruth moved away in the direction of the Yanks who had started walking up the road.

"But did ya hear? I'm to guard the plane. It's a B-17 bomber," Dennis tried again.

"That's great. You guard that plane," yelled Ruth over her shoulder. "Come on, Imelda! We don't want to miss this."

The Yanks walked past them, still surrounded by little boys. As Les Wagner drew level with Imelda, he smiled and waved. Imelda smiled back and fell in step with the crowd of people following them.

Dennis stood to one side looking puzzled. Imelda dug her elbow into Ruth. Ruth looked up, laughed, and waved gaily back at him.

"Goodbye so, Just Dennis," she giggled under her breath.

Chapter Nine

⚫•⚫

They carried Beau through the kitchen and laid him on the sofa in the front room. Mary got an extra blanket from the tea chest and covered him. As soon as they had him settled, Tommy went off to fetch the doctor, leaving Mary alone with the Americans.

It was cold in the front room. She hadn't lit a fire in here for months. She was aware of the musty slightly damp smell and she wished she had aired out the room that morning. Sure, how was she to know her house would be full of strangers? Seeing the Yanks standing there amongst the armchairs and the knick-knacks made the familiar surroundings seem unreal. It was unnerving. Back at the marsh it had all felt like a bit of fun. But here she was with three foreign men in her house. Mary stood in the middle of the room, feeling flustered.

"Maybe I should make a fire," she said softly.

"A fire?" echoed Matt.

"Don't you find it cold?" asked Mary, adding, "I'm afraid we don't use this room very much."

The Chief pointed to the chimney and nudged Matt, who seemed suddenly to understand.

"Sorry, Mary. It's a good idea. Where I come from we don't do much fire-lighting." He grinned. "But you just sit over here and tell us what to do. I'm sure the Chief here knows all about fires."

"You've been watching too many cowboy movies," joked the Chief.

"No, really. I don't mind. I've a fire lit in the kitchen. It won't take a minute." said Mary, glad to have an excuse to leave the room.

Mary put some embers in a bucket and got kindling and turf. She lingered as long as she dared. She would much rather stay in the kitchen but the thought of the injured man drew her back into the room. As she walked in, both airmen reached out to take the bucket and bundle she was carrying. They stood in the middle of the room, waiting for instructions. They looked so willing, yet so clearly unsure of what to do next that Mary could not help but smile. She motioned them over to the chimney, and quickly set the kindling alight, laying the turf so that it would catch easily. She knelt in front of the hearth and blew softly until the tiny flames grew and she was satisfied that the fire would work away unattended.

"You put a Cherokee to shame," commented the Chief.

"What's the brown stuff?" asked Matt.

"Turf," answered Mary. "You get it from the ground."

"Like coal?"

"Not really, you don't mine it. You cut it from the bog. We can't get any more coal these day. It's rationed."

"The bog?" echoed Matt.

Mary tried to think of how to explain it but was saved by the Chief.

"It's peat. From a peat bog. It's decomposed organic material. Like coal, only closer to the surface and of course not as old. It's like young coal."

"I swear this guy is a walking encyclopaedia," laughed Matt.

"Are you really an Indian?" asked Mary, feeling more comfortable. The Yanks' easy-going manner was hard to resist, and the familiar crackle of the fire was relaxing her.

"Yes ma'am. A full-blooded Cherokee Indian."

"Absolutely," added Matt. "He left his headdress in the plane. But if you want, he'll do a raindance."

"A raindance!" exclaimed Mary. "Heaven forbid!

The last thing we need around here is more rain. We've enough as it is, thank you very much."

"Those are Hopi Indians who do the raindance," corrected the Chief. "You don't have to worry."

Mary glanced over at Beau lying on the sofa. They had tried to make him comfortable by loosening his jacket and removing his shoes.

"It would be great to get him into a clean shirt." Matt noticed her looking.

"Maybe wash him up a little."

"Of course," said Mary "I can give you one of my husband's."

By the time she came back with a clean shirt and a basin of warm water and cloths, they had his jacket and shirt off. They lay in tatters on the floor. They must have been cut off him, thought Mary. Afternoon light came through the tiny window and fell in a single shaft across the sofa. It illuminated his strong jaw, and cast a shadow on his naked shoulder. Mary felt herself blush as she took note of the curve his neck made. She hid her embarrassment by fetching a side table to lay the things on. She pulled up a chair and very gently took his chin in her left hand while she wet the cloth with her right. His skin was cool to the touch. She could feel a slight stubble underneath her fingertips. Mary forced herself to concentrate on the gash on his forehead, dabbing at the dried blood.

The gash was small and straight, but he had an ugly bruise the size of an egg.

"The cut isn't deep. He might need a stitch, though," she commented.

"We can do that, if you'd rather," offered Matt.

"Nonsense. It's a woman's job."

"Isn't lighting the fire a man's job?" asked Matt slyly.

"Not here it isn't," answered Mary smiling. "But don't women do all the jobs anyway? Men just pretend to do half of 'em."

Beau stirred and grimaced. Mary reached out her hand and smoothed his hair. The curls rippled under her open palm. Beau sank back and relaxed. Mary continued to wash him, patting him dry as she went so he wouldn't get cold.

Matt and the Chief called his name. Beau seemed to be trying to wake up. He would start to open his eyes and then close them again as if he hadn't slept in days. She hoped he wasn't badly hurt. The cut was nothing but he still wasn't fully conscious. She wished the doctor would come. He looked so helpless just lying there. And beautiful. Like a sleeping angel. That was it. It wasn't a Roman soldier. He reminded her of a picture of an archangel she'd seen in her religion book. The angel had been asleep on a hillside. He had smooth long muscles and white fluffy wings. The sound of a car driving up caught her attention. Mary realised that she had been lost in her thoughts. She finished drying Beau and covered him quickly with the blanket.

"That'll be Dr Moloney," she said, going out to the hall to greet him.

"Hello there, Mary girl," the doctor greeted her fondly.

Mary had known the doctor since she was a child and he never really seemed to change. He was a large corpulent man with a shock of white hair that used to fascinate her when she was little. He smiled and winked at her kindly.

"I've been told to come up by Garda Coughlan. He's still down with the others. They're all walking back into town. You should have seen them. The Yanks looked like pied pipers with a rake of children tagging along and half the town behind them. And that monkey jumping from one to the next."

"A monkey?" exclaimed Mary.

"Seems he's the plane's mascot. Now where is this fella who took a knock on the head?"

Mary showed him into the front room and introduced him to Matt and the Chief. The doctor gave them a cursory nod and quickly went over to Beau. He threw back the blanket and examined him carefully, concentrating on his neck and head. After a few minutes he looked up, smiling.

"No serious damage here. Nasty bump on the head but nothing is broken, thank God." He forced Beau's eyelids apart and slapped him gently on the cheek.

"Come on now. Wake up, man," he said softly.

Beau groaned and shook his head.

Dr Moloney searched his big black medical bag and pulled out a small bottle.

"It'll do no harm to try some good old-fashioned smelling salts," he said, opening the vial under Beau's nose.

Beau's eyes flew open instantly and he pulled away from the bottle.

"Steady now. Steady," said the doctor. "Don't get up. You've had a nasty fall."

Beau looked at the doctor and then around the room. His eyes rested on Mary and she looked straight back at him. His eyes were very dark. He seemed to be confused and trying to focus, but he held her gaze. Mary found she could not look away. Dr Moloney spoke up and Beau turned to face him.

"My name is Brian Moloney. I'm a doctor. Do you understand?"

Beau nodded slowly. His hand reached up to his forehead and gingerly touched the bruise. He winced in pain.

"Now so," said the doctor, "tell me your name. Do you know who you are?"

"Beauregard St Soucis." Beau answered still touching his head. The doctor looked at Matt for confirmation.

"Fair enough. And do you know where you are?" asked the doctor, adding quickly, "Of course you don't. Do you remember what happened?"

"We were going to land. I was trying to catch the monkey. I'd just remembered something," said Beau. "But I forget what it was. I can't remember anything else."

"That's all right. You'll feel a bit groggy for a while. That's enough for today. Just lie there and relax for now. You're in good hands."

Beau lay back and closed his eyes. Mary wondered if he had fallen asleep. Dr Moloney rummaged in his big bag again. He handed Mary a small box.

"There's some tablets if he complains of the pain. He can have two every four hours. He's not to be moved for forty-eight hours. He seems fine but his brain has had a mighty wallop and we won't know if it's done any harm for a few days. He can have water but it's just as well if he doesn't eat just yet. Maybe some broth, or light tea. Nothing heavy. You'll be all right, won't you?"

Mary nodded silently and took the boxes.

"Right, so." The doctor turned to Matt and the Chief. "I'm to bring you back with me."

"I'm afraid we can't do that," said Matt, shaking his head.

"Well, afraid or not, you're going to have to," answered the doctor.

"We have orders from our pilot to stay with this man," said the Chief.

"Sorry, lads. The garda says you're to come with me. Sure you can talk to your pilot when you get into town. They all went off together."

The two men looked at each other, trying to make up their minds.

"Don't worry about this fella here. He's in good hands. And I can tell you he won't be going anywhere tonight."

Matt and the Chief went over to Beau.

"I just want to sleep," he said, "and to get rid of this awful headache."

"Mary'll give you something for the head. Won't you, Mary? You'll be grand," said Dr Moloney. He looked at Mary. Mary nodded again. "You're a great girl. I'll call in tomorrow."

Before she had the time to respond, she found herself showing them to the door and waving them off.

Mary wondered what to do next. The front of the house lost its light early in the day and the hall was getting dark. She peeped into the front room. Beau seemed to be asleep. Then he shifted and groaned. Mary remembered the tablets and scurried into the kitchen. As she passed the stove, she put the kettle on.

She came back into the room quietly. The light from the window now illuminated a spot on the wall behind Beau. His face was in the shadows. Mary was startled to hear him speak.

"Hi there," he said lazily. His voice was a surprise. It was warm and purring. His accent was unlike anything Mary had ever heard. The "r" slid like honey, so different from the rough throaty "r's" of West Cork.

Mary held out the tablets and a glass of water shyly.

"The doctor said you were to take these. They'll help ease your head."

He took them with a nod of thanks, wincing again as he moved.

Mary was relieved to hear the hiss of the kettle faintly through the open door.

"Would you like a cup of tea?" she asked quickly.

"Thank you very much. I don't mind if I do."

"And a pillow, maybe?" she added.

"I would be much obliged." He smiled and closed his eyes.

Mary busied herself getting everything ready. It

helped her sudue the tiny fluttering in her stomach. She wondered if she should put a cloth on the tray. It had been so long since she had served tea to anyone, she didn't even know where the dainty cloths her grandmother used to have were. Then she remembered: they were in the front room. Just like the good china which never came out of the little mahogany cabinet, except when she gave the place a good dusting. Well she wasn't going in to get them. She'd just have to make do.

She searched every cup to find the one that was least chipped and had a saucer to match. A white tea towel would do to cover the tray, and the milk would have to go in the big pitcher. She made the tea and went to get a pillow. When she came back she found Imelda standing there looking at the tea-tray.

"I thought I'd call in to see how you're getting on before I went home," said Imelda.

"I'm grand," said Mary. "They've left the one who was hurt here. The doctor says he can't be moved for forty-eight hours."

"That looks lovely," said Imelda pointing to the tray. "Is it for him?"

"He's not to eat anything. The doctor will call back in the morning."

"Do you want me to stay with you?" asked Imelda. "I could maybe come back later."

"Thanks, but I'll manage. He has a bad bump on the head but he should be all right."

"What's he like?" asked Imelda.

"Well, his name is Beau. And he speaks funny," said Mary. The memory of his voice made her stop and smile.

"Why does he speak funny?" continued Imelda.

"I don't know. They all do. And they all sound different. You know the two others who were here? One was a Red Indian. And the other was an Italian. This one here's French, or so they tell me. I ask you!"

"One of 'em is Irish. His name's O'Mahoney. Can you believe it? It seems they ran out of petrol. And one of 'em's from Wisconsin," said Imelda her eyes lighting up. "I went all the way to town before Tommy caught up with us. He's gone off to see what's happening. I thought I'd better get back to the girls. Ruth Bennett was there. Loads of people came out when you left. The town must be in a tizzy. Did you see the monkey?"

"No, but the doctor told me about it."

"His name's Tojo."

"Come here," said Mary, picking up the pillow. "I should go in with this. The tea will be cold. Give me a hand."

Imelda stopped her chattering at the door. She hesitated to go in. Hiding her own nervousness, Mary urged her on. She motioned her to lay down the tray on the little table. Beau was fast asleep. The light was fading fast, but she could tell by the steady rise and fall of his chest that he was peaceful. Mary carefully placed the pillow under his head without waking him. The thought struck her that it was the second time today she had done that.

"Doesn't he look just like a film star?" Imelda whispered in Mary's ear.

"Sure what would you know, Imelda Tanner?" she answered under her breath.

"That's what I said to Ruth Bennett," continued Imelda as they both crept out of the room. "But ya know what? I've never been to the cinema but I think Ruthie is right – that's what a film star should look like."

"You girls are full of nonsense," said Mary sternly. But then again, thinking he looked like a film star was no more foolish than thinking he looked like an angel.

Once Imelda was satisfied that there was nothing more for her to do, she said her goodbyes. Mary found herself alone again.

She stood, caught in the silence of the hallway. What was wrong with her? The day's excitement had left her giddy and bewildered. Mary could feel her heart pound as if she'd just run up the stairs. She told herself to be calm.

Opening the door silently she was enveloped by a smell that made her heart speed up again. It was warm and lemon-scented. She knew instantly that it came from him. She had first smelled it when she sat washing him. It smelled like he spoke.

The light was almost gone. Mary watched it creep up the wall and then cross over to the other side of the room before fading altogether. The fire cast flickering shadows on the figure asleep on the sofa. The draped folds of the blanket and the outline of his curls reminded her of an angel again. She smiled at herself for being so silly.

The pills Dr Maloney had given him must have been powerful. Safe in the knowledge that he was out cold, Mary let herself breathe in the air. How could a man smell of lemon? She stood beside the sofa and let herself look at him. She had never thought of any man as being beautiful. Handsome of face perhaps, but never beautiful. The blanket had dropped to his waist and Mary let herself contemplate him without prudery or embarrassment. She took her time, let her eyes drift from his strong shoulders, across his chest, and down to his tapered waist and flat belly.

Her fingers remembered the silky feel of his hair, the touch of stubble on his cheek. She relished the thought and yet it scared her. What was happening? The man had barely spoken two words to her and she longed for him to wake and speak to her again. And yet she was terrified that he might do just that. Maybe she was going mad. She had to get her mind off these thoughts of angels and lemon. They were giving her a fright.

She decided to douse down the fire in the kitchen and build up the one in the front room. Before leaving the room she leaned over him and pulled the blanket up over his chest. She couldn't help noticing the curly tuft of jet-black hair that nestled there, nor avoid feeling the satin smoothness of his skin. As she tucked the blanket around him, she inhaled deeply.

Catching sight of the untouched tea-tray she reached out to take it. Her hand faltered and she knocked over the cup. It crashed to the floor, shattering the silence. She jumped back with a cry, holding her hand to her mouth but it was too late. Beau's eyes fluttered open and searched the darkened room.

"Oh, you're back," he said groggily.

Mary smoothed her apron and took a step back.

"The tea is cold," she said pointing at the tray. "Will I make some more?"

"No thank you, miss."

"My name is Mary. Is there anything else I can get you?"

"Well, Mary, could you be a darling and turn on a light for me?"

"Of course," she said as she headed for the door. She was slightly unsettled by his familiarity.

"Where are you going?" he said, as if admonishing a child. He raised his head, and then finding it too heavy, settled back on the pillow.

"To fetch you a lamp," Mary snapped. She instantly regretted the sharpness in her tone.

"Can't you just switch it on?" he asked wearily.

"What do you mean?"

"Can't you just switch on the bedside lamp for me. I can't seem to find it." His voice was still sweet but the words were slightly slurred. Mary realised he must be even more confused than she was.

"Do you know where you are?" she asked softly. Beau stared blankly around the room, and then looked back at her. He seemed to be having problems keeping his eyes open. Mary felt herself relax.

"You're in Ireland." she said taking a step back into the room. "In West Cork, near Clonakilty."

"Ireland? Oh, I remember," he said, sleepily waving his hand dismissively. "Thank you very much, Mary. That'll be all."

Mary stifled a laugh. He must think she was some sort of chambermaid.

"I hope you're comfortable, sir," she said, playing along. "Do ring if you should need anything."

"Well, I have to admit the bed is somewhat lumpy. But other than that, it's a charming establishment. Now be a good girl and run along." His voice was fainter with every word. By the time he'd finished he was fast asleep again.

"I'll mention the lumpy bed to the innkeeper, shall I then?" whispered Mary as she sank down in the armchair by the fire and watched him sleep.

Mary sat and watched him as the evening melted into night. She fetched a lamp, and kept the fire going, but other than that she just sat and watched him. She searched his profile for clues. Who was he? Was he married? Did he have a family? What did he do for a living? All she knew was that he smelt of lemon, he came from Louisiana and he was going to fight a war. What was it like to be so far from home, knowing that you mightn't make it back? She shuddered at the thought. The war was something you read about. She didn't like being confronted with it. She wouldn't let herself think about what might happen to these Yanks once they got to where they were going.

Instead she watched Beau sleep. It was comforting to sit with only the fire for company and the soft rhythm of his breathing. Her mind drifted aimlessly in a way that it hadn't since she was a child. Curled up in the big armchair, she remembered things she hadn't thought about in years. Her father lifting her high up above him, telling her to catch a cloud for him. And her grandmother, sitting in this very chair, reading Robert Louis Stevenson to her as Mary stared into the fire and thought she could see pirate ships and hidden gold blazing in the glowing embers.

Later, as the wind picked up outside, Beau tossed and groaned. Mary reached out and lay a hand on his brow. He smiled and took the tablets she offered him without a word, gulped down the glass of water and fell instantly back asleep.

He didn't stir after that. The dog scratched at the door and Mary let him in. He paid no attention to Beau and curled up at the foot of her chair. Mary let herself slide into a pleasant calm as she stared into the fire. The flames licked languorously at the glowing blocks of turf. Her breathing matched the steady rise and fall of the blanket which covered Beau. Mary was smiling as she fell asleep.

Beau was having a very strange series of dreams. He

knew he was dreaming because none of it made any sense. He wished he could wake up because his head throbbed with pain. He had been in a small enclosed space and then suddenly all he could see was grey sky. And then a beautiful woman with dark red hair and eyes that matched the sky was smiling down at him. A chattering sound rang in his ears and he knew he had to catch a monkey. Why a monkey? A doctor who looked like Santa Claus was giving the beautiful woman instructions, but he couldn't make out what he was saying. Then for some reason he was back in his hotel except that he couldn't find the light and the chambermaid was offering him tea.

Beau was thirsty. He willed himself to wake up so that he could reach for his glass. The housekeeper always left an ice-cold pitcher of water when she turned down his bed for the night. As he slowly pulled himself up, he realised he wasn't in his bedroom. This was too narrow to be his bed. He looked up. Instead of the familiar canopy of his four-poster bed, he saw only a low ceiling. Shadows flickered across rough plaster. He was dizzy and disoriented. A soft sigh made him look over at a glowing fire. A dog was curled up asleep at the foot of an armchair. Beau realised he must still be dreaming. Why else would the red-haired woman be there? She was fast asleep, curled up like a cat in the armchair. Fickering flames of light darted over her face which seemed impossibly white, her hair a sharp contrast of colour and brightness as it reflected the red glow of the fire.

Chapter Ten

•—•

They had all walked back together, following the coast for about two miles. The group had grown in size as they met more people and even more children who were on their way out to the plane. By the time Les saw the church spires poking into the sky above the grey line of buildings in the distance, the group had become a throng. They slowed down to a snail's pace as people met and stopped to chat excitedly. Children and barking dogs darted in and out among the crowd, while horses and carts and bicycles blocked the road.

Tojo was a great attraction. He seemed to relish being the centre of attention. The children shrieked with delight as he leapt from shoulder to shoulder, chattering and pulling people's hats off. It was like the Fourth of July and the circus coming to town all rolled into one.

Ruth walked alongside Les, asking questions and pointing out landmarks. She explained that the man in charge was Pat Coughlan, from the gardaí, which is what they called policemen in Ireland. She seemed to have appointed herself Les's personal guide and went on to explain that no cars were on the road because petrol was rationed, that the estuary used to be a big port back in the days when Clonakilty was a linen town, that Clonakilty meant "the stone of kilty" or "the stone in the woods" in Irish, and that she was sixteen and working at the local hotel.

Les smiled pleasantly as she talked, but all the while he tried to keep an eye on Imelda who walked silently behind Ruth. Somehow he lost her in the crowd as they came into town.

They walked up a steep hill, lined on both sides by little grey two-storey houses. Some of them were only one room wide, but an astounding number of family members spilled out onto the street to wave as they passed by.

Their destination was a large square building which served as the police station and local jail. Only Barry Kingston and the crew were let in. Pat Coughlan managed to close the door behind them.

After taking down their names, the garda was clearly

confused as to what to do next. Barry Kingston was still arguing that the thing to do was to let them fly off again but Pat Coughlan thought it best to call Cork for instructions. It seemed that his superior was gone for a few days along with the District Officer who constituted the army presence in the town.

"The superintendent and Lieutenant Dinneen won't be back until tomorrow night at the earliest," the garda said thoughtfully. "In their absence it would be proper to contact Collins Barracks in the city."

"Of course ya will. But there's no rush, like. In any case ya can't keep 'em in there," said Barry Kingston, pointing at the two little cells at the back of the room. "And we're all starving by now. It's way past everyone's dinner time. You'd better take them down to the hotel where they can wait just as well as in here, but with a good feed and a decent bed."

Pat Couglan was considering this proposal when the door burst open. In walked a large man with a shock of white hair, followed by Matt and the Chief. Les recognised the doctor and remembered Beau. He wondered how he was doing. Ignoring the garda, the doctor walked straight up to Charlie Hansen and addressed him.

"Your man has a nasty bump on the head, but no permanent damage as far as I can see. Still, I thought it best to leave him where he is for a day. Heads weren't made to be knocked about like a *sliotar* – that's the ball we use when we play hurling. Then again, you probably wouldn't know the game in America."

Charlie Hansen shook the doctor's hand warmly.

"Thank you for your help, doctor. It's a relief to know that Sergeant St Soucis is going to be all right."

"Right, so." The doctor turned to the garda, "What are we doing, Pat?"

"We were just saying how a good feed down at O'Donovan's hotel was in order," Barry Kingston butted in.

"That's a marvellous idea," said the doctor. "Not to mention a drink," he added, turning to the crew lined up along the wall. "I don't know about you, lads, but I'm hanging for a pint."

"I'll run down and tell 'em to expect us, will I?" said Barry Kingston to Pat Coughlan who still looked doubtful. With a quick nod and a wink he was gone out the door.

"We'd certainly appreciate a meal," said Charlie Hansen, smiling his most dazzling East-Coast smile. "We haven't eaten since we left early this morning."

"That settles it, so." The doctor slapped the garda playfully on the back. "Come on, Pat. You must be starving as well. Sure, you can't think straight on an empty stomach, can you?"

Garda Coughlan had to concede that the good doctor was right. And so they all filed back down the hill and into O'Donovan's hotel where half of the town was waiting for them.

Les looked hungrily at the steaming plate in front of him. It was piled high with potatoes and what looked like cabbage and bacon. The girl, Ruth, had shovelled a mountain of food onto his plate despite his protests. He had to admit he was ravenous, and by the looks of it, so were the rest of the crew. The food smelled wonderful and tasted even better. They all spoke little while they ate. Even Matt, who never missed a chance to tell everyone how nothing compared to Italian food, wolfed it down.

To Les, the meal tasted like the first real home cooking he'd had in months. It was just like the good solid German fare his mother cooked back in Wisconsin. He wondered how they were all doing back home. It worried him to think that they had no idea where he was. They'd certainly never have guessed he was sitting in a hotel dining-room in Ireland. Though the room was crowded with people, the thought made him feel lost and a little lonely.

Hansen was huddled in deep discussion with a group of men at the other end of the room. Les could tell from the pilot's alert manner that nothing had been worked out yet.

Ruth came up with the serving-platter and offered him another helping.

"You'll have a bit more bacon to go with them spuds," she said, not waiting for an answer.

"No, thank you. I've had more than enough," Les stammered.

"Ah, you will! A tall fella like yerself," she said, disregarding him completely.

"And you'll have some more cabbage, won't ya?" she added, heaping a full plate in front of him again.

"She's taken with you, kid," said Matt as Ruth walked away. "You be careful. I could tell you stories about Irish women that would break your heart."

"Stop it, Matt," said Les embarrassed.

"What's a matter, kid?" said Matt nudging him. "Don't you think she's pretty?"

"She's not as pretty as the other one," Les said, before he could stop himself.

"What other one?" asked Matt intrigued.

"The girl with the pony. The first one we met." Les lit up just at the thought of her riding on that old cart, her eyes blazing and her braid bouncing in the wind as she galloped up. "She's the prettiest girl I've ever seen. Her name's Imelda," he added.

"That's her brother over there," offered the Chief nodding towards a boy who stood in the doorway. Les recognised him as the scruffy kid he'd met at the marsh.

"Are you sure that's her brother?" he asked, lowering his voice.

"Yeah. His name's Tommy," said the Chief.

Les looked over again and waved. The boy flicked his head in recognition, but hesitated as the Chief called him over.

"Come over and sit down with us," said the Chief encouragingly as Tommy came up to them.

Tommy's eyes glistened as he looked down at the plates of food.

"You're Tommy, right?" Matt pulled out a chair. "You remember me and the Chief? And this is Les Wagner. He's our best gunner."

"We never got a chance to thank you for helping us," said the Chief.

"'Twas nothing," mumbled the boy, taking the seat.

"Nah," said Matt. "You were great. We couldn't have got Beau up to that farm without you."

Tommy beamed with pride, but his eyes were still cast down on the table.

"You hungry, kid?" asked the Chief.

"I'm fine thanks," Tommy answered quickly.

"Forget it. I'm sure you missed lunch and it's almost time for dinner. I bet you're starving."

Tom laughed and shook his head.

"What's so funny, kid?"

"In Ireland dinner's long past and 'tis time for tea," he explained.

"Whatever," answered Matt as he pushed Les's full plate up to Tom. "Eat. That's all my mother ever said when I was a kid. Eat! *Mangea*, Mateo!"

Tommy didn't wait to be asked again. He started in on the plate of food with a vengeance.

Matt rose and patted him on the back. "The Chief and me are gonna go and see what's cooking over there with Charlie Hansen. He's our pilot. You sit here with Les and make sure you've cleaned that plate by the time I get back."

Les watched Tommy while he ate his way methodically through the mass of food in front of him. He wondered if he could just come right out and ask about his sister?

Tommy noticed him and smiled. "This is beautiful," he said, holding up a forkful and waving it at Les. "Are ya really a gunner?"

"Sure am," said Les.

"I'd never seen an aeroplane before today," Tommy added, eating quickly. Every once in a while he would sneak a look around the room, as if he was going to get caught.

"There aren't many planes where I come from either," said Les. "In fact I saw my first plane when I finished basic training and went to gunnery school."

"What's it like being a gunner?" asked Tommy. He was eating so fast he was already halfway through the meal.

"It's great. I'm in the top turret. That's the one on the roof of the plane," said Les, wondering how he could bring the conversation around to Imelda. "You stand on a ledge with your head and shoulders sticking out into the sky. It feels like you can see forever."

"That must be marvellous. Are you the only gunner, then?" asked Tom. He pushed the plate away with a satisfied grin and leaned back in his chair. "That was mighty."

"No. There's one in the nose and one in the tail. Then you've got the two in the waist – that's what we call the middle of the plane."

"How old are ya? Ya look like a young fella."

"I'm just eighteen. How old are you?" answered Les, relieved to change the subject. Maybe he could ask Tommy how old his sister was, he thought.

"Seventeen."

"That's how old I was when I enlisted." That was

the wrong thing to say, thought Les. They'd be back to talking about planes if he didn't watch out.

"I'd love to fly. Sweet Jesus but I'd love to," Tommy said with true longing.

"Do you live here in town?" asked Les quickly.

"No. We're Travellers, tinkers." Tommy looked towards the door and sat up straight. He was watching a plump lady who was coming into the dining-room. Les had been introduced to her earlier as Miss Aileen O'Donovan, one of the O'Donovans who owned the hotel. She was making the rounds of the dining-room, greeting the members of the crew.

"Travellers? Tinkers?" repeated Les with a puzzled look.

"We live in caravans or tents," Tommy explained quickly. "The whole family like. We sleep out on the roads. We might stay a while in one town, but then we move on. After a time we come back again. It's our way."

Les nodded, but he didn't quite understand. She lived in a caravan? That was amazing. She was some sort of gypsy girl? For some reason that made her even prettier.

"I've got to be going now," said Tommy abruptly. He stood up and held his hand out to Les, still keeping an eye on the woman who had stopped to chat at another table. "Thanks for the grub. Maybe you could show me the plane, if you're still around like?"

"Sure. I'll ask the pilot. I could take you out and show you around," said Les playing for some more time. His heart started to pound. He couldn't just let him leave like that.

"Great stuff." Tommy turned to leave. "I'll see ya, so."

"Maybe I can take you out there tomorrow," blurted Les. "And maybe you could bring your sister," he added lamely.

Tommy stopped and turned back to him. "Me sister?"

"Imelda."

Tommy laughed as if it was a really odd idea. "Sure what would Imelda want with a plane?" he said, still chuckling. Then as Miss O'Donovan approached he winked at Les and sprinted out the door to the street.

Les felt like a fool. He tried to brush the feeling off as Matt and the Chief returned to the table. After all, they'd probably be leaving in a few days. What was he doing trying to get to know some girl when they had more important things to do? Like get to England and fight a war.

"Why so glum, kid?" asked Matt as he sat down. "Did her brother give you the runaround?"

Les shook his head. "So what's happening?" he asked half-heartedly. The girls were clearing off the dinner plates and replacing them with bowls full of apple-pie and jugs of custard. Les couldn't eat another bite. He pushed his dessert away as soon as the girls had gone.

"They seem to have come to a sort of truce about calling the army in. At least until tomorrow," explained the Chief as he ate his pie. "They've decided we're staying here tonight. We can move freely inside the town limits, as long as we're accompanied by one of their guys. That's about a three or four-mile radius."

"That guy, Barry Kingston, has arranged for all our stuff to be taken off the plane. So we can wash and change our clothes," added Matt. "They're also sending out the Local Defence Force – seems to be a sort of Home Guard over here – to guard the plane tonight."

"Will they give us some gasoline so we can take off again?" asked Les.

"I don't know, kid." Matt looked doubtful. "I don't think anyone knows."

"But why not? Wouldn't just be easier to give us some gas and let us go?"

"It's not that simple," the Chief explained patiently. "Ireland is a neutral country. They can't seem to be helping one side and not the other."

"But that's just plain stupid," said Les.

"And to make things worse, gasoline – or petrol as they call it – is rationed," continued the Chief. "Only the army and a few civilians providing vital services are allowed any."

"It's still stupid," said Les grumpily.

"Stupid or not, let's hope Charlie Hansen manages to talk his way out of this one. Or we may end up spending the rest of the war here." Matt looked over to the pilot's table. The men around them had finished their meal and were starting to get up. As they stood to follow, Miss O'Donovan reached their table and shook hands with them warmly.

"I hope everything was to your liking," she said. She stood with her arms crossed over her ample bosom. Her hair was in a loose bun. She wore a snow-white blouse with a large lace collar, and a long dark wool skirt from under which two tiny shoes peeped. A thick gold chain hung around her neck with a small bar attached to it.

"That was by far the best meal we've had in months," said the Chief graciously. "Thank you very much for all your kindness."

"Not at all," she said, her rosy cheeks flushing even more. "It's not every day we have visitors dropping in from the sky. You gave us quite a fright, I can tell you."

"I hope we can make it up to you." Matt flashed his most charming smile.

"The Air Corps wouldn't like it if they found out we'd been frightening beautiful ladies in Ireland."

Miss O'Donovan chuckled with pleasure. "I hope that boy wasn't bothering you," she said to Les.

"On the contrary," said the Chief. "We were thanking him. He helped us take care of our injured companion."

"Dr Moloney said the man isn't badly hurt, thanks be to God," said Miss O'Donovan. Then she added, "I knew that boy's father. He was an honest man, and the mother, bless her poor soul, was a good woman. But you never know with them sort. Still, 'twas tragic to have both parents taken away, with the children being so young and all."

Les was trying to absorb this new bit of information about Imelda when Barry Kingston announced that they were all retiring to the bar. Matt offered Miss O'Donovan his arm, which she accepted as if she were about to dance a waltz. Les stood, his heart racing again. Imelda was a gypsy, and an orphan, and she lived in a caravan! She sounded like a fairytale character from his childhood. The Chief nudged Les out of his thoughts and urged him out with the others.

The dining-room had been full, but the bar was overflowing. People were crammed into every available seat and nook and cranny. The place was buzzing with excitement. Children of all ages ran around laughing, while their mothers sat demurely to one side, occasionally grabbing one by the neck and forcing them to calm down. The men at the bar were three deep. They passed the pints high over their heads to those waiting behind.

Charlie Hansen was up at the bar with Pat Coughlan, the guard, and Dr Moloney. As the rest of the airmen walked in, a hush fell over the room. For the space of a heartbeat every pair of eyes was staring at them. Then the room burst into spontaneous applause, rising to a crescendo as the crowd parted to let them through. A space was made at the bar for them and ten black pints were lined up, a third of the way full, waiting to be topped.

As Matt walked up with Miss O'Donovan on his arm he was slapped on the back by a dozen men and shook hands with a dozen more. The clamour was so loud that he caught very little of what the people greeting him were saying. They leant in close, their faces animated, and pumped his hand vigorously before standing back and letting another take their place. He heard names which he would never remember, as one pair of bright light eyes was replaced by another. Many seemed to be telling him of family back in America and he heard several cities being mentioned. He finally squeezed in beside Dr Moloney.

"Hello there," said a man, standing aside to let him pass. He had a mop of curly hair and twinkling eyes that seemed to be smiling at some private joke. "My name's Con O'Leary. I see you've already got the measure of the town. You've got yourself the best catch. I tell you there's many a man who's waited years to walk in with Aileen O'Donovan on his arm."

"Con, you're a devil," said Miss O'Donovan fondly as Matt laughed.

"Take no notice of him."

"You must be the Italian fellow," Con O'Leary said as the barman swiftly took each pint glass and filled it, lining them back up on the bar with a nod towards the Americans.

"How did you figure that out?" asked Matt, intrigued.

"News gets around a small town. And I like to think of myself as having a flair for faces. Seems you've an Italian, an Irishman named O'Mahoney – local name that – and a Red Indian," chuckled Con O'Leary eyeing the pints. "You're definitely not Irish. You're very dark of complexion, and your man over there must be the Indian. So you must be the Italian." The back pints glistened like patent leather. The froth stood upright above the rim, thick and creamy. Yet no one made a move to take one. Con noticed Matt looking around. "They're not ready yet," he explained.

"You've got to wait till it settles. They're nearly done by the looks of it."

As if on cue, Barry Kingston raised a glass and encouraged the others to do the same. Matt took a tentative sip. He'd tried a great number of alcoholic beverages in his time but this was a first for him. It tasted flat and slightly bitter, but not unpleasant.

"It's not bad," he said.

"The second one goes down a lot easier," Con O'Leary smiled. He drank a big mouthful and smacked his lips, which now sported a brand-new moustache. Matt did the same and he had to admit that it did get better. The barman was lining up another row of smaller glasses. He then produced two bottles of whiskey.

"A gift on the house," said Miss O'Donovan grandly as she waved to the barman to pour.

"Now that," said Con O'Leary, leaning in close to whisper in Matt's ear, "is a rare sight. In fact I'd say that an American bomber nearly taking the steeple off Clonakilty church hardly compares!"

The drinks were replaced before anyone had a chance to empty their glass, and soon rows of pints and shots of whiskey stood waiting at the bar. Matt paced himself and checked around to see how the rest of the crew were doing. Each one was surrounded by several men, with more peering over their shoulders to catch the conversation. The Chief seemed to be holding his liquor as he talked with Dr Moloney, while Les, with Tojo on his shoulder, was sitting with the girl, Ruth.

Charlie Hansen sipped at his drink and Matt thought he was probably making sure he stayed sober. The pilot and Barry Kingston stayed close to Pat Coughlan whose features had softened somewhat, while his cheeks glowed with the shots that kept being poured for him.

The noise level reached an even higher pitch and then died down somewhat as a man sitting in the corner near the fire pulled a fiddle out of an old battered case and tuned up. After a few notes he struck up a jaunty tune. The music was wild and fast. Matt couldn't keep from tapping his foot in time. Tojo liked it as well. He bobbed up and down to the rhythm to everyone's delight.

"Will ya look at that!" said Miss O'Donovan, beaming. "The little fella's dancing!" She tapped her foot and clapped her hands and was immediately imitated by Tojo. A space was cleared in the middle of the floor, and, like a true star, Tojo leapt in and pranced to the music, turning somersaults and leaping high into the air. The room was rocked with laughter. Even Pat Coughlan doubled over watching Tojo perform. Then as the music came to an abrupt halt, Tojo jumped up and snatched the cap off the fiddler's head and passed it around.

"I bought him off a guy on the street in Marrakesh," Matt explained as copper pennies were thrown into the cap. "But I never knew he was so talented."

"Nor so handy, I'd wager. You'll never go hungry with him around," laughed Con O'Leary as Tojo walked up and handed Matt the cap. He turned to the barman and shouted, "Line them up there, Tony! Drinks are on the monkey!"

They raised their glasses to Tojo who sensed the occasion and did a few more somersaults. The fiddler was about to strike up another tune when Barry Kingston took a step forward and raised his glass.

Cries of "Silence! Shush, now!" went up around the room. With great flair for the dramatic, Barry Kingston stood, his pint high in the air, and waited for the room to quiet down. When he was satisfied that he had everyone's attention, his great voice boomed out.

"Ladies and Gentlemen, today was a momentous day in our history. In any case, I can tell you it was a momentous day in my history – I nearly had a heart attack when I looked up and saw this great big aeroplane dropping out of the sky above me. And I know for a fact that I wasn't the only one to be scared witless today. By all accounts Miss Aileen O'Donovan here was certain 'twas an earthquake!" The crowd laughed.

"And rightly so," continued Barry Kingston more sombrely. "And rightly so. For who knew what awaited us when the door of that great green giant opened? I certainly had no idea if the young man who leapt out, revolver at the ready, was friend or foe. And he was as wary as I was." Barry Kingston paused for effect. It was not lost on the crowd. They were hanging on his every word. He pointed to Les who was following the speech with interest under the proud gaze of Ruth Bennett. "Little did I know that the young man was Les Wagner from Wisconsin. And as he told me himself, they thought they had landed in a hostile country and did not know what lay waiting for them. They only knew their lives were at stake." Les blushed at this dramatic rendition of events but Ruth seemed to be quite taken by the story. She leant over and squeezed his hand quickly.

"Did he really ask ya if ya spoke English?" shouted the fiddler.

"That he did," answered Barry Kingston. "And he asked me where they were. And I told him: Ye're in Paddy White's bog!"

The room broke into good-natured laughter again.

"What a relief it was," Barry Kingston continued,

"for all of us to find that we were among friends. So I would like to take this opportunity to welcome the crew of *T'Aint a Bird* to Clonakilty. You are among friends. More than friends, in fact."

Applause rang through the bar. Barry Kingston silenced it and then paused once again.

Matt saw Charlie Hansen stand up straight and listen closely, as if he sensed that something important was coming next.

"Yes, you are not just among friends here in Clonakilty, but among family. For who among us does not have a loved one who has crossed the ocean to seek a better life in America? Who does not have a brother, a son, a cousin, or a nephew over in America? We welcome you as our own – sure isn't there even a fellow called O'Mahoney? A Cork name if I ever heard one!" A murmur of assent rippled through the room. Barry gestured to Charlie Hansen to stand up beside him.

"On behalf of the people of Clonakilty I wish to welcome you and your crew to Ireland. Your visit will go down in history as one of the great moments of our town. I have no doubt that fifty years from now we will still remember you. So we wish you all safe home. And let it never be said that the people of Clonakilty did not do everything in their power to help you on your way."

There was wild cheering as the two men lifted their glasses to each other.

"A toast to our visitors and may they find safe home," shouted Barry Kingston. The bar became a forest of arms as all those present toasted the Americans. The fiddler started up and Tojo leapt in to dance.

Charlie Hansen shook hands all round. The members of the crew were slapped on the back again and again. The music was getting into everyone's blood, and though there was no room to speak of, a few people joined in to dance with Tojo. Mahoney had been carted off to a corner of the room and was being introduced to a large group.

"Those'll all be O'Mahoneys from Ardfield," explained Con O'Leary. "The poor man is going to have to endure the tale of exactly how he is related to each and every one of 'em."

"Things could be a lot worse," said Matt laughing. "We could have been in a German jail tonight."

"That they could, man," said Con O'Leary shaking his head. He reached out his hand and caught Matt's in a firm grasp. "Safe home to you. God willing."

"Here's hoping," answered Matt and raised his glass once again.

Chapter Eleven

---◆---

Mary woke with a start. The sun was blinding her. She brought her hand up to shade her eyes and felt an awful pain in her neck. That's when she remembered that she had fallen asleep in the armchair. She looked over at the sofa and her heart skipped a beat. He was gone! Had he just left without as much as a goodbye? She had a sinking feeling in the pit of her stomach. Then she heard the whistling. It was coming from the kitchen. She hurried out of the room without even bothering to put her shoes on.

She stopped dead in the doorway. Beau was over by the sink at the window. He was drying himself vigorously with a towel. Mary's hands flew to her hair. It had come undone and she desperately tried to pin it back up before he saw her. She silently cursed her unruly locks as Beau turned and caught her at it. He beamed a beautiful open smile and Mary forgot how silly she felt. He deftly pulled on the shirt she had fetched the night before.

"Good morning," Beau said. "I took the liberty of washing. I also took this shirt. I hope you don't mind."

"You shouldn't be up, you know," said Mary. If anything he was even more handsome as the bright sun streamed in behind him.

"It's a beautiful day," he said.

"The doctor said you shouldn't be up," she repeated. "How's your head? It looks pretty bad."

"Ah, but the good doctor has come and gone," he answered, looking very pleased with himself. "You were sleeping so peacefully we decided it would be a veritable sin to wake you. And the head is fine, thank you. It looks a lot worse than it feels."

"Dr Moloney was here? And I was sleeping?" said Mary, flustered. "What did he say?"

"He said I shouldn't be up!" Beau laughed. It was a ringing infectious laugh and Mary had to join in.

"I can see you're going to be a difficult patient."

"Don't you worry yourself. I'll be as good as gold. The doctor said I was all right and to take it easy today. He'll be back this evening. I told him taking it easy was the one thing I am exceedingly talented at."

Mary's mind was racing as she thought of what

needed to be done. She must put the kettle on. And see about breakfast. No, she must start up the fire first.

"But seriously, I believe an apology is in order," continued Beau.

"An apology?" echoed Mary.

"I was confused about where I was. I thought I was in a hotel," he said, a grin playing at the corners of his mouth. "It made sense at the time. And I'm afraid that I mistook you for the chambermaid last night. I hope I didn't offend you."

"No offence was taken," said Mary, charmed by his manner. "And I promise to do something about that lumpy bed."

"I am truly sorry." he said crossing the room. "Of course, by the light of day – and with a much clearer head – I can see that you could never be mistaken for a mere chambermaid. And I must make amends." He reached out and took her hand, turning it ever so gently. "Beauregard St Soucis at your service," he said clicking his heels and bending his lips over her hand. Mary could feel his breath on her skin, as his lips brushed her hand. "I am forever in your debt, ma'am, for helping me in my hour of need."

Mary giggled and took her hand away. He was a bit of a chancer, but a very charming one. She took a step back. Enough of this messing. It was time she got on with the morning chores.

"Did the doctor say if you could eat?"

"I can't say that I remember him mentioning it, but frankly, I could eat a horse!"

Mary moved swiftly through the kitchen. What could she cook that was both quick and worthy of her guest?

"You just sit there. I'll have the fire going in no time at all," she said.

Beau did as he was told, a smile playing on his lips. Mary cracked open the caked ashes of the fire with a poker. The red embers had kept alive from the night before. In a short time she had the turf burning merrily. She picked up the black iron kettle. Mary could tell by its weight that it was empty. The can on the sink was empty as well. Beau must have used up the water washing.

"I'll have to go for water," she said.

"I'm terribly sorry. It didn't occur to me. How inconsiderate! Here, let me help you." He picked up the second can and fell into step with her as she lugged the can out the door. Mary noticed that he was limping slightly.

"Did you hurt your leg?" she asked as they crossed the courtyard to the pump.

"It's nothing. My ankle is slightly swollen. I must have twisted it as I fell."

"What happened to you?" asked Mary as she started to work the pump. After a few shakes, the water gushed out, icy cold and clear. Mary put her hands in the flow and bathed her face. The water stung, but it felt wonderful.

She waited for his answer but he said nothing. He was watching her. Mary felt herself blush slightly.

"How did you fall?" she repeated.

Beau told her about the parrot and about Tojo peeing on Russell. He made it sound so comical that Mary laughed with him as the can filled.

He leaned back and watched her work the pump as he spoke. When the first can was full, he moved in the second one as naturally as if he'd been doing this all his life. Mary forgot herself as she soaked up his every word. The sound of the water gushing matched the cascade of her laughter. By the time the cans were full his soft accent and easy gestures were almost familiar.

As Beau finished his story, he looked up and noticed the landscape for the first time. He stopped in mid-sentence and looked around. Still limping, he walked to the gate and looked out at the estuary. The tide was just turning. The water was a deep turquoise under an impossibly blue sky. The sun beat down as if it was July, bleaching the sand-dunes a brilliant white. Across the estuary, the green hills, with their tidy little fields, were bathed in gold. She watched him take it all in and knew that his heart was filled with the beauty of the place.

"Is that the sea?" he asked, as if to himself.

"Yes," she answered softly, not wanting to break the spell.

"But what's that land just across there?" he continued, trying to make sense of the geography. "Are we on a peninsula?"

"We're on an island. Inchydoney Island, in County Cork."

"An island!" he exclaimed. "How romantic. Shipwrecked on an island!"

"Well, we're not really an island any more. The causeways link us to the mainland. You landed in the marsh between them. That's where the sea drained out."

She watched the disappointment cross his face. He looked like a little boy who had just been denied a promised treat.

"But we often get flooded," she offered. "When the storms come in then we get cut off from the mainland again."

Beau brightened up immediately. To Mary's surprise, he struck a pose lifting his arms to the sky:

"Blow winds, and crack your cheeks! Rage! Blow!
You cataracts and hurricanes, spout
Till you have drenched our steeples," he recited. Then he turned and winked at her. "Do you think it'll work? It's Shakespeare! *King Lear.*"

"I have no idea," she answered laughing. "But you never have to wait long for it to rain in Ireland. In the meantime I'd best get on with breakfast."

He wouldn't let Mary carry the water in, so she left him to it and busied herself cooking. The griddle was good and hot and she quickly melted some butter and fried up two thick rashers. She flipped slices of bread in the fat before breaking three eggs into a corner of the griddle.

"You'll have to wait a minute for the tea. But have a glass of milk while you're waiting," she said as she put the plate in front of him.

"Won't you be joining me?" he said as if he was addressing a grand lady in a fancy restaurant. Mary was suddenly aware that she still had no shoes on.

"I'll wait for the tea," she said. "I've loads to do yet."

When the tea was boiled, she served them both a cup but she didn't sit down. She felt uncomfortable and he didn't insist. Instead she got out the big mixing-bowl and started making the day's loaves.

"What are you doing?" asked Beau as he began to eat. He ate with quick elegant movements. None of the slurping and loud chewing she was used to.

"I'm baking bread," she answered as if stating the obvious.

"How do you bake bread?" he asked.

Mary looked at him to see if he was mocking her, but he seemed really interested. Hesitantly at first, then with more confidence, she answered each question that Beau asked. He was fascinated that she cooked over the fire and admired the bastible and the skilful way she put the embers on its lid so that the bread would bake evenly.

"My grandmother was renowned for her light fingers," Mary said. "I'm not as expert as she was, but my baking isn't half bad."

"I'm sure it's wonderful, just like breakfast was." Beau stood up and clapped his hands. "So what do we have to do next?" he asked, as if embarking on an adventure.

"You should rest now," she said, shaking her head. He really was a strange devil, she thought, and then laughed to herself. Last night she'd thought him an angel and today she was calling him a devil.

"I feel great. And it's a beautiful day," he said brightly.

"It would be an offence to sleep through a day like this."

"You'll be bored to tears," she countered, getting into the game.

"My mama always said that I was easily amused," Beau taunted.

"It's very smelly and messy."

"Try me."

"I have to let out the chickens and feed them. Go for the eggs, milk the cow, and clean out her stall," she listed woodenly. "Oh, and the hounds. I must see to the hounds."

"Sounds wonderful,"

"You'll hate it," she promised, more pleased than she cared to admit.

"I'll love it," he beamed, knowing that he had won. "By the by. A young man named Tommy dropped in to say he'd walk the hounds later on in the day."

"Tommy was here as well? Next thing you'll be telling me the whole town was up with a brass band while I was sleeping!" she said, leading the way to the chicken shed. Beau followed her around, asking questions about everything she did.

"Are ya naturally mad, or is it the bump on the head?" she asked as she watched him running after the chickens.

"Oh, it's quite natural." He laughed. "It runs in the family."

Mary had to concede that he was the most charming madman she had ever met. She looked forward to spending the day with him. And yet it made her shaky inside to feel him so close as he helped her with her chores. But sure, what harm? He was having a laugh and she was enjoying the first real company she'd had in years.

After milking, Beau followed Mary as she led the little black Kerry cow out to a field close to the house. They sat in the sunshine and enjoyed the view. From where they sat, Beau could see the B-17 down in the marsh. There seemed to be a number of men in green uniforms chatting with civilians on the road. He wondered how the crew were getting on, but he didn't really care. They'd come and get him soon enough, and in the meantime he was enjoying himself. It reminded him of the farm on his uncle's plantation, though it was smaller. He'd loved to visit when he was a child, but even back then they'd had indoor plumbing and electricity. And an army of farm-hands and servants to do all the work. He glanced over at Mary, as she sat in the sunshine, and marvelled at how she did this every day, apparently on her own.

Mary answered every question asked, and he asked

many. She knew a lot about the history and people of the countryside around them and was generous with detail. She only became vague when speaking of herself. Beau did not press her, though it was in his nature to be curious. When he had visited Ireland with his father he'd wondered about the people who lived in the tiny cottages and farms they passed. Here was a chance to find out. He often thought that he'd been born in the wrong century. He should have been one of those gentlemen scholars, travelling the world and taking notes. No wonder he'd enjoyed the last month's roaming so much. The thought of returning to his father's side in the dark mahogany-panelled office was less than appealing.

When they returned to the courtyard, Mary swiftly caught a chicken and wrung its neck in one sharp tug. Beau thought she must have very strong hands. He remembered her hand when he took it earlier. It was small-boned and feminine, but he had felt the rough callouses on the palm and fingers.

No matter how much he insisted, she wouldn't let him sit and watch her pluck the chicken. He was dismissed and told to go inside and have a rest. He had to admit that he was tired.

Beau wandered back into the room he had slept in and looked around. The kitchen was sparsely furnished but someone had gone to some trouble and expense to decorate this room. Though the walls were rough plaster like the rest of the house, there was the large red velvet sofa he had slept on, along with a few good solid Victorian pieces. In the corner was a small delicately-turned rosewood cabinet crammed with china pieces. Beau wondered if the little cups and saucers with their tiny pink rosebuds had ever been used? That in turn got him wondering about the people who lived in the house, and Mary in particular. Beau liked to think of himself as an expert on women. He liked their company and knew that he could charm both young and old. But Mary was different. She was very beautiful in a wild, strong way. She was totally different to the hothouse flowers he was used to. No one would ever describe her as delicate, a high form of praise in Louisiana. She was solid, he thought, with wide hips and generously proportioned breasts. He had caught himself watching her several times that morning. She moved naturally, with no pretence or flirtation, as if unaware of her attractiveness. Mary had a beauty that radiated from within. It caught him by surprise when she laughed, when she bent down to pick up something heavy, or when she sat soaking up the sunshine. Her eyes were a remarkable grey-green when they sparkled. But Beau sensed a shadow beneath the brightness and he wondered what that might be.

She had mentioned in passing that her husband was away, soon to return. She didn't go on to describe him or her family, as would be natural, but changed the subject quickly. Beau let it pass. He was not out to seduce this strong woman with the flaming red hair. There was something about her that commanded his respect. Maybe it was the way she worked the water pump, or the swift manner in which she had wrung the chicken's neck, he thought laughing to himself. Whatever it was, he knew it wasn't the simple gold band on her finger. He had always found that to be an advantage, rather than an impediment when setting out to seduce a beautiful woman.

An upright piano stood against one wall and on impulse Beau opened it. He ran his fingers up and down the yellowed ivory and was pleased to hear that it was only slightly out of tune. Perfect for playing some honky-tonk and ragtime, he thought.

He started off with the slow Scott Joplin pieces that he loved. He could hear Mary moving around in the kitchen. She'd probably be in soon, he thought, as he changed to a faster swing tune. He finished it and started another but still he could hear pots and pans banging in the kitchen, and he was a little hurt that she was so unimpressed with his playing. It was only after a long while, when the smell of cooking wafted in the door, that she appeared. Beau immediately went into a rollicking rendition of "Ain't she sweet?", singing lustily.

"Is that what ya call resting?" She looked down at him sternly as he banged out the last chords.

"Music eases the soul as well as the body," he said, his hands picking out a few bars of a melody.

"What was that music you played first?" she asked. She sat herself down on a chair beside the piano.

"So you were listening!" he exclaimed happily. "That was Scott Joplin. A very talented Southern man."

"Play it again," she asked.

And he did. He picked out the notes slowly and lightly. And as he played he told her about the black man who had written them, and how his music described the south better than any he knew. He told her about the gentlemen tipping their hats, and about the Southern Belles flirting behind their parasols as they walked down the fine avenues of New Orleans.

Mary closed her eyes and felt herself transported. She could almost smell the magnolia trees, though she had no idea what they looked like. It was pure bliss, sitting there in this room she never used, enjoying this handsome man's company as the dinner cooked on the fire.

All morning Mary had felt herself slide into the easy rhythm of his company. She had worked away in the kitchen listening to him play, her heart filling with joy as she cooked. She had waited to join him, not wanting to stop the pretence. Mary felt her whole body relax into the quiet domesticity of it.

She tried to hang on to the feeling, but she couldn't help but compare this moment to the harshness she was accustomed to. She knew this was just a game that would soon end. As Beau started playing another ragtime tune, Mary felt her heart contract as if a sharp cold wind had blown on her soul.

Chapter Twelve

•◆•

Les wandered into the bar. He wasn't yet fully awake. Tea just didn't have the same punch as a good strong black cup of coffee, he thought, as he spied Matt and Tojo sitting at one of the tables with some guy from the night before. Ruth had told him that you couldn't get coffee in Ireland for love or money. As his eyes grew accustomed to the semi-gloom, he realised that most of the crew were dotted around the place.

"Am I the last one to get up?" he asked.

"Pretty much," answered Matt. "The Chief is still snoring up a storm upstairs. He was pretty bad last night."

"I spent a good bit talking to him," said the man sitting next to Matt. "He's a very sound fella. Has a lot of learning."

"Well, I'd wish he'd learn to drink. I carried him up the stairs again. It's a good thing he's not very big." Matt laughed. "You remember Con O'Leary from last night?"

Con turned to Les. "I enjoyed your rendition of 'My Darling Clementine'."

Les blushed.

"However, it seems we won't have the pleasure of your singing for long," added Con. "We've managed to find you some petrol."

"Is that true?" asked Les.

"Things are looking good," said Matt.

"Your pilot and co-pilot are in the snug this very minute, making the arrangements." Con pointed to a little walled-off corner of the bar. Behind the frosted glass Les could make out four or five men seated together.

"It seems that a delivery was scheduled for today," said Matt, "and Charlie convinced them to let us have some."

"What about the police guy? The garda? He didn't seem too happy about the idea," said Les.

"Pat Coughlan is in there too, but I'll bet that with the hangover he has, he won't remember what he did or didn't agree too," said Con O'Leary. He lifted his glass to the barman. Les noticed that it was still a third full.

"What are you drinking?" Con asked.

Les declined, but Matt nodded, "It's kinda early but what the hell."

After a while the barman brought over the pints of black stout. Les noticed that Con O'Leary's pint had only one swallow left as the next one was set in front of him.

"You timed that pretty well," said Les.

"It takes years of practice to know exactly when to call the next one," said Con as he took the final swallow. Matt reached out for his glass, but Con stopped him. "Wait 'till it settles. Did I not teach you anything last night?"

"How do you know when it's ready to drink?" said Matt.

"That takes years more," he answered laughing. "But here, I'll show you a trick. Listen carefully now." He took a coin from his pocket and tapped the edge of the glass. It was a hollow dull sound. Con kept tapping and Les heard the sound change ever so slightly every time.

"Here. Listen here now. Can you hear the pint singing?" Con bent his ear towards the glass. Les was amazed. The hollow sound had changed to a pure note that rang each time the glass was tapped.

"Hurry now," said Con O'Leary, handing the glass to Matt. "Or you'll lose that lovely head it's got."

Matt accepted the pint with a laugh. He took the coin and tapped the glass himself. "Well, I can tell you it's a lot easier back in New York. You just crack open a cold one and drink it!"

The men came out of the snug. Charlie Hansen came up and told them that he was going out to the depot with the co-pilot and the engineer Tate. The rest of the crew had the afternoon off. They could come and go as they pleased within a three-mile radius as long as they were accompanied. Each man had been assigned to a member of the Local Defence Force.

As the group left for the depot, the church bells started to ring. Everyone in the bar rose. The Americans looked around and followed suit, perplexed. Les was confused but when he turned to Matt, he found him with his eyes downcast and his hands held in front of him. He seemed to be praying. After a minute the bells stopped and the bar relaxed.

"That was the Angelus, wasn't it?" asked Matt delighted. "I haven't heard that since I was in grade school. My mother's gonna love this. Which reminds me, there's something I gotta do." He rose and finished his drink. "Hey Mahoney!" he yelled across the room. "We gotta go light a candle or our mothers will kill us!" Mahoney waved him off but Merdeza came up.

"I'll come with you," he said. "But aren't we supposed to wait for our escorts?"

"There they are," said Matt, pointing at three little boys who had just popped their heads in the door and were pointing excitedly at Tojo. "Do you boys think you can guard us to the church and back?" Matt asked them.

All three nodded their heads energetically.

"That settles that." Matt turned to Con O'Leary who was clearly amused. "If anyone asks for us we've gone to the church under the strict supervision of Clonakilty's finest."

"So what is your church called?" asked Matt, letting the boys lead the way.

"Our Lady of the Immaculate Conception," said the boys in chorus.

"Oh boy," said Matt laughing as he went out the door. "Is my mother gonna love this!"

"Hang on," said Con O'Leary, rising. "I'll join you. 'Tis time I did something for my immortal soul."

Les sat back and let his thoughts wander. They conjured up the picture of Imelda on the cart. He'd thought about her as he drifted off to sleep and he'd thought about her when he woke up and remembered where he was. He figured he had it pretty bad. He wondered how long it would take to wear off after he left.

"A penny for your thoughts?"

"Oh, hi Ruth," said Les, startled.

"This is Dennis Crowley," she said, introducing the tall handsome young man at her side. "He's your LDF escort. We thought you might want to go for a walk. 'Tis a very fine day."

As the trio walked down the main street and out to the edge of town, Les could see that Dennis was clearly quite taken by Ruth. The poor guy's got it bad too, thought Les. She practically ignored him, saving her most charming and witty remarks for Les. Ruth was a pretty girl, but Les could think only of Imelda. He had watched out for her all night in the pub but had only caught a fleeting glance of her brother Tommy. He had stood in the doorway for a moment before disappearing into the night.

They left the last row of tiny houses and started to climb a hill that rose above the town. Les stopped and looked down. It looked like a little toy town. The sound of hooves caught his attention and his heart jumped as he saw Tommy Tanner drive around the corner. Two little girls were sitting next to him. They looked identical except that one was slightly bigger than the other. Both stared openly at Les as they drew up.

"How are ya?" said Tommy. "I was just in town to pick up some holy water and honey. My baby sister

Nellie's down bad with the cough and Auntie Helen swears by honey and holy water."

"Is she very bad?" asked Ruth.

"Imelda's been up with her all night," answered Tommy. The little girls tugged at his frayed jacket and whispered in his ear.

"They want to know if yer the Yank with the monkey," said Tommy to Les.

"Nope. He's gone to church to light a candle," said Les kindly. "My name's Les. What are your names?"

The little girls just giggled and hid behind Tommy.

"The bigger one's Margaret and the other's Nora. So what are you lot up to? Do ya think ya could show me the plane?" said Tom.

"Sure," said Les. "But shouldn't you get that stuff to your little sister?"

"It's on the way," said Tommy. "Hop on."

"Great!" said Les jumping up on the cart. Ruth and Dennis climbed on beside him. Les was delighted. Now he had the perfect excuse to see Imelda again.

Imelda sat in the half-light of the barrel-top and looked down on the sleeping child. She was such a little dote. Nellie was her sister, but Imelda felt as if she was her own child. Hadn't she practically raised her from birth? Nellie looked so small tucked up with all the ticks and blankets around her. The bright blue blanket Mary had given Imelda was pulled right up to Nellie's face, off-setting her soft reddish curls and apple cheeks. Imelda knew that her cheeks were rosy with fever and not health, and she felt a panic rise at the thought that the child could take a turn for the worse. Her mother had lost two babies before she died herself. Every winter there would be news of one or the other family who had lost a child. Imelda remembered asking her mother why God took little children when they had done no wrong? Her mother had looked at her with a sad smile and told her that sometimes He needed new angels in heaven. And Imelda had thought it very greedy of God to do such a thing. Imelda crossed herself and prayed that He would not be needing Nellie until she was old and grey.

At least Nellie was sleeping peacefully. The fever had dropped a bit, though she was still coughing from time to time. Imelda was wondering where Tom had got to when she heard a commotion outside. Peering out of the front of the caravan, she was surprised to see Ruth standing at the campfire with Just Dennis and Les Wagner beside her.

Les caught sight of her and strode up.

"Hi," he said, flushing slightly. "I heard your little sister is sick. How is she doing?"

"She's better, thank God," said Imelda quickly. Behind her Nellie started coughing again. It was a dry hacking cough. Imelda popped back in to soothe the child back to sleep.

Les followed her. "She doesn't sound too good," he said, concerned. "Have you seen the doctor?"

"We don't have much to do with doctors," she answered curtly. "She'll be fine. Let's just leave her sleep."

"But I really think she should see a doctor," insisted Les, looking at the child's red cheeks and fevered brow.

"Listen, Les Wagner," she said, pushing him gently but firmly out of the caravan, "we've no money for to pay no doctor. And anyway, 'tis bad luck to pay for a cure. We have our own ways and we'll be just fine with them."

Les looked hurt and puzzled but he let it drop. Imelda felt bad that she had spoken to him so harshly. But who did he think he was, coming in and telling her what to do? Sure, wasn't she trying her best? She sent Bridget to beg some tea and sugar off Auntie Helen, and put the tea-can on the fire to boil. Les followed her every move but did not speak to her again, just nodded his thanks as she offered him a jamjar of tea.

Tommy suggested they all go over and visit the

plane. Les jumped at the idea, but Imelda said no, she had to stay near Nellie.

"Nonsense. I'll mind her," said Auntie Helen who had come over as they were drinking the tea. "The child is asleep and you could do with a bit of fresh air. You've been cooped up in there since yesterday."

Imelda sat with Ruth and the girls as they drove out, avoiding Les. She could see the plane as they started across the causeway, and again marvelled at how big it was. The sun was reflected off the top turret, making it sparkle, and Imelda remembered that Les had told her he sat up there.

"Yer man's taken quite a fancy to you," said Ruth, nudging her in the ribs.

"What are ya on about, Ruth Bennett," said Imelda.

"The Yank. Les Wagner. He doesn't stop looking at ya."

"Don't be a fool. What would he want with me?" said Imelda trying to sound annoyed.

"Seriously," continued Ruth, whispering in her ear, "I tried to get his attention all last night. He was really polite and all, but he just wasn't interested. He even asked about ya."

"He did not!"

"He did. A few times. Honest, girl! Ya just have to look at him to know. He's been following you around like a puppy-dog ever since we arrived. I suppose I'll have to settle for Just Dennis," she concluded giggling. "I'll end up Mrs Crowley, the West Cork farmer's wife, and you'll be Mrs Les Wagner, the pilot's wife from Washington."

"'Tis Wisconsin, and he's not a pilot. He's a gunner," said Imelda smirking.

"See! What'd I tell ya? Ya like him too!" exclaimed Ruth in a loud whisper as she shoved Imelda playfully.

Imelda did not answer, but she was smiling broadly as she stuck her tongue out at Ruth and shoved her back.

There were crowds of people at the landing-site. It was such a fine day, people had come out to see first-hand this marvel that had dropped out of the sky. The LDF men kept everyone on the road, but after a word with Les and Dennis, they let their little group cross the marsh to visit the plane.

Tommy ran ahead with the little girls, followed by Dennis and Ruth, who was not being very discreet in her efforts to leave Les and Imelda on their own. Imelda shot her a dirty look as Ruth took Dennis's hand and strode purposefully a few yards ahead. Ruth just winked back.

"Was that the caravan you live in?" asked Les as they walked.

Imelda nodded.

"It reminds me of the covered wagons. You know the ones that went out west. My grandparents went out to Wisconsin in one. They lived in it for a year until they'd staked out a homestead."

"Where were they coming from?" asked Imelda.

"They were from Germany – Bavaria. Most of the people where I live are of German stock. Except the Indians of course."

"And how is it they ended up in Wisconsin?" asked Imelda. She found the fact that his people had also travelled both comforting and intriguing.

"I don't know. I guess they just landed in America, hitched up the wagon and headed west until they found a place they liked."

Imelda wondered what it would be like to set out in one direction and just travel in a straight line without a notion of the road ahead. She had only ever travelled in circles visiting familiar places. She had never thought like that before. For the first time she was aware that she lived on an island surrounded by water beyond which there were whole new worlds.

"It's ironic really," continued Les thoughtfully. "I'm the first Wagner to return to Germany, and it's to go to war."

Imelda looked at him, slightly startled. She had

forgotten that they were going to war. The fact that he was going to fight Germans was shocking.

"Don't you feel strange fighting your own people?" she asked incredulously.

Les laughed. "We're Americans now. Everyone on this plane was from somewhere else originally: Matt's Italian, the co-pilot's Scottish, Merdeza came from Yugoslavia. Mahoney's from Ireland. Hell, the only native is the Chief! But we're all Americans now. I don't even speak German. Except for a couple of words."

"Did you not know your grandparents?" she asked, still trying to make sense of it. How could he not be what his grandparents had been before him? How could he not even speak their language? Imelda had spent her whole life learning the ways and words of her people. She hung on to who she was. It was her lifeline. It was the only thing she had.

"I grew up with them. Granddad only passed away a few years ago and Grandma is still living at home. I guess they worked so hard to learn English and make a new life that they wanted to leave the past behind. They wanted us to be different, to be Americans."

They arrived at the plane. The others had waited, not daring to go in until Les arrived. Les climbed up the stairs urging them to follow.

Imelda hung back a little. She was deep in thought. How could a person decide to be someone else?

Imelda's little sisters yelled at her to come and see. Les was showing them the plane from the tail to the nose. He stopped and explained things, and answered the little girls' questions. They had lost all shyness and were tearing around the place. Les showed them what looked like a little round room in the middle of the plane. He told them it was the ball turret and explained how the gunner was lowered in it until he was hanging under the plane. He even let Tommy get inside. Everyone laughed as Tommy crouched, his knees up around his ears, pretending to shoot the guns. Dennis and Ruth went ahead to the pilot's seat. Just Dennis had cheered up considerably, thought Imelda, as she followed them. Les stopped her before she could cross into the next compartment.

"Have a look out of here. This is the top turret," he said, showing her how to step into the little dome above their heads. Imelda looked out and saw the marsh, the people on the road, the island and the estuary. She could even see Mary's house.

Les slid in beside her and Imelda felt slightly wary of being so close to him. It was a very small space and Les had to hold her shoulder lightly to steady himself.

"You know, when we're flying, and I'm up in here, it looks like the sky just goes on and on forever," he said quietly.

Imelda looked up and saw him smiling. She felt the same sense of wellbeing that she had the first time she had seen him smile. Before she realised what was happening, he bent down and kissed her gently.

"Not here," said Imelda. She quickly looked over to the people on the road but no one outside seemed to have noticed. Thank God.

"Where then?" said Les, looking intensely at her.

"Nowhere," she answered in a loud whisper.

"You're the prettiest girl I've ever seen."

"You must be daft." Imelda looked worriedly around to see if anybody was coming.

"Or in love," pondered Les. He thought about it for a minute and declared: "I'm in love, that's it."

"You don't even know me."

"That proves it," said Les. "Matt says you can fall in love just like that. You see a girl and bam. I thought he was kidding but he's right."

"I've got to go," said Imelda. She could hear the others laughing in the compartment beyond.

"Of course you do," he said brightly. "Just wait a minute." Les pulled her to him and kissed her again.

This time she kissed him back. Then seconds after her lips had touched his, she was back with the others, her heart pounding as if she'd just run up a hill. Tommy was back inside the ball turret, messing about and making the others laugh.

She was relieved to see that no one was taking any notice of her. She tried to join in the fun but her head was reeling. She willed herself to stop blushing. He had kissed her! The cheek of it! She felt a flush rise up her neck.

Thankfully the little girls discovered a large bag of oranges. No one had ever seen an orange before, and they marvelled at the large round fruits as they were passed around. They were so round, both bumpy and smooth, and a colour that Imelda could not recall ever seeing, much less eating, before. She turned the orange in her hands and found herself for the second time that day thinking of what lay beyond the ocean that surrounded them. What tree did this strange and wonderful fruit grow on? What people had picked it?

Les coaxed the little ones to try them. Nora took a big bite and made a face. Les laughed and explained that the peel was bitter and needed to be removed. He took a pocket-knife and carefully cut the fruit into sections, showing her how to suck it. Instantly the plane was filled with the most wonderful perfume. Les offered Imelda a section. She wished he would stop looking at her that way. Surely someone was bound to notice. Sure enough, she saw Ruth smiling at her.

Imelda accepted the orange. The smell of it was only a pale shadow compared to the taste of it. Imelda let the sweet juice run down her throat and closed her eyes, almost swooning with the delight of the smell, the taste, and the kiss she still felt burning her lips. When she opened them again, Les was standing there watching her with those pale smiling eyes. Imelda laughed out loud. The excitement in the plane was mounting as everyone tasted the oranges and commented on them. The girls had juice running down their chins and were shrieking with pleasure.

Their shouts of glee were interrupted by a louder noise outside. Everyone rushed to the windows to see. A large lorry was pulling up outside with a number of men hanging off its sides. Dr Moloney's car was right behind. Dennis explained that they were going to try and get the plane off again.

"When?" asked Imelda softly, surprised at the stab of pain she felt.

"I guess they'll give it a go tomorrow," said Dennis.

Imelda turned away. She was confused. He had stolen a kiss when he knew he would be leaving the very next day. But then again, hadn't she kissed him back, knowing full well he would be going soon? She willed herself to forget it, pushing the brightly coloured worlds full of oranges and wagons away back into the ocean.

Les looked delighted with himself as he herded everyone off the plane and across the marsh. He instructed Tom to bring the oranges, along with some other bags and crates that he pointed out.

"Have you ever tasted figs?" asked Les beaming. "They look really ugly, but they're delicious."

"I have to get back to Nellie," she said softly, averting her eyes.

"Of course you do," said Les. "Just wait a minute, though. I have an idea. I'll meet you on the road."

Imelda watched as he bounded across the marsh, his long legs jumping over the tall grass as he waved to his companions on the road.

When she climbed back on the road, Les was standing at Dr Moloney's car. The doctor was inside and had the motor running.

"The doctor will drive you home. He says he'll be glad to examine Nellie," said Les. "We're going up to see Beau. Tommy can take us."

Imelda felt trapped. He had had his way once again. She was too down-hearted to fight.

"I've really no money," she whispered.

Les placed his hand softly on her shoulder. His eyes pleaded for her to agree. "You don't need any money. Just let him have a look at her. Please?"

Imelda was too upset to discuss it. She slid silently into the car and pointed the way home.

Chapter Thirteen

◆━◆

Mary stood humming at the kitchen table. As she mixed the batter for an apple-cake, she strained to remember the Scott Joplin melody Beau had played earlier. Its lopsided rhythm wasn't like anything she'd heard before. The tune was firmly in her mind, but when she tried to sing it, she just couldn't. It drifted in her head like a dream. She smiled as she tried to recapture the tune and found she could only really remember Beau's hands as he played, and the serious way his dark eyebrows knitted as he tried to explain what made ragtime so different from other music.

She had three small crab apples left that had dried for months up on the shelf over the hearth. They were shrivelled and wrinkled, but Mary knew that they would be perfect in a cake. Behind the tartness there would still be the linger of sweet summer.

If they had calm weather this spring, there would be a fine crop of apples this year. She had noticed the hundreds of buds just waiting to flower as she showed Beau the orchard earlier that day. She had also shown him the little vegetable patch she kept, with the few young plants already poking their shoots out of the ground.

She had always been secretly very proud of her garden, her little Kerry cow, her orchard and chickens. It was wonderful to share that with someone else. Beau had seemed so interested, and had admired the hard work she put in. He had commented several times how surprised he was that she did it all on her own, and each time Mary had winced behind her smile remembering Gerald. He was like a bad dream that she wanted to banish. But in her heart she knew that today was the dream. Her life with Gerald was only too real.

Mary finished cleaning up the kitchen. There wasn't much to do as Beau had insisted on helping her until she finally managed to shoo him away. She could see that his head was hurting and he seemed tired after eating his meal. He'd been asleep for over an hour. Mary looked in on him regularly, taking advantage of the fact that she could look at him openly. When they were together Mary only dared look at him out of the corner of her eye. There was something in his gaze which made her act differently, walk differently.

Dark clouds rolled in from the sea, blotting out the bright day. Mary sat in the kitchen and thought about herself. She was acting like a schoolgirl. It was pathetic, really. It had been such a long time since anyone had looked at her like that. She didn't know what to make of it. Of course he was very handsome and very charming, and very young and exotically foreign. But after all, he was just being himself and probably had no notion of the effect he had on her. At least she hoped he didn't. The fact was that he was the first man to walk into her house and pay her some attention in years, and she was a sad and lonely woman. But she couldn't help feeling happy, knowing that he was asleep in the front room while the cake she was baking for him started to fill the kitchen with the sweet smell of apples.

Mary heard the sound of a cart turning into the yard and remembered that Tommy was due in. She was annoyed at having him intrude on her fantasy. She hoped that he'd just take the hounds and not come in at all.

Voices laughing outside made her realise that more

people than just Tommy had driven up. The yard was full of people. Tommy was helping his two little sisters get down, while Matt and the Chief unloaded a few bags off the cart. A third Yank accompanied them in, introducing himself as Les Wagner. She also recognised Con O'Leary from town. He tipped his cap as he greeted her. Mary had known him well as a child but had not spoken more than twice to him since she'd married. Ruth Bennett and a young man came in behind them.

Tommy Tanner asked if Mary would mind his little sisters while he saw to the greyhounds and she quickly agreed. Everyone was in high spirits and Mary felt herself swept in along the wave of good humour.

She rushed to put the kettle on and was glad of the cake. Hospitality was always very important to her grandmother. God forbid Mary let any visitor leave without a cup of tea and something to eat. She hadn't had many opportunities to offer that hospitality in the past twelve years.

Ruth chattered away as she lent a hand and introduced the young man with her. The little girls ran around laughing, while the men sat and chatted. As she laid out cups, bread and butter, and the apple-cake, Mary was again filled with the sense of pleasure that had been with her all day. Her house felt like a home.

Mary stood back and called her visitors to the table. She couldn't remember the last time her kitchen had been so full. The table looked lovely. The Americans had brought oranges and fresh figs: strange round purple fruits that Mary had never seen before. Though the rain started splattering the window, the gloom she had felt earlier was gone. Her heart felt as light and warm as the fire crackling in the hearth. Mary felt a presence behind her that sent a shiver down her back. She knew it was Beau.

"Am I missing a party?" he drawled. "How come I wasn't invited?"

Mary laughed. Everyone inquired how Beau was feeling. He smiled and put his arm around Mary's shoulder in a friendly gesture.

"Thanks to my very own Florence Nightingale, I am feeling very much improved," he said. "Not only do I owe my life to her, she graciously put up with me all day as I got in her way. I'm afraid that I'm a dismal failure as a farm-hand."

He soon had the room laughing with his account of their day on the farm, where he described Mary as a pillar of efficiency while he made a mess of things.

The table sparkled with laughter and good talk. Beau showed Mary the plate of figs and told her about the great fig-trees in his parents' garden. He said they were hundreds of years old and bore so much fruit that they had a boy employed just to pick them. He carefully chose one and made two sharp crossed cuts in it, opening it like a flower before he offered it to her. It looked like a strange creature, almost frightening as it lay curled, exposing the pink and black flesh within. It smelled sickly sweet but enticing.

Mary bit into the fruit and again wondered about Beau. She'd already gathered that he was rich and well educated. Apparently he wasn't a member of the crew, but was just hitching a lift. Mary took that nugget of information and placed it alongside the other bits and pieces she did not even realise she was collecting.

His charm was almost palpable. It flowed around the table, captivating them all. And yet Mary felt as if the charm was for her alone. But what harm? Hadn't they said that the plane would take off the next day? Feeling herself drop back into the gloom of reality, she decided to force herself to enjoy the present company. She reached out for another fig and smiled.

The men were lighting up cigarettes and the kettle was back on for another pot when they all heard a car drive up. It was Dr Moloney. Imelda was sitting in the front carrying a child wrapped in blankets. The young Yank called Les ran out to help her. They all came in and Dr Moloney came in after them and shook himself like a large sheep dog, his white mop of wet hair flying.

"This child has a very bad chest," he said, directing Imelda towards the fire.

"She needs to be kept warm and dry. A leaky caravan is no place for a sick child. She needs to be looked after properly."

Imelda flushed at the slight. Mary thought that she had brought the child against her will! Les stood protectively at Imelda's side and Mary saw something between them that made her wonder.

"Imelda stayed up all night nursing her sister," he said, defending her.

"I didn't mean to say you hadn't done all you can," said Dr Moloney gently. "I'm just worried that she might develop pneumonia. Just keep her here until the danger has passed."

"We'll make her up a bed by the fire," said Mary. She opened the bench by the fire. There was a small bed underneath. Imelda looked at her gratefully. The talk of pneumonia had clearly scared her. She held out the child to Mary. "If you hold Nellie I'll make up the bed."

Nellie peeped out from under the blanket. She

had bright inquisitive eyes. Mary felt a lump in her throat. The child was about the same age as Séan had been. She wanted to push the child away and yet she couldn't help but melt. She took her in her arms and felt her brow.

"This child is burning up," she said.

"Unwrap her a bit," instructed Dr Moloney, helping himself to tea and cake. "Keep her warm but not too hot. I see you have oranges. Excellent. Excellent. Make her some hot juice. As much as she wants. As many times as she'll have it."

The Americans were soon cutting up oranges and squeezing them. Mary and the girls busied themselves making up the small bed and clearing away. Nellie first made a face when she tasted the juice but she was soon drinking it up.

The men had drifted off to the front room. Mary could hear the sound of the piano. She was glad that they had all stayed on.

"Sounds like a bit of a session starting up," said Ruth, her eyes dancing with merriment. Imelda looked happy as well, now that Nellie had settled in. Mary caught the girls by the arm, filled with anticipation of the evening ahead.

"Why don't we join them, so?" she said and marched them into the front room.

The evening was a marvellous success. Con O'Leary sang sad songs of lost love and exile in his sweet tenor, and the doctor made them all laugh with his renditions of some old Dublin tunes. Bottles of rum the airmen had brought clinked alongside some of Gerald's poitin. The music and the drink flowed until all were flushed with it. Mary had two rums and she was beginning to feel it. She looked around at all the happy smiling faces and felt her own smile beam back.

Beau sat at the piano and played the fast frantic music he called swing. The armchairs were pushed aside as the Americans took turns teaching the others how to dance to the music. They were soon all laughing and catching their breath.

Matt called out for someone to sing "When Irish Eyes are Smiling". Beau handed the piano over to Con O'Leary who complained that it was a dreadful song, and that he would play it only to oblige their visitors. Beau came to stand by Mary as the Americans started singing. She was pleased to have a chance to be alone with him. He'd been at the piano all evening.

"Romance is in the air," he said grinning.

Mary blushed and then realised he didn't mean her. He was pointing at Imelda. She was openly smiling at Les as he sang to her. Ruth also seemed to be very interested in her companion, whose eyes followed her every move. Mary brushed off her embarrassment with a quick laugh.

"They're very pretty girls," Beau continued. He fetched her another drink of rum without asking her if she wanted one.

"They're young," she answered casually. "They're entitled to have some fun."

Beau stopped and looked pointedly at her. "I don't remember Irish women being so beautiful. I must have visited the wrong part of the country the last time I was here."

"Where did you go?" asked Mary, accepting the unspoken compliment despite herself.

"Mainly Dublin," he said.

"That explains it so," she said mischievously. The rum was making her bold.

"Do they hide all the beautiful girls in County Cork?" he asked smiling.

"At birth," she retorted and giggled.

Beau watched her laugh. His smile faded suddenly as if he had just remembered something.

"I'll be sorry to leave so soon," he said, uncharacteristically serious.

"Nonsense," said Mary, trying to sound light-hearted. "Ye'll all go off and forget all about us."

"No, I won't," he said, sounding hurt. "I will always remember your kindness to me."

"That's a line from a song!" Mary exclaimed. Without thinking twice she closed her eyes and sang softly so that only he could hear her:

And if ever I meet you by land or by sea,
I will always remember your kindness to me."

Her voice was sweet and pure. His eyes asked an unspoken question. The lamplight made them look even darker. Mary found she had to pull her gaze away. The moment was saved by Dr Moloney calling on Beau for a song.

Beau's eyes never left Mary as he sat down to play: "This one is for my charming hostess and nurse. It's a popular song back home. It's called 'It's Only a Paper Moon'."

The keys tinkled a long syncopated introduction. Mary tapped her foot. The music was infectious. By the time Beau started singing they were all tapping their feet and clapping to the rhythm. Matt grabbed the Chief and started dancing, swinging him in wide circles. Les coaxed Imelda to join him, and Ruth and her fella tried to dance a waltz to it.

Mary stood out of the way, near the fire, as Beau's voice rang out:

"It's only a paper moon hanging over a cardboard
sea –
But it wouldn't be make believe, if you believed
in me."

She couldn't help noticing how he looked over his shoulder at her as he sang. It was a simple tune and she found herself humming along. Her faced was flushed with the heat of the fire and the warmth of the drink. She was caught in the moment. Beau played louder, emphasising the beat:

"Without your love it's a honky-tonk parade.
Without your love,
It's a melody played on a penny arcade!"

The drink was going to her head. Thoughts flashed through her brain like lightning, tripping on the notes Beau was playing. She could only catch a flash before it was gone. She was struck by how different her life might have been if she had married someone like Beau. What would life be with a man like him? Not so young, not so foreign, but with his kindness, and lightness, and sense of fun? Mary watched Ruth waltzing with her tall fella. She wished them well. She prayed with all her heart that they would always be as happy as they looked right now.

Beau finished with a flourish and was immediately ordered to play it again. This time everyone sang along.

"It's only a paper moon hanging over a cardboard
sea —
But it wouldn't be make believe, if you believed
in me."

The fire leapt with the music, casting the dancers' shadows crazily over the plaster walls. Mary set down her drink. The music was too loud, the laughter too high-pitched. Beau's smile was too wide. Imelda's eyes were shining as she danced. The sight of her made Mary desperately want to cry.

"We'll be heading home soon." Dr Moloney came to stand next to her as Beau finished playing. "It's great to see you looking so well. God knows you've had your fair share of troubles," he said, dropping his voice as he patted her hand. "It's good to see you smiling."

Mary turned away to mask her confusion. She was reeling and her heart was beating loudly in her head. She leaned back against the wall for support.

She didn't like anyone to know her business. She knew many thought her haughty, but she didn't care. Dr Moloney was different. He had always been kind, and he knew better than most what her life was like. Still, she wished he'd not make it so obvious that he pitied her.

She hated that. She swallowed hard and forced herself to smile.

It put a sour taste in her mouth so that when Beau asked charmingly if he could avail of her hospitality one last night, she merely nodded. The Americans put the furniture back in place and everyone readied themselves to go. Mary struggled to remain as clear-headed as she could, hanging back as everyone said their goodbyes and headed off into the night. She barely heard them as they made arrangements for the next day. She hadn't had a drink for a long time and she had been tricked by the strength of it.

When Imelda went off to settle in with Nellie, Mary headed up to her room. Halfway up the stairs she paused, glad that she had the bannister to hang on to. Beau was standing in the middle of the hallway looking up expectantly.

"Mary," he called softly. The sound of his voice was hypnotic. He looked like a hazy dream in the lamplight.

Mary clasped the bannister tightly and took a deep breath to clear her head. When she felt that she could focus, she looked back down at him. His eyes were blazing and this time she did not look away. She drank him in, committing to memory the image of him standing there. A sad little smile played on her lips.

"Good night, Beau," she said primly and then purposefully turned and climbed the stairs.

Mary was glad she made it to her room without stumbling. She hadn't turned around even once as she climbed the stairs, though she knew he was still standing there. Once she was inside however, the room started to spin. She tripped as she miscalculated the distance to the bed. The cheek of him, she thought, as she collapsed on top of the bedclothes giggling to herself. She felt her indignation rise as she made several attempts to sit up straight. Who did he think he was, dropping out of a plane like that with his fancy ways, singing to her about paper moons?

Mary hummed the tune to herself as she struggled to take off her dress. The buttons were impossible, so she gave up and pulled it off over her head. The abrupt move made the ceiling flip and Mary had to cling to the side of the bed for fear of falling off.

That Beau fella was a right chancer. Pure cheek, she thought, once the room had stopped spinning. And she was even more the fool to be taken in by it. Whatever was she thinking? Flirting like a drunken schoolgirl on her first night out? Sure, he'd been especially charming to her, but what would you expect with a foreigner like that? He was probably charming to sheep.

Mary threw her dress on the floor and clumsily got under the covers without bothering to undress any further. She buried her head in the pillow, relishing its coolness. She was roasting. Maybe she'd caught that cold of Nellie's. It made her think of the pair sleeping downstairs in the kitchen. Mary thought of checking on them, but she abandoned the idea when she lifted her head and found that the room was spinning again.

Her body felt very heavy, and she let it sink deep into the mattress. As she drifted between sleeping and waking, it occurred to her that she was almost directly above where Beau slept. Mary saw Beau at the piano, smiling at her, heard his voice as it sang. There had definitely been something there. Something just for her. She knew it. And tomorrow he would leave. Tomorrow he would be nothing more than the pretence of a dream she hoped she would quickly forget. Mary tossed and turned all night, listening to the pounding surf and whistling wind, until she saw the dawn peep behind the curtain. Only then did she finally fall into a deep, dreamless, sleep.

Chapter Fourteen

·—·

Word had got out that the Americans were taking off and people had walked down to watch. Some carried baskets of food and looked as if they planned to make a day of it. A line of bicycles piled up along the stone walls. A bunch of small boys hovered near the Americans, clearly excited at the prospect of seeing the great B-17 bomber lift off into the sky.

Martin Kelleher was dressed and ready at the crack of dawn. Since the moment the plane had swooped over the steeple of Clonakilty Church, life had been one great big adventure. He didn't care that his mother had gone on and on and on about the terrible sin he had committed by skipping out of school. He didn't care that the Master would probably make his displeasure more painfully clear once Martin showed his face in the classroom again. And as for Father Collins, hadn't he been just delighted to see Martin bringing the Americans to his church? That surely would count for something.

Martin caught sight of Matt and boldly walked over to him. The Barry boys followed along behind.

"Hey, mister?" he said. "Remember me?"

"Martin Kelleher – am I right? How could I forget my escort?" said Matt kindly. "So what's up, guys?"

"We just came out to see ya off," said Martin.

Matt sat up on the wall and lit up a cigarette. He really looked grand, thought Martin. His leather jacket had a long zip up the front and sheep's wool on the collar. He held his cigarette between his thumb and forefinger and squinted up his eyes as he took a pull. Martin made a mental note to practise that skill in front of his bedroom mirror.

"Good-looking guys like you? You should be out chasing girls," teased Matt.

"Girls are stupid," said Joe Barry, and made a face. The others nodded their heads in agreement.

Matt laughed. "You won't be saying that in a couple of years." He searched in his breast pocket and pulled out a packet and passed it around. The boys stared at the bright silver paper in their hands.

"It's chewing-gum," explained Matt. "Put it in your

mouth and chew. It tastes good. Just don't swallow it."

The boys did as they were told, their expressions going from suspicion to surprise to pure delight as they tasted it. The five of them stood in a line chewing methodically. Martin wondered why they couldn't swallow it, but he didn't dare ask.

"Come 'ere, mister?" said Pat Barry, pushing his scruffy freckled face forward. "Do ya really think ye'll get her off the ground?"

"Hell! I sure hope so," chuckled Matt.

"She looks pretty well stuck to me," mused Martin importantly. He was very proud to have been remembered by name. That would go a long way to impress the Barry boys. "I reckon she won't budge an inch."

"Wanna bet?" asked Matt, with a twinkle in his eye.

Martin's eyes grew wide. He could feel the Barry boys' respect growing with every word. He leaned casually against the wall with his hands in his pockets like the men standing outside the church after Mass every Sunday.

"I don't mind," he answered casually as if he bet with Yanks every day of the week. "What are we betting for?"

"I'll tell you what," said Matt, taking something out of his pocket. "You see this jackknife? If we don't take off you can have it." He handed it over to Martin who dropped his man-of-the-world pose and stared at it in delight. The other boys jostled around to see.

"Are ya serious?" said Martin, handing it back.

Matt nodded "Yup. You hold on to it for me. If we don't take off, you win."

"But what happens if ya do?"

"Well, then I guess you can keep it," said Matt smiling. "For services rendered to the American Army Air Corps."

Martin couldn't believe his luck. He quickly dropped the knife into his pocket before Matt changed his mind.

Matt was watching a large group of people that were ambling up, chatting and pointing at the plane. He let out a low whistle.

"Now *there* is one good reason to hang around for a while," he said, looking at a small trim woman striding down the road. She had jet-black hair tied up in a high bun and bright blue eyes which Martin knew only too well.

"Are ya daft, man?" exclaimed Martin. "That's me ma! Oh Jaysus, Mary and Joseph! She'll have the skin off my back. Sorry. I've gotta go. See ya! Thanks for the knife." And he scurried like a mouse to hide behind the big truck that had brought the Americans out in the morning.

Beau jumped off the open cart and saluted the group of airmen. Tommy had been sent out to pick him up early and they had left almost immediately. There had been no time for more than a quick goodbye to Mary.

The marsh was alive with activity as men went back and forth to the plane. A few local men in green uniforms tried to keep the curious at bay. Beau shook hands with Tommy and said goodbye to Imelda and the little girl. Nellie was clearly better after her night by the fire and was babbling away as the cart drove off down the road.

Les came running up from the marsh.

"Damn," he said, catching his breath in big gulps. "I missed them. I wanted to say goodbye."

"Sometimes it's better not to say goodbye," said Beau, vexed by this morning's rush. There had been no time for more than curt platitudes. It had left a bad feeling in his belly.

"Love 'em and leave 'em. That's my motto," said Matt trying to cheer Les up.

"Come on, kid, we've got work to do! There's lots of other fish in the sea. Did I ever tell you about English women? Wait till you see them. Long legs, and I mean long long legs!"

But Les looked bereft as he watched the cart cross the causeway in the distance.

Beau wandered through the growing crowd to where the pilot and co-pilot were conferring with the engineer. He saluted Charlie Hansen smartly.

"Sergeant Beauregard St Soucis reporting back, sir," he said with a grin.

"Beau! I'm glad to see you back on your feet again. How's the head?"

"I'm fine, Charlie," Beau answered. "So when are we taking off?"

"You should first ask: *are* we taking off?" interjected engineer Tate wryly.

"Is there a problem?" asked Beau.

"Actually I wish we only had one problem," answered Charlie Hansen. "To start with, the fuel is really low-octane."

"And the landing gear is sunk halfway up," added the engineer.

The co-pilot waved the rest of the crew over. They ran up and formed a semicircle around the pilot.

"OK, men. We're gonna try and fly this bird out. But I can tell you it won't be easy. We've got really low-grade fuel. That means we can't use the turbo superchargers. It's gonna be hard to get enough power to take off. We'll try to lighten the load as much as possible but I don't know." Charlie Hansen shook his head.

"It's gonna take a helluva a lot of power. It's like

jello out there. We're gonna have to suck that baby out of it," the engineer elaborated.

"Could we try and put planks or something under the wheels?" asked the Chief.

The engineer shook his head. "There's at least three feet of mush. Your planks would just get swallowed up. I've heard of a soft surface but this is ridiculous."

"Anyway we'll give it our best shot," said Charlie Hansen. "We'll warm up the engines real slowly and carefully. Then we'll push her as far as it's safe."

"The engines could detonate if we push them too far," explained McKnight. "They weren't designed for this grade of fuel. Tate and I have calculated the load and such, and frankly I'm not certain this will work."

Charlie Hansen looked over at the people on the road. They had all retreated a respectful distance while the Americans talked.

"They've been very kind to us. Not to mention that they've bent a few rules to get us the fuel. So we owe it to them to give it a try," he said. "I know how badly you guys want to get out of here and see some action, but I've got to be honest with you. I hate to disappoint you, but the chances of flying out today are pretty slim. We might get stuck here a little while longer while we figure another way out."

Beau looked at the circle of faces. They listened grimly to what the pilot was saying but their eyes belied their sternness. Sly grins played at the corners of their mouths. They looked far from disappointed. In fact Les Wagner looked positively delighted.

The men dispersed and Beau found himself alone. There was nothing for him to do but wait to be called. He leaned back on the wall and smoked his first cigarette of the day. God, but this was a beautiful place. He remembered someone saying that Ireland had forty shades of green. And then some, he thought. Beau was surrounded by grey and green. Dark pine-green that was almost black, rich mossy green that looked like velvet, the brown dusty green of the gorse, and the soft vibrant green that was just starting to show on the hedges and trees. He wished he wasn't leaving so soon.

Beyond the pines he could see the top of the farmhouse and again felt a twinge. Yesterday had been so perfect and then he had to go and spoil it. Mary was a lovely woman who had taken him into her house without question. She was a simple farmer's wife and he had treated her as if she was some flighty debutante. He felt ashamed. He was sure that he had offended her with his behaviour. It was clear by the way that she had avoided him in the morning. He had mistaken her kindness for flirtation and stupidly reacted to it. But there had been such a change in her as the drink had danced in her eyes. Her body had softened as her smiles grew more open. He had been captivated by the way she looked at him from under her lashes, a mixture of shyness and forwardness. Beau tried to swallow his discomfort. After all, he would never see her again, but it saddened him that she might think badly of him.

A movement behind the pines caught his eye. It was Mary's dog running up the hill. Presently a woman's silhouette emerged from the tree-line. She stopped for a minute and looked out over the marsh. Then she quickly walked up the hill and disappeared behind a ridge. Beau hurried over to Charlie Hansen.

"You don't mind if I go for a walk to stretch my legs?" he said. "I'm feeling kinda useless."

"No problem," answered the pilot.

Beau smiled and gave him the thumb's up.

"I'll be back in a half an hour. Don't leave without me!" He ran across the road, jumped the gate, and started walking rapidly up the hill.

The dog came up to greet him before he reached the top and led him to where Mary was. She sat in a little dip, protected against the wind, leaning against a stone slab. He knew that she had seen him, but she didn't turn to face him. She just sat very still, her arms hugging her knees which were pulled up tightly against her chest. Her copper hair was flying loose, a bright contrast to the grey green landscape. The wind blew her hair around her face but she made no move to put the loose locks back in place. She just looked out to sea intently as if studying it.

"What are you doing?" asked Beau softly. He sat himself down on the stone ledge above her.

"I'm counting the waves," she answered, not moving. "I'm looking for the seventh one. They say it's bigger than the rest."

The sea was as grey as the clouds. The swell of the waves started far out and rolled majestically in, one wave behind the other, getting fuller and faster as they approached the shore. Beau tried counting them but found that he could not take his eyes off Mary.

Beau was at a loss for words. He wanted to thank her for her hospitality and apologise for his boorishness. He wanted formally to say goodbye. He toyed with the usual phrases but they all sounded hollow to him. Impeccable manners seemed totally inappropriate to these wild surroundings. Most of all they were wrong for the woman sitting there looking at the breakers crashing on the beach below.

"Do you come up here a lot?" asked Beau.

"Most days," she answered. "It helps to take my mind off things."

Beau saw a tiny shadow pass over her face. It was as if a sharp pain had crossed her brow. He reached out and tucked a wayward bright curl behind her ear.

"Mary, I'm so sorry," he began. His voice was unsteady, gruff.

"Don't," she said firmly and turned to face him. For a brief moment she held his gaze before turning away again. Her eyes were the same colour as the sea: grey-green. In the morning light he could see a criss-cross of little lines around her eyes that he hadn't noticed before. He had to look away for fear that he might kiss her. He wanted to take her in his arms and tell her everything was going to be all right. This was going terribly wrong. He stood up and cleared his throat.

"You'll be leaving soon, I expect," she said, almost to herself.

"They're busy getting the plane ready," Beau answered woodenly. "I wanted to thank you for all your hospitality. There wasn't much time this morning. You have been most kind."

Mary rose and held out her hand. Her smile was bright and her voice was cheery.

"There was no need. You already thanked me last night. Remember?"

"I remember," said Beau taking her hand.

"Goodbye, so," she said.

"Goodbye." But he did not let go of her hand. Instead he pulled her close and kissed her lips softly. Mary stood stock-still, neither giving in nor pulling away. Beau cupped her face in his hands, kissed her again and felt her body relax. Her arms went around his shoulders and she held him tightly. They stood for a long while like that, not saying anything. Finally she pushed him gently away.

"You'd best be going now," she whispered.

Beau could only nod.

He did not look back at her as he ran down the hill. Down on the marsh he could see a figure turning the propellers by hand. They were starting to warm up the engines. By the time he got to the road the air was filled with the sound of them. Then Beau remembered what Charlie Hansen had said about their chances of taking off. He knew it was all terribly wrong but he hoped like crazy that the pilot was right.

Getting the plane ready took the best part of the morning. Twenty LDF men kept the crowd orderly and in good humour. After a while they all became used to the engines revving and then slowing and the conversation drifted to upcoming weddings, past funerals, and the always interesting subject of rationing.

Dr Moloney had taken the liberty of driving out, though it could hardly be called a medical emergency. He had brought Barry Kingston and Pat Coughlan with him. Con O'Leary and Miss Aileen had also come along. She had sat regally in the front, forcing the three men to crowd into the back. She was now sitting in the car with her hands over her ears, her bosom trembling with each rise in the pitch of the engines. Con O'Leary had his box camera and was busy trying to get a good shot of *T'Ain't a Bird* for posterity.

The chattering crowd quietened as the engines revved up a notch. All eyes were glued to the plane. Charlie Hansen leaned out of his window in the cockpit and waved goodbye. The crowd cheered and waved back and then all covered their ears as the engines revved even higher, the sound echoing back and forth across the marsh.

The tension rose. Everyone held their breath. The propellers were just a white blur on the wings. Miss Aileen was quite overcome by it all and got her rosary tangled in her cameo brooch as she attempted to pray.

"Lift!" ordered Barry Kingston under his breath. "Lift!"

"Holy Mother of God," implored Miss Aileen, her rosary beads flailing in front of her nose. "Would they ever get on with it? I'm having the palpitations."

"Go on! Go on, now!" yelled Con O'Leary. The call was echoed up and down the road as they all willed the big bomber off the ground.

Martin Kelleher lay under the truck. He could barely see over the stone wall, but managed to keep one eye on the plane and the other on his mother, who was craning to see over the crowd as it backed away from the noise. He could hardly contain his excitement. He was torn between the desire to see the big plane fly and that of meeting Matt again. The Barry boys crouched beside him, their eyes glistening.

"So what do ya think?" Pat Barry whispered loudly in his ear. Martin took a copper coin from his pocket and held it up.

"Heads she flies. Tails she stays stuck in the muck."

"Heads so," chose Pat Barry.

"I'll take tails," said Martin as he spun the coin on the ground. It rolled out from under the truck and stopped at the heel of a bright black boot.

Its owner took no notice. His attention, along with that of all the others crowding the road, was caught by a slight change in the rhythm of engines. One by one the big propellers slowed and then stopped. An audible sigh and clucking of tongues was heard along the road as it became clear that the attempt had failed.

Martin wriggled out from under the truck to regain his coin and then slid quickly back under as he recognised Pat Coughlan, the garda. To make matters worse he was soon joined by a pair of sturdy legs that Martin recognised as belonging to his uncle Barry Kingston.

His uncle and the garda leaned up against the truck, forcing Martin and the Barry boys to lie low. Was there no end to his troubles, thought Martin, as he scanned the legs milling about, for his mother's trim ankles.

"'Tis an awful shame altogether," said Barry Kingston. "An awful shame."

"'Tis that and a nuisance as well," affirmed Pat Coughlan.

"I suppose there's nothing left but to bring them back to the hotel?" inquired Barry Kingston.

"You can do whatever ya please with 'em as long as they stay in town. It won't be my problem for long,

CRISTINA PISCO

thanks be to God. I've a call that the Superintendent will be back soon, and he's bringing the army with him. They'll be a lot of explaining to do once they get here."

Martin could tell that the Americans had come back onto the road. Their long green trouser-legs could be seen around the truck. The boys soon found themselves hemmed in on all sides. Martin could stand it no longer.

"I'm going to make a run for it," he said grimly.

"Yer ma'll kill ya!" exclaimed Pat Barry.

"She'll have to catch me first," said Martin bravely. "I'll tell ya what. You fellas crawl out the back and I'll head off in the opposite direction. We'll make our own way into town and meet at the back of the hotel." He noted with pride Joe Barry's silent approval of his plan.

Martin waited to hear the shouts of surprise as the Barry boys emerged and then wriggled out into a small clearing in the forest of legs. He darted through the crowd, looking over his shoulder to see if he had been spotted and ran straight into Matt.

"Hey, *bambino*! Where's the fire? You won the bet!"

Martin gasped and looked frantically around.

"You still hiding from your mama?" asked Matt,

grinning. Martin nodded. Matt turned to the tall blondy Yank standing beside him. "Did you ever play hooky, Les? I used to do it all the time. And did I get it when I came home!"

"I can't say that I did," laughed the tall fella. "Say, do you think the same rules apply as yesterday? We can wander around within a three-mile radius as long as we have an escort?"

"I should think so," answered Matt. "Why? What's cooking?"

Les didn't answer. He leant down to Martin and asked: "Do you know a guy called Dennis Crowley, my escort?" Martin nodded. "Well, could you find him and tell him that Les Wagner is looking for him." He turned back to Matt and beamed. "I think I feel a long walk coming on."

"Would that be a long walk over the causeway?" asked Matt matching his smile. Les beamed even more. Matt laughed and mimed a fiddle-player. To Martin's surprise he then batted his eyelashes coquettishly and burst into song, his voice trilling like a girlie: *"I looove yooou hums the April breeze. I looove yooou echo the hills . . ."*

"Cut it out," said Les blushing but clearly pleased about something.

Martin didn't understand what they were on

about. But he couldn't give a toss. He was back in the action. He'd find Dennis Crowley in a flash, in a hail-storm, in a blizzard! He trotted off, still keeping an eye out for his ma. But he didn't care if she found him. He was on top of the world. He could feel the jackknife slap against his leg. He had important business to attend to, and nobody was going to get in his way.

Chapter Fifteen

‒•‒

Mary left Dr Moloney sitting patiently in the kitchen with a cup of tea while she went upstairs to get changed. He'd driven out to invite her to a dance that was being held in the airmen's honour. Before Mary could comment, he informed her that he wouldn't take no for an answer and that, seeing as Mrs Moloney was feeling poorly, he would be needing an escort. Besides, the pilot had insisted that she attend as he wanted to thank her personally for helping Beau. Mary felt a shiver of excitement at the mention of Beau's name. The roar of the engines had stopped down at the marsh hours ago, and she had known then that they hadn't taken off.

Mary sat down on the bed. It had been a most extraordinary day. She'd woken up with a heavy head and a parched mouth that felt like sandpaper. She was sick and bothered. She knew it had less to do with the drink than with the feelings she had been having ever since she had first set eyes on Beau, as he lay unconscious on the cart. She was embarrassed by herself. She had kept her eyes averted over breakfast. Beau had said little apart from a quick goodbye.

As the cart echoed down the road, taking him away, Mary sat at the table and tried to stop her hands from shaking. The sick feeling in her stomach was becoming a tight ball. The whole damn thing had left her breathless and fearful. She was scared and she didn't know why. So she'd climbed the hill as she'd done so many times before to find comfort in the sea, and the sky, and Séan's memory. And then Beau had come and taken her in his arms and kissed away all her fears.

It was as if a veil had been ripped from her eyes. Even as she heard the engines revving up in the marsh, she knew a sense of calm she had never felt before. She thought she would never see the handsome young man from Louisiana again. But she felt no remorse. He was leaving her with much more than a kiss.

Mary remembered poor Dr Moloney waiting downstairs. It was time she got a move on. What was she going to wear? On impulse she took out the dress Gerald had given her. It was a light-green watered silk. Mary held the dress up to her body and looked at herself in the mirror as she did a little twirl. "Chartreuse silk, if you please," she said out loud. "Very grand altogether."

With a growing sense of excitement she turned the dress inside out to check if the original seams were still there. She found them tucked behind the perfect little stitches she had so carefully sewn the night her life had changed forever. Mary got her sewing scissors and ripped the stitches out.

Mary slipped the dress on. It fitted perfectly. It felt good. As she quickly pinned up her hair, she swore that she would never let Gerald lay a hand on her again. She did not know how, she did not know when, but she knew in her heart that she would some day be free of him. He was an evil man who she had endured for no reason except that it had never occurred to her not to. Now that she knew, she could never endure him again. Mary found her good black shoes. They were a bit worn but they would do fine. She had no idea what would happen when she saw Beau again, but it didn't matter. He had already changed her.

Mary walked into the big hall on Dr Moloney's arm.

She was surprised to see so many people there. Chairs lined the hall and a large group was already dancing to the céili band playing on a little platform up at the front. The bar was crowded with people dressed in their Sunday best, drinking and laughing loudly. Mary took a step back. The doctor sensed her nervousness and gently guided her into the room. Green uniforms seemed to be everywhere, some of them Yanks and others from the LDF. Mary searched the crowd as Dr Moloney went off to get them a drink, but she could not find Beau amongst them.

And then she saw him. He was up near the band with one of the local girls. Beau leaned down and said something and the girl exploded into giggles. Mary's heart sank. Oh God, she thought, they look so good together. They were a perfectly matched pair. A dashing young airman and a pretty girl – that's the way it should be. Beau had shaved and changed into a fresh uniform and was devastatingly handsome. The girl was so young and pretty. She was laughing and looking up at Beau with the kind of sparkling open eyes that carried nothing more than the joy of being alive. Mary knew she had lost that look forever.

Mary felt overdressed and old, and out of place in this hall where everyone seemed not to have a care in the world. Beau and the girl chatted away, unaware that they were being observed. They were interrupted by Miss Aileen O'Donovan who invited Beau to dance a waltz that was just starting up. He was a graceful dancer who managed to make even Miss Aileen look like a slip of a girl in his arms.

"May I have the next dance?" said a voice on her right. Matt and the Chief were standing there surrounded by a group of little boys. The smallest one held a small furry bundle in his arms.

"Don't you worry, Matt," said the little boy importantly. "I'll mind Tojo for ya."

Mary laughed, despite herself. "So this is the monkey? He seems a very quiet little thing."

"He's normally much more jumpy," explained the boy. "I think he's tired. He'd better stay with me."

Matt held out his arm to Mary. "So whadya think? Shall we?"

"Sure, it's been a long time, but I'll give it a go," she answered, letting him lead her out to the dance floor.

"And I insist on having the one right after," said the Chief as Matt led her away.

"That was Martin Kelleher, my official escort," explained Matt as they started to dance. "Him and his friends have been following us around since this morning." Matt was a competent dancer and Mary found she had little to do but follow his lead.

"Well, you know you've created quite a stir," said

Mary. "I'd say those boys will never forget this as long as they live."

"They're great kids. I've enjoyed their company," continued Matt. "It's one of the things we miss, being in the military – kids. Everywhere we've been, South America, Africa, or on the bases, we're always happy to meet some kids."

"Martin Kelleher? Does his mother have the small sweet shop on Pearse Street? I went to school with her," said Mary, still keeping her eye on Beau as he danced on the other side of the room. "Poor Kitty was widowed very young. But she seems to be doing well. Still, it must be hard, raising the children on her own."

Over Matt's shoulder she could see Beau escorting Miss Aileen back to her seat. She was talking a mile a minute, evidently much charmed by him.

"Widowed?" said Matt, raising an eyebrow. "And her name's Kitty?" He did not elaborate and Mary wondered what he meant.

When the dance was over they went back to the others. Dr Moloney had returned from the bar and was talking with the Chief and a tall American who was smoking a pipe.

"Ah, Mary, there ya are," said Dr Moloney. "This here is Lieutenant Charles Hansen, the pilot. He's been wanting to meet you."

"I wanted to thank you for your help," said the pilot, shaking her hand. He pointed to Beau. "As you can see, Sergeant Beauregard seems to be fully recovered."

Beau was being introduced to a group of older ladies by Miss Aileen. He took his time to smile at each of them, much to the ladies' delight. He asked one of them to dance and was soon gliding across the floor again.

"He certainly has a way with the ladies," said Dr Moloney smiling.

"It's the accent," joked Matt. "That soft southern accent gets 'em every time."

"Indeed," said Mary wryly.

The Chief claimed his turn and Mary was on the dance floor again. It was a foxtrot and Mary had to concentrate to keep up with her diminutive partner as he held her tightly. It caught her by surprise when she suddenly realised that Beau was dancing beside her. Her heart caught in her throat as she looked up and saw him beaming back at her, looking like the happiest man alive.

"Mary!" he exclaimed. "You made it!" His partner craned her neck around to see who he was addressing. Mary met her curious gaze coolly and just stared right back. Nosy old bird, she thought.

"I'll see you in a minute," Beau called over his

partner's shoulder as they danced away. Mary tried to calm herself enough to finish the dance. The Chief made polite conversation about their attempt to take off that day, but Mary just nodded. She could feel Beau watching her from across the room. It felt like the longest foxtrot in the world, but it finally ended and Beau was at her side.

"I was starting to worry that you wouldn't come," he said breathlessly. He took a step back and looked at her. "You look wonderful."

Mary was speechless. She felt herself glowing under his gaze. She didn't know if she looked wonderful, but she certainly felt wonderful. Beau discreetly took her arm and started guiding her away from the others.

"Come on. Let's get out of here," he whispered.

They had reached the edge of the crowd when they heard Beau's name being called. Dr Moloney was standing on the little platform with Con O'Leary. They were calling out for Beau.

Beau turned back and waved half-heartedly. "What do they want?" he asked under his breath. The doctor and Con were waving at him to come forward.

"I think they want you to play," answered Mary. "You'll have to go up."

Beau looked trapped. He gave her arm a little squeeze. "I'll be right back. Don't you dare go away."

Mary watched him walk away as the crowd parted to let him through. His smell lingered beside her and she could still feel his touch on her arm. What in heaven's name did she think she was doing? It was as if she lost all sense when he was near her, and got a slap in the face the minute he was gone. Mary was filled with a confused mess of joy and regret. Beau was conferring with the musicians. He sat down at the piano. Then he looked over the crowd at her and began to play. He played it slower than he had the night before, but Mary recognised the tune instantly. It was "Only a Paper Moon" and she knew he was playing the song for her alone.

The crowd moved onto the dance floor and Mary found herself on her own. She felt very exposed standing there alone. Slowly, she started moving backwards to the less well-lit part of the hall. Beau looked over his shoulder and searched the crowd. A frown crossed his brow when he could not find her. She needed some air. Her back hit a door behind her. She felt for the handle and slipped outside.

She was in a small service alley. It was very quiet and still compared to the noise inside. She sat on a barrel and took a deep sharp breath of cold air to clear her head. The moon was shining brightly, bathing the alley in a silver glow. She could still hear Beau singing over the muffled sound of shuffling feet and clinking glasses. Paper moon indeed, she thought. A damn silly notion if she'd ever heard one! Then the music rose as the other musicians picked up the tune, adding their own embellishments to it.

Suddenly the door flew open and Beau burst outside. He looked around wildly until he found her sitting there.

"Thank God!" he said. "I thought I'd lost you."

"I needed some air," she said hesitantly.

Beau drew her to her feet and held her shoulders. His eyes searched her face. "Are you all right?"

"I'll be fine." Mary felt her body tremble and wondered if he'd notice. He was staring at her with both desire and concern.

"Do you have any idea how beautiful you are, here in the moonlight?" he asked.

Mary shook her head slowly and then looked deep into his eyes. "No, I don't." she said plainly, her eyes never leaving his. "Tell me."

"You are far, far, too beautiful," he answered slowly, emphasising every word.

Mary closed her eyes and smiled. When she opened them again he was still staring at her. Mary pulled back. "Beau, I wish," she started, stammering slightly, and then tried again, "I wish that . . . I mean, I'm . . . " His eyes willed her to go on. Mary took another deep breath. "Beau, I can't," she said simply. "I just can't."

He pulled her close against his chest and cradled her like a child. Mary felt herself melt into the warmth of his embrace.

"I know. I know you can't," he whispered softly in her ear. "It's OK." He pulled away and forced her to look at him.

"I want you to listen to me," he said intently. "I would never hurt you. I don't want to force you into anything. I understand. You don't have to run away."

He drew her down to sit on the row of barrels again, taking her hand in his. "I'll admit that I am totally infatuated, but that's all right, isn't it? You must be used to men falling head over heels in love with you at first sight. Why don't you just enjoy it? You know you're beautiful – why, if you were a Southern Belle, you'd have gentlemen lining up just to catch a glimpse of you at the window, and you wouldn't even have to turn and say hello."

Mary laughed. What was it about him that made everything seem so light and easy? "Yer a devil, ya're," she sighed.

"I know," he said grinning. "I have even been called a handsome devil on several occasions. And a damn charming one too!"

"Don't be so cocky."

"And why shouldn't I be?" he asked laughing. "Look

at me sitting here with a beautiful woman and a great big old full moon while the music's playing in the background."

"Did you just jump up and leave them all back there?" she asked.

"Of course not," he said, as if offended at the suggestion. "I finished singing and gave them my most sweeping bow before I ran out after you."

"By the way, the moon's not full yet," she corrected. "It won't be till Sunday."

"Whatever. We can sit and watch it then." Beau jumped up excitedly and pulled her to her feet. "I'll tell you what. You know what would make me the happiest man in the whole wide world?"

Mary shook her head.

"Dance with me. Come back inside, and dance with me."

People were crowding the dance floor as Mary and Beau came back into the room. He held her hand until they stepped into the light and Mary felt a pang of regret as he let go. The leader of the band was calling for couples to form. Dancing partners lined up in rows as the leader called out for more people to come and fill in the gaps.

"What's going on?" asked Beau.

"They're going to dance 'The Siege of Ennis'," said Mary. "Come on! This will be fun."

He followed her on to the floor, intrigued. They joined another couple forming a line of four. There was a lot of shuffling about, and changing of partners until the lines were rearranged to the leader's satisfaction. When the pattern was complete, sixty-four people were on the dance floor in eight pairs of four that faced each other. As the music started, Mary took Beau's hand and held it up in front of them. She counted out the beat along with the other one hundred and twenty-eight hands held aloft. Then the whole floor moved as one.

"Front," said Mary, as they hopped forward two paces. "And back," she said as they danced back.

"This is like a jumpy minuet," said Beau.

"Not really. Now cross to the side, and back," said Mary, laughing as they bumped into the couple next to them. All around them the Americans were bumping into other dancers. Everyone laughed at their clumsiness. The dancers crossed back to their original position so that each person was facing a partner.

"Now what?" asked Beau, tapping his foot to try and keep to the rhythm.

"Now you swing," said Mary pointing him towards the very large lady facing him. The woman hopped over eagerly and grabbed Beau around the waist. She was as tall as he, but twice as broad. Beau looked over at Mary in mock fright. Mary's partner swung her until the room was spinning around her. She caught a glimpse of Beau and nearly lost her balance from laughing. He was gallantly trying to hold on to the woman's broad waist. She spun him around, lifting him almost off the ground.

In the confusion of the swing Beau lost his place as each line moved up a notch in the pattern. He tried to return to Mary's side but another had taken his place. Mary waved him in alongside his large companion. The woman took his hand in a steel grip and held it up.

"What happens now?" Beau called out to her.

"We do it all over again," she said laughing.

Beau held her eyes as they danced forward towards each other and then back again. He'd managed to get the pace of it and kept up with his sour-faced partner as the line moved sideways and back again. Then they were facing each other for the swing. Mary reached out and showed Beau how to lock arms with her. They spun faster and faster, tightening their grip so as not to fall, laughing loudly at the thrill of it. Mary's heart soared as a fit of giggles caught her by surprise making her even more out of breath. Almost as soon as it started, it was over, and Beau moved forward into the line behind her.

The pattern was repeated over and over. Beau was dancing clockwise as Mary's line moved in the opposite direction. The huge circle moved up a notch every time. For a while they danced further and further apart, until they were on opposite sides of the hall. Then each section brought Beau and Mary closer together. They searched for each other over the tops of the dancers' bobbing heads, losing their bearings at every swing and then smiling across the crowd as they found each other again.

Mary could feel the gap between them closing. He was only four lines ahead. Beau had it learnt by now and was really dancing. It was as if his eyes were reaching out for her. Mary danced in anticipation of the moment when they would face each other again in the swing. But as he took his place in front of her, the music stopped.

They stood catching their breath as the dancers dispersed around them. They said nothing, not wanting to break the spell. It was only when Beau took her hand and put his own on her waist, that Mary realised that the music had started again.

It was a slow waltz to allow the dancers a rest after the wild energy of the last set. Dancing with Beau was like floating. He held her lightly but firmly, the slightest pressure moving her gracefully around the room. Their bodies did not touch but still they moved as one.

"You're a very good dancer," said Mary.

"I should be. I cost my parents a fortune," he quipped.

"You had lessons?"

"Every Tuesday afternoon from when I was six to when I was twelve. I'd be driven into town, and forced to attend. The dancing teacher was this appalling woman called Miss Lily Rose, a bit like my dancing partner back there, but with more ruffles. She held tea-dances every week and taught deportment, dancing, and what she called decorum. The idea was to teach us genteel manners as well as dancing. All the girls were taller than the boys, and looked like overdressed chantilly desserts. At least they enjoyed dressing up. The poor boys were miserable. We were scrubbed and stuffed into suits and ties. It's a very Southern form of torture. Disgraceful really. I hated it intensely."

Mary laughed. "Why did you keep going?"

"Oh, I wanted to stop, but my mother wouldn't hear of it. Then when I was twelve I decided not go any more."

"And your mother?" asked Mary.

"I guess you could say I omitted to inform her of my decision," he answered with a wicked grin.

"So how did you manage it?"

"It took some doing," he began, "I forged a note saying I would not be attending due to a medical condition and mailed it to Miss Lily Rose. Then I bribed the maid who was chaperoning me, and got the driver to keep quiet by telling him I knew he kept a bottle of scotch in the glove compartment. So every Tuesday I'd hop out of the car and pretend to go into the building, but instead I'd scoot down an alley and go off an play poker for pennies with the boys from the rougher part of town. It's sad a tale of corruption, really," he said shaking his head. "I committed a multitude of sins. Lies, forgery, bribery, extortion and gambling! And I was only twelve years old."

"And how long did ya manage to keep that up for?" asked Mary.

"Only one term," answered Beau. "Miss Lily Rose paid a visit to my mother to enquire if my medical condition was any better and the game was up. There was hell to pay, I can tell you. But it was worth it. I never did have to go back to dancing classes."

"In all fairness, you *did* learn how to dance," Mary added as he twirled her one final time just as the music ended.

"That's true. And I must say that thanks to Miss Lily Rose, I do deport myself decorously should the need arise," he acknowledged smiling. Beau took a step back still holding her hand. "Thank you very much for the giving me the pleasure of this dance, madame. I am eternally in your debt." Then he bowed gracefully and brushed a light kiss over the top of her hand. Mary giggled and did a little curtsy.

As the music started up again, Lieutenant Hansen stepped up to ask her to dance. He warned Mary that he had two left feet, but managed to dance with her nonetheless, unlike Dr Moloney who cut in for the next dance. He was a heavy dancer and apologised profusely each time he stepped on Mary's foot. The women of the town were lining up to dance with the Yanks. Beau was a very popular dance partner as was the Chief. Mary noticed Matt dancing with Kitty Kelleher under the astonished gaze of young Martin, while Miss Aileen O'Donovan took to the floor with Con O'Leary, complaining loudly that her new shoes were killing her and he'd best be careful not to step on them. Beau looked over at Mary often. At the start of each new dance, he tried to get over to her side of the room. But every time either Mary or Beau was whisked off by a different partner.

Mary danced with each member of the crew, one after another. They were all courteous and friendly, though none was as charming as Beau. She noticed that the young long fella, Les Wagner, was missing. She asked about him when Matt danced with her again. He smiled and said that he'd "gone for a long walk" and Mary wondered if Imelda had anything to do with it.

The hall was full of laughter and dancing. Mary couldn't remember when she had enjoyed herself so much. As the evening progressed worries were forgotten, slights forgiven, and troubles denied by all. Mary chatted with people she hadn't talked to in years, and more than one told her how happy they were that she was looking so well. For the first time, in a long time, she felt a part of the town and its people and it warmed her heart to be back.

Tojo rallied to the general cheer and started dancing on the little platform. Martin Kelleher and his mates danced with the monkey as people formed a circle and clapped, urging them on. The little boys were all wearing the airmen's caps cocked saucily to one side. Mary stopped to have a rest and take in the scene. She hadn't been sitting long before Beau sat down next to her.

"You are definitely the Belle of the Ball," he said. He put his hand to his heart in a gesture of mock hurt. "I've been trying to cut in for a dance for over an hour but you have utterly ignored me. I thought

I'd have to beat them off with a stick to talk to you again."

"I'm not the 'belle' of anything. 'Tis just the fancy dress," said Mary, delighted to be in his company again.

Beau leaned over in what Mary recognised as an an exaggerated imitation of Matt. "As they say in Brooklyn: It ain't the dress, lady, it's the hanger. I even saw Charlie Hansen putting the moves on you."

"Your pilot is a lovely man," said Mary. " He's very keen to get over to England and get on with the war."

"Oh, they all are, I suppose," Beau said distractedly.

"He said that your crew would be very pleased to see you."

Beau just shrugged. Mary thought that perhaps he preferred not to talk about the war. The thought of Beau risking his life made her shudder.

Beau noticed her change of mood and asked what was the matter.

"It just makes me ill to see young men go off to war," she said sadly. "I'd hate to think something might happen to you," she added softly.

To her surprise Beau just winked and laughed.

"You don't have to worry about me," he said cheerfully.

"But you could be shot down," Mary whispered seriously. "We hear about how bad it is sometimes.

The papers are censored, so are the letters, but word gets out. "

"You still have nothing to worry about," he said smiling. "I have as much chance of getting shot down as I do of getting hit by a bus."

Mary was confused. What was he going on about?

Beau turned to her with a conspirator's grin. "Can you keep a secret?"

Mary nodded slowly.

"I'm not really an airman," Beau whispered in her ear.

"What do you mean?" she asked, pointing to his uniform. Beau looked down at himself as if he'd only just noticed that he was wearing it.

"Oh that? That's only make-believe."

"What are ya then?" she asked bewildered.

"I'm just a handsome Louisiana devil. Just don't tell anyone." Beau paused to emphasise his point. "Promise?"

"I don't believe a word of it," said Mary primly, though her eyes were dancing again.

"Promise you won't tell?" he insisted.

"I suppose I could pretend to believe ya, if it makes ya happy," said Mary, throwing up her hands.

"Well, that settles it," said Beau leaning back in his chair and stretching out his long legs in front of him. "You pretend that I'm not and I'll pretend that I am, and somewhere in there we'll make some sense of it."

Mary looked to see if he cared to explain, but Beau had nothing more to say. He just raised his eyebrows at her and started to whistle as if he hadn't a care in the world while he watched Tojo and the boys dance. He kept stealing glances over at her with a big silly grin on his face and she realised that he was whistling that "Paper Moon" song. He looked like butter wouldn't melt in his mouth.

"You are a Louisiana devil, that's for sure," she said shaking her head.

Beau pretended not to hear her and sang softly under his breath, *". . . But it wouldn't be make-believe, if you believe in me . . . "*

"Ya really think yer cute, don't ya?" said Mary sternly, but she couldn't stop herself from smiling.

Beau sat up straight and faced her.

"No, ma'am, I do not *think* I'm cute," he said seriously. "I *know* I am. In fact, when I was born my mama said there wasn't a cuter baby in the whole state of Louisiana!" Then he threw his head back and roared with laughter.

Chapter Sixteen

◆•◆

Les shone his flashlight down the muddy path. It was so overgrown that he could have easily missed it in the dark if he hadn't been there before. Dennis had walked out with him in the afternoon, but Imelda and Tommy had both been "gone for the day". Their aunt asked them to call in later. Les was disappointed to have missed Imelda, but it made him even more determined to see her again. It took some convincing but Dennis finally agreed to go back out to the tinkers' camp that night.

Ruth had been very easy to persuade. She'd told her parents that she had to stay late at the hotel because of the dance, and got off work to come along. Dennis had got a hold of a bicycle for Les so that they could all ride out to the marsh together.

Les wasn't sure if they had a curfew, but he didn't bother to ask. He slipped out under the "sometimes forgiveness is easier than permission" principle and asked Matt to cover for him if anyone started asking questions. The whole expedition had an air of secret intrigue as they rode out of town in the dark, stifling their laughter and taking roads where it was unlikely that Ruth would be spotted by anyone she knew.

Les dropped his heavy knapsack on the ground and called the others over. "It's down this way. It's pretty dark, so be careful."

"Do you want a hand with that," said Dennis. "It looks heavy."

"No thanks. I'm OK," said Les, hoisting the bag back on his shoulder.

"What have ya got in there?" asked Ruth.

"I just got a couple of things from the plane and stuff I bought in town. You know food and fruit. I found some chocolate for the kids. And I got a bottle of rum from Matt."

"Rum! That'll make sure we're welcome," said Dennis.

"Jaysus, I've sunk down to me ankles in the muck," shrieked Ruth. "Me shoes are ruined. How am I going explain that?"

Les shone the flashlight on Ruth. She had missed the path and walked into the marsh. The sight of her struggling to get loose from the mud was so funny that Les and Dennis couldn't stop from laughing.

"Go away home and mock yer own!" she said giggling. The more she flayed around the more they laughed. "Shut up and help me, ya eejits!" she shouted.

Dennis reached out and grabbed her hand. "Come on girl. I'll pull ya out." Ruth popped out like a cork as Dennis pulled her out like a fish on a line.

"Holy Mother of God – I've lost them altogether now!" Ruth stood barefoot looking helplessly at the black muck. Les shone the flashlight over it but there was no trace of the shoes. It was as if the marsh had swallowed them up.

"Wow!" said Les. "That stuff is like quicksand."

"It *is* quicksand once you get closer to the sea. The estuary can be treacherous at low tide," said Dennis.

"Treacherous?" exclaimed Ruth. "I'll give you treacherous! You want to see me mam when I come home with no shoes on! She'll swallow me up faster than any quicksand."

"Here, I'll carry ya," said Dennis swinging her up into his arms with a whoop.

"Put me down!" ordered Ruth. They could hear dogs barking down the path.

"Come on, you two. Let's get going," said Les.

A pack of growling dogs met them halfway up the

path and held them at bay until a man following behind called them off. It was Imelda's Uncle Paddy. He welcomed them and guided them down to the clearing as the dogs sniffed at their heels. Two small campfires burned brightly, shooting sparks up into the night sky. People stood around warming themselves in small groups. Les could just about see the outline of the two caravans and the small stone shed. In the shadows to his right he saw that a third caravan had pulled up alongside Imelda's. A large low tent was rigged up beside it. Larger shadows moved slowly behind the tent, and Les realised that half a dozen horses were tethered out there.

Children ran out to meet them as they came into the clearing. They were soon surrounded by at least a dozen kids and even more dogs. Les saw Imelda standing next to her aunt. He walked up and gave her the knapsack.

"It's a few things for the kids," said Les shyly. "And there's a bottle of rum for your uncle."

Imelda nodded her thanks and gave it to her aunt.

"There's a doll in there too," Les added. "I bought it for Nellie. I hope she's feeling better."

"She's much better, thanks," said Imelda shooing away the children and dogs.

Auntie Helen opened the bag and found the doll. It was quickly taken by Imelda's sisters who ran off to the caravan yelling for Nellie to see what the Yank had brought her.

"That'll keep 'em quiet for a while," said Imelda. Auntie Helen was emptying the bag out. Each item brought a murmur of approval from the group of women and children who crowded around to see what was going on. Les looked around and counted at least thirty people camping at the site.

"Are these all your family?" he asked Imelda.

"More or less," she answered. "These lot are cousins up from Skibereen. They'll be moving on to Cork in a few days and then they'll be gone off to Clare for the summer."

"All tinkers are related," said Ruth, coming up with Dennis. "Sure, they only marry amongst themselves, you know," she added.

Les had no time to comment as Tommy came up and pulled him and Dennis away to one of the campfires. He introduced them to a group of men that were standing there. The men nodded and grunted a gruff welcome as they shook hands. Tommy pulled up a small three-legged stool and a wooden crate and gestured for them to sit down. Les was hoping that the girls would follow, but he saw Ruth and Imelda walking over to the other fire where the women were settling back down. Imelda was pointing at Ruth's feet and Ruth was laughing.

"Why do the men and the women sit apart?" Les asked Tommy.

Tommy shrugged as if it was something he'd never much bothered with. "I dunno. They just do."

"How do they ever meet each other," joked Les.

"Meet? We don't have to meet. Sure, we know everybody," said Tommy, clearly bored with the conversation.

"But, how do you – you know – find a girl?" Les continued. Tommy looked at him and scrunched up his nose, not understanding.

"I mean, how do you find a girlfriend? A sweetheart? You guys get married, don't you?" Les looked over at Dennis who just shook his head and laughed.

"Married!" exclaimed Tommy. "Is that what yer on about? Of course we get married, but that's all sorted by the old folks. Sometimes they sort it out when yer born, sometimes only when yer older, like."

"You have arranged marriages? I didn't know they still existed. What if you don't get on?"

"It always works out in the end," said Tommy matter-of-factly. "The old folks know best. They know the young people and they know the families, and they make the best match they can. But enough of all this – didn't I hear you say there was a bottle of rum in there with all that stuff you carried in?"

Tommy hailed his aunt, who sent Imelda and Ruth over with the bottle along with a can of tea and some jamjars and cups to drink it in. The men around the campfire all grunted their approval. The bottle was passed around and lifted in the air before each took a long swig. Imelda did not speak to Les, but she smiled as she poured him out a cup of very sweet milky tea. The flames caught the ginger highlights in the thick blond braid that hung down her back. Les thought she looked even prettier than he remembered. Ruth tried to stand near Dennis, but Imelda pulled at her sleeve and brought her back to the women's campfire.

"Did Ruthie fall in the muck?" asked Tommy as he watched them walk away.

"She did," confirmed Dennis. "It took her shoes clean off her."

"She was lucky to get off so lightly," said Tommy seriously. "Isn't that right, Uncle Mick?" he added addressing a very old man sitting on a bucket near the fire. He seemed to be sleeping with his chin resting on his hands as he balanced on a short stick held in front of him. He wore a heavy black overcoat that was encrusted with mud over a collection of thread-bare clothes whose original colour was lost long ago. Surprisingly, thick grey curls tumbled out from under his weather-worn cap.

"Uncle Mick knows all the old stories, don't ya Mick?"

The old man opened his eyes at the sound of his name and grinned a wide toothless smile. One eye was clouded over, but the other flashed like a bright blue beacon shining out from a sea of grey.

"Hey, bey!" the old guy whistled through his gums as he pointed his stick at Tommy. He looked like some character that had crawled out from under the root of a tree. His hands were gnarled and twisted and as black as coal.

"Tell them about the marsh, Mick," prompted Tommy. The other men settled back as if anticipating a good story.

"'Tis de dead, bey!" said the old man. "'Tis the dead in de marsh. Dey'll schuck de mayte off ya and schpitt out yer bones!" The men all laughed loudly and raised their cups as if toasting the old man. They called for him to tell a story and then yelled for all to be quiet and listen up. The women at the other campfire stopped talking and hushed the children. When all was quiet the old man began.

The old guy was reciting something with great expression. Les couldn't understand what he was saying. It had a rhythm and a rhyme and he paused often to let those listening laugh or gasp, which they did loudly. The women called out to him and were enjoying the story immensely. Les could only catch a word here or there. At times it sounded as if he wasn't speaking English at all. Les could tell that some of it was scary and some of it was funny. The old man held his audience enthralled, hanging on his every word and every twist and turn of his face. Les nodded and smiled whenever it seemed appropriate. They were all having such a good time that Les laughed along with them, delighted to be in their company.

The clouds parted overhead and a pale moon appeared behind the old man like a ghostly backdrop. Les felt as if he had jumped into the pages of a book. The campfires, the women wrapped in their shawls, the little children playing barefoot in the dirt, and the old toothless man waving his stick in the moonlight, all looked like pictures in a fairytale. And in the middle of it all sat Imelda, like the gypsy princess.

The old man finished his story with a flourish and a wild stab of his stick. He had everyone rolling with laughter.

Boy, thought Les, he couldn't be further from Wisconsin if he'd dropped down into deepest darkest Africa.

The old man took a sip from the bottle of rum and held it out to Les. He said something loudly. It was a toast or a greeting of some sort.

Les grinned and took the bottle. "Thank you," he said, grinning. He hoped he hadn't agreed to anything. "Thank you very much."

"Did ya enjoy the story?" Tommy asked.

"Oh, I enjoyed it," answered Les. He laughed and passed the bottle to Dennis. "I didn't understand it but I enjoyed it. Was he speaking English?"

"Sometimes," said Dennis with a grin. "With a bit of Irish mixed in."

"Uncle Mick's getting old. He goes from English to Irish without noticing but mostly he speaks in the gammon. 'Cant' we call it."

"What's that?" asked Les.

"'Tis the tinkers's language," explained Dennis. "It's old Irish or something, like."

Les looked to Tommy who shook his head. "It's more than that. It's got the Irish all right. But sometimes words are back to front or inside out. Or they rhyme. It's handy if you don't want anyone to understand."

"So it's like a secret language?"

Dennis and Tommy nodded.

"Do you understand it?" Les asked Dennis.

"Nah!" snorted Dennis with contempt. "I'm no tinker!"

Tommy looked down at the tips of his boots and Dennis took a deep breath. An uncomfortable silence followed. Les realised he'd hit a sore point there, but he let it pass.

"We used to have a secret language at school," he said cheerfully. "We called it Pig Latin."

Tommy and Dennis both jumped at the chance to break the gloom.

"Pig Latin?" repeated Dennis.

"Do ya speak it?" asked Tommy.

"It's very easy," explained Les. "You take a word and stick the first consonant on the end with an 'aye' sound. Word becomes ord-way. So pig Latin is ig-pay atin-lay. U-day uo-yay eak-spay ig-pay atin-lay?"

Dennis and Tom looked blank for a moment and then burst out laughing as they got the gist of it. "Es-yay!" they both shouted.

The three of them were soon trying out sentences and explaining Pig Latin to the other men round the fire. The women lent an ear to hear what was so funny and soon they were trying it out for themselves. Les smiled over to Imelda who was having a whispered giggle with Ruth. She caught his eye and smiled back from under her lashes.

The clouds had disappeared and the moon bathed the camp in light. Les could see almost as well as if it were the middle of the day. He caught sight of a young boy who was trying to catch Tommy's attention. He turned away when he saw Les watching him.

"I think someone's looking for you," Les said to Tommy.

The boy stepped out of the shadows and came over shyly to whisper something in Tommy's ear before slinking off to wait behind the caravan.

"That's my cousin," Tom explained. "He's a bit simple like. Not the full shilling, if ya know what I mean. But he has a gift with the animals. One of the ponies is loose. I must go help 'im."

Les followed Tommy down to edge of the campsite and watched them walk into the marsh. They didn't seem at all worried about any marsh dead catching them, though they walked carefully through the long grasses, calling softly to the ponies. Les was startled by Dennis who he hadn't noticed coming up behind him.

"Ruthie's got to go home," he said. "We'd best be going now."

Ruth and Imelda were standing a few yards behind him waiting. Les felt a stab of panic. He'd hardly even talked to Imelda all evening. From what he'd learnt about these people's ways, it wasn't going to be easy to see her again. People were lining up to say goodbye. He walked mournfully back to the edge of the fire. Imelda watched him with a smile on her face.

"I'll walk ya back to the road," she whispered as he passed. Les felt his heart soar. He was going to get a chance to be alone with her. He shook hands vigorously with everyone, even all the little children. The old man grabbed him with strong bony fingers and pronounced something before giving him a slap on the back. Everyone laughed and pointed. Les smiled back and nodded. He still didn't understand a word, but he didn't give a damn.

Saying goodbye took ages but finally they found themselves walking up the moonlit path on their own. Ruth and Dennis only waited to be under the cover of the trees before they put their arms around each other. Les reached out for Imelda's hand, but she slapped him away.

"Not here," she whispered loudly. "They'll all still be watching us."

As they walked up the muddy path Les made several teasing attempts to take her hand. Imelda laughed and pushed him playfully away. As they came to the end she stumbled on a rut and Les caught her around the waist and swung her around laughing.

"I-ay ink-thay ou-yay are-ay onderful-way," he said as he put her gently back down onto the road.

"What are ya on about, Les Wagner? That's too long for me to figure out." Imelda's eyes were shining brightly.

"I think you are wonderful," he translated. He still

had his arm around her waist and he pulled her closer and kissed her softly. She kissed him back without hesitation and then she turned and ran down the causeway road.

Les followed her to where she sat on the stone wall looking out at the estuary with her back to the marsh. Ruth and Dennis had gone further down and were busy kissing. Les took Imelda's hand in his, and she did not push him away.

The tide was out and a strong smell of the sea was coming off the estuary. Les could hear the roar of the surf in the distance. Birds cried out in the marsh as if calling to each other. Far on the other side, he could make out tiny lights and he figured they were the local men guarding the plane. *T'Ain't a Bird* was clearly visible in the moonlight. The bright light reflected off the gun turrets making it look like a giant fairy castle.

"I wanted to bring you a present," he said. "But I couldn't find anything good enough in town."

"It makes no difference," Imelda said.

Les wondered how she could sit so still. She looked like a statue in the moonlight. It struck him that she was both very young and very old at the same time. Les let go of her hand and fumbled with the top of his shirt.

"No really, I want you to have something." He unpinned his flight wings and gave them to Imelda. "Here, take this. It's not much, but it's something to remember me by."

Imelda looked down at the shiny silver pin.

"I can't take this. 'Tis too precious. You'll get into trouble for sure," she said, shaking her head.

"I want you to have it. I'll tell them I lost it. Don't worry," Les said, closing his hand around hers. And before she could say anything more, he wrapped his arms around her and kissed her again.

They rode their bicycles a small ways together. Ruth and Dennis were joking in Pig Latin to each other but Les just pedalled slowly trying to see how long he could keep the taste of Imelda's last kiss on his lips. At the crossroads they stopped. Dennis kissed Ruth goodbye for the third time, before she finally started down the road that would lead her home.

Dennis and Les stood and waved until she disappeared round a bend. Then they slowly laboured up the steep hill. It was hard going, and they spoke little to each other, both lost in their thoughts, and too proud to get off the bikes and walk. Les thought of Imelda by the campfire's glow. She really did look like a gypsy princess. His mind was filled with strange languages, and arranged marriages, and ghost stories he could only feel and not understand. But it kept going back to the image of Imelda standing in the moonlight as she waved them goodbye.

At the top of the hill they stopped to catch their breath. The town lay below them, its little rows of grey houses shining silver in the night. The church spire towered above the rooftops reaching up as if to skewer the moon.

Les took out a Lucky Strike and offered one to Dennis. They stood together smoking, sharing the thrill of being there while the world lay fast asleep at their feet.

Dennis flicked the butt into the ditch and grinned.

"This bit is really steep," he said, pointing to the road that curved sharply down into town. "Do ya think yer up to it?"

"It looks pretty steep all right," said Les, grinning back, "but I think I can manage it."

"I'll race ya, so!" yelled Dennis, jumping on his bike and taking off like a shot.

Les pedalled furiously down behind him, spraying gravel as he skidded around the sharp bends. Dennis had a headstart but Les was gaining on him. Dogs started to bark from the small enclosed yards. The two young men laughed wildly and shouted at each other. They were young and reckless and they didn't care if they woke up the whole county. Their whoops echoed down over the town as they raced in the moonlight. They were neck to neck as they swung into Emmett square and flew over the bridge past the church.

An old man walking his dog had to jump back so as not to be run over as they took the corner into Pearse Street. He waved his cane menacingly at the two lads flying past, but Les could see that he was smiling as he cursed them.

Chapter Seventeen

◆

The hotel staff were stacking the chairs in a corner of the hall and picking up the empty glasses. The musicians had retired to the bar along with some of the Yanks and a few of the local men. Beau stood with Mary and a small group saying their goodbyes.

Mary was exhausted but happy.

"It must be way past your bedtime," Beau said gently.

Mary hid a yawn behind her hand. "'Tis past three," she said. "I'd usually be getting up in a few hours."

"That's when I'd usually be getting to sleep," answered Beau. "How about one for the road?"

"I don't mind," said Mary. She knew she had to leave but she was glad to stay just a little while longer.

"Surely you'll let me offer you a nightcap before you go?" Beau asked Dr Moloney.

"I've an early start in the morning and I still have to drive this lovely lady home," mused Dr Moloney. "Still, I'd say we can have just the one before we go."

"You don't need to drive," said Mary. "I can walk home. It's a lovely night."

"You can't walk home in dancing shoes," teased Beau.

"Of course not," answered Mary. "I'll take them off. I like walking barefoot. They're killing me anyway."

"Nonsense. We can't have you walking home barefoot in a fine frock," said Dr Moloney. "We'll have the one and then I'll drive you home."

Matt was standing to one side talking to Kitty Kelleher. Matt wasn't a big man but he had to bend down to speak to her. Martin was hanging around them holding Tojo asleep in his arms. There was a striking resemblance between the boy and his mother. Matt was being very gracious, opening the door for her and talking softly in her ear.

As he pulled the door open they all heard a crash. Everyone ran out to see what had happened. Les and Dennis were collapsed in a heap on the street, laughing. Two bicycles lay on the ground, their wheels spinning crazily.

"Woaw boy! Where's the fire?" asked Matt helping Les up.

Les pulled Dennis up and threw an arm around him. "You won," he said.

"No, no! It doesn't count if the contestant is flat on the ground at the finish line. You won by default," said Dennis, shaking Les's hand.

"Nah! You won it fair and square."

"Whatever!" said Matt before they started in again. He looked at the pair sternly. "You boys been drinking?"

This only made them laugh more.

Matt threw up his hands and shook his head. "Kids!" he said to his petite companion. She laughed knowingly as Matt turned to her son. "Would you allow me to escort your mama home?" he asked formally. "It's kinda like escorting the escort," he added with a wink.

The boy nodded, but looked slightly bewildered at the idea.

"What a beautiful night," declared Matt as he offered his arm to Kitty. "Hey, Les! Will ya quit fooling around and take care of Tojo for me? The little guy is pooped. Too much dancing!"

"Sure," said Les as he took Tojo in his arms. "We'll put the monkey to bed, won't we, Dennis?"

"Es-yay ir-say!" yelled Dennis, snapping to attention. "Monkey to bed!" And the pair marched into the hotel, still hooting and laughing.

The bar was quiet, the low hum of conversation broken every now and then by a burst of laughter. A small group sat in the back around the fire. The tall engineer called Tate was slumped in his chair, nodding seriously to an old man who was whispering intently to him.

Mary spotted Merdeza, the Yugoslavian gunner, with Mahoney and the Chief. The other Yanks must have gone off to bed, she thought. She looked around and realised that she was the only woman in the bar. A shiver ran down her spine as she remembered the last time she'd been in here with Gerald. She steadied herself. He would be coming home sooner rather than later. God only knew what she'd do, but she knew she had to do something.

Beau came back from the bar with a glass of port for her. His eyes searched her face, but she just smiled.

"You really are remarkably beautiful," he said under his breath.

"If you keep saying that, I'll end up believing it and then what will become of me?" she answered, sipping her drink.

"Then you'll be even more beautiful."

"Are you saying that women who know they're beautiful are more beautiful than those who don't?" she asked.

"Definitely," he said and then paused as if puzzled. "Except you."

Tony the barman asked if they minded going to the back as he was closing the bar for all except the residents. Beau took Mary's elbow and guided her over to a seat next to the small group by the fire. The Americans all stood up as she joined them. Mary stifled a giggle as she noticed that some of them, especially Tate and the Chief, had a good drop taken and were having a bit of trouble balancing as they stood. Mary sat back as the men chatted.

She thought about what Beau had said. Was she beautiful? What was beautiful anyway? She supposed she was pretty enough, but what difference did it make? She'd never really been courted except during those spendthrift days with her father, and even then she'd been too young to notice. Mary remembered young men asking her to dance at a dinner-dance in a Dublin hotel. They had slicked-back hair and shiny shoes but they hardly spoke a word. Did they pick her because she was beautiful? She supposed they must have – after all, they had little else to go on.

She watched Beau out of the corner of her eye. He was beautiful – and he knew it. But not in an arrogant way. He just knew it, like he knew how to play the piano. Or how to dance. Maybe you were taught to be beautiful. Her grandmother had taught her a lot of things but certainly not how to be beautiful. It had never seemed important. If she ever mentioned looks she made them sound more like a curse than an asset. She wondered what it would be like to be one of those ladies that Beau described. Southern Belles, he called them. They seemed a very petty sort, with their fancy parasols and flirting and fainting. Yet behind all the preening, Mary felt the power they must have. She was sure *they* all had lessons in being beautiful.

Con O'Leary leaned over to Mary and Beau. "Did ye enjoy the dancing?"

"Very much," replied Beau. "The people in this town all seem to be great dancers."

"Yer not so bad yerself," said Con. "And a great one at the piano. I enjoyed that tune. What was it again?"

"'It's Only a Paper Moon.'"

"That's right," said Con. He started humming it, adding a few extra *diddly-die-dums*.

"You make it sound like an Irish jig," said Beau smiling.

"The tunes in America were all Irish to start with. A bit like yer man here," he said, pointing to Mahoney. "A good West Cork lad if ever I saw one."

Mahoney laughed and raised his glass. All heads turned towards him with interest.

"Just look at the cut of him!" continued Con as everyone started laughing. "Get rid of that uniform, stick a cap on his head and a good strong coat tied up with a bit a twine, and he'd fit right in!"

Mary laughed as she looked at the ginger-haired young man. He had pale blue eyes and a face full of freckles. Con was right – he looked the part.

"Sure he's the image of my cousin Donal from Inchigeela!" joked one of the musicians. He whipped his cap off and threw it to Mahoney who put it on.

"Well, I'm Irish through and through," said Mahoney. "My dad's a Mahoney and my mom's a Murphy."

"O'Mahoney," corrected Dr Moloney. "My wife's an O'Mahoney from round Rathbarry."

"O'Mahoney," repeated Mahoney, slurring slightly. "We're probably related!"

"And a Murphy!" exclaimed Con. "Another good Cork name. With two names like that, boy, you're probably related to half the county."

"Where are you from?" asked one of the locals.

"Chicago," answered Mahoney.

"Is that so?" asked the old man who had been

talking to Tate. The engineer was asleep with his chin on his chest. "And was it yer own father that left Ireland?"

"Nope, it was my granddad."

"That would have been in the mid-nineteenth century," calculated Dr Moloney. "About the 1860s. After the famine."

"The famine," repeated Mahoney as if he was remembering it. His slurring was getting more pronounced. "The famine. That was terrible." He looked like he was going to cry.

"That it was. That it was," said Dr Moloney solemnly.

The men all nodded their heads slowly and then grunted their agreement. They sat, heads bowed, barely managing to keep their glasses straight while Mahoney sat there with the cap thrown on his head as if it were a bit of laundry drying on the hedge.

Mary sat back and watched the men. Every now and then she exchanged smiles with Beau. She was really enjoying watching this show, which was usually confined to an all-male audience.

Matt bounded back into the bar. "So is this when the serious drinking starts?" he said, rubbing his hands together. He looked at his crew members: "Let's show these Irish guys what we're made of. I'm glad to see the Catholics are still up! We might have a chance."

"I'll have you know that I was raised by God-fearing Protestant missionaries," said the Chief, raising his index finger.

"Is that so?" asked the old man turning to the Chief with interest.

"Absolutely. In Oklahoma," answered the Chief, carefully enunciating every syllable.

"Well fair play to ya!" said the man, reaching out to shake the Chief's hand vigorously.

"You don't count," said Matt. "You don't know how to drink. You're not even on the reserve team."

"It's the white man's fire-water, *kimosabi!*" said the Chief, holding his glass out in front of him.

"That's right, Tonto! What's your poison?"

"It's whiskey," declared Mahoney. "Good Irish whiskey!"

"Good lad. Good on ya!" The men around the table yelled out encouragement which had Mahoney grinning from ear to ear.

"I'll drink to that," said Matt calling the barman over. "What d'yah say I trade you a bottle of rum for a bottle of good Irish whiskey?"

"Fair enough," said Tony, shaking Matt's hand. A round of applause broke out.

"So here's the deal," Matt said, spreading his arms to the assembly. "We get the bottle, or bottles as the case may be. We drink it. The last guy standing wins.

So who's gonna be on Uncle Sam's team? I can see that Tate isn't going to be on the winning side, and Merdeza here is just a dumb-ass Yugoslavian coal-miner."

"Is that so?" said the old man, leaning over and wavering as he tried to reach Merdeza's hand. "Are ya from Yugoslavia? That's something else now!"

Cries of "Mind the pint!" echoed around the table. Merdeza reached out to steady the old man, knocking a glass over. Arms flashed out to save their drinks.

"I'm from Pennsylvania. And I could drink this Italian greaseball under the table," said Merdeza, turning to Matt as he added, "I thought you said you were glad to see the Catholics?"

"Yeah, I know, I know. But you guys don't *really* count," said Matt. "You see, you're not Italian. My grandmother, who was a saint, may she rest in peace, always said that God only spoke Italian. She would drag me down to hear Mass in Little Italy because otherwise it didn't count. So all of you guys are gonna burn in hell anyway!"

"I'm going to bed after this one," said Merdeza.

"Well, I guess it's just you and me, Patrick my boy," said Matt to Mahoney.

"Though I'm not really sure what side you're on tonight, considering the present company. What about you, New Orleans? You playing?"

Beau looked at Mary who smiled back. She was delighted. They all seemed to have forgotten her as they sat around drinking and she was enjoying their company. Most of all she enjoyed the way Beau was attentive to every thing she did.

"I'll certainly join you for a drink but I'm not sure if I'll be with you for the duration," said Beau.

Tony came back with the bottle and Matt filled all the glasses on the table. He held up the empty bottle and peered into it.

"So, Tony my friend! Do we have a deal for another bottle?"

Tony nodded and was applauded again by the men. "I'll match ya bottle for bottle. That stuff you have is like gold dust over here."

Matt raised his glass to the company. "To good Irish whiskey and to the good people of Clonakilty. Salute!"

Beau raised his glass to Mary before joining Matt's toast. She couldn't avoid drinking though she didn't like the taste of whiskey at all. It burnt her throat as it went down and she shuddered when the alcohol hit her belly. She tried to hide it but her face pulled into a grimace and tears smarted in her eyes. Beau laughed and patted her on the back. His hand lingered just that little bit too long and she was glad of it. Tony brought over another bottle. Mary quickly covered her glass as Matt started to pour.

Beau leaned over and whispered in her ear. "Are you sure you don't want another drink? Your cheeks have gone all rosy after the last one and your eyes have taken on a lovely glow."

"Are you trying to get me drunk?" Mary said, pretending to be indignant. Her head felt light after the shot of whiskey. Beau's soft breath on her neck wasn't helping.

"I'm mortally offended that you could even suggest such a thing," said Beau accentuating his accent.

"'Tis common enough," stated Mary.

"A southern gentleman would never stoop so low. We are raised never to take advantage of a lady no matter how inebriated she might be. You're as safe with me as with my own dear mama," he protested with his hand on his heart.

"I'll have a small one, so," Mary said, enjoying his posturing.

One of the musicians struggled to rise, thought better of it, and sat down again. Instead he raised his glass high and slowly drew a circle with it over the table stopping in front of Mahoney. Mary raised her tiny measure of whiskey to join in the toast.

"To these brave boys from across the water. And

especially to our very own Pat O'Mahoney, come home after a hundred years."

The small group toasted Mahoney loudly. "And may we never lose the mind we have for it!" yelled the old man, his wide grin revealing the few teeth he had left.

"I'll drink to that," exclaimed Mahoney.

"You'd drink to anything," smirked Matt.

Mary saw Les enter the bar. His mood had changed from sunshine to rain. He waited for the rowdy toast to end before tugging at Matt's sleeve.

"Something's wrong with Tojo. I think he's sick."

"He was kinda quiet most of the evening," said Beau. The news spread around the table rapidly. All the men were very concerned and expressed their dismay that the poor creature had taken ill.

"Can we call a vet?" asked Matt.

The men all shook their heads. Mary knew that there wasn't a vet for twenty miles.

"Maybe the doctor could have a look at him," she suggested.

"Sure it'll do no harm," said the doctor, rising from his seat.

Les and Matt led the way. The men all trooped up the stairs behind Dr Moloney. They hushed each other loudly as they tried to walk quietly down the narrow hallway, bumping into furniture. Mary and

Beau followed behind them, exchanging wide smiles. The room was a small one and was soon filled. Mary and Beau squeezed their way to the bedside. Tojo lay curled up with his eyes closed and his little hands held up to his face. Every now and then a shiver ran through his body from head to tail.

"Will ye all move away and give him some air. I can't see a thing with all of ye crowding around," exclaimed Dr Moloney, waving them away.

"He doesn't look too good," ventured Con O'Leary.

"I know nothing about monkeys, now," said one of the men in the doorway.

"But if that were a cat or a dog, I'd say it was sick all right."

A general discussion ensued about whether a monkey was more like a man or more like a dog. It abruptly came to an end when Miss Aileen O'Donovan appeared and pushed herself into the room, loudly admonishing them for all the noise and commotion until she noticed the small group round the bed and the small black and white animal lying there.

"Ah, the poor little dote," she said sadly. "What's the matter with him?"

"I don't rightly know," said Dr Moloney, "but if I said he had pneumonia, I don't think I'd be far off the mark. I'm afraid there's nothing I can do for him."

"Will ya look at the poor crater," said Miss Aileen. "He looks as if he's praying."

The sight of the pathetic creature nearly broke Mary's heart. He looked so small and helpless lying on the white coverlet. The shivers seemed to be increasing.

"Give him a drop of brandy," suggested one of the men.

"No, a shot of whiskey. Or better yet poitín. That's the best for dogs. If it doesn't kill him it'll cure him for sure," said another. The noise level rose as each suggested a suitable cure.

"You'll give him nothing of the sort," said Miss Aileen waving her arms at them. "Now go away with ye. Mary and me will sit with him." They were silenced immediately and started shuffling backwards out of the room.

"Aileen is right, lads," said the doctor. "He needs some peace and quiet."

Mary had tears in her eyes when she came back down an hour later. The men were drinking quietly. They all looked expectantly at her. A few had fallen asleep on their chairs. Tony had curled up on a bench in the corner. Mary gently put her hand on Matt's shoulder.

"He gone," she said softly. "I'm so sorry for your loss." The men all shook hands with Matt and Les in turn. Dr Moloney and Con O'Leary stood up and stretched their legs.

"'Tis a terrible shame," said Con." And to die so far from home."

"Poor Tojo," said Dr Moloney. "At least he went quickly."

"Miss Aileen is sitting with him," Mary said. "She has him laid out with his little head on the pillow and all."

"I'll go pay my respects," said the doctor," and then I think it's about time I got you home, girl."

The men went upstairs to see Tojo leaving Mary and Beau in the bar. Mary was shattered. The dawn would be rising soon, she thought. She hated to watch anything die. The memory of the monkey curled up on the bed overwhelmed her and the tears she had been holding back spilled down her face. Beau took her in his arms and she cried freely, the sobs shaking her. Beau held her tighter, cradling her head against his shoulder.

"Miss Aileen had me say a rosary with her," Mary sobbed, laughing and crying at the same time. "It was silly kneeling there praying for a monkey, but he was such a dotey little pet!"

"You did the right thing," said Beau still holding her.

"I don't usually cry," said Mary sniffling to try and stop the tears. "'Tis just that I'm exhausted."

"It's good to cry. It clears the brain. Now you'll go home and sleep like a baby." Beau loosened his hold on her. He held her at arms' length so that he could look at her face.

Mary had to stop herself from pulling him back. "But I don't want to go home," she said, surprising herself.

They looked at each other. Their eyes reached out to one another and acknowledged what they could not say out loud. He smiled and his smile was the most wonderful she had ever seen. It warmed her to the marrow.

"I'll come out to see you. May I come out to see you?" he asked. "We'll both get some rest and then I'll come as soon as I can. Say yes."

Mary nodded.

They both turned as they heard someone coming down the stairs. It was Dr Moloney.

"You get some sleep, you hear?" said Beau as she rose to leave.

"See you, so," said Mary. Then she followed Dr Moloney out into the crisp air that was heavy with the smell of the night's peat fires, her heart filled with such a mix of sadness and happiness and longing that she felt it was going to burst.

* * *

The delivery-van from the creamery pulled up just as the men were stumbling down the stairs after viewing Tojo. They all accompanied the driver and the young fella up to the little room to pay their respects. On their way back down again, they met the boy from Houlihans' bakery with his tray of fresh-baked bread. So they all went back upstairs again. Miss Aileen had arranged Tojo as best she could, putting his head on an extra little pillow and covering him with a small lace tablecloth. Matt and Les were both very touched by the sympathy they recieved, though they sometimes had trouble keeping a straight face. Miss Aileen ordered them to round up the Yanks and get them to bed, as the next day would be busy. So they said goodnight and went off to wake the Chief and Tate who were still sound asleep in the bar.

By the time the first guests arrived for an early breakfast the news of Tojo's sudden death was spreading around the town, carried by the various delivery men who stopped off at O'Donovan's before continuing their rounds. A small queue had formed in the narrow hallway. Miss Aileen had appointed herself chief mourner and would not leave her post by the monkey's side. The arrival of Mickey the postman insured that every citizen of Clonakilty and the surrounding areas would know of it before the morning was out.

At eight o'clock, with the queue growing, Miss Aileen sent one of the girls to fetch Father Collins. Her presence in the little room leant an air of formality and respect to the proceedings. She let them in, in small groups of twos and threes, solemnly shaking each person's hand and accepting their condolences before inviting them silently with a small wave of her hand to collect their thoughts at Tojo's bedside.

When Father Collins arrived he was quickly ushered upstairs. Miss Aileen closed the door behind them and told those still waiting to be quiet. Barry Kingston arrived at the hotel about the same time, crisp and freshly shaven. He was considering whether to have a second breakfast when he heard the news. Abandoning his thoughts of a good fry, he strode past the people in the hallway and walked in on Miss Aileen and Father Collins who were having a heated discussion. Martin Kelleher, waiting at the end of the queue, took this opportunity to slip in unseen.

"I want you to bless him, Father," Miss Aileen was saying firmly. She was seated on a small chair by the bed with her arms folded resolutely across her ample bosom.

"I can't bless a monkey," sighed Father Collins.

"You bless houses. You bless cows and you bless

tractors. Why couldn't you bless this poor creature and say a prayer for his immortal soul."

"But Aileen, I don't know if a monkey has an immortal soul."

"And a tractor does? It's bound to have more of one than a tractor," argued Miss Aileen.

Martin crept past the priest and looked down on Tojo. He looked like he was sleeping. Martin fell softly to his knees and started to cry.

"Isn't it one of God's creatures?" continued Miss Aileen. "Is a monkey not part of His glorious plan?"

"Be reasonable, Aileen," said the priest, shaking his head.

"Is He not the God of all things?" Miss Aileen looked at the boy who was quietly crying. "Now look what you've done. You've upset the boy."

Martin lifted his tear-stained face. "But Father, you said God made everything. The sky and the sea and all the beasts and birds. The flowers and the fields." He was enjoying putting Father Collins in a tight spot. Martin searched his memory for an appropriate verse or prayer, but could find nothing that mentioned monkeys.

"Would it be a sin if I said a little prayer for him, Father? A *Hail Mary*, maybe?"

"Of course it wouldn't," snorted Miss Aileen. "Didn't

I pray the rosary for him when he passed on? I'm sure God did not look upon me with disfavour."

"Ah, go on, Father," said Barry Kingston, a small smile playing on his lips.

"Sprinkling a little holy water never hurt anything. And the boy's right. The monkey is one of the Lord's creations."

Father Collins relented and took a small vial from under his cassock. He uncapped it and sprinkled the contents over Tojo. Then he made a small and rapid sign of the cross over the monkey's body. The others in the room crossed themselves as well.

"Now we have to decide how to put him to rest," said Miss Aileen.

"I'll not bury him in the churchyard," said Father Collins quickly.

"No. I suppose you won't," said Miss Aileen, eying the priest as if sizing him up for a suit. "We could bury him in the garden. That would be nice. But we'd need some kind of service. You could preside."

"I'm not sure about that," stammered Father Collins.

"Well, I can tell you that it will not be taken lightly by the good people of this town if you don't," said Miss Aileen. "Isn't that so, Barry?"

Barry Kingston nodded solemnly but his eyes were twinkling with delight. Martin caught his amusement and tried to hide the smile that was spreading across his face by burying his head in his hands and starting to recite the *Hail Mary*. There was only one party better than a funeral and that was a wedding. Martin thought that Tojo's funeral might turn out to be the best party yet.

Chapter Eighteen

◆━◆

At ten o'clock the bar opened again and was soon packed. The tea room and lobby were also beginning to fill up. News of the funeral was the main topic of conversation. All agreed it was a sin not to give the animal a proper burial. He wasn't just a pet, he was a mascot, a member of the crew as it were. In fact, one could say he was a military monkey.

Beau walked in just as Barry Kingston was suggesting that a funeral with full military honours was the only thing truly befitting the occasion. Beau had only managed to catch only few hours' sleep but he was astounded at the change in the hotel in that short space of time. The bar was full. He recognised some from the night before and figured they hadn't been to bed at all. Others seemed to have come in from their jobs, and yet more had the distinct look of day-trippers out for an excursion.

"You remember that German who was washed up on the Long Strand at Castlefreke, back in 1941?" asked a man to the general assembly up at the bar. "Wasn't he put to rest with a military funeral?" They all agreed that that had been the case.

"So that settles it," said Barry Kingston. "We'll bury our dear little friend in the back garden with full military honours."

Beau went over to the guys in the crew. "So what do you think of all this, Charlie?" he asked.

Hansen was following the proceedings with interest. "I think it's great," answered the pilot with a wink. "If nothing else it'll buy us some time. After yesterday I don't think we'll get out of here without some official intervention. Anything that keeps us in this hotel and away from some internment camp is OK with me."

Beau couldn't agree more. As soon as he could, he was going to find a bicycle and ride over to Mary's. With a bit of luck they could have a whole day together.

Barry Kingston came up with Garda Coughlan and several LDF men in tow.

"I expect you'll all want to be at the service," he said. The Americans nodded. "Good. We've decided to hold it at two o'clock this afternoon. I thought we could have a guard of honour when the corpse comes through and then perhaps a few words. Some music would be lovely as well."

"Well, Tojo sure loved music," offered Beau smiling.

"That he did. That he did," said Barry Kingston, shaking his head. Then he stopped to think. "Maybe we could bring the piano out if it stays fine. You could play us something appropriate. And the American national anthem, of course. I could get some of the local lads to lead us in the Irish anthem, maybe play a slow tune as well," he mused.

Everyone thought that was a splendid idea and Beau had no choice but to agree. He was annoyed at having to put off his trip out to the island. He would stay for the funeral, and slip out as soon as it was over. That thought cheered him up and he went off to see about getting some breakfast.

All morning people arrived to view the monkey. The queue soon grew and snaked down the stairs and into the lobby. By lunchtime they were lining up along Pearse Street. People were arriving from all over West Cork and even further afield. The news of the plane's landing three days before had spread out from Clonakilty to the surrounding areas and beyond. They came from as far as Bantry to the west and

Inishshannon to the east. They came by foot and by bicycle, with carts, carriages, and all manner of horse-drawn vehicles. They came down from Cork city on the train. They had come to see the plane and maybe catch a glimpse of the Americans, and were delighted to get a wake to boot. Pearse Street was more crowded than at Corpus Cristi. Women with small children chatted away to old men with dogs. Two brothers from Glengariff rode up on bicycles and proceeded to have an impromptu picnic on the pavement outside the hotel as they joined the queue. They had got up at three in the morning to ride the seventy miles to Clonakilty and were thrilled to have picked such a good day for it.

The hotel was doing a bustling trade in teas and sandwiches. When Ruth Bennett came in to work, she was told to to run down to Houlihans' Bakery to see if they could get more bread. The bar was full to capacity. The Americans were all downstairs milling around with the crowds.

Ruth bumped into Les in the lobby. He was signing autographs for the people queuing up the stairs.

"How did things work out with your mom?" asked Les. "I see you found another pair of shoes."

"These are my sister's, and they're killing me," said Ruth, giggling. "I told me ma that I'd stopped for a call of nature on the way home from work and lost them in a bog. She was angry but at least she believed me. She'd a killed me if she knew I was down at the tinker's camp with you lot."

"Why are they called tinkers?" asked Les following Ruth out into the street.

"Because a lot of them are, like. They make pots and pans and repair buckets and such. Most people hate 'em. I'm not really bothered. I've known Imelda for a long time and she's all right, like."

"Why do they hate them?" asked Les.

"I dunno. They're different. We keep to ourselves and they keep to themselves. When we mix there's often fights."

"Last night was incredible," commented Les. "It was like going back in time out there. I felt like I was in the middle of a fairytale."

"A fairytale? In a tinker's camp?" exclaimed Ruth. "'Tis no fairytale, I'll tell ya. It's wet and cold and hungry. That's what it is. Have you seen Dennis?"

"He left real late last night and he hasn't been back yet."

"Not to worry," said Ruth. "I expect he's sleeping in. He'll show up soon enough."

The day was bright, with an impossibly blue sky dotted with tiny fluffy clouds that looked like smoke-signals overhead. The sunshine was as hot as in the middle of summer. People had discarded their coats and were relishing the heat in their shirtsleeves and dresses. Les took his sunglasses out of his breast pocket and slipped them on.

Ruth nodded to everyone as they made their way down Pearse Street. It was slow going as each person wanted to stop and chat with her tall companion. Many offered their sympathy about the monkey and wished Les well. Ruth was rather chuffed at being seen walking with Les in his uniform and smart-looking sunglasses. There'd be talk for sure, but she didn't give a toss.

At the corner of Rossa Street they heard the distinctive sound of a pony's sharp hooves. Tommy was driving up with a number of people balanced on the cart. Martin Kelleher stood up at the front.

Tommy reined in, in front of them. His passengers got off and followed Martin up to the hotel.

"What're you two up to?" asked Les.

Tommy grinned. He pulled a load of coins from his coat pocket and started counting them. "We're bringing people out to see the plane. Martin has got his mates to stand in the queue for the monkey, so that people won't lose their place. He's a great head for business, that one. He's gone off to get another load."

"Where's Imelda?"

"She's minding the girls."

"Did ya tell her the poor monkey died?" asked Ruth.

Tommy just shrugged.

"They're going to have a funeral at two o'clock," said Les. "Don't you think Imelda would like to go?"

"I suppose she might," answered Tommy.

"I'll tell you what," said Les, hopping up beside Tommy. "I'll get Imelda when you bring the next group out to the marsh, and you can pick us up on the way back. We'll be in time for the funeral then."

Tommy agreed with a quick nod. Then he flicked the reins and started the pony back up Pearse Street as Ruth waved goodbye.

"This place is starting to look like Grand Central Station," said Matt as he surveyed the lobby. "I didn't even think they had this many people in the town."

"They're apparently coming in from around the countryside," said Beau. "I was talking to some people who said they'd travelled twenty miles just to see the plane."

Beau and Matt sat in two overstuffed armchairs as they waited for things to shape up for the funeral. Every now and then someone would come up and introduce themselves and shake hands with them.

"It kinda reminds me of Mardi Gras," said Beau.

"Come to think of it, this reminds me of a real New Orleans funeral. All we need is a good Dixieland band."

A man stepped up and held out his hand. Matt and Beau stood up to greet him. "My name's Brian Murphy," he said. "I live just down the road on the way out to Inchydoney. I thought you were going to take the roof off my house when you landed!"

"Well, I'm sure glad that we missed it," joked Matt.

"So am I," said the man laughing. "The cows took a terrible fright. They'd never heard anything like it before. Then again, neither have I."

"I hope the cows are all right now," said Beau.

"Ah, they're grand. They've been enjoying all the traffic along the road. They'll probably miss ya when you're gone," joked the man. "I won't be taking up any more of your time, now. I just wanted to say hello. Oh, and I'm sorry for your loss," he added. "I didn't get to meet him while he was alive, but by all accounts he was a grand little thing."

Beau and Matt smiled as the man walked away.

"I tell ya, when I die, there ain't gonna be half this many people at my funeral," said Matt.

They looked into the hall they could see Barry Kingston ordering five big guys who were pushing the piano across the floor. After much discussion they opened the side door to the garden and rolled the piano into the alley. Beau remembered holding Mary the night before in the little alley, and felt a thrill at the thought that he would be seeing her again soon. It was about time they got this monkey buried, he thought, smiling to himself. His wish was granted as one of the young men came up and asked them to join the others in the hall.

The rest of the crew members trickled in and joined the group of local men who had already assembled. Miss Aileen O'Donovan had rested and changed and was resplendent in a black dress.

Barry Kingston called them over to where he was discussing final preparations with Garda Coughlan and the pilot. "Pat here has pointed out that we can't fit the whole town into the garden," he said, "so we have decided that the funeral should be limited to family and friends only, if you see what I mean. That means the crew, the local defence force who will form a guard of honour, local officials and some of the hotel staff. Is that all right with you all?"

"How are ya going to keep the rest of 'em all out?" asked one of the local men.

"We thought we would post two men at the big garden gate, and another here at the side door." He turned to Beau. "We've put the piano in the alley where it has the advantage of blocking the door. Members of the public could follow the service from in here if you don't mind."

"That's fine by me," said Beau, grinning.

Nothing really got started before half past two that afternoon. Looking at the crowds lining the stairs and hallways of the hotel Miss Aileen realised they would have a problem manoeuvring through the lobby. She saw a group of little boys lounging around by the front door and had an idea. Recognising Pat Barry, she caught the freckle-faced young gurrier by the scruff of the neck.

"Aren't you an altar boy?" she asked as he wiggled.

"No! Not me!" he answered. "But Martin Kelleher is. He should be back soon. Or I could get my big brother Joe."

"Never mind. You'll do," said Miss Aileen, releasing him. "You're to come with me, boy. I'll give you a little bell. When I say, you'll come back downstairs ringing it. Do you understand?"

"Why would I want to do that?" he asked.

"You're to tell people that the body is coming down, and that they are to shut their gobs and pay some respect. During the service I'll signal you and you will ring it. No messing, just a short little ring."

This idea seemed to please Pat Barry and he eagerly followed Miss Aileen upstairs.

The little bell worked wonders, and a respectful hush descended on the hotel as Tony the barman emerged from the room carrying the corpse followed by Miss Aileen. A titter ran through the silence as people realised that Tojo's body had been laid out on a large silver serving-tray covered with a white cloth. His head rested on a little pillow and his prostrate body was covered with the lace tablecloth, from underneath which his long tail curled out.

"I'm not sure if he's being laid to rest or served up for dinner," Ruth whispered to Dennis as he pushed his way through the crowd to stand near her. He stifled a guffaw and glared at Ruth to shut up before she started them all laughing.

The Americans waited at the front door and filed in behind Miss Aileen as the small cortege proceeded out into the street. Martin Kelleher arrived just in time to fall in step with Pat Barry who was walking several yards ahead of the corpse ringing his little bell with great gusto. A small tussle ensued as Martin tried to take the bell from him, but Pat Barry held on firmly and Martin conceded defeat.

From his position behind the crew, Beau had an excellent view of the proceedings. Matt walked behind Miss Aileen, between the pilot and co-pilot, with the rest of them lining up behind them in two rows. People reached out to shake hands and say a few words as they passed. The occasion was both solemn and comical as men uncovered their heads and Tony advanced holding the tray with the prostrate monkey out in front of him. Beau caught snatches of conversation as he passed and he could tell that the crew were having as hard a time as he was in keeping a straight face.

"Ah, he's in a better place," said one woman to another.

"He looks well," commented her companion, "and didn't he have a lovely tail?"

"Taken in the prime of his youth," chuckled a man further down. "Poor little fella should be swinging on trees chasing after little girleen monkeys."

They followed the high wall that enclosed the garden until it tuned sharply to the left. As Tony turned down the small passage, Beau saw Tommy drive up with Les and Imelda riding in the front with him. Les jumped off the cart and fell into step beside Beau, pulling Imelda along with him by the hand. She followed reluctantly, keeping her eyes lowered.

They paused at the big gate while two LDF men, armed with rifles, cleared a way through the crowd. Ten others stood in two rows at the entrance of the garden, forming a guard of honour. After Beau passed through the arch, the two men closed the gates and posted themselves behind it. Beau slipped away and took his seat at the piano.

Tony laid the tray on a little table set up alongside the grave that had been dug in one of the flower beds earlier that afternoon. Father Collins stood uncomfortably beside Tojo as the rest of the procession took up their positions. The Americans lined up to one side, while on the other the local officials and hotel staff had already assembled. Miss Aileen raised her eyebrows and nodded significantly to Beau. He had no idea what would be appropriate and so settled for "Amazing Grace" with a slightly upbeat tempo. He was reassured by Miss Aileen's smile of approval.

As the last chords rang out Barry Kingston took a step forward.

"We are gathered together this fine afternoon to say a final farewell to a most surprising friend. Tojo wasn't with us long, but I think I speak for all when I say that he will be sorely missed. I will now ask Lieutenant Charles Hansen, the pilot of *T'Ain't a Bird*, and Sergeant Matt Russo, who knew Tojo well, to say a few words. Father Collins will bless him. We will then have the American national anthem before laying him to rest."

Barry Kingston motioned to the two Americans to step up.

"I would like to take this opportunity," began Charlie Hansen, "to thank, once again, the kind people of Clonakilty for their warmth and generosity. And to tell you how touched we all are for this gesture to our mascot. I will now hand over to our waist gunner Sergent Matt Russo."

Matt walked over to the little table and looked down at Tojo. He made no effort to conceal the wide grin spreading across his face.

"When I first saw this little guy he was dancing in the street in Marrakesh. He had a little red hat on his head and a cute little waistcoat. I traded him for a bottle of rum and a couple of packs of Lucky Strikes. I don't know why I did it. I'd had more than a couple of drinks? It seemed like a good idea at the time? Who knows? We certainly didn't need a monkey on board – we already had a whole crew of them! And I can tell you now, he was a handful. Always jumping all over the plane and making a ruckus." The mourners were hanging on his every word, their smiles and chuckles matching his. "Little did I know what a good buddy he would turn out to be. And who could have guessed that Tojo and me would end up here, in Ireland? But one thing I do know is that he helped to bring us all together." Matt paused for effect.

Then he looked down again at Tojo lying there. "I'm gonna miss ya, little guy."

Pat Barry rang the little bell loudly without waiting to be told. He knelt down alongside Martin Kelleher as Father Collins blessed the corpse. Miss Aileen dabbed at her eyes with a lace handkerchief and loud sniffles were heard from one of the chambermaids. She was quickly hushed by Ruth who poked her in the ribs. Beau looked at the group standing in the brilliant sunshine and wished that Mary was there to see it. She would have enjoyed it. He couldn't wait to get away so that he could tell her all about it.

A loud cough made him look up and Beau realised that the priest had finished and was signalling for him to play again. "The Star Spangled Banner" was not in Beau's usual repertoire but he managed it honourably, slapping out the accompanying chords as he slowly picked out the melody. As he played he thought he heard several trucks drive up. He took no notice of it until he remembered that there were no cars on the road because of gasoline rationing. Several people in the assembly had heard the trucks as well, and looked towards the noise. Beau finished the national anthem with three crashing chords.

Tony and Miss Aileen wrapped Tojo up in the cloth. Matt carried him and gently laid him in the grave.

A scuffle seemed to be breaking out behind the high closed gates. Someone was loudly demanding to be let in, while other voices argued that no one could pass.

Matt bent down and picked up a handful of earth and threw it into the grave. All the Americans snapped to attention and saluted. Barry Kingston signalled four men in uniform who raised their rifles in the air.

As a volley of rifle shots echoed through the town, the big gates swung apart and a large group spilled into the garden. At its head was a red-faced man in uniform brandishing a revolver. He looked wildly around the place, taking in the extraordinary scene of the priest, the Americans, and the Local Defence Force, and making no sense of it. Behind him were more soldiers surrounding three frightened-looking men in suits, and behind them was a very angry-looking crowd.

The funeral party faced the group of soldiers. Everyone held their breath. Pat Barry and Martin Kelleher stood stock-still, their eyes popping out of their heads and their mouths wide opened. The only sound was from the chambermaid who had started up sniffling again. This time Ruth was too astonished to hush her. The stand-off was broken by Barry Kingston who walked up to the man with the revolver.

"This is a private affair," he declared. "Would you be so kind as to wait outside, please?"

"Are these the Americans who landed?" asked the man with the revolver.

"Of course they are," answered Barry Kingston. "Do they look like a camogie team?"

"I am Captain Éamonn Carroll and I am here to take these men into custody."

"Well, they're not going anywhere just yet," said Barry Kingston. "Would ya ever stop waving that thing about? You could hurt someone."

The Captain looked at the revolver in his hand. "I heard shots," he said.

"Of course ya did. 'Tis a military funeral."

"Someone died? Who died?"

"A member of the crew."

"Who shot him? On whose authority?"

"Nobody shot him. For feck's sake, man, he died of pneumonia. Put the bloody thing away!"

Charlie Hansen made a move forward. He was stopped by Miss Aileen who strode up between the two men.

"Now listen here, Captain, whatever yer name is. Enough is enough. Have you no respect for the dead? Either get out or come in, and let us bury this monkey once and for all!"

"What monkey?" wailed the army captain.

"That monkey. The one who died. The one in the grave."

The army captain looked into the little grave and saw the small bundle lying there. He slowly put his revolver back in his holster. He shrugged and, shaking his head, signalled for his men to line up alongside the Americans.

"That's better," said Miss Aileen. Everyone sighed with relief. Pat Barry rang his little bell loudly as Barry Kingston threw a handful of earth into the grave. They all lined up behind him to pay their last respects as the piper started up a slow mournful tune. Beau fell in line behind the hotel staff. As he threw his handful of earth over Tojo he took a good look at the guys in suits who had come in with the army. One of them looked far too dark to be an Irishman, and Beau could swear that he was wearing a Brooks Brothers suit. And as for his shoes, Beau would know those wingtips anywhere. He had a pair just like them in his closet at home.

Chapter Nineteen

•-•-

By the time Mary had reached home early that morning the sun was rising to the left of the island. It was like a big ball of fire shooting red flames over the mainland. The hills and fields blazed under the lurid pink canopy of clouds that held up the sky. Up above hung the pale shadow of the moon as if someone had pasted it up there as an afterthought. Mary remembered the moon in the alley. She could feel Beau's arms holding her and shivered at the thought of seeing him again.

"Red sky in the morning, shepherds take warning," said Dr Moloney. "It'll be a fine day at first, but the weather will change by tonight."

"Thank you for bringing me home," said Mary, getting out of the car.

"Not at all." Dr Moloney smiled as he waved goodbye.

Mary took her shoes off and carried them as she walked up the lane. She let the chickens and the ducks out. They scratched around her bare feet squinting up at the rising sun. Mary did a little twirl in the middle of the yard and laughed as the ducks waddled away and the chickens scattered, squawking in surprise. She wondered how long before Beau would come out. It would probably take a long time, she reasoned. He surely wouldn't make it till the afternoon, maybe early evening. Then again he might make it out in the morning if they had to inspect the plane or something.

She wasn't going to count the hours. He'd be there as soon as he could. She knew it. Mary resolved to fill her day so it would pass quickly. As she changed back into her work clothes, she decided that after her usual chores she would give the house a really good clean. And after that she would make them something really nice to eat. A stew of some sort.

The morning passed quickly. The sunshine was blazing down as if it was the middle of July. Mary went around the house opening all the windows wide to let in the sea air. Dust-motes danced in the sunlight as she swept. The house smelt fresh and bright. She would definitely repaint the house this summer, she thought. It had been a while, and it needed some cheering up. Looking out beyond the estuary Mary could see big grey clouds forming. Dr Moloney was right. The weather would turn before long.

By four o'clock she had everything done. A thick stew was bubbling away on the fire and her house was so clean that you could eat off the floor. Tommy hadn't come in for the hounds so Mary went out to feed them again and clean out the pens. Though she loved animals, Mary had little affection for the greyhounds. It wasn't that they were Gerald's. They seemed to her like stupid inbred animals, raised only for men's pleasure. They spent their lives penned up, every aspect of their existence measured against a short burst of speed after a stuffed rabbit. They couldn't even mate without assistance. Still, their beady little eyes followed her every move, craving her touch. She bent down and gave each of them a good rub, feeling their hearts thumping below their ribcages.

There was nothing left to do so she had a wash and changed her clothes again, choosing the crisp blouse and plain skirt that she normally wore to Mass. Mary was religious and prayed often, but she had made her own peace with God and felt sometimes closer to Him out on the hill than in any church.

The light was fading fast. The kitchen would soon be in darkness. Mary lit a lamp and on impulse lit three more which she arranged around the room. They cast a lovely warm glow, adding to the brightness of the fire in the hearth. She wondered whether to set the table. It would be nice to have everything ready when Beau arrived. Maybe she should take the good china out?

She busied herself laying a pretty table and then changed her mind. What if he had already eaten, she thought. Or if he was delayed even further? She didn't want him to feel uncomfortable, or to think that she was upset in any way by his lateness. She decided just to put the plates on the sideboard, ready to be set should they be needed.

She watched the clock as she put the plates away. She felt a stab of disappointment. It was getting late. Maybe he wouldn't be able to come out.

She felt her tummy grumble and realised that she hadn't eaten all day. She cut a small slice of bread and sat at the kitchen table to eat it. The fire was roaring. The wind was rising, pulling the flames up the chimney. The smell of the stew filled the kitchen. Mary felt cozy and warm and safe. She felt herself dozing off and lay her head on her arms. She deserved a little rest, she thought. It wasn't his fault if he hadn't arrived yet. He'd get out as soon as he could. A wistful smile played on her lips. Maybe when she woke up, Beau would be there.

Les sat with Imelda in the hotel. After Tojo's funeral most of the townspeople had drifted back to their normal lives, but quite a number were still crowding the bar and tea room. The Irish army captain had taken over a meeting-room upstairs. He was up there with Charlie Hansen and the three guys in suits. For some reason that Les couldn't figure out, Beau was up there with them. He had introduced himself to one of the guys, who turned out to be from the American embassy in Dublin. The others were from The Irish Foreign Office. They had been up there for five hours. Plates of sandwiches and trays of tea had been sent up at regular intervals, but no one had come down yet.

The rest of the Irish soldiers had left in their trucks to go out to the marsh and guard the plane. The army had taken over the entire operation, which didn't seem to please the local defence force men, or the gardaí. Most of them waited in the bar drinking with the crew. The noise level had increased in there as the hours passed.

Les didn't have any idea what was going on but he didn't really care. He'd spent the whole time sitting in the lobby with Imelda. They talked about everything, jumping from subject to subject. They didn't feel the time pass. They both looked up as the big clock chimed the hour.

"I'll have to be going soon," said Imelda.

"Can't you stay a little longer?" asked Les. "Please?"

"I have to get back to the girls," she answered, "but I'm sure we can see each other tomorrow."

"That's gonna depend on what's happening up there, I guess," said Les. "We might be arrested or deported or whatever they do in these cases."

"They won't do that will, they?" asked Imelda, alarmed. "You're just saying that so I'll stay."

"I wish," said Les seriously. He looked around. No one was looking at them. Les shifted his weight on the sofa and took Imelda's hand in his, placing a pillow on top so no one could see. She tried to pull away, but Les pleaded with his eyes, and her little hand relaxed in his.

"Listen to me," he said seriously. "You are the most wonderful girl I have ever met. We'll get arrested or they'll find some way to get us to England. Either way I'll be leaving."

Imelda felt tears filling her eyes. She just hadn't thought. She'd known he would be going but she hadn't thought it would come so soon.

"I'm not gonna to lose you," Les said intensely.

Imelda just shook her head and looked away. He hadn't a clue. There was no way.

"I don't know how to contact you. You have no address. So you're gonna have to keep in touch with me. OK?" Imelda was confused. She looked back at him, not understanding. Les let go of her hand and rummaged around in his pocket.

"I've got a plan. Look. I've written down my name, rank and serial number," he said, showing her a little piece of paper covered in writing. "I'm in the 95th Bomb Group of the 8th Airforce. OK? I don't know where in England I'll be stationed, but if you address the letter to the bomb group I figure it'll get there."

Imelda didn't dare to speak. She just nodded.

"I've also written down my parents' address in Wisconsin. If we lose touch you write to them. They'll always know where I am. You'll write them, won't you? You promise?"

"I can't write very well," said Imelda blushing. "I can read," she added fiercely, "I just don't write much."

"I don't care. Just don't forget me, Imelda. Promise me you'll write. You can get someone else to write for you if you want."

Imelda smiled weakly and nodded.

"You can tell me where to write back. And I will. I'm sure you can get a post-office box. Just don't lose that piece of paper. OK? If worse comes to worse, just go to Wisconsin."

Imelda burst out laughing. "And how in God's name am I meant to do that, Les Wagner?"

"I don't know. Beg, borrow or steal. Whatever it takes. You'll find a way."

"And I'll show up in Wisconsin, just like that!" she said, snapping her fingers.

"Well, it's a lot easier than me going the length and breadth of Ireland looking for you. But if you're gonna be stubborn, I'll just have to. I'll come back and find you. I told you, I'm not going to lose you."

Ruth hailed them from across the hall. Imelda and Les waved back and she came over to join them. "I'm dying here, like. I've been on my feet since this morning," she groaned, flopping into an armchair.

"Still wearing your sister's shoes?" joked Les.

Ruth made a face of agony and they all laughed remembering the incident in the marsh.

"So how are the two lovebirds getting on?" she whispered wickedly.

"Speak for yourself," said Imelda smiling. "What have ya done with poor Just Dennis?"

"Just Dennis?" asked Les.

"Never you mind about my lovely Dennis," said Ruth. The she leaned down and cupped her hand to her mouth. "Actually this is pure secret but he's asked me to marry him!"

"What did you say?" asked Imelda. Her heart was thumping. The thought of someone actually asking you to marry him was romantic beyond her wildest dreams. Then her heart beat even faster. Wasn't that what Les had just done?

"I told him I'd think about it," said Ruth grinning. "But I'm mad about him. So I'd say it's a yes. We won't tell the folks for a while yet. Dennis thinks that if we save, we should be able to get married in about four, maybe five years."

"Isn't that a fierce long time to wait?" asked Imelda, her eyes sparkling.

"Not really," said Ruth. "My grandma and granddad waited ten years. And they were very happy. They thought it was going to take fifteen. He left for America and she promised to wait for him. They figured it would take fifteen years of scrimping and saving. But they got lucky. Granddad was a gambler, and one night he won so much in a poker game that he was able to come home five years early and buy the home place!"

"Is that true?" asked Les laughing.

Imelda laughed with him. She felt as if she were flying. The future suddenly opened roads where anything was possible.

"Sure, we're still living there," said Ruth. She hugged herself and looked dreamily into space. "Don't ya know anything is possible when you're in love."

Les and Imelda both nodded enthusiastically.

"Well, I'd better get back to it," said Ruth, jumping up. "It looks like they're finally coming down." she pointed to a group of men coming down the stairs. "I'll see ya, so."

The men looked tired but pleased. Whatever had happened up there was working out OK, thought Les. Unless the pilot was still just humouring them. Then Beau came down the stairs. He looked worried and grim, but he broke into a smile as soon as he saw Les and Imelda. It only took two long strides for him to reach them.

"I'm really glad to see you," he said, addressing Imelda. "Are you going back out to the island?"

"What happened up there?" asked Les urgently, before Imelda could answer. "You look really worried."

"Everything is going to be all right." Beau lowered his voice. "I was just worried because I told Mary that I was going out to see her today and I've been stuck in here. She must be wondering what happened."

Matt appeared at Beau's side. He couldn't contain his excitement.

"So? What gives?" he asked "Is it true what I hear?"

"That depends on what you heard," said Beau, teasing him.

"A little bird told me we were flying out. Am I right?" said Matt, raising his eyebrows.

"That's right," said Beau, his southern drawl slowly pulling out the vowels. "They have kindly agreed to let us fly out and continue on our way."

"How are we going to fly out?" asked Les, astonished at the thought. "That bird is stuck solid. She's probably still sinking."

"They're going to build us a runway," said Beau with a wink. "But don't put it in the headline news. It's a highly irregular situation."

"Get outta here! What're you talking about?" declared Matt. "How are they gonna build us a runway? They don't even have cars."

"They're bringing down one of those runways that you put together, from Air Transport Command. There's a US airbase up in Belfast. The Brits are helping out. Like I said, for a neutral country, this is a highly irregular situation. In fact, we are all gonna have to swear we never set foot in Ireland."

Matt considered the situation. "Why do ya think they're doing this?" he mused. "If it's so irregular."

"I guess that's the difference between war and diplomacy," said Beau philosophically. "The diplomats

337

can bend the rules a little more. Then again," he added, "maybe they just find us charming."

"How come you were in there, buddy boy?" asked Matt.

"Yeah, how come you were in there?" echoed Les. "I thought you were a waist gunner?"

"The guy from the embassy knows my father," said Beau slowly as if measuring what he was saying. "My father knows a lot of people high up. We pulled some strings."

Matt let out a low whistle. "They must have been pretty high strings."

"High enough."

"Well, they're certainly too high for a Brooklyn boy," said Matt. "Nice going, New Orleans. I've gotta go and clean up. I've got a date in about fifteen minutes."

They all looked at him inquisitively but Matt only laughed and wagged a finger at them. Then he sauntered up the stairs.

Beau turned to Imelda again. She had been following the conversation, but had understood little of what was going on except the fact that they would be flying out instead of being arrested. She did not know whether to be upset or relieved.

"I was hoping to get a message to Mary," said Beau.

"I'll be going back soon. I could drop in if you want," she offered.

"I'd be very much obliged if you did," said Beau smiling kindly. "You're sure that it isn't too far out of your way?"

"Not at all," said Imelda.

"Well, just tell her I'm really sorry. I've been stuck in a meeting here all day. I hope to get this finished real soon so I can visit with her this evening."

"I'll tell her so," said Imelda as Beau rose to join the others who were beckoning to him from the bar.

. . . Mary was dancing in a great ballroom. Her frock swirled around her legs as she danced. The room was sparkling with light from a big crystal chandelier hanging above her. Elegant men and women waltzed sedately around the room. She could feel her partner holding her close. She buried her face in his neck and smelled the sweet tang of lemons.

The music changed to a reel and she was off, skipping through a chain of hands held out to her. She knew her partner was just out of sight and she craned her neck to try and catch his attention. She tried to call out to him. She could feel her mouth moving but found that she could not utter a sound.

The music was getting wilder. Mary was out of breath, but still the dancers pulled her on through the chain.

Suddenly Beau was facing her. He held out his hands and clasped her. They went into a swing and Mary felt a thrill of excitement rush through her. They swung faster and faster. The room was blurring around her and she could no longer make out Beau's face.

They were going too fast.

Mary was frightened. She tried to tell him to stop but her voice caught in her throat. His hands held her in a tight grip. She was afraid to let go, but he was holding her tighter and tighter. It was hurting her. She looked wildly around, but all the elegant men and women had disappeared. The light dimmed. Beyond the dance floor were only shadows. She thought she saw faces leering back at her.

She could still feel the hands digging into her. If they didn't stop swinging soon her heart was going to burst. Mary tried to make out Beau's face but all she could see was a gruesome grimace. This wasn't Beau, she thought. These were not his hands. She saw a figure step out of the shadows. It was pale and wispy and very scared. She realised it was Imelda. Something bad had happened to Imelda. She had to get away from this creature who was still swinging her. She had to get to Imelda.

Mary pulled away, trying to break the mad swing, but he just held her tighter. His laugh echoed through the empty ballroom.

Then it stopped.

She was alone. She looked around for Imelda but she was gone.

Mary's heart gave a jump. A man walked slowly out of the shadows. She recognised the green uniform and ran into his arms. But when she looked up at him, she stared at a grotesquely distorted face. He smelt rank and evil. She tried to push him away but he held her tightly.

"Where's my dinner, woman?" he whispered in her ear . . .

Mary woke with a start.

She felt a rush of air on her face. She rubbed her eyes and tried to focus, still groggy and beathless from the nightmare. What she saw chilled her to the bone.

Gerald was standing at the end of the table. The door was wide open behind him. Mary could hear the wind picking up outside, whistling in over the shed from the east. It was an ill wind which made her shiver.

"I said, where's my dinner, woman," he repeated smiling. His tone was jovial but she could hear the hard edge in his voice. She gripped the table top until her knuckles were white and tried to supress a shudder that ran down the length of her back.

"I'll get it now," she said, pushing her chair away from the table. "Let me shut the door. You'll have us freezing. Sit yerself down." Her voice was slow and measured as she tried to silence the scream she heard in the back of her mind. This was wrong. This was all wrong.

Gerald did as he was told. He watched her in silence, still smiling as if considering some small private amusement.

She had to calm down. She had to get a hold on herself.

"Now this is what I call a warm welcome," he said, leaning back on his chair and surveying the room with pleasure. "I'm glad to see you learnt your lesson the last time. What smells so good?"

"It's stew," she said, the words catching in her throat.

It's not for you! she wanted to scream. She had to stop herself from grabbing the pot off the fire and throwing it. She could feel a whirlwind growing inside her. It was a force so great she feared she could not contain it.

She tried to stay as far away from him as she could. She kept her head down and her movements small and quick. She served him up a plate of stew and brown bread and turned back to the fire. She forced herself to take deep breaths and stand up straight. The whirlwind subsided into her belly, but she could still feel it churning.

"I'll put the kettle on," she said quickly, glad to have something to do.

"Don't bother with the tea. I'll have it later," said Gerald pulling two bottles of stout from his pocket and handing them to her. She stood well away from him as she poured, but as she set the glass on the table he reached out and patted her backside. Her body froze and she felt as if her spine was going to snap.

"This isn't bad at all. I must come home more often."

He started to eat, shovelling the food quickly into his mouth. She stood behind him, unable to watch. He ate as if he didn't have a care in the world, keeping up a steady monologue all the time.

"I did very well. Very well indeed. I was up at the race track in Cork and I've sold the small tan bitch for a tidy sum. Made a nice little bet on the side while I was up as well. I've just come back to sort out some transportation."

Mary felt the words spin through her head, only

catching a phrase here and there. Gerald ate and chatted as if it was the most natural thing in the world. As if he owned the place. As if he belonged here.

"But before that I did a lovely bit of business." He waved a fistful of bread at a bag on the floor. "Bring that here and have a look."

The bag was heavy. Mary dropped it on the table, making the plates and glass rattle. Gerald took no notice as he finished wiping his plate with the bread.

"Go on. Open it," he ordered.

There was several boxes of tea and sugar, three bottles of whiskey and tobacco. At the very bottom was a small bundle wrapped in a dirty cloth. She laid them all out on the table without saying a word. Gerald motioned her to unwrap the bundle. It was as thick as a pound of butter and contained a stack of English notes. Mary drew her fingers away as if she had been burned.

"What's this?" she exclaimed. The whirlwind was tight in her belly. She watched it coil round and round, only half-hearing Gerald as he talked.

"A bit a this and a bit a that. But mainly a good bit of something else." Gerald laughed at his own joke mightily.

Mary felt herself smile. But it was like someone

else was pulling up the corners of her mouth. The tight coil relaxed inside her, turning into a black smoke that slowly weaved long tendrils through her body.

"I was doing a bit a business up at the border. I had some information that was worth something to someone. Tea coming down. Beef going up. That sort of thing. Names, faces. There was this cute hoor from Fermoy who undercut me on a partnership a while back. You could say I got *three* birds with the one stone. I got paid for the trade and then made even more on the information. And that fecker from Fermoy won't be bothering me anymore. As I said, a lovely bit a business."

"Sounds like a dirty bit a business to me," said Mary. She flinched in anticipation of the blow she was sure would come. Let them come, she thought. She almost welcomed the blows. They would be better than this farce. This pretence.

But Gerald just threw his head back and roared with laughter.

"Well, it's a lot cleaner than shovelling shit on a farm and it pays a good deal better! Get me another glass. I'll have a shot of whiskey to finish this off."

Mary got the glass and set it down carefully afraid that she might shatter it. Gerald poured himself a generous measure and pushed his plate away. He held the whiskey up to the light and watched it as he swirled the glass.

"Come here. I stopped in town for a few pints. What a commotion! Did ya see that plane? It's an American bomber. I didn't see it properly in the dark. I'll go have a look tomorrow."

Mary felt her heart start to thump in her chest.

The black smoke swirled wildly though her head, clouding her vision.

Oh, dear God. Oh, dear God, no.

What did Gerald know? Was he playing a game with her? Was that why he was in such a good humour?

Mary stood behind him and looked down at the back of his head as he sipped the whiskey. She had to bite her hand to keep from whimpering. What if Beau suddenly arrived? What would she say? She couldn't let him see her this way. He would know right away. She could not bear the shame.

"They had a monkey that died. The fools went and buried him today. The Army came in and broke it up, so I heard," continued Gerald. "I saw a few of the Yanks in the bar. You should have seen them, acting as if they owned the place. I wonder what that sort of information could be worth?"

The whirlwind was growing. Pulling strings. Pushing

levers. Mary felt her nails dig into her palms as she clenched her fists, but she welcomed the pain. This was real. The pain was real.

"The women were all like bitches in heat sniffing around those Yanks. I've never seen such a carry-on. I saw that little hoor as well. That Imelda. She was as bad as the rest. I saw her with a tall blondy Yank, looking at him like her knickers were going to melt right off her. She's ready for it, I tell ya. Wouldn't mind giving her a taste of it myself." Gerald took a match from his pocket and started to pick his teeth.

At the sound of Imelda's name Mary felt her vision clear. She saw Gerald for what he was, a stinking piece of filth that had beat her and cheated her and made her life a misery. There was no way she was going to let him anywhere near Imelda with his dirty paws. She wouldn't let him even think of the girl. He tainted Imelda by just speaking her name.

Gerald let out a large belch and undid his belt. He patted his stomach with a satisfied grin. "I'll have that cup of tea now," he ordered, carefully pouring himself another measure of whiskey.

"Get it yourself, ya filthy bastard," Mary hissed.

The bottle of whiskey smashed to the floor. Gerald turned around to face her, his face red and angry. He started to rise but stopped, his eyes wide in surprise.

Mary stood looking down at him. She could feel all the hate and the anger she had kept bottled up inside pouring out of every pore. In her hand she held the long black carving-knife.

Chapter Twenty

•◆•

They faced each other in silence. Time stood still. Gerald was like a trapped animal ready to pounce. Only his eyes moved, assessing the situation.

Mary held her breath.

She dared not make a move.

She could hear the pulse beating in her temples, drowning out her thoughts. The wind outside, the steady tick of the clock on the mantle, were very distant and faint as if far, far away in another world.

"You'd better leave," she said slowly, never taking her eyes off his face. "Take your money and leave. Leave now and never come back."

The sound of steps in the courtyard made Mary turn her head. Gerald noticed and moved forward.

She instantly turned back on him and held him at bay as the door swung open.

Imelda stood stunned on the threshold. Mary heard her gasp.

Imelda's eyes quickly swept around the room, saw the contraband and the pile of money, the bottle smashed on the floor, Gerald on the edge of his seat and Mary standing there, with the knife in her hand.

Gerald started to chuckle. He got off his chair very slowly.

"Don't you touch her," Mary commanded. "Don't you even look at her."

Gerald raised his hands slowly in a gesture of surrender. She followed his every move with the knife. Gerald nonchalantly turned his back on her and faced the wall. He took a cigarette from his pocket and lit it.

"What have the two of you been up to, I wonder," he said in a low voice. "Did ya have this all planned? Did ya? You and this bastard daughter of a tinker?"

Mary felt as if she were going to explode. Gerald's calm manner frightened her. He could turn and hit her at any time. Her arm ached from holding the knife so tightly. Her head was reeling from the pressure on her temples. She tried to focus only on Gerald, to be prepared if he made the slightest move. He still had his back turned to her and was smoking casually. She remembered the shotgun in the shed. Maybe she should tell Imelda to run and get it. She didn't even know if it was loaded, and it might just make matters worse.

She missed it when it came.

Gerald moved with a swiftness that was extraordinary for such a heavy man. Imelda cried out a warning but it was too late. Before Mary knew what was happening Gerald had grabbed her wrist and was twisting it.

"Ya didn't really think you would get away with it? Did ya? Did Ya?" he yelled into her face. Her arm was screaming with pain. Her hand opened and the knife dropped to the floor.

"Leave her alone," screeched Imelda, rushing across the room. She flung herself onto Gerald's back and started to pull at his hair, her fingers scratching for his eyes. Gerald shoved Mary away and spun around wildly, crashing into the furniture and overturning the chairs. He knocked Imelda up against the wall and she lost her grip and fell.

"I'll deal with you later," he snarled, looking down at her. Then he turned back to Mary.

She was waiting for him. She had picked up the knife and was holding it out in front of her.

"Leave now," she screamed. "What more do you want of me? Just go away and live your life."

Gerald's eyes blazed. He crossed the room and

swept the knife from her hand. It flew across the room and clattered along the slate floor.

"I'll kill ya before I leave ya," he growled.

"Run Imelda. Get out now!" Mary cried. Imelda was getting up. She rubbed her left arm and looked confused.

Gerald grabbed Mary by the shoulders and held her at arms' length. He seemed to be measuring the distance carefully as she struggled to break free.

Then he punched her hard in the stomach. Mary crumpled instantly. As she went down she tried to call out to Imelda, but she found she could not speak. She could not breathe. She struggled to raise herself but could not move.

Gerald was towering above her. She curled up into a ball and covered her head with her arms as he started into kicking her. She squirmed under the table where the blows could not reach her. Then Gerald let out an almighty roar. From under the table Mary could just make out the flash of Imelda's wellington boots as she fled out the door.

Gerald gave her one last kick and ran out the room after Imelda.

"Run, little hoor!" he barked. "Ya won' get far."

Mary gasped trying to get her breath back.

This wasn't happening. This wasn't real. This could not be happening. It just could not be happening.

Please God, make it stop. She gulped for air but it stuck in her windpipe. From the sounds coming from the yard she knew that Gerald had caught up with Imelda.

"Now I've got ya," she heard Gerald sneer. "Now I'll teach ya a lesson. And yer going to like it!"

Mary heard Imelda screaming. She fought the pain and sat up, still holding her belly. Imelda's screams grew more shrill. Mary could hear Gerald's throaty laugh, thick with lust. A blind rage seared through her body. The black whirlwind ran through her veins, fuelling her to rise.

Mary picked herself off the floor. Strength returned to her limbs, pushing out the pain and numbness. God wasn't going to stop this. Only she could end it.

Beau was delighted with himself. He had managed to get out of the bar quickly, with the excuse of a headache and lack of sleep. They would probably be celebrating all night and wouldn't miss him. He borrowed a bicycle from Les and slipped out of the hotel unnoticed. Apart from Les, they'd all think he was upstairs, fast asleep.

Beau rode silently over the causeway. The cross-winds were strong and he battled to keep up the pace. His ankle had started bothering him again. It had seemed all right the day before, but all that dancing had probably strained the bruised muscles. It throbbed each time his foot pushed the pedal.

The moon was the biggest he'd ever seen. It sat on top of a hillside across the estuary, bathing the marsh in its light. Fat clouds raced across the sky, plunging the landscape into darkness as they covered the moon. Beau kept to the shadows. He could make out the tiny lights of the sentries. The army had set up a series of tents around the big bomber but no one noticed him as he rode silently past.

Beau felt his heart beat faster as he saw the road bend to the left. Mary's house was just around the corner. He rode through the curve and realised he had been mistaken. It was still at least another fifty yards away. He could see the palm fronds that marked the entrance. The lights were out on this side of the house but he could see smoke rising from the chimney.

Beau paused to catch his breath and looked out across the estuary. It was starting to rain. Beau jumped back on the bike and sprinted up the road. If he hurried he could get inside the house before the downpour started.

It was steep and dark in the shadow of the house. As he got off the bicycle he thought he heard a muffled scream. He stopped to listen. He heard shouting and a crash. There was no mistaking it. It was coming from the house. He heard Mary's voice, and then a gruff male voice. Something bad was happening. Beau threw the bicycle on the ground and started running. The rain pelted his face, making it even more difficult to see where he was going. He swerved just in time to avoid running into the cart. The shaggy brown and white pony snorted with surprise as Beau slipped, twisting his ankle. A shot of pain made him stumble and fall. Someone was screaming. The screams rose shattering the night.

Then a single shot rang out.

He pulled himself up and ran, ignoring the pain in his ankle, turned the corner and stopped at the entrance to the tiny yard. Mary was standing in the doorway silhouetted in the lamplight that shone behind her. She was staring straight ahead at a small boot lying in the middle of the yard. The rain was slashing down in striaght diagonal lines that bounced off the ground.

Beau took a step forward and saw Imelda sitting on the ground, hugging her bare knees, silently crying. One foot was bare. Her face and dress were covered in mud. Beside her Beau could make out the legs and feet of a large man prostrate on the ground. The rest of his body lay in the shadows. In the light from the kitchen he could see a dark stream of blood washing away into the rivulets of water flowing across the yard. Beau understood everything in a flash. But he could see no gun. Mary seemed to notice him for the first time. She looked him up and down. Beau suddenly realised she too was trying to puzzle out where the shot had come from.

Then Tommy stepped out of the shadows between the sheds. He was soaked to the bone. His blond curls stuck to his forehead and his clothes were dripping. He held a shotgun in his right hand.

"I'm sorry, missus," he said. His tears were lost in the rain pouring down his face. "I kil't him. I had ta. I'm sorry."

Mary walked over to the body lying there. She took no notice of the rain drenching her. Her face was a stone mask. Beau was too stunned to speak. He wanted to reach out to her but it was as if an invisible barrier surrounded her.

Then Mary kicked the body viciously with her foot. He did not move. She held her head high and spat down on the dead man.

"He was a bad man, Tommy," she said. "I hope he burns in hell."

Beau persuaded them to come in out of the rain. Tommy busied himself making tea and picking up the chairs that lay strewn around the room. He kept throwing scared sideways glances at his sister. Imelda had covered herself with a cardigan she found hanging on a hook and washed her face and hands. She sat by the fire as Tommy fussed over her.

"Are ya sure yer not hurt?" he kept asking.

"I'm fine. Just a little shook," she said, her chin trembling slightly. "He's not the first to try and mess with me."

"Who else messed with you?" Tommy asked fiercely. He looked at her but she just shook her head.

"Don't you worry, boy. None of them got me," she said in a disgusted tone.

Mary stood staring into the fire. She refused a cup of tea, and flinched every time Beau tried to comfort her. An uneasy silence fell on them. Beau noticed the whiskey on the table and filled a glass and gave it to Mary. She took it, but did not drink. After a moment she looked at it as if wondering where it had come from and set it down on the mantlepiece.

Beau tried to collect his thoughts. The whiskey had cleared his brain somewhat and he was faced with the reality of the situation. There was a dead man lying outside. Should they call the police? The man had obviously tried to rape Imelda. Surely it was a matter for the police. Mary seemed to read his thoughts.

"We have to do something about Gerald," she said still staring into the fire. "We can't leave him lying there."

"Who was he?" Beau asked softly.

"Gerald Burke." Mary spat out the name. "My husband."

Beau was astounded. "Don't you want to call the police?"

Mary considered it for a moment and shook her head.

"We have to get rid of the body. Tommy, you'll have to help." Tommy nodded silently. "It's high tide, isn't it? He could go out with the tide."

"But Tommy was defending Imelda," Beau argued.

"The police must know nothing about this," she said in a tired voice. She pointed to the things on the table and gave a little shrug. "They'll start snooping around, asking questions. They'll see tinkers and money. They'll ask what you were doing here." She turned to Beau and searched his face. He could hardly bear to see the despair in her eyes. "Nobody knows he was here. He comes and goes. It's better this way. Will you help me?"

"In any way I can, Mary. Just tell me what you want me to do," Beau answered.

Mary looked up at the clock. She noticed the whiskey on the mantlepiece, picked it up and took a sip. She grimaced and then drank the whole shot down, closing her eyes as a shiver ran down her. When she opened them again they burned brightly with a wild determination.

"You and Tommy have to get rid of the body," she began again. "Imelda should get home. Just go home and pretend this never happened."

"I'll walk back," said Imelda.

"It's raining pretty hard out there," said Beau with concern.

"I'm sure it's not the first time she's been rained on," snapped Mary. A look of pain crossed her brow. "I'm sorry," she said softly before continuing. "The danger is Tommy and Imelda. They have to go away." She faced them. "Can ye just up and leave?"

"But no one saw us. No one knows we're here," argued Tommy.

"Except Les," said Imelda blushing. "But he won't tell anyone."

Mary ignored Imelda's remark. "Listen to me. That body is going to wash up, hopefully later rather than sooner. No one will link you to it, but it's better if no one even remembers you were around. If ye leave they'll forget ye."

Imelda looked at her brother. Mary was right. It was better to be safe. Tommy gave a quick nod of agreement.

"Can ye just up and leave?" Mary repeated.

"We've a family camping with us," Imelda said slowly. "They'll be going to Clare soon. We could go with them."

"Good. That's good," said Mary. "You and the girls can go with them. But Tommy should really get away. Far away."

"Could you leave the country?" asked Beau. He understood what Mary was trying to do. She wanted to remove every trace of this horrible night. He wondered if there would be any place left for him when she was done, and felt a stab of sadness darken his heart. He looked at Mary and saw her wild beauty, but he could find none of the soft sweetness that he loved.

"How could I leave the country, like?" exclaimed Tommy. "I've no money for a passage and nowhere to go."

Mary walked over to the table and sat herself down. She pointed to the notes still lying there. "This will get you as far as you could ever want to go," she said.

Chapter Twenty-One

·◆·

Beau and Tom worked in silence. Imelda had left quickly, disappearing down the road as she kept to the ditch. The wind had calmed down but the rain still fell. They were soaked to the bone in minutes. It was hard getting the body onto the cart. Gerald was a heavy man and it was awkward trying to lift him up. Beau was surprised at the boy's strength. Tommy was half his size but he bore most of the weight as he grabbed the body around the chest, leaving Beau to pick up the feet.

After a lot of pushing and heaving Gerald finally lay on his back on the cart. Beau forced himself to shine the lamp on the dead man. He was shocked to find how old he was. He must be over fifty. His features were coarse and vulgar as if years of dissipation had been etched on his face. His eyes stared blankly at the moon peeping through the clouds. Beau took a handkerchief from his pocket and put it over the dead face.

Tommy had found an old coal-bag and was ripping it up into large squares. He had argued with Mary half-heartedly about the need to escape, until Imelda had reached over and taken the money. Once the decision was made Tommy had worked without stopping, with no need to consult with anyone.

"What are you doing?" asked Beau.

"I'll tie these around her hooves and stuff 'em with some straw," Tommy explained. "So you won't hear her on the road."

The boy bent down and ran his hand down the pony's leg whispering to her. The pony ears flicked attentively and she lifted her hooves one after the other as Tommy tied the straw-filled rags on. Beau admired the skilful way he worked with the horse.

Looking around, Beau saw a dark patch of blood still staining the courtyard, the shotgun beside it as if bearing witness.

"We must wash this down," he said.

Tom nodded. "The rain'll get rid of most of it. But I'll throw a bucket of water over it to be safe, like."

Beau picked up the shotgun.

"Is this yours?" he asked.

"Nah. It belongs to himself," said Tom, cocking his head towards the body on the cart. "It's usually hanging in the little shed where he keeps the things for the greyhounds. We'll put it back."

Beau nodded. He wiped the shotgun all over with a bit of sacking, carefully holding it by the barrel so that his own fingerprints would not get on it. It was probably an unnecessary precaution but it gave Beau something to do. Overcoming his disgust, he tried to get Gerald's hand around the stock. The hand was large and meaty and was starting to stiffen up. It was cold and rough, the fingernails bitten down to the quick. Beau shuddered as he thought of those rough hands on Mary. He felt a fool. He hadn't given a second thought to Mary's husband, or about what sort of a life she led with him. He'd been enchanted by his own illusions of a rustic life lived on this romantic coast, and of the beautiful woman dancing in his arms. She was a mirage which had little in common with the woman who had stood in the pouring rain and spit on her husband's dead body, cursing him to hell.

Mary had hardly spoken to him. He could see her though the window, sitting by the fire. When he'd tried to approach her she was cold and distant, and just kept saying that the body needed to be moved before the tide went out. Beau felt as if he had been dreaming and had woken up only to find that he was caught in a nightmare. It all seemed so unreal, the dead man on the cart, the woman sitting silently by the fire. He knocked on the window to say goodbye, but Mary only nodded.

The pony plodded slowly down the road which became a stony path with a stream running through it. They followed the path as it wound its way around, encircling the island like a belt. A hill rose steeply before them and the pony laboured, its hot breath smoking from its nostrils. The pony picked its way over the stones carefully and the cart rocked as they splashed up the hill.

At the top the pony stopped to take a rest and Beau could see the inky expanse of the Atlantic Ocean. The clouds raced past the moon which hung over the water, fat and ripe, and outrageously big. Beau could not help but be mesmerised by the hypnotic swirl of the moonlight on the waves as it formed patterns that melted and changed.

The track led down to the beach and beyond to where a rocky ledge jutted out into the sea.

"That's the bank," said Tommy pointing. He gave the reins a little shake to get the pony going again. "Virgin Mary's bank they call it."

"Why's that?" asked Beau.

"Because Our Blessed Lady appeared there once.

Some say it couldn't have been her. Some call it Cliona's bank. Cliona was a sort of goddess in the olden times. You see there were sailors out in the bay and, according to the story, they saw Our Lady praying on the bank and they laughed and made fun of her. So she sank their boat and they all drowned. But Our Lady wouldn't do a thing like that, now. She prays for all sinners and would forgive them. But Cliona would."

"She was a more vengeful type, I gather," said Beau.

"You could say that, all right," said Tommy solemnly. "But there's also some shells wash up sometimes on the beach down here. They have a picture of the Virgin Mary on them. So you never know," he added.

They drove the cart out on to the promontory as far as it could go. The edge was stony and Beau could see steps cut into the rock leading into the sea. The waves crashed against the bank, sending spumes of foam shooting up into the night sky. Tommy was walking along the edge peering into the water.

"I think we should drop him in here," he said, pointing to a little inlet. Beau went to have a look. A natural pool swirled below him, churning up froth.

"It's very deep. Have a look what happens when the wave breaks," continued Tommy. Beau watched a swell moving towards the bank. He followed it closely as it crashed onto the rocks. A wall of water was pushed into the little inlet and pulled away almost immediately. The current would be very strong.

They lifted the body off the cart and rolled it along to the edge. Beau was surprised at how calm he felt. The extraordinary scenery made it all seem unreal and he felt no compunction as they rolled the body over the edge and watched it drop with a splash into the black water. It bobbed there as the smaller waves came in, pushing it back and forth in the little pool. Beau watched the horizon for the seventh wave. He felt drugged by the steady movement of the sea as it reflected the moonlight. Then he thought he caught sight of a really big wave. It came in majestically, gaining both speed and size as it rolled in from far out in the Atlantic. It broke before it hit the bank and long fingers of frothy surf reached out like a hand to scrawl at the cliff. The body was instantly submerged and disappeared as the water pulled back.

Beau and Tommy stood on the edge watching. Beau thought he caught a glimpse of the body out to sea but he wasn't sure. Then all he could see was the moonlight spreading its eerie patterns over the water.

"The crabs'll be at 'im," said Tommy. "I saw a girl that was washed up once. She'd fallen in just a few hours before. Her face was gone. Covered in crabs."

Beau gave a shudder of disgust.

Tommy looked at him and shrugged his shoulders. "Ah, well. If the crabs don't get ya the worms will."

At the top of the hill they stopped and looked back one last time. Beau gazed at Tommy's face in the moonlight. He saw the blond curls hanging damply over his brow, the pale blue eyes and freckles and thought that he looked not much more than a child. But Tommy's calloused hands resting lightly on the reins were those of a full-grown man.

"How old are you?" Beau asked.

"I'll be eighteen by Christmas," Tommy answered.

"Have you thought about what you're going to do now?"

"I dunno," answered Tommy shaking his head. "I suppose Mary's right. I should leave. I don't know where. Maybe England."

"You could go anywhere in the world. You're bright and young. You could be anything you want," said Beau.

"I dunno," repeated Tommy. "I've never thought of leaving before, of doing anything else, and now I have to. At least I know Imelda and the girls will be taken care of. I hate to leave 'em but they'll be fine. We take care of our own. I could send them money. They'll be needing it if I go."

"You have a lot of money," Beau remined him gently. "Remember?"

"Yeah, right," said Tommy sounding confused. "It feels strange. I've never had any, so I'm not sure about it now."

"Believe me, you'll get used to it. Just be careful not to lose your head. It's only money. It doesn't own you. You own it."

Beau held out his hand. "I wish you and your family all the best."

Tommy shook his hand and nodded. They rode the rest of the way back in silence.

Mary was sitting in the dark by the fire when Beau got back. He stopped at the window before going in. The kitchen looked like a painting by a Dutch master. The red glow of the fire lit Mary's face and hands while the rest of her melted into dark shadows. She stared blankly into the dying embers. Her eyes showed no trace of emotion, her breathing was slow and regular. Beau felt a well of tenderness fill his heart and was taken aback that it could hurt so much.

Beau called to her softly as he entered the room. He didn't want to startle her. She sat like a china doll as he walked slowly up to the fire. He was afraid that she might shatter if he broke the stillness that surrounded her.

She turned slowly and looked at him. She paused a minute and contemplated him standing there.

"You're wet," she said finally.

"It doesn't matter, sweetheart," Beau answered in a low whisper.

"You should change. You could get ill," she continued in a detached voice. A shudder shook her body and she closed her eyes.

"Don't you go worrying about that. I'll be just fine." He reached out and gently took her hand. "You come with me."

Mary looked at her hand in his as if wondering how it had got there. It lay lifeless and small and very white against the dark tan of his hand. He slowly closed his fingers around it and pulled her to her feet. Mary followed him, stopping to carefully close the door behind her.

Beau made his way up the stairs, talking softly all the while. "Don't you worry, sugar. I'm here now. I'll take care of you." The sweet nothings his mama and nursemaids had used to calm him as a child tumbled out in a flood. Beau didn't know if she heard him, but he kept it up.

Mary sat on the bed as Beau lit the little lamp at her bedside. She did not protest as he took her shoes and she lifted her arms like a child as he removed her damp clothes and slipped her nightdress over her head.

He tried not to give in to the arousal he felt on seeing her naked.

She lay back and looked up at the ceiling. She looked small and helpless and so very distant that it scared him. He covered her with a thick eiderdown which he found at the foot of the bed.

Beau took off his own damp jacket and trousers and lay down beside her on top of the eiderdown. He did not know what to do. Mary lay stiff and still. She flinched involuntarily as he reached out and stroked her hair. He lay his hand across her cheek. He felt her tremble ever so slightly.

"Hush now," he whispered, hearing his own voice shake. "Everything is going to be all right."

He felt cold lying there on top of the bedclothes. He listened to the rain pummelling the roof and the wind rattling the window frame. Bucketfuls of water poured down the pane. He cradled Mary's face and continued to stroke her hair. She lay very still, but he could sense her thoughts as they swirled crazily around her mind.

He remembered Gerald's dead eyes staring out at him, the blood washing down the yard, and the soft splash as the body hit the water. He felt the horror of it all rise in the back of his throat. Beau found he was shivering and slipped under the eiderdown.

He ached for her warmth. The dead man's eyes

had stared at him and he'd covered them with a handkerchief. Mary seemed not to notice Beau as he reached out for her. Beau felt his body tremble. He pulled her close, feeling her cold and dead in his arms. He buried his face in her hair and tasted the tears running down his cheeks. Mary stirred. Her body relaxed and he pressed her closer.

"I don't know what to do. I love you so much and I can't do anything to help you. Mary, talk to me," he implored.

Mary's eyes were brimming with tears. Her arms went around him and clutched him as the sobs racked her body. They clung to each other, their tears mingling as they kissed. Beau's passion rose like a flood catching them both by surprise before sweeping them away.

They made love as the storm raged outside. They felt the horrors of the night swirl around them, and they cleaved to one another until their cries had exorcised the demons and they lay safe in each other's arms.

They slept as if their bodies had been moulded together, neither one stirring nor waking the other. At dawn they awoke together and kissed before opening their eyes.

"Hi there, beautiful," Beau whispered softly. "Are you OK?"

She nodded slowly. She sighed and he saw a flicker

of anguish cross her face. "I can't believe he's really gone," she said.

"He's gone," Beau said, feeling the disgust rise again in his throat. He'd seen the bruises on her body. Beau hadn't needed to ask where they'd come from. He cupped her face and softly kissed her eyelids. "He'll never hurt you again."

Mary stared at him earnestly.

"What did you do with him? Where did you put him in the sea?" she asked.

"Off the bank. Off Virgin Mary's Bank."

"Will you show me where?" she asked. Beau nodded. Mary made a move as if to rise, but Beau pulled her back into his arms. He would show her where they had dropped the body. But first he needed to make love to her again. This time it would be slow and sweet.

Chapter Twenty-Two

◆◆◆

It was going to be a glorious day. The storm had chased all the clouds away, leaving a brilliant blue sky in its wake. The tide was out and the beach spread out for a quarter of a mile before it finally caught up with the surf.

Mary walked lightly down the stony path. Beau held her hand and guided her across the difficult bits though she could have easily jumped over them. She felt like a newborn, not daring to open her eyes too wide for fear that the sunshine would be too bright.

Mary remembered the hatred that had raged through her the night before. The knife was in her hand before she knew what she was doing. The hateful feelings had overpowered her, had burned and consumed her until the shot had rung out.

She'd been numbed, yet she hadn't felt cold. She didn't felt anything at all until she found herself in Beau's arms. She was a ghost woman, observing yet not seeing. She'd stood apart from it all, watching herself move around, arranging things, talking to Imelda and Tom, following Beau up the stairs. She was still stunned to have woken up to find that it had all really happened: the joys of Beau's embrace, the horrors of Gerald's death.

It was too much at once. She had to take it one thought at a time. Mary tried not to think about anything at all apart from getting herself down on to the bank. She knew she would do her thinking once she got there.

Beau walked her out to the edge. The water surged down below them. Mary walked down the steps on to a rocky flat ledge and sat on a large rock. She looked around idly at first, reading the incriptions carved into the rock ledge marking the death by drowning of half a dozen people over the last century. Some of the incriptions were so old only a crude cross could still be made out. The names and dates had been worn away into faint lines by the pounding tides.

She braced herself and thought about Gerald.

If he would ever have a place to mark his grave it would be here.

She made herself think of him lying in the yard.

374

She imagined Beau and Tommy throwing his body into the sea. She waited to be overcome by grief, or by anger, or by fright, but nothing came.

She was surprised to find that where all the pain had been there was only a vast emptiness left. She knew that pain and hatred and sadness were still there lurking in the dark corners of her mind. But she knew they had changed. They were no longer quite the same sorrows that had been the faithful companions of her days, colouring even the happiest times in their sad hues. They had moved from the present to the past.

"Would you rather be alone?" Beau asked softly.

"No. Stay," she said laying her hand on his arm.

Beau stood behind her and held her against him. She leaned her head back onto his chest and looked across the water.

"He didn't beat me at first, but he was never kind," she started slowly as if to herself. "I never wanted for anything. I never went hungry. Sometimes he would even throw some money down and tell me to buy something for myself. Some people were far worse off. I don't know why I let him hurt me. I don't know why I never did anything. I just let him. I lost a baby once because he threw me down the stairs. It was a little girl and I hated myself because I was relieved. I couldn't stand the thought of her growing up and seeing her father beat her mother. I really wanted to die that day." Mary paused for a minute lost in her thoughts.

"And then Séan came. Gerald was away a lot. He didn't pay too much attention to the baby, but he seemed proud enough to have fathered a son. I thought maybe with time he would change. Séan was the sweetest little boy. I could have stood up to the world for him. He was only two years old when he died. I stopped feeling after that, and I was happy for it."

Mary felt Beau stroke her hair. She closed her eyes and let herself relax into the soft caress. She was surprised to find that silent tears had filled her eyes. She willed herself to continue. She wrapped her arms around Beau's as if she were holding on to a life buoy.

"When Gerald started talking about Imelda. About how he'd like to have her . . . " Mary paused as a shudder went through her. "I don't know, something snapped. It woke me up. It made me realise what a monster he was. And then you came. You made me feel different. But it had started before you ever came. You just reminded me what it felt like to be alive."

They sat for a while and watched the tide coming in. The sea inched its way across the rocky ledge and lapped at their feet before they got up and walked down onto the beach. Beau had said little all the while. He'd just held her, giving her all the time she needed. But when he jumped onto the sand his mood seemed to change. He sauntered down the beach and then stopped to take his shoes and socks off, splashing back to her through the rising surf. He ran up and kissed her and then ran off again. Mary sat in the sun and kicked off her shoes.

She watched him and smiled. She marvelled at this young man as he did somersaults and clowned around for her. He stole glances at her, checking to see if he was being apreciated. His dark features and black hair where in stark contrast with the white sand. A thrill ran through her as she noticed how effortlessly his lean body moved. She remembered their lovemaking and found the desire for him rising in her belly.

Beau stopped and peered down on the sand at a pile of white shells. He let out a yelp of pleasure, picked one up and came running back to her. He held out the shell like a child, delighted with what he had found. It was small and more of a ball than a flat shell. It was so delicate you could have crushed it between two fingers. On the top was a faint pattern. Mary knew the shells well. She had combed the beach for them as a child, and always felt it was a sign of luck to find them.

"Look! " he exclaimed pointing to the top. "It's the Virgin Mary."

"And how would you know that, ya heathen?" she asked grinning. His smile was wide and sparkling. It crinkled up the corners of his mouth and she was surprised at how much she wanted to kiss him.

"I am not a heathen," he said, flopping down beside her. "I am a very happily lapsed Christian who intends to have a wonderful time and return to the fold on his death-bed."

"Isn't that cheating, like?" asked Mary.

"No, Ma'am. It's in the basic contract. Sinners can always repent. I'm counting on it," he said laughing.

She laughed with him and didn't resist as he pulled her down on the sand and kissed her. They lay looking up at the clouds.

"This is bliss," sighed Beau. Mary nodded. She couldn't ever remember feeling happier.

"I wish we could just lie here forever."

"It's too bad that we can't," Mary said with a sad little shake of her head.

He propped himself up on one arm and smiled. "Who says we can't?" he asked insistently. "Why can't we?"

"Well, for one thing, the tide's coming in. Not to mention that you'll be flying off more than likely."

"You have a point," said Beau. "Which reminds me – they're bringing down a runway from Belfast. It'll be here soon. I'll have to get back." He checked his watch and smiled. "But not quite yet. It's only six in the morning, I don't expect anyone will be up yet."

"What do you mean – a runway?" asked Mary.

"They have this sort of runway that you can put together very quickly. The army uses them in remote outposts or if they need to set one up somewhere fast," he answered but Mary could tell he was thinking about something else.

"How long will it take them?" Mary asked, but Beau wasn't listening.

"Forget the runway," he said, his voice rising with excitement. "Forget the runway and the army and everything. They'll be here soon enough. Let's forget about it all for now. Just pretend none of this ever happened. Then we can lie here forever."

"What are you talking about?"

"Just you and me," he said taking her in his arms. "If you pretend we can lie here forever, if you really believe it, then for whatever time we have left it'll be true."

"But it won't be true, because it'll have to end," Mary argued.

"Come on! You can do it. Pretend there's only you and me. Like right now. Like last night."

"Last night was wonderful," said Mary kissing him softly, "but it can't go on."

"Why not?"

"Because it can't."

"It's easy," he said jumping up and pacing around to emphasise his point. "Just pretend. Just for now. Pretend that it *can* go on. That it will go on forever. This is real. This is now."

Mary looked around. She saw only the dunes and the sky and the sea. They might as well have been alone on a desert island. But this was not just any island. This was Inchydoney Island in West Cork, where everyone knew your business. Where if you stopped to talk to a man on the street, the tongues started wagging before you'd even said goodbye. They'd probably be gossiping already. Nobody could have failed to notice her with Beau at the dance. Mary shook her head and laughed softly to herself. She didn't give a toss what they thought. She would share as much of this new joy with them as she had shared the old sorrows.

"Come on Mary," pleaded Beau. "Didn't you ever

pretend when you were a kid? Don't you remember what that was like?"

Mary rose and shook herself. What the hell, she thought. She could pretend with the best of them. Hadn't she done it for years like? She unpinned her hair and let it fly loose in the breeze. Her naked toes dug into the sand and she remembered the gritty feel of summers long gone. Beau stood and watched her, puzzled. His look turned to surprise as she pulled her dress up over her shoulders and threw off the rest of her clothes.

"I remember," she said smiling and unashamed. "I used to pretend I was a mermaid."

"You must have had a vivid imagination," said Beau grinning as he reached out for her. But she slipped out of his embrace and started walking rapidly towards the sea. He followed and she slowed down, letting him catch up before she raced away.

"What are you doing, you wonderful crazy woman?" yelled Beau running after her.

"I'm going swimming," she yelled back over her shoulder. "It's what mermaids do."

"It's freezing in there!" Beau protested.

"Not at all," said Mary splashing into the surf and letting out a shriek. She bent down and let the surf run over her fingers. The water was freezing all right.

She licked her hand and tasted the salt as she looked at Beau. He had rolled up his trousers and was standing in the surf alongside her. Beau could not take his eyes off her.

"It tastes wonderful," she said smiling.

"It might taste wonderful, but my toes are going to fall off. Us southern boys are more accustomed to balmier climates." He reached out and put his arm around her waist and kissed her neck. "You're not really going in, are you?" he asked.

"Are ya coming?" taunted Mary. Beau shook his head in disbelief.

She could feel him watching her as she waded a few more yards into the surf. The cold against her legs made her gasp. She walked slowly on tiptoes and lifted her arms as the water came up to her waist. Then she stopped and watched the waves, floating up and over as they swept past her. She picked one and waited for it. Her legs were numb and her heart was racing like the wave rushing towards her.

Mary took a deep breath and plunged in just as the swell rose before her. She cut through the ice-cold water and came up gasping, whooping and laughing.

Beau jumped up and down on the beach, cheering. He had taken his shirt off and was waving it above his head. She saw him hop off and start taking off his clothes. Mary dived in again and felt the cold water flow over her. She imagined herself as some sort of sea creature. She gave a kick and swam deeper still, cutting through the water and swirling around till she lost her sense of direction. She was one with the ocean, cleansed and sharp.

She broke through the surface and looked around. Beau was nowhere to be seen. She bobbed in the water and turned, realising she had been disoriented by her dive. Then she spotted him a few yards from her, swimming strongly. She could hear him cursing.

"Jesus H Christ!" he said, his teeth chattering as he swam up alongside her. His lips had turned a dark purple and his face was flushed. "This is damn cold! Pardon my language, but my nuts have just disappeared into my nether regions! I thought only the Scandinavians were loony enough to try something like this!"

Beau's accent got thicker the faster he spoke. The southern accent and the chattering teeth together were the funniest thing Mary had ever heard. She laughed so hard she missed a wave as it broke over her, sending her sputtering and choking into Beau's arms.

"Now see what you've done?" said Beau, laughing

and shivering as he held her. "You're drowning and I'm freezing! You tell me what was so wrong about sunbathing on that little old sunny beach?"

Mary just gulped for air, still laughing.

"What's so dddamn fufufunny?" Beau stuttered.

"You are," said Mary catching her breath. "Come on, so. We'll go back."

They swam until they could stand and walked out of the sea hand in hand.

Mary scanned the sand for her clothes. The beach looked different. Something was wrong.

"Oh, my God! The tide came in!" she yelped. "My clothes!"

She ran madly ahead, leaving a trail of splashing water. "Oh, my God! Oh, Sweet Jesus!" She zigzaged back and forth along the waterline, dropping to her knees to peer into the surf.

Beau was standing off to one side. He was bent over double from laughing. He reached down and pulled out what looked like a wet rag from the water.

"My dress!" howled Mary running up and snatching it from him.

Beau laughed. "You looked like a chicken I once saw that had its head cut off and was still running around the yard!"

"It's not at all funny," said Mary giggling as she remembered her panic. "I must a looked a sight!"

She was suddenly aware of their nakedness and she held the dress up to cover herself. It was cold and full of sand and she shivered all over. Beau looked at her apreciatively.

"My my," he said in a low voice, "You people blush *all* over." Mary felt herself blush even more. Beau took her by the hand and led her to a sheltered spot, picking up his clothes as he went. A tiny voice in Mary's head asked her what she thought she was doing? But she hushed it as she looked into Beau's eyes and they began to make love on the sand.

Chapter Twenty-Three

Imelda sat by the little lamp and waited for Tommy to get home. She had arranged to travel out with the family going to Clare. They would be leaving in a day or two. She had not mentioned anything about Tommy. She let them think he was coming along as well.

He arrived in, drenched and weary, and she wished she'd kept a fire going so she could get him a cup of tea. He gratefully accepted some milk, gulping it down in one go. They quenched the lamp and sat in the dark for hours talking in low whispers.

They decided not to tell anyone, not even the family, about what had happened that night. Tinkers were hot-headed and God only knows what Uncle Paddy or Auntie Helen might do if they found out.

One thing was for sure: they would take the money for safe keeping. Imelda had tucked the thick wad into her shirt. She had no idea what they were going to do with it, but she knew it wasn't leaving her body.

Imelda and Tommy had been on their own since the parents had died, but what tinker was ever really on his own? Tinkers were like a web stretching out across the country linked one to another by birth or by feud. It was a comfort that cushioned every event from the smallest broken jamjar to the many tragedies that befell them as they travelled the roads. For the first time Imelda and Tommy considered what they might do without consulting or including anyone else, and it was lonely and confusing. They wandered, lost in a fog of half-sketched possibilities. They thought of one plan only to reject it the next minute. When the silences became longer than the talk they decided that it was best to sleep and talk again in the morning.

The wonderful time she had spent with Les seemed years away and Imelda could hardly believe she had been so happy only a few hours before. Talking with Ruth about getting married she had felt a door open. It was a mad idea, but Les made it sound so easy. She'd wait for him, write to him, and then some day find him again. She'd let herself imagine going to

America with Les. She'd brushed aside the hundreds of reasons why it could not be, and relished the happiness she felt.

Imelda lay thinking about how stupid she'd been. The little piece of paper was in her pocket. She took it and smoothed it out, trying to read it by the light of the moon. Dark clouds kept drifting by and she could barely make out Les's writing. She didn't want to think about what he had said. If she started thinking about it, believing in the way he said it, she'd start imagining it could really happen. She'd have to tell Tommy and she didn't know what he'd do. They'd enough to worry about without going on a wild-goose chase after some Yank she'd only met a few days before.

Imelda wondered if she'd get a chance to say goodbye to Les before she left for Clare. It made her very sad. Imelda had considered leaving her own people that night, yet it seemed a less painful idea than the thought of never seeing Les again. She put the piece of paper away and searched her pocket until her fingers closed around the small pin Les had given her. She traced the flight-wings in the dark, feeling the eagle engraved in the middle. She pricked her finger with the pin to try and distract herself from the heavy ache in her heart.

Imelda hardly slept that night. She kept drifting off

for a few minutes only to awake fitfully and feel for the large wad of bills pressing against her chest. She had no idea how much was there, but she knew it was enough to do whatever they wanted. It was probably more money than any tinker ever saw in his entire life. It was probably enough to get them all to America.

The storm rose, screaming through the trees and shaking the caravan, as she tossed and turned. The ordeals of the night kept running through her head but they were overwhelmed by the uncertainties of the new day that would dawn in just a few hours. Her only comfort was the little girls, softly breathing around her, as they cuddled together for warmth. She thought of Tommy lying underneath the caravan, alone in his blanket, and wondered if he had managed to get any sleep at all.

The dawn came quickly through the caravan's little window. Imelda watched the sun rise over Inchydoney across the marsh. She couldn't see the plane from where she lay, but she knew it was there. She remembered the top turret where Les had kissed her, Tommy messing in the ball turret, the smell and taste of the oranges.

She was wide awake when she heard a soft knock on the side of the caravan. Before she could answer, Tommy had popped his head in.

"Meldy? Are ya awake?" he whispered. "Do ya want a cup a tea?"

Imelda leaned against the caravan door and watched her brother as she drank her tea. He sat poking at the fire. It occurred to her that, though she loved him fiercely, she didn't really know him. Tommy was cocky and sure of himself. He never failed in his care of her and the little girls, but he kept to himself. He sported the arrogance of being born a man, like a shield. He moved in the men's world, she moved with the women. They exchanged few words, knowing their place and getting on with it. Imelda had no idea if her brother had dreams that went further than selling a pony at a good price, or meeting up with old friends at Puck Fair. Last night was the most they had ever talked together since their parents had died.

Imelda had no doubt that Tommy had saved more than her chastity last night. He had saved her life. Mary's too, probably. Gerald had been like an angry bull, his face turning from red to white rage as he ran after her. She'd tripped and lost her boot and Gerald had caught her, grabbing at her clothes. He held her arm with an iron grip and she couldn't free herself no matter how much she kicked and struggled. She had heard the shot and watched Gerald fall back, but she did not understand until Tommy stepped out of the shadows. There was no way he deserved to get done for that. He had to go away. It was the safest thing to do.

"Have ya thought about what yer going to do?" she asked.

Tommy just shrugged.

"I've been thinking about it," she said. "Mary's right. Just go on as if nothing happened and at the first chance ya get, go away and let them forget ya."

"I suppose so," said Tommy, still poking the fire. "I could lay low and wait. Go far up the country. I could go to Clare with ya and then move on for a bit. We could come back through when everything calms down. If anything happens at all."

"What if we never came back?" Imelda asked hesitantly.

"What'er ya talking about. Never come back here, like?"

"I mean go away and never come back. Far away. All of us. What if you and me and the girls all went to England. Or even America."

Tommy looked up at her, squinting at the sun. He said nothing and waited for her to continue.

Imelda took a deep breath. "What do ya want outta life, Tommy?"

"I dunno," he answered. "Why are you talking about leaving?"

"People have been doing that for a long time, ya

know. Leaving. Trying to go some place else to find a better life."

"A better life?" echoed Tommy.

"I don't know if this is what I want," said Imelda, waving at the caravan and the campfire. She searched for the right words.

"What's wrong with this, then?" Tommy asked. "This is what we are."

"Maybe we could try something else. Maybe this thing that happened was meant to be. You'd never have thought a leaving. We'd never have the choice if it wasn't for the money."

"I don't want to go work at some job in England,or America," Tommy said sullenly.

"Why can't we chance it?" Imelda asked, surprising herself with the question.

"What about the ponies?" Tommy asked. "I can't leave the ponies. What about proper clothes, and the girls, and all?"

"We can plan it all, Tommy. We can find a way," Imelda answered grabbing her blanket and pinning it on.

"Where are ya going now?" asked Tommy, thrown by her sudden decision to leave.

"I'm going to see Mary."

"Why?"

"I want to see Mary. I'll feed the dogs so you don't

need to come out. Tell Bridgit to mind the smallies. Nellie's had a good night. She hardly coughed at all. She'll be right as rain by tomorrow. Tell the girls to go to Mass with Auntie Helen. You go into town and do whatever it is you do. I'll meet ya at Mass."

"But what are we going to do, Imelda? We haven't decided yet. One minute yer talking about going to America and the next yer going off to feed the hounds."

"Don't you worry," said Imelda over her shoulder. "When I meet you in town I'll know what we're doing."

Mary went around doing her chores, still relishing the salty taste of Beau's kisses. She wanted to hang on to the memory for as long as she could.

Beau had grabbed an old coat and cap to cover his uniform, in case anyone saw him riding over the causeway. He looked like a local farmer until you caught the flash of his dark eyes under the brim of his cap. They had kissed goodbye a dozen times before finally managing to pull away from each other.

"Are you sure you'll be all right?" Beau had asked again and again as he kissed her. "I don't like leaving you on your own."

"I'll be just fine. You get back. They'll be wondering where you've got to," she said, but she did not let go of him. She nuzzled his neck and smelt the scent of lemons mixed with that of the sea.

"They'll all be so busy I'd be surprised if anyone noticed, honey," he said. "I'll just make an appearance and find out what's happening and then I'll come straight back to you."

"Maybe it's better if you wait until dark," said Mary. "Then maybe you can stay longer."

Beau pulled her closer still, and ran his hands over her back. "Oh God, I want you again," he said and they laughed as they embraced. Mary felt ripples of passion rising through them. She kissed him on the cheek and gently pushed him away.

"Go now, before we change our minds," she said grinning. "And come back soon."

Mary let the chickens out and watched them as they scratched around the yard. The air was very still, with only a soft sea breeze to lightly rustle the leaves in the trees. She sat on a little bench in the sunshine and stretched her legs out in front of her. She wiggled her feet, feeling the gritty sand between her toes. She had changed into a simple dress but she had not washed. She could still feel their lovemaking all over her. She remembered them lying entwined. Mary felt a small twinge of guilt but it was quickly pushed aside by the thrill that ran through her as she thought about their bodies coming together. Mary knew that she would have to confront the guilt one day. She would have to make peace with all these new feelings, and find a place for them alongside the disgust she still held for Gerald.

But not now. Not while Beau was still here. She would follow Beau's lead and pretend it was never going to end. She closed her eyes and gave herself up to the night's discovery of lust so sweet that time and place, and who they were, and where they came from, and where they were going, were forgotten as his body melted into hers.

A soft cough startled her. Imelda was standing shyly at the edge of the yard. Mary hadn't heard the pony pull up. She rushed and put her arm around Imelda's shoulders.

Imelda looked as if she hadn't slept a wink. Mary was stunned at how small she was. She looked no bigger than a child. Her dress was dirty, still smudged from the night before, and Mary wondered if she had another to change into. Her plait was loose and her blonde hair framed her face, accentuating the dark circles around her eyes.

"Are you all right, pet?" she asked, worried. "Come in and have a cup of tea."

Imelda followed her quietly into the house. Mary noticed her shudder and hesitate a moment before she crossed the threshold. She led her to a seat by the fire and made her some tea. Imelda cradled her cup of tea and watched Mary as she cut them some bread and buttered it.

"Are ya hungry? You must be hungry. Let me cook ya some breakfast," said Mary. She suddenly felt ravenous, and remembered she had not eaten since the day before.

Imelda let herself be served, quietly eating whatever Mary put in front of her. She seemed to be wrestling with a thought and Mary let her be and waited patiently, keeping an eye on her as she ate.

Finally Imelda cleared her throat.

"I'm sorry for your troubles, Mary." She kept her head down and Mary had to strain to hear her. "I was so scared," Imelda whimpered. "I thought he would kill us both."

Mary stood up and hugged the girl as if she were her own. Imelda was trembling. Mary stroked her hair and spoke softly to her, feeling the words catch in her throat.

"He's gone, Imelda. He won't ever hurt anyone again," Mary whispered. "You're right. He would've killed us both. Tommy was very brave." Mary's eyes filled with tears and she was grateful as they spilled down her face in a flood of relief. "I can't believe he's really gone. I'm scared I might wake up one day and find him there."

"Did ya love him?" Imelda asked, looking up as if to check if she hadn't overstepped her place. Mary hesitated a moment. Imelda blushed and lowered her eyes again. "I'm sorry. I didn't mean to be nosy," she said quickly.

Mary picked up a brush from the press and stood behind Imelda. She slowly undid her plait and started to brush her hair. Imelda was not yet fifteen but she deserved an answer. She was no longer a child.

"No," said Mary. "I never loved him. My father gave me away. I had no say in it. I'd hardly met him before I married him. I thought I'd grow to love him, but I never did."

"He beat you, didn't he?" Imelda asked, her voice barely a whisper.

Mary separated three thick strands of golden hair, brushing them out until they shone before starting to weave them into a plait.

"He beat me and he raped me. He made my life a misery."

"Why didn't you just run away?"

"I had nowhere else to go. But that wasn't the reason. I never thought of it. He was my husband. What could I do? I knew nothing else. Until last night I just took one day at a time." Mary tied the end of the plait and smoothed it along Imelda's back.

Imelda nodded solemnly. Her eyes held a look far beyond her years. Mary felt her heart leap in her chest. She wanted to hold Imelda and protect her from it all. She wanted to buy her pretty dresses and take her to tea rooms and make her smile.

She thought of the small camps she had passed along the roads all her life without giving them a second thought. She saw the children playing in the dirt, the hard men who came around selling their wares, and the tired faces of the women as they walked from one house to the next, carrying their babies wrapped in threadbare shawls. It was not her place to change that.

Mary bit her tongue, but could not stop from speaking. They were in it too far, the two of them. Imelda's life had become enmeshed in her own and it was too late to pull back. She turned Imelda so that she was facing her. Her nails dug into the girl's shoulders.

"Don't let them give you away, Imelda," she said fiercely. "Don't let them do that to you."

"It's our way. It's our life," Imelda said weakly, but Mary could tell that her heart wasn't in it. "I want to raise the girls right first," Imelda continued. "I'll make them wait, but if they say I have to, then I have to."

"It's no life for a girl like you. Don't let them do it.

Take the money and leave with Tommy. There's more than enough. I can't stand the thought of you being forced to live with some brute."

"He could be good. Me ma and da were happy together," Imelda argued.

"But he could be awful, and he wouldn't be your choice. They could give you away tomorrow and you'd have no say."

Imelda said nothing but her eyes were shining. She reached into her pocket and held out her hand. Mary looked down and saw a piece of paper and a little pin shaped like two wings. She did not understand.

"It's Les. Les Wagner, the American. He said I must write to him. He says he doesn't want to lose me. He said he'd walk the length and breadth of Ireland to find me if I didn't write." The words tumbled out of Imelda.

Mary thought of the tall gangly Yank and how he'd looked at Imelda. He was smitten all right. That was as clear as a summer's day. "And would ya go with him?" she asked, looking intensely at Imelda. "If he came to find ya, would ya go with him?"

Imelda nodded. "I would. I think I would. But I don't know him at all. I've only just met him and he says he loves me."

"Do you love him?"

"I dunno. I think I do," Imelda paused. Her eyes were shining brightly as she looked up to Mary. "I know I could."

"That's more than you're ever going to get if you stay here, girl," said Mary hugging Imelda close to her. "That's more than you're ever going to get."

Chapter Twenty-Four

— • —

Les wandered around the town. It was strangely deserted. Only a few men lounged on the street corners. Two stray dogs ambled right down the middle of the street. He had been looking for Imelda. He was sure she'd be coming into town. He needed to see her. They had precious little time left together. The runway would be arriving by tomorrow morning and they would be taking off a day after that if everything went well.

He wondered where all the people had gone. The town had been full the night before. The hotel bar had stayed open late and many a round was bought before the last man had staggered home to bed.

Les had stayed up a while after Imelda left, but

had called it an early night and gone off to bed to dream of her instead. He woke late and called in to see Matt but he was already up and gone. Beau's bed looked as if it hadn't been slept in.

The church bells started ringing, startling Les. He remembered that it was Sunday. That's where all the people were, he thought. At Mass. Maybe that's where Imelda was.

The church was packed with people who spilled out onto the yard. A large group of men followed the Mass from the doorway, and still more stood around outside furtively pulling on their cigarettes as they talked in hushed whispers.

Les leaned on the iron railing and lit up a Lucky. Several of the men nodded to him. He noticed that kid, Martin Kelleher, hanging around with his friends.

Les waved and they all trotted up eagerly. He searched his pocket for candy and then remembered he'd given all he had away to the kids in the tinker's camp.

"Have ya got a smoke?" asked a tall kid with freckles.

Martin followed behind him and gave him a hard poke in the ribs.

"Don't listen to this eejit," he said to Les.

"You're too young to be smoking," Les said, shaking his head.

"Sure it does no harm to have a smoke now and then."

"How old are you anyway?"

"I'm eleven," said the kid.

"It'll stunt your growth if you start smoking too young."

"Stunt your growth? You smoke and look at the size of ya."

"I only started smoking when I joined the Air Corps. You've still got a lot of growing to do to catch up with me." He cuffed him playfully on the head.

Martin was clearly annoyed with his friend.

"Hey, Martin, how are you today?" asked Les. "Have you still got the jackknife?"

Martin nodded and took it proudly out of his pocket. "I hear you're going to try again soon. Maybe I can win another bet," he said brightly. His friend rolled his eyes to heaven.

"You're not meant to be spreading that around too much, you know," Les lowered his voice. "It's kinda confidential."

"You can trust me. I can keep my mouth shut," Martin said with a wink. Then he added, "But I wouldn't be too sure about this eejit."

"Sure you think you're the bee's knees since you got that stupid knife," said his friend. The boys eyed each other like two terriers.

Les tried to change the mood.

"Actually Martin, I was wondering if you've seen Tommy Tanner or his family anywhere?"

"What would ya want with the likes a them?" asked the kid.

Martin glared at him and the boy stuck out his tongue. "Tommy's in the back of the church," said Martin still glaring. "I think some of his lot are inside but I wouldn't know. Matt's in there."

"Matt? That's the first time I've seen him get up early and go to Mass," said Les smiling.

"His ma dragged him in," sneered the first boy.

"She did not. You shut yer gob, Pat Barry, or I'll thump ya!" yelled Martin, shoving his friend.

Pat Barry laughed and stuck out his chin in a show of bravado.

"Ya would, yeah?"

"Yeah! You mocked my mother. No one mocks my mother," said Martin, shoving him again.

Pat Barry shoved him back. "I don't give a toss about yer mother. She can go to Mass with the friggin Pope for all I care!" he yelled. Martin was on him in a flash. The boys fell and rolled around at Les's feet. He stepped in and pulled them apart, holding one in each hand.

"Cut it out, guys," he said. "I thought you were buddies. You should be helping each other, not fighting."

The boys looked sheepish and hung their heads. Les let go of them and dusted them off.

"Now shake hands," he ordered.

The boys glared as they faced each other, catching their breath.

"He started it, like," said Pat Barry. Martin took a step forward.

"It's over," declared Les. "Come one, let's shake on it."

Martin reluctantly put out his hand. Pat Barry shook it.

"I didn't mean to mock yer ma," he said.

Martin's answer was lost as the bells started ringing and the people started to pour out of the church.

Les patted the boys on the back.

"You guys stay buddies," he said smiling. "I gotta go now. I'll see you later."

Les searched the faces as the people congregated in little groups. He was surprised at how many he recognised. The sun was shining down on the church-yard and no one seemed particularly rushed to get home. Les walked through them, stopping to chat every now and again, still scanning the area for Imelda or her family.

Charlie Hansen, and the co-pilot, McKnight, were standing together along with the Irish Army captain and officials that had come down two days before. Barry Kingston was talking animatedly as usual while Miss Aileen O'Donovan and Con O'Leary looked on. Con called Les over and gave him a big bear-hug.

"How are ya, man?" he asked jovially. "We missed your singing last night."

"I was tired out," said Les grinning. "You guys are too much for me."

"Well, you missed a mighty one. Come here, they say that the runway will be arriving tonight or tomorrow. So you'll be off soon, then?"

Les had no time to answer before the Irish Army captain stepped up, looking unhappy, and addressed Garda Pat Coughlan.

"There's too much talk about this runway," he stated. "I've heard several people mention it this morning."

"'Tis very difficult to contain," Pat Coughlan said formally. "We had to appeal to Father Collins not to announce it at Mass. He wanted to wish the Americans well before they left."

"Sure, the whole town knows by now," said Barry Kingston, spreading his arms wide. "You can't keep this type of thing a secret in a small place like Clonakilty. If ya sneeze on Pearse Street everyone knows about it before you've turned the corner to Emmett Square. This is the most exciting bit a news to have happened in years. That plane practically took the steeple off the church in the middle of the day. Ya can't expect to keep it under wraps."

"Still, 'tis highly irregular," said the Irish Army captain. "I don't want crowds of people down there at the marsh. We need to carry out this operation as quickly and quietly as possible."

"Well, if our landing was anything to go by, I'd say keeping people away is going to be damn near impossible," interjected Charlie Hansen.

"And you've even bigger crowds now. They're pouring in from all around the county for a look," added Con O'Leary. "The rumours are flying fast and furious. There's no way you can disguise those trucks from the North once they start rolling into town."

The small group paused to consider the situation. Les still searched the people coming out of the church. Most stopped to shake hands with the priest and he concentrated on them, hoping to see Imelda.

"We'll just have to set up a road block at the causeway, or even before, and stop them coming out," said the Irish Army captain. The locals shook their heads.

"That'll never work," said Barry Kingston, turning to Garda Coughlan beside him. "I'm sure Pat Coughlan here will back me on this one. You could have a riot on your hands. I even saw a couple of lads from the papers sniffing about. If this gets into the press you'll have the entire population of West Cork to manage on that causeway."

"Don't you worry about the press," said the Irish Army captain. "This is the Emergency. The press won't print a word that hasn't been cleared up above first. The problem isn't the press. It's the rumours. You can't censor them as easily."

"Hang on a minute there," said Barry Kingston, scratching his head. "I feel an idea coming on."

The whole group turned and looked at him expectantly. Barry Kingston motioned them to come closer as he dropped his voice to a loud whisper.

"The way to do this now, is to fight fire with fire," he said, emphasising his words with a stab of his hand. The Irish Army captain looked perplexed.

"What exactly do you mean?" he asked wearily.

"Start yer own rumour," whispered Barry Kingston intensely. He nodded slowly as he surveyed the group with a satisfied look, prompting their approval. All the locals were nodding back, beaming wide smiles, while the others still looked confused.

"That would do it all right," said Con O'Leary chuckling.

"I still don't understand," said the Irish Army captain, clearly annoyed.

"You start yer own rumour, boy," repeated Barry

Kingston under his breath. "Ya let it be known that the plane will be taking off at a given date, say on Thursday or Friday. Whatever suits. Maybe ya even add some official-sounding instructions to put them off the scent. Ya know, like that members of the public will only be allowed to go as far as the first causeway. That the road will be closed at such and such a time, and that it is dangerous to be on the marsh before that. Ya give 'em something to talk about. Then, and here's the beauty of it, ya leave in the early morning the day before you've announced it, when everyone's fast asleep dreaming of the lovely picnic they're gonna have!" He stood back and crossed his arms over his wide belly and gave a wink.

"'Tis brilliant!" Pat Coughlan was beaming.

"It could certainly work," said Charlie Hansen, laughing. "It's not very ethical, but it'll work. Do you think they'll forgive us?"

"Ah, they will!" declared Barry Kingston. He turned to the Irish Army Captain. "So what do ya think?"

"It's better than anything I've heard so far," answered the Captain slowly.

"But how do you propose to start such a rumour? Or were you thinking of putting up some sort of official notice?"

"Never you mind any official-notice nonsense," said Miss Aileen O'Donovan. "I'll see to it that by teatime tonight every person in Clonakilty thinks that plane is leaving next month if ya want it."

"No better woman!" said Con O'Leary, delighted.

"Would Friday suit, so?" Barry Kingston asked smiling broadly. The captain nodded slowly. Everyone else was chuckling at the plan.

"It'll take about twenty-four hours to get the runway set up. I'd say we could try for a departure on Tuesday at dawn," said Charlie Hansen. "And we'd still have more than a day to spare if anything goes wrong."

"Friday it is, so," said Barry Kingston shaking the Irish Army captain's hand. The group dispersed quickly.

The last people had left the church and some of the groups were saying goodbye and moving off. Les hadn't seen any of Imelda's family. He was wondering what to do next when Charlie Hansen called him aside.

"Have you seen Sergeant Beauregard?" he asked Les.

Something prompted Les to cover for Beau. "He got up early," Les answered. "He's gone for a long walk. I'm sure he'll be back soon. Is anything wrong? Do you want me to find him?"

"No. Everything is going smoothly. If you see him just tell him that the local big shots have organised a

Sunday lunch for the officers," said Charlie. "He's expected to attend because of the way he helped out during the negotiations. It's at two o'clock, in a house on Emmett Square. Tell him to ask Miss O'Donovan."

"Will do!" Les sauntered off. The churchyard was almost empty and he could hear the sound of horses around the back. Maybe Imelda had gone out a side door, he thought. Les didn't get very far before he was stopped by Matt, who caught him as he rushed by.

"Hey kid! Where's the fire?" Matt was standing with a tiny black-haired woman. "Let me introduce my good buddy Les Wagner from Wisconsin. Les, this wonderful lady is Kitty Kelleher. She's taken it upon herself to save my soul this morning. So in exchange, I'm taking her out to lunch."

Kitty Kelleher held out her hand. Les shook it and was astonished by bright blue eyes that danced merrily.

"I've done nothing of the sort," she said smiling. "I'm very pleased to meet you, Les Wagner."

"Would you like to join us?" asked Matt. "You look kinda lost there."

"Thanks, but no. I'm actually looking for Imelda. Have you seen her anywhere?"

"Imelda?" Matt repeated. "So that's what all the

hurry is about. I'm sorry, kid, but I haven't seen her."

"Was she at Mass?" Les asked hopefully. "Maybe I missed her as she came out."

"I didn't see her, but there's a string of carts around the side. Maybe she's there," said Matt.

"Thanks!" yelled Les over his shoulder as he ran off.

"Poor kid," said Matt smiling. "He's got it real bad." Then he held out his arm to Kitty who giggled and slipped her arm through his. "Alora, *bellissima Signora*, shall we go?"

The horses were causing a traffic jam with carts and traps and all manner of carriages trying to get into position and drive out the churchyard gates. Curses flew as the drivers yelled at their animals.Les felt a panic. Maybe she'd left. Maybe he wouldn't see her again.

The noise was overwhelming and Les jumped up to try and see the carts up front. He caught sight of Ruth and Dennis and ran up to them.

"How's it going?" said Dennis warmly.

"I'm fine. Have you seen Imelda?" Les asked catching his breath.

"No, but I thought I saw her brother earlier," said Dennis. "What's up?"

"Nothing, I'm just trying to find her. Where was Tommy when you saw him?"

"He was walking down Pearse Street with a scowl on 'im that would cloud a sunny day," said Ruth.

Les said a quick goodbye and ran down the street, dodging people as he went. At O'Donovan's hotel he nearly collided with Beau who was just coming out the door. Beau looked fresh and clean-shaven, in a new uniform. Les could smell his after-shave.

"Charlie Hansen was looking for you," Les said, still craning his neck down the street. "He says you're invited to lunch at two o'clock. Ask Miss O'Donovan, she'll tell you."

Beau didn't look too pleased at the invitation. In fact he looked like going to lunch was the last thing he wanted to do. Les had no time to ponder Beau's problems. He had to get to Tommy before he left town.

"I'm sorry but I gotta go," said Les "I've got to catch up wth Tommy Tanner."

Beau's frown turned to concern.

"Tommy Tanner? Why, what happened?" he asked.

"Nothing," answered Les, perplexed. "I just wanted to find Imelda."

"Is she all right?" Beau asked urgently.

"I guess so," said Les, even more puzzled. "Why shouldn't she be?"

Beau paused a second as if considering something. Then he smiled and patted Les on the shoulder.

"Hey, it's nothing. Don't worry about it. Thanks for the message, I guess I'm going to go to lunch then."

Les was worried. What did Beau mean? Beau winked at him and went back into the hotel. Les did not consider it further, but started walking fast down the main street. As he reached the little square his heart gave a leap. He could see Tommy Tanner walking ahead of him.

"Tommy, am I glad to see you! " said Les as he drew level with him.

"How's it going," mumbled Tommy.

"Fine. Just fine. Is Imelda in town?"

Tommy shook his head. Ruth was right, thought Les, Tommy seemed to have lost his usual sunny smile. The boy gave a nod and turned away.

"I'll see ya, so," he said, ending the conversation.

Les wasn't about to be put off by Tommy's bad mood.

"Hey, are you going back to the camp? Maybe I could come out with you?"

"I don't think so," said Tommy, shaking his head. He started walking out of the square. "I have to head away."

"Well, maybe I could go on my own," Les continued,

following Tom. "I'm sure I can find it. I could go and visit with Imelda and the girls."

"It's no use. They'll be busy. She's heading away as well. She'll be going up to Clare. Maybe she's gone already."

Les ran ahead of Tommy and faced him, forcing him to stop. He tried to look into Tommy's eyes but they were downcast, his mouth set in a thin line.

"What's the matter, Tommy?" asked Les. "What do you mean 'she's gone'? What happened?"

"Step outta my way, Les Wagner," Tommy growled. Les was surprised at the hard edge in his voice. "You'll go away and mind yer own business if ya know what's good fer ya."

Les was amazed. Tommy's body was tense and ready to pounce, his arms hung loosely at his sides but his fists were clenched into tight balls. If Les made a move, he was sure they have a fight. Les didn't want to fight with Tommy. He didn't understand what was going on or how to stop it.

The sound of sharp hooves made them both look up. Les's heart jumped in his chest as he saw Imelda coming up the street in the cart. She was standing up in the front like the first time he'd seen her, but her face was set with fiery determination as she searched the street. Tommy relaxed and unclenched his fists. He shrugged his shoulders as Les waved wildly to her. Imelda caught sight of them and flicked the reins for the pony to speed up. The pony's shaggy coat was wet with sweat and he snorted as Imelda pulled up alongside them. Her eyes were shining brightly and she glowed with a sense of excitement and urgency which immediately infected Les. Before he knew what he was doing he was up on the cart beside her.

"Come on, now," she called to Tommy. "Get up here."

Tommy leapt up beside them. No one spoke as Imelda skilfully turned the pony and cart around and headed back out of town. Once they were on the coast road Imelda urged the pony to pick up its pace. She looked straight ahead as she drove the pony on.

"What's going on?" asked Les. "What happened?"

"Did ya see Mary?" Tom cut in before Imelda could answer. "And what's he doing here?"

"Shut up, the pair of ya," she said, still keeping her eyes on the road. "Just wait until we get there."

"Where are we going?" asked Les. "Are we going back to your camp? Why did Tommy say you were leaving?"

Imelda still did not look at him but Les heard a softness creep into her voice as she answered and it warmed him.

"You'll see when we get there, Les Wagner."

They were following the road the crew had walked when they first came into town. The tide was low, but it was coming in. Far out by Inchydoney island he could see the surf sparkling bright white in the sunshine. The sky was a brilliant blue with hardly a cloud. Thousands of birds were feeding on the mud flats of the estuary as they drove by. Les watched a flock of long-beaked birds take off in a single squawking cloud and fly high above their heads, the cloud expanding and contracting as the birds circled the estuary. He wondered what type of birds they were, but thought it best not to ask. His two companions did not look in the mood to discuss the local wildlife.

As they came to a little wooded area on their left, Imelda slowed the pony to a walk and turned onto a path that headed into the trees. Les figured that they weren't far from the marsh. It must be just over the hill. The path was overgrown, with bushy trees on both sides, and they were soon hidden from the road. Imelda stopped the cart and tied the pony to a tree. Jumping off, Les could see a pair of tracks leading further into the woods. He looked at Imelda who smiled at him for the first time that morning.

"It's an old mine down there," she said sweetly. "No one ever comes down here anymore."

Tommy still sat on the cart looking miserable. He

pointed to a small bundle beside him. "What's this then," asked Tommy sullenly.

"Food and blankets," Imelda answered. Les couldn't figure out what was going on. He searched Imelda's eyes but she nodded for him to wait and turned her attention to Tommy instead. She grabbed her brother's arm and forced him to look at her.

"We have to tell him, Tommy. We can't do this on our own. He'll help us."

Les couldn't contain his questions any further. He stepped up to the cart and reached for Imelda's hand. She gave it readily and squeezed tight.

"What happened, Imelda? Tell me what happened. I'll do anything I can to help you, but I don't understand."

"Why would ya help us? We're just tinkers," Tommy spat out. "Yer not family. Yer just some some Yank, out fer a laugh. What would you know?"

Imelda's voice was low and hesitant, but she turned and faced Les, looking straight up at him.

"If I needed you, would you come and help me?"

Les felt a lump in his throat just looking at her. He had to cough and clear his voice before he spoke.

"You know I would," he said, taking both her hands in his. "I'd die before I let anything happen to you."

"What are you two going on about," Tommy said angrily. "Why would ya bother with her, Les Wagner?"

"Because I love her."

Tommy sat gobsmacked on the cart. He looked as if all the wind had gone out of him as he openly stared at Imelda and Les holding hands.

"You have to trust him, Tommy. I do. He's been places. He'll know what to do. Trust him, Tommy. Tell him everything."

It took over an hour for them to tell him all that had happened that terrible night when Gerald had been killed. Les felt his nails dig into his palms as he listened. By the time they had finished he knew what they had to do. It was so simple it almost seemed too easy. But Les could see no reason why they couldn't pull it off. The important thing was that no one should know. It had to be their secret if it was going to work.

He reached over and hugged Tommy who looked exhausted and shrunken from telling his story.

"I don't know how to thank you, Tommy. I'd die if anyone hurt Imelda. I would've killed him myself. You're a brave man."

Imelda held his hand and looked up to him expectantly. Her face was as open and as trusting as a child's. Les could see the love in her eyes. She was counting on him, and he had no intention of letting her down. He looked around at the little clump of trees.

"Is this where you're going to hide out?" he asked Tommy.

"I thought he'd be better off at the old mine," said Imelda. "There's shelter and you can hear people coming a long way off."

"Let's go help him set up then. We have a lot of planning to do before you leave to Clare tomorrow." Les felt a pang as he said it and he put his arm around Imelda's waist to steady himself. Then he led her by the hand up the worn out rail road track as Tommy followed carrying the small bundle.

Chapter Twenty-Five

•◆•

Lunch took a lot longer than Beau had hoped. It was practically seven o'clock before he was back on his bicycle riding out to the island. The sun was already starting to set and the marsh was lying in the shadow of Inchydoney.

As he got to the open countryside he had slipped the coat and cap back on. He took the second causeway out. It meant a longer ride but it was farthest from the army guarding the plane. He pulled the cap down over his head and lowered his eyes as he started to cross. If anyone noticed they didn't react. Beau thought that they'd probably seen him riding over in the morning and imagined he was a farmer on his way back home.

The greyhounds started barking as Beau rode up

the lane into the little yard. It lay in the half-shadow of the house, the red rays of the sunset illuminating the top of the sheds. He half-expected Mary to come rushing out, but the place was deserted. Only the twin columns of smoke coming out of both chimneys hinted that somebody was in. Beau smiled as he thought of Mary lighting the fire, her quick gestures and surprising strength for such a small woman. He was sorry he hadn't been there to help her with the chores. He had thoroughly enjoyed taking part in Mary's daily tasks.

Beau looked in at the window. The kitchen was spotless and cosy, with a small fire dancing in the hearth, and the day's bread propped up on the sideboard to cool. He tapped lightly on the window but got no answer save from the dog who sniffed at the door and wagged his tail.

Beau let himself in and wandered into the hall. The front room was open and there was a fire lit in there as well.

Mary was sleeping curled up in the armchair, like the first time he had ever laid eyes on her. Beau remembered thinking he had been dreaming. But Mary was even more fantastic than any dream he could have had. He'd had quite a number of women since the first time his father had taken him down to the French quarter when he was fifteen. Sex had always been one of life's pleasures since then. Beau prided himself at being a good lover. He'd thought he'd fallen in love several times, the first with the fancy lady his father had arranged for his education. But though the thrill had always been delightful, it was always short-lived.

Mary was different. Watching her sleep, Beau realised that he had been slightly bored with the women he frequented. At twenty-two he already felt that love was nothing more than an elaborate parlour game. Whether it was fancy ladies or high society girls, and sometimes their mothers, it was all too easy.

He knew he was good-looking. Women had always swarmed around him. He hadn't ever had to go searching for them, he just reached out and they were there. Beau had welcomed their advances but lately it had felt as if he were just playing a role. Beauregard St Loucis, rich playboy, slightly roguish but always charming. He wondered if he seduced them mainly because that was what was expected of him.

Mary's hair was down and framed her face. She was wearing a simple cotton skirt and a white blouse. At her neck hung a tiny gold cross on a chain. Her breathing was barely audible. Only the slight rise and fall of her chest disturbed the stillness. Beau remembered her running naked on the beach and felt a yearning stir in his belly.

What was it about this woman that made him desire her so? Granted she was very beautiful, her body had both a strength and a softness he had never encountered before. But he knew that it was not the ripe curves that drove him to want to make love to her right there and then. It was something in her eyes. He wanted to take her as she slept in the armchair and see her eyes flash open in surprise.

Beau knelt beside her and softly kissed her lips. Mary was startled and pulled away. Then she looked up and smiled. Her arms pulled him to her and she kissed him back. Beau lay his head in her lap, letting his cheek sink into the softness of her legs.

"You took yer time," Mary said as she stroked his hair.

"I had to go to a lunch in our honour. Charming people I'm sure, but I just couldn't wait to leave. I missed you every minute I was there."

"I missed you, too," Mary said softly.

Beau kissed her knees gently through the thin cotton. He planted a row of kisses up her leg and felt she tense as he slipped his hand under her skirt. He let it rest casually on her thigh until he felt her relax again. He checked her face. She was blushing deeply but she was smiling. Beau kissed her again and skilfully undid the buttons on her blouse.

The light was fading. Beau leaned over and lit the little lamp as Mary let her clothes fall to the floor. He stopped her as she reached out to undo his shirt.

"You just lie back there, darling," he said, his voice husky. "Let me see just how beautiful you are."

Mary's skin trembled at his touch. The flicker of the lamp cast little shadows all over her milk-white body. Slowly he started kissing her legs again, stopping every time he felt her tense until she relaxed of her own accord. Soon Mary was lying back, her eyes closed, her breathing getting deeper and faster.

Beau pushed aside his own rising passion as he concentrated on Mary's pleasure. He let her set the pace. His mouth, and tongue, and hands, moved of their own accord, feeling the slightest shift of her body, the faintest intake of breath and adjusting to it. The rhythm of his caresses grew faster. Mary gasped. Her eyes flew open and she arched her back, her body rising off the armchair.

Beau could hold back no longer. He ripped off his clothes as she lay back panting. He kissed her face, her eyes, her hair.

Her arms went around his neck and he felt her soft breasts against his naked chest. He reached for her hips and lifted her to the edge of the seat. She wrapped her legs around his waist as he entered her. Their bodies melted into one, the rhythm of their lovemaking as natural as the swell of the waves in the bay. As they climaxed they clung to each other as if to save one another from drowning.

They remained locked in an intimate embrace until their breathing had calmed down and they finally parted. Beau lay his head on her breast as she cradled him. He heard her heart thumping, matching the same beat in his chest.

"You are the most wonderful lover," he said, kissing her sweetly.

"Yer not so bad yerself," she giggled. "Where did you learn to do that? You know? What you did to me?"

"Oh, you could say I'm just naturally gifted. It runs in the family," Beau answered grinning. He got up and stretched. "It's also considered part of a well-rounded education back in Louisiana."

"Don't tell me you had lessons in that as well?" she teased as she watched him pace the room.

"Well, to tell the truth, I guess you could say I had but I'm not about to discuss that in the present company. Suffice it to say that a southern gentleman should be well-versed in the art of lovemaking."

Mary threw her legs over the armchair and let

them dangle over the side. She threw her head back and looked at Beau upside down and laughed. She felt like she had never felt before. Beau was walking around naked in the front parlour as if it were the most normal thing in the world, and Mary was surprised to find she had no urge to cover herself either.

"You look just like a fancy lady in the French quarter with your hair falling on your shoulders, and the reflections of the fire," Beau said, looking at her. "Wait. Don't move."

Mary obeyed as Beau went out of sight behind her. He came back with the small bit of lace Imelda had given her. He unrolled it and tied a bow around her neck leaving the ends trailing over her body.

"There. *Vous êtes trop belle, madame*," he said, blowing her a kiss.

"What does that mean?" asked Mary glowing with his attentions.

"You are too beautiful."

"And what's a fancy lady?"

"A lady of the night," Beau answered slowly.

Mary shook her head, not understanding.

"A courtesan. A lady who makes a man's pleasure her business."

"You mean a whore, don't ya?" Mary blushed deeply and pulled at the lace.

"No, no, no. That's too cheap and vulgar a term for the fancy ladies of New Orleans."

"Is that who taught you to make love?" she asked eying him. "A fancy lady?"

"Don't you worry about that," said Beau, looking embarrassed for the first time.

"I'm not angry Beau," Mary said, touched by his confusion. "I'm just interested. I've never heard of fancy ladies. I've never really known much about men and women and love. Or else what I knew was too harsh and without love to be anything but horrible."

Beau sat on the sofa across from her and stretched his long legs out in front of him.

"Her name was Fifi. It sounds like a poodle, I know. But Fifi was very beautiful, and a true expert. She had skin the colour of caramel. And she was kind. Very kind to a scared, though completely thrilled, fifteen-year-old boy."

"You were fifteen, and you went to see a who— I mean, a fancy lady?" Mary's eyes grew wide at the thought.

"No, I did not. My father brought me for my birthday."

Mary gasped and then shook her head. "I didn't know such things were possible. Imagine that!"

"Well, I did tell you that we appreciate a well-rounded education."

Mary considered the information. A look of concentration crossed her brow.

"If you were only fifteen, then that means you must have been with more women since then."

"I have had the pleasure of many a fine lady's company," Beau said.

Mary frowned and Beau crossed the room and took her in his arms.

"But believe me, Mary, I can truly say that I'd never really made love until I met you. Ever."

He kissed her. Mary felt herself go weak as his lips pressed down on hers.

"Did you feel that?" he asked, looking deeply into her eyes.

Mary nodded.

"Well, I've never felt like that before. Believe me."

"Neither have I," whispered Mary, letting him kiss her again.

They held each other quietly until Beau jumped up, pulling her up with him.

"Come here," he said, leading her to the hall. "There's something I want you to see."

"But I'm naked!" protested Mary.

Beau was trying to open the front door. The key was slow to turn and the hinges were rusty. Finally the door swung open, squeaking mightily.

"That door sure didn't want to be opened," Beau said laughing.

"I'm not surprised," said Mary. "I don't think it's been opened in fifteen years."

"Why not?"

"I guess because it's the door for visitors and nobody ever visits."

"Well, it's open now. Close your eyes and give me your hand," Beau said pulling her towards the doorway.

"But someone could see us," Mary objected, but she closed her eyes.

"Nonsense. We're shipwrecked on a desert island, remember?"

Mary let herself be led outside. She felt the cold sea breeze on her naked skin and felt the grit of earth beneath her toes. The smell of the sea was mixed with that of the garden.

"OK. You can stop now, honey." Beau stood behind her and wrapped his arms around her for warmth. Mary could feel his body pressing against her. Beau rested his chin in the crook of her neck.

"Now. Open your eyes."

Mary caught her breath. The moon was hanging over the sea like giant balloon, all round and white, cutting a path over the water and showering the little garden with its light.

"I saw it through the window," said Beau as he nuzzled her neck. "I had to come out and show you. It's our moon."

"A paper moon?" Mary sighed.

"Well, if it is, then it's the biggest, brightest, roundest, most solid darn paper moon I've ever seen."

Somewhere she could feel a pang at the thought of him leaving creep in and spoil her happiness. Mary wished the thought away and leaned her weight back on him. The warmth of his body cleared her mind of anything but the feel of him, the taste of him, and the incredible passion he had created in her. He nuzzled her neck again and whispered in her ear. It tickled delightfully and Mary squirmed in his embrace. He was humming the tune, his lips against her neck. It buzzed and tickled. Mary giggled and tried to pull away but Beau wouldn't let her go.

"We better go back inside. Someone might see us," she said laughing.

"The only one watching is the man on the moon," said Beau pointing. "And as you can clearly see, he's got a big ol' smile on his face. He doesn't look as if he minds two butt-naked lovers one bit. In fact, I'd say he looks positively charmed by us."

When it got too cold, they finally ran back inside, shivering and laughing, and tried to warm themselves by the fire. Beau decided he was going to cook them something and he marched off to the kitchen as Mary got dressed.

He was standing over the table, dressed only in his underpants, with a collection of bowls and eggs spread out before him. Mary laughed to see him there.

"What's so funny? Have you never seen a man cook in his underpants before? Just call me the naked chef!"

"What are ya cooking?" asked Mary, still giggling.

"I was going to whip up a Bayou omelette but I can't find any spices. Have you got any pepper, honey? I found some salt, but that seems to be the only condiment around."

Mary shook her head. Pepper was difficult to come by these days and she'd never really cooked with spices.

Beau shrugged his shoulders and started breaking eggs and chopping onions.

"My father always travels with an assortment of condiments. His valet has a whole range packed whenever we leave. And it doesn't matter if we're staying in the finest hotel, Papa will just slap the hot sauce on anything that's served up to him."

"Your father travels with a valet? You must be very rich."

Beau said nothing. He concentrated on his

cooking and considered how much to tell her. He realised that the fact that she knew so little about him was very important to him. She saw him for what he was and nothing more. He found that he was scared that she might not like him quite as much if she knew more. He wished he'd had the foresight to never mention fancy ladies, and valets and dancing-lessons.

Mary sat herself down on the chair by the hearth and poked the fire to get it going again. She threw a few blocks of turf on and watched the flames jump up to grab them.

Mary had an ageless beauty as she sat tending the fire. She was not a young pretty thing who would be easily impressed by his family's wealth and possessions. On the contrary, she'd probably think him spoiled, which of course he was. Mary must have sensed his confusion and she let the question hang unanswered between them. Instead, she came up and kissed him lightly on the back of the neck.

"So what was this big lunch you went to?" she asked. "Did all the crew go to lunch with ya?"

"No. Only the officers and myself. I was invited because I helped with the negotiations." There it was again, at every turn he ran up against the wall of his background. Beau continued slowly, a weariness in his voice. "My father has some very highly placed friends both here and in the British chain of command.

And, of course, back home. It helped in securing the runway from Belfast."

"That's wonderful," Mary said, her eyes gleaming. "I'm very proud of you, Beauregard."

"I didn't do much, really. I have to tell you though, it's all very secret."

"Why? What's wrong with getting your plane back up in the air?"

"We're all at war, honey. And Ireland is neutral. So it wouldn't be right if the Irish and the British got together to help the Americans retrieve a plane to go fight the Germans. You understand?"

"I don't see why not," Mary shrugged.

"Well, the Germans wouldn't be too pleased if they found out."

Beau was making an almighty mess of things and Mary ran around him, cleaning up. They had a laugh when Beau tried to cook the omelette on the griddle hanging over the fire, refusing to let Mary do it. In the end he produced two delicious, if slightly charred, plates of fluffy eggs and onions. They ate hungrily, cutting thick slabs of bread and butter to go with it.

"So when is this runway arriving?" Mary asked, looking up at him from under her dark lashes as she finished her meal.

"Tonight maybe. Tomorrow at the latest. It'll take at least a day to put it together," Beau answered. He could not bring himself to state the obvious: that once it was set up *T'Ain't a Bird* would fly off to England. He suddenly realised that he could not bear to leave this woman. Mary caught his sadness and reached over and gently put her hand on his arm.

"That means we still have a a day and a night together, maybe two," she said sweetly.

"I don't know." Beau's voice dropped. He was surprised to find his eyes smarted and he had to clear his throat to continue. "I'm fine for tonight. We all are pretty free to come and go as we please. No one even knows I'm gone. If I get back to the hotel for breakfast no one will notice. But things could be different when the runway arrives. I don't know if I can get out here again."

"Don't you start, Beauregard St Soucis!" Mary said sharply. She squeezed his arm. "We still have all night. Wasn't it you who said to forget the runway? Didn't you say we can have forever if we pretend it's just you and me?"

Beau held back his tears and nodded. He smiled despite himself at her pronunciation of his name. Her West Cork accent ran all the syllables into one another and crunched them up.

She was looking at him fiercely, her eyes blazing.

"We still have tonight. We can make tonight last forever."

Beau thought that she had never looked so beautiful. He reached out and took her hand as if asking her for a dance. Their eyes locked as they rose from the table and fell into each others arms. Then they silently went up the stairs hand in hand.

They made love all night as the moon continued to shine through the little bedroom window, wrapping their bodies in a silver glow. Mary found that she did not just reach out to hold Beau as before. This time her hands explored his body, delighting in every curve and line as she made love to him. It was a voyage of discovery and Mary felt herself awed at every turn. Her body seemed to know just what to do and she let it go, following the path of passion and tenderness and lust with a wild abandon that surprised and elated her.

They lay tucked into each other's arms, content and calm, and talked in whispers. Then their need for each other rose again and swept them away to a place where only they belonged.

Mary lay back exhausted and happy as Beau propped himself up on one elbow and smiled at her. He traced the curve of her hip with his hand and she revelled in the feeling of his fingers on her skin.

"You know that I've fallen in love with you, don't you?" he said softly. Mary held his gaze and waited for him to continue. "And you can deny it all you want but I know that you love me too."

Mary nodded. "I wasn't about to deny it. Sure 'tis plain as the nose on my face. It makes no sense at all, but there ya have it." Her hand reached out and brushed his cheek.

He grabbed it and kissed her wrist.

"It makes perfect sense to me," he said.

"You're my beautiful dreamer, you are," said Mary sweetly.

"No, Mary. This isn't make-believe. This is real. I know I promised we wouldn't talk about tomorrow, or after, but I can't stand the thought of leaving you alone here."

"I'll manage, don't you worry."

"What are you going to do?"

"I haven't really thought about it yet," she said, looking up at the ceiling. The plaster was old and cracking. This room could use a lick of paint, she thought. The whole house could, really. Mary let herself drift into plans for the future. It was a new sensation and she felt her excitement rise at the thought of getting the place fixed up. She was talking out loud as she planned. "In my grandmother's day, this place was a working farm," she said dreamily. "Maybe I could build it up again slowly. I have some money. If I was careful I could buy some stock, maybe even get back some of the land Gerald sold – or at least rent it."

Her eyes were gleaming. She saw barley waving in the south field, and potatoes blooming below where the soil was black and peaty.

"The land is very good out here. My family's been chucking seaweed on it for a hundred years. You could grow anything you like it. And cattle, you could raise cattle as well."

"Or you could just sell it," said Beau.

"Why would I want to do that?" Mary asked.

Beau took her face in her hands and kissed her. When he spoke again his voice was filled with a frantic urgency. "You could sell the farm and come to Louisiana."

Mary's heart melted. Beau's eyes were like two black holes burning into her. She saw his strong jaw, long nose and full lips. He waited for her answer and Mary could feel the love pouring out of him willing her to agree. "What would I be doing in Louisiana? I'm too old to be a fancy lady," she said trying to sound light-hearted.

"You could marry me."

"Oh, my darling," she cried and held him close. "I'd never fit into your world."

"Yes, you would," he argued. "I could teach you. We could be happy together."

"I would never fit in. Just like you could never fit in here."

"Who cares! Aren't we perfect together? Isn't this perfect, right here, right now?"

"Yes, it is," she said and she kissed his eyes softly as if calming an unruly child. "But we can't live in this room forever. Not really. This was never meant to be. It is the most wonderful trick of fate that it did come to be. You belong in your world and I belong in mine."

"We could run away then. Make our own world." he objected.

Mary got up and walked over to the window. She looked out over the estuary. The moon had moved above the hills of Ardfield and was much smaller. Tomorrow it would look as if someone had cut a tiny sliver off its side and by next week it would be gone altogether.

"No, my love, we couldn't. You'd end up hating me and I'd resent you. And if I did as you say and tried to fit in to your world then I would change. I wouldn't be the woman you fell in love with any more."

"I will love you forever, no matter what," Beau declared.

"Of course you will. And I'll love you. You made me whole again, when I didn't even know that a big piece of me was missing. No one can take that away from me. No one can erase what we had here. It will remain in our hearts forever."

"Please, Mary," he said simply, his arms reaching out for her. "Please come with me to Louisiana."

She fell into his arms and breathed the lemon scent of him deeply. She felt as if she were on a precipice, high above the sea, and that Beau was far below calling to her. She steeled herself and imagined that she closed her eyes and leapt into the void. But she knew she could not do it. Not really. She kissed him hard and tasted the saltiness of tears. She did not know which one of them was crying. Maybe they both were.

"I could never leave," she whispered softly. "Too much of me is here. I could never sell the place. My baby is buried up on that hill. I could not leave him alone to strangers."

Beau tried to persuade her again but she smothered his protests with kisses. Slowly she felt his body harden and arch towards her. When they made love this time it had all the bitter-sweetness of the love they shared.

Beau fell asleep in her arms, but Mary did not sleep. He didn't know it yet, but she had made the right choice. Maybe he would not know it until years from now when he was settled and married with a family of his own. Mary hoped that in the years to come he would not hold it against her, nor suffer too deeply. But she knew that one day he would understand that it was only because she loved him so much that she could not go with him.

The hours passed until the dawn crept in through the window. She lay alongside Beau, feeling the whole length of his body pressed up against hers, hearing his soft breathing as he slept, listening for the strong beat of his heart as she lay her cheek on his chest. And all the while her hands traced the long muscles of his legs, the curly hair, the line of his jaw. She ran her hands over his body like a blind man trying to perceive with his fingers what his eyes could not see.

By the time the first rays of sunlight crossed the bed, Mary had memorised Beau's every detail, committing them to her memory where she knew she would keep him forever.

Chapter Twenty-Six

Imelda woke up just as the grey dawn started to lighten the sky. Her breath made little patches of fog and she snuggled back under the blanket to try and capture a last bit of warmth before she got up.

They were leaving today.

She couldn't believe it was Tuesday already. The day before had started so slowly and then it had just rushed into today.

In less than an hour they would be striking camp and heading up the road to Cork. If they made good time they would camp that night just outside the city before moving off across the country the next day. It could take them days, maybe weeks, before they got to Ennis where Uncle Paddy had some work lined up with a farmer there. Imelda didn't care how long it took. The longer the better – then she'd stand a better chance of finding a letter from Les waiting for her at the post office.

Imelda had packed everything up the day before. It had not taken long – tinkers were always ready to leave quickly. She fidgeted at tasks, speaking sharply to the girls. They were over-excited and difficult. Nellie was back on her feet and giving more trouble than the rest of them put together.

No one had questioned her when she announced that Tommy had been offered some casual labour and gone off on his own. She said she didn't know where, but that he would catch up with them in Ennis, or send news if the work was good enough to stay the summer.

She tried to keep herself busy, but every few minutes her mind would drift to Tommy hiding out in the mine, or to Les back at the hotel, and her heart would sink. Then she'd remember their promises and take heart that everything would be all right.

She heard the clanging and clanking all day. Shouts and banging, and the rumble of trucks back and forth over the causeway, had echoed across the marsh as the army built the runway.

She'd also thought a lot about Mary. She wanted to go and say goodbye, but Tommy and Les thought it best if she just stayed in the camp as much as possible. Imelda worried that Mary would be hurt, or worse, by her sudden disappearance. Then she hit upon the idea of writing her a letter. She smiled to herself. That was Les's fault, she thought. 'Twas Les that had put notions of letter-writing into her head. Letter-writing and so much more.

She had to scour the camp in search of a pencil and a scrap of paper. She took herself off to a quiet spot behind the caravan from where she could see Inchydoney Island. Imelda had never written a letter before and she didn't really know where to start. She wanted to tell Mary how sorry she was to leave her, and how happy she was about Les, and how scared she was about it all. She wondered whether she should tell her about their secret plan? No, she mustn't. Not yet. Maybe some day when everything was over. Who knows what could happen to a letter? Who might read it?

She licked the pencil and slowly started to write, but ten minutes later all she had written was *Dear Mary*.

Imelda scratched her head and thought hard. *I am well*, she wrote, quickly adding *So is Tommy*. What else could she say? Her words tumbled through her head but refused to take shape on the paper. Imelda was angry that writing was so difficult and she vowed to write every day from now on. And read. She'd find some books and read them. If she was going to write to Les then she'd have to get better at this writing business. And if she was some day going to be Les Wagner's wife and live in America she'd have to get educated. She wouldn't let him down.

I am leeving to Clare, she wrote, painfully rounding out each letter. Her hand felt cramped and she shook it before continuing. *Les is leeving to Amerikay. We will write*. She could think of nothing else. Anyway she was running out of paper.

Imelda wrote her name at the bottom. The words were all big and uneven. Her writing had been far better than that for her Confirmation, five years ago. She hadn't written anything since really. She was definitely going to practise. She folded the piece of paper and then stopped before she put it in her pocket. She smoothed it out and added a note on the back. *Write me at Ennis post ofis*.

Then, with the excuse of getting some things in town, Imelda had hitched up the cart and driven to the post office. Clonakilty was said to be the only place in the world that had a post office in a church. Imelda had certainly never seen anything like it in any other town. She knew it was an old Protestant church that had been deconsecrated years before but it still felt strange. Imelda had never been in a post office before and she stopped and stared at the high arches above her head, until the woman behind the little counter coughed for her to hurry up. She bought an envelope and a stamp and posted it under the eagle eye of the postmistress. Imelda wondered if the old bag ever read people's post. She wouldn't put it past her.

Imelda walked the pony slowly through town, wanting to gallop out instead. She was meeting with Les and Tommy at sunset. It made her heart ache to think that it was probably the last time she'd see the pair of 'em for a long time. She was stopped by Ruth who wanted to chat. Imelda explained that she was leaving, and Ruthie had given her a big hug and made her promise to call in when she came back to Clonakilty. Imelda waved a quick goodbye so that Ruth wouldn't see the tears filling her eyes. She thought to herself that she'd probably never set eyes on Ruth, or Clonakilty, ever again.

Imelda tied up the pony to same tree as the night before. The place looked deserted. Slowly she began walking down the tracks that led to the mine. She stopped and hooted like an owl to let Tommy know she was coming. She'd just started down the track again when a figure stepped out from behind a tree. Imelda gave a shout which caught in her throat as she saw Les holding out his arms to her.

They kissed for a long, long while. Les was so tall that Imelda had to stand on tiptoes to reach his lips.

"I'm scared, Les Wagner," she said, finally pulling away. "What if someone finds out? What if they find him?"

"No one's gonna find him. We've got everything covered."

"We? Who's we?" she asked, frightened at the thought that he'd told some one.

"Just Matt. I needed some back-up. It'll be easier if there's two of us. If anything goes wrong – and nothing will – one of us can create a distraction."

"And he agreed?"

Les nodded. "He's my buddy. You can trust him."

Imelda started to cry. She couldn't help it. It all had seemed so simple but now she saw the countless things that could go horribly wrong. Les held her close, hugging her tightly.

"Don't cry Imelda. Everything is going to be just fine. I'll write to you the minute I get to England, and you'll write back. And before you know it, my tour will be over and we'll all be together in Wisconsin."

"But what if something happens to you?" Imelda moaned. "What do we do then?"

"Nothing's going to happen to me," Les said, smiling tenderly.

"But you could get killed. The war could go on for years and years."

"I'm not going to die." Les held her chin and forced her to look up. "Look at me, Imelda. I'm not going to die. I don't know how long this war is going to take. But I have twenty-five missions to fly and then I'm going home. And so are you."

Then they walked hand in hand to where Tommy waited.

Imelda still couldn't believe what they'd done. Or were going to do. Before she got up she closed her eyes and said a prayer for all of them.

It took less than an hour to get the ponies hitched up and everyone sorted out with breakfast. Imelda sat herself in the front of the barrel-top and picked up the reins. She followed her uncle's caravan as it set off down the boreen. Bridget drove the cart with the extra ponies trailing behind her, and the family from Clare brought up the rear.

As they came up onto the road Imelda stopped and listened. She could hear a low hum. It rose in intensity filling the air with a mighty roar. The birds in the estuary rose all at once and the trees by the road were filled with cries and flapping wings.

Imelda's heart skipped a beat and her hands were

trembling so much that she had to put the reins in her lap to stop them from shaking.

"What's that big noise?" Nellie called from the back of the caravan. "Is it the plane? Can we go and see the plane?"

"It's the plane all right. It's leaving today. But we can't go see it," Imelda said unable to stop her voice from trembling. Tears were falling freely down her face. She was glad to be in the shadow of the barrell-top awning, where no one could see her crying.

"You girls stay in the back and be good, now," she called over her shoulder trying to sound as natural as possible. "You can come and sit with me once we're on the road to Cork."

Imelda flicked the reins, urging the pony to move out. Her face was wet with tears and her lips moved silently, mouthing the words of the rosary. She prayed as she had never prayed before. She prayed that everything would turn out just like Les said it would. But most of all she prayed for Tommy. Imelda begged God and Our Blessed Lady and all the saints to watch out for her only brother as he sat huddled hiding somewhere in the belly of that big plane, while the engines roared around him, scared out of his wits by a whole new life that was just beginning.

Chapter Twenty-Seven

◆

Two hours before, Martin Kelleher had dragged himself from a deep sleep when someone shook him.

"Wake up Martin! Wake up, boy!"

He rubbed his eyes and tried to adjust to the dark.

His mother was standing fully dressed by his side. She motioned him to keep quiet. "Get dressed and come downstairs," she whispered.

Martin threw on his clothes in the dark. What was going on? Why would his mother be waking him up in the middle of the night, like? He would have been scared except that his mother's voice had been light, almost jovial, as if he was in for a big treat.

She was waiting for him in the hall, holding a small lamp which she lifted to shine some light as he came down the stairs. Her eyes were smiling as she pointed him into the tiny kitchen.

Martin shivered. The fire was cold, with only a few embers left from the night before. He stood by it nonetheless trying to warm himself. He took the cut of bread his mother gave him.

"Have a quick bite to eat," she said. "Hurry now. We've got to leave soon."

"Where are we going? What's up?" Martin sensed his mother's excitement. She could barely keep her voice down and her eyes were dancing.

"We're going to see that plane take off, lovey."

He thought his mother must have gone mad. What was she on about? The plane wasn't taking off today. Everyone knew it was taking off on Friday!

He'd heard the trucks roll into town at dawn only the day before. Leaning out of his tiny bedroom window, he'd seen them line Pearse Street before heading off in the direction of the marsh. He knew it must be the runway the Yanks were waiting for. He'd tried to follow them, but had been turned away by the army who was keeping everyone away. Pat and Joe Barry and himself had run all over town trying to get news. It had taken them all day to find out what was happening.

"The plane is leaving today?" Martin asked in amazement.

"That it is," she replied with a satisfied smile.

"But it can't leave today! Everyone knows it's leaving at ten o'clock on Friday morning. The master even said it. He even said that if we were really good he might take us down to watch it take off!"

"That's what they want everybody to think. But a little bird told me that it's leaving today at dawn. It's a very big secret!"

Martin's mouth fell open.

"Close yer mouth, Martin," she ordered. "You look like a cod fish. I've told ya a thousand times if I told ya once never to chew with yer mouth open."

Martin's jaw snapped shut and he tried to swallow as fast as he could. He looked at his mother with new-found respect. She was tapping her foot impatiently, still smiling like a cat who had just stolen the cream. Martin thought to himself that he'd never really noticed how pretty she was with her hair up.

"So how is it that we're going?" he gulped finally.

"We have a special invitation to watch the departure," said his mother, putting on her coat. "Mateo arranged it all and he asked for you to come along."

"So ya mean we'll be the only ones there!' Martin glowed with pride.

"I expect there will be some others. But we're among the chosen few. Everyone else in town is probably fast asleep. Now get your coat. There's a truck waiting at the hotel and I don't expect it to wait for long."

Martin didn't need to be asked twice. He grabbed his coat and was out the front door in a flash. He couldn't wait to get out on the marsh. He couldn't wait to see that giant bomber lift off into the sky. But most of all he couldn't wait to tell Pat Barry and watch his mouth drop down to his boots.

A thin veil of mist hung about a foot above the marsh, shrouding the undercarriage of the plane. Martin thought that it looked like a giant mythical sea creature swimming through steaming waters,with its tail-fin sticking out and the small lights in the nose and cockpit shining like a ghostly face with a leering grin. The monster rumbled as the propellers slowly turned over. Every once in a while they would go up a notch, stopping everyone on the road dead in their tracks. Martin knew they were warming the engines. He felt a knot of excitement in his belly that got tighter every time they revved up.

The army had cleared their small camp of little white tents and stowed everything away in the row of trucks lining the road. Soldiers were rushing to and fro, looking very busy. Further down the road, Barry Kingston and Garda Couglan were deep in conversation. Only the Yanks looked relaxed as they leaned against the wall smoking cigarettes, the tips glowing brightly in the pale dawn light.

Martin caught sight of Matt chatting away and he pulled at his mother's hand.

"Come on Ma. It's Matt!" Martin tugged at his mother as he tried to speed it up, but she slowed to a regal pace as if walking into a ballroom and calmly lifted her hand in a little wave. Martin let go and ran up.

"How's it going for ya?" he said brightly.

"Hey! Glad you could make it!" Matt said, patting Martin on the back. He turned to Kitty who was just strolling up. He reached out and took her hand.

"Kitty, what a pleasure to see you again," Matt said kissing her hand. "It's so early I could understand if you hadn't made it out."

Kitty giggled. Martin wondered what had got into her. His mother never giggled. Coming to think about it, she didn't smile much either.

"I wouldn't miss it for the world, Mateo. Such an occasion!" she answered, batting her eyelids. What was it with adults? Why couldn't they speak like normal people?

Just then Les walked passed. Martin tugged at his sleeve and Les stopped, but he didn't seem to recognise Martin at all. He looked distracted and moody. Matt reached out and slapped Les's shoulder.

"Hey, kid!" he said laughing. "Wake up. Rise and shine!"

Les smiled wanly. "Sorry. I guess I'm not awake yet."

"You OK?" asked Matt, eying Les closely.

"Yeah. Sure. I'm a little nervous, but what the hell!" He laughed, but Martin could tell he didn't think anything was particularly funny.

"Everything's great. Take it easy!" said Matt grinning.

Les nodded. He turned to Martin and smiled.

"So you've come to wave us off?" he asked. Martin nodded happily.

Their conversation was cut off by the tooting of a loud horn. They looked up and saw Dr Moloney drive up. The car seemed crammed with people. Miss Aileen stepped out of the front seat, complaining loudly of her sciatica while from the back spilled Con O'Leary, Ruth, Dennis, and Tony the barman. Martin's mother smirked as she saw Ruth and Dennis emerge from the car hand in hand.

"I wonder if her mother knows what she's up to?" she sniffed under her breath.

"Kitty, don't be so harsh," said Matt in a soft voice that turned her frown to a smile. "They're young and in love." Martin made a face. His mother was beaming, Les was blushing, and Matt's eyes had gone all funny. Martin decided to go and have a closer look at one of the army trucks up the road. It was more interesting by far.

"'Tis a fine day for it," said Con walking up and down to stretch his legs. "Fine and dry."

"'Tis very low," added Miss Aileen in a worried voice." Will they ever take off with the clouds so low? I thought they couldn't fly in fog?"

"'Tis mist. It should clear off once the sun starts shining," commented Tony the barman. He was squinting up at the sky, shading his eyes from the long streaks of light piercing the clouds above.

"Still, they make an awful noise," continued Miss Aileen looking out at the plane. "I should have stayed in town. The noise nearly drove me demented the last time they tried."

"Go on Aileen, you know you couldn't miss it," said Dr Moloney affectionately.

The little group stood discreetly apart from the bustle like the privileged guests that they were, not wanting to get in anyone's way, yet straining to hear what was going on. A few of the crew noticed them and ambled over.

The first one to reach them was the Chief. He was looking no worse for the long nights he had spent drinking in the hotel bar. His dark copper-colour skin gleamed and he looked sharp and dapper in his fresh uniform, his cap cocked jauntily to one side. He went straight up to Tony and gave him a big bear hug.

"So there you are, you devil Irishman! It's good to see you! I'm glad you could make it."

"How could I not say goodbye to my best customer?" Tony teased. The Chief cuffed him playfully and the two men jostled each other laughing.

"You've got my address, remember?" said Tony.

"I most certainly do," said the Chief.

"And you said you'd write."

"I believe I made a solemn vow," said the Chief laughing. "Though I must admit some of last night is a little hazy!"

"You certainly looked hazy when we carried you up the stairs," joked Matt, walking up. "Whadya say Tony? Is this guy putting on weight or what? It must be all that great food at your hotel."

Miss O'Donovan tittered with pleasure. "Well, I certainly hope you all enjoyed your stay," she said.

"It was a delightful break from the drudgery of army life, especially army rations," said the Chief. "And the company was far better!"

"Well, we all hope you can visit us again sometime," added Miss Aileen, shaking the Chief's hand vigorously.

"You never know, ma'am, I just might do that."

Miss Aileen turned her attention to Matt who was talking with Dr Moloney. She took his hand in both of hers and patted it for a long time. Her eyes swam and her face went even more pink. She spoke in a hushed whisper, bowing her head as if she were in church.

"I am still so sad about poor Tojo," she said, shaking her head. "I can tell you I'd not have felt sorrier about that dotey pet dying like that if he were my own. I'm so sorry you had to lose him in our establishment."

"Miss Aileen, I can honestly say that he died a very happy monkey. And I can't think of a better place to have passed on," Matt said solemnly with only a hint of a smile. "You were magnificent. I don't know how to thank you."

"'Twas nothing, really," said Miss Aileen modestly but she clearly was well pleased.

"That runway is a fine bit of engineering," stated Dr Moloney.

"A marvel," agreed Con O'Leary. "But tell me, lads, do ya think its long enough?"

"To tell the truth we could use an extra hundred yards," said Matt. "It's just about the minimum required."

"But don't you worry," said Les, who had just come up. "Our pilot Charlie Hansen is a real ace. He'll get us off the ground this time."

"We'll fly this baby out all right," said Matt. "We'd better. I'm not sure I could take any more parties! And anyway, I've traded all my bottles of rum. Ain't that right, Tony?"

"Best trade I ever did," said Tony nodding.

Les took Dennis's hand. "Thanks for everything. You were great."

"O-say ere-way ou-yay!" declared Dennis proudly.

"You've really caught on," said Les smiling. "So now you can speak Pig Latin."

"'Tis great. We have a secret language now!" said Ruth. She took Les's arm and whispered in his ear. "I saw Imelda yesterday. She was leaving. Did ya get a chance to say goodbye?"

Les nodded. "We said goodbye yesterday," he said sadly. "She promised to write."

"Never you worry. She's sound. I know she'll write," said Ruth. She reached out and took Les's hand. Her voice was strong and clear. "I wish you well, Les Wagner."

Les shook her hand and then moved on up the small line of people saying goodbye.

"We'll miss yer singing," teased Con O'Leary, "but not too much, like."

Dr Moloney reached out his hand and shook Les warmly.

"Mind yerself," he said, his voice a bit shaky with emotion. "You all mind yerselves over there."

He regained his composure and waved at Beau who was sitting apart from everyone on the wall. He'd been sitting there since they'd driven out to the marsh, smoking one cigarette after the other and looking over at a small ridge of trees on the opposite hill. Beau noticed them looking his way and came to join them.

"How's my patient doing?" asked Dr Moloney.

"I'm fine," said Beau, shaking the doctor's hand. "Thanks to your kind care, that is."

Beau shook hands all around, saying a word or two to each person, and formally bowing to the ladies present. He started to walk off and then turned around and took Dr Moloney aside.

"I wonder if I could ask you a favour?" he said formally.

"Of course you can!" declared the doctor.

"I hate to impose, but I never got a chance to say goodbye to Mrs Burke. I was wondering if you could be so kind as to convey my regards to her and to thank her for her hospitality."

Dr Moloney took a long look at Beau, but he said nothing. He nodded his head sharply and grunted.

"Of course I will, man. Of course I will."

The pitch of the engines went up a tone. The plane

was throbbing. The mist was almost gone and a pale yellow light filled the marsh. Big fat clouds hung like a giant tent in the sky above. Martin pushed through the circle of people all saying goodbye and shaking hands.

"Right, lads!" said Barry Kingston rubbing his hands together as he came up to them. "It's time to go. Yeer pilot asked me to get ye all sorted."

The noise level rose as everyone said goodbye all over again. Martin could see that the Irish soldiers were lining up on the road. His excitement knew no bounds. He searched for Matt, peeking through the forest of legs, and found him standing off to one side with his mother.

"Goodbye, so," he said, holding out his hand.

Matt got down on one knee so that his face was level with Martin's.

"You take care of your mama. OK? I know I can count on you. Am I right?"

Martin looked at his mother. Her eyes were gleaming, and he thought he heard her stifle a sniffle. He nodded to Matt but found that he had a big lump in his throat.

"And you take good care of yourself," he said standing and taking Kitty's mother hand in his. "Don't forget to write. It'll mean a lot to me when I'm over there."

"It'll mean a lot to me too, Mateo," she answered, her eyes glistening even more.

Some of the crew were lining up in front of the Irish soldiers and calling for the others to join them. Charlie Hansen shook hands with the Irish Army captain. They stepped back into their respective lines and saluted smartly.

Miss Aileen sniffled loudly and then snorted into her oversize white linen handkerchief.

Martin felt a big lump in his throat grow bigger as he watched the crew of *T'Ain't a Bird* cross the marsh. He counted them one by one. Ten crew members and one passenger, eleven in all. Before each man ducked around the tail, he stopped and waved.

Cries of "Goodbye! Safe home!" rang out and Martin yelled so hard he knew he would be hoarse for days.

Matt waved the longest, giving a special salute to Martin and his mother. The last one to disappear was the one called Beau. The passenger fella. He waved at them all and then stopped and looked out for a few seconds at Inchydoney Island before ducking around the tail.

The plane sat there for what seemed like an eternity. No one spoke but Martin knew everyone was wondering if something had gone wrong. If this was another false start. Then the engines roared louder than they ever had before. Martin threw his hands up over his ears and noticed that most of the people on the road had done the same.

"'Tis moving!" screamed Martin. "The tail is moving. Look! The wings are too!"

His mother put her arm around his shoulder and held him a little too tightly, but Martin was too engrossed to care. He watched in fascination as the huge plane moved ever so slowly on to the runway. It advanced a few yards and then stopped.

Then, unbelievably, the engines screamed louder still and the plane started to move. It was gaining speed as it went. Beyond, about a quarter of a mile away, was the second causeway. Martin realised with horror that they would have to be airborne before they reached the causeway wall.

The tension was unbearable. The plane was speeding down, heading straight for the wall. Gasps were heard as it hurtled down the narrow metal mesh. Someone was praying a *Hail Mary* out loud, and Martin found himself echoing the words.

Then, with only fifty yards to spare, the great green giant lifted. It cleared the wall by no more than the height of a two-up-two-down cottage.

A wild cheer went up from the people on the

road. Martin's mother was waving her little white handkerchief wildly. Martin looked around and saw that most of them were crying.

Martin climbed up on to the wall. He continued to jump and yell and wave goodbye, long after the plane had disappeared into the grey clouds above Ardfield.

Chapter Twenty-Eight

• ◆ •

John Joe O'Mahoney stopped on the doorstep and tried to balance the chamberpot again before stepping outside. The night's collection sloshed ominously, and John Joe did not want to spill it. His ma had gone mental when he'd slipped one morning and dropped the entire contents on the kitchen floor.

John Joe held his nose as he emptied it out. He hated doing it and wondered when he would be old enough never to have to do it again, like his father and older brothers. He shivered as a light breeze came in from the sea. He had slipped on his trousers over his nightshirt and his feet were wet and cold from the dew. He'd better make sure his ma didn't catch him barefoot. What with his "fragile constitution" and all.

Feeling a call of nature again, John Joe decided to relieve himself on the hedge. It was a dull morning with low clouds, but far off above the sea a thin blue line of sky shone. John Joe looked forward to the breakfast he knew was at this very moment being cooked on the fire.

A faint noise to his left made him stop and listen.

It didn't take long for him to recognise it. It was the plane! The plane was flying!

John Joe waited as the sound grew louder.

All of Ardfield had talked of nothing else since it had landed less than a week before. He had been to visit the B-17 bomber in the marsh with his father the very first day, and had carefully copied out the number and markings on the tail. By the light of his lamp he had sat up in bed drawing it over and over until he was satisfied it was correct.

John Joe had carefully measured his drawing to scale, putting in the top turret and ball turrets, and the wonderful nose turret. As he drew, he often stopped to try and imagine what it would be like to be sitting in there flying 10,000 feet above the ground.

Finally he had carefully written *T'Ain't a Bird* on the nose and 90-2340 on the tail below a little yellow triangle. He had pasted the picture on to a bit of cardboard and pinned it over his bed.

The noise was getting louder. It seemed to be just behind a huge grey cloud. John Joe raised himself up to try and catch a glimpse of it. He heard his mother calling him from the kitchen but he didn't move. Breakfast could wait.

Then, as if by magic, the B-17 emerged from the cloud and flew right over his head. It was as if the little picture on his wall had come to life right in front of his very eyes. John Joe could hardly contain himself. He could see a little figure behind the cockpit window. He could even see a silhouette in the nose.

When his mother came out to see what was happening she found him with his trousers down around his ankles, still waving wildly, bits of broken chamberpot strewn around his bare, wet feet.

Mick O'Sullivan waited at the sea wall and hoped the throbbing in his head would stop soon. He tried hard not look at the swirling water below. The waves crashing against the lighthouse embankment were turning his stomach. He had no one to blame but himself, as herself had pointed out repeatedly both last night when he'd staggered in and this morning when he'd limped out of bed. The woman had no pity.

He was actually glad to be on duty at the look-out

post in Galley Head. It only seemed right. He'd spotted it first when it had landed and now he would be the last person to see it before it left Ireland. And who knows, maybe the sea air would clear his head as well.

Mick chuckled to himself remembering the mighty craic they'd had in O'Donovan's bar. The dancing, and the music. And the monkey! He would never forget the sight of that monkey laid out on the bed, or of Tony carrying him on the tea tray through town. He would remember those nights for as long as he lived. It was worth the sore head and sour stomach.

Mick was checking his watch when he first heard the rumble in the clouds. The plane was flying up the coast. He knew they'd be looking out for the lighthouse before banking off over to sea.

He needed no binoculars to spot it. As the plane flew closer he was again taken aback at how big the damn thing was. There was no need for exaggeration with this story. That plane was as big as a mansion.

Mick pulled his cap off his head and waved, ignoring the pounding in his skull. He wished them all well and said a quck prayer for them silently.

The plane seemed to hang for a minute overhead, then it slowly started banking left. As it flew out towards the horizon, Mick saw it wag its wings ever so slightly. He watched until his eyes smarted from the glare and he could not even make out the smallest speck.

Mick took out his little notebook with the pencil attached to it with a bit of string. But he didn't write anything. Instead he flipped back a few pages until he found the entry he was looking for:

April 7, 1943 12:37 Large aircraft sighted flying Seven Heads to Galley Head in the direction of Mizen Head. Seen returning over Galley Head and heading back from whence it came to the east. The aircraft seems to be losing altitude and may attempt to land.

Mick carefully ripped out the page and crumpled it up. He watched it as it fell twirling into the sea and was immediately lost in the swirling froth.

The entry would remain typed up in some army file in Dublin, marked "Strictly Confidential". Mick had no doubt that the people of Clonakilty would still talk of the time the B-17 landed in White's Marsh and had taken off again for years to come. But there would be no mention in the newspaper, no record of it open to the public view.

Officially, as far as the governments of Ireland, Great Britain and the United States of America were concerned, it had simply never happened.

Epilogue

◆━◆

Mary got the last letter five years after she had sat on the hill and looked out to sea as the roaring of the bomber's engines had filled the sky.

The first year alone took up a entire shoe box. She kept them bundled by year, each bundle tied with a ribbon, each letter unanswered.

At first the letters were full only with his love and longing for her. They had come at least once a week, sometimes two or three at the same time. Then after the first year, Beau's letters did not arrive quite so often, but when they did they were long and witty and full of amusing little stories.

He wrote about life in New Orleans, the parties he went to and the trips he took with his father. Sometimes they were from New York city, or even further afield.

One summer after the war was over she received a postcard from Paris, then one from Rome, and finally one from London. Her heart had jumped at the thought that he was only a short skip across the sea.

Mary knew each letter by heart. If ever she felt a little lonely, or needed a treat, she would take her box out and read one at random. That always filled her with love and well-being and the wonderful scent of lemons.

Beau never asked her to join him again. He always finished by saying that he knew she would not write back but that his love remained undiminished. He had made his peace with Mary's decision and respected it. If ever she needed him, she knew that he would be there for her.

The last letter arrived a year after she thought he'd stopped writing.

Beau's elegant handwriting, full of fancy loops and swirls, fairly covered the front of it. Mary held the writing against her breasts and remembered Beau's soft southern accent, his hands caressing her, the smell of him, the taste of him, the sweet nothings he had whispered in her ear.

A letter from Imelda arrived at the same time. Mary opened Imelda's letter and placed Beau's on the sideboard.

Imelda was full of news about the baby. They'd

called her Mary, and Les was delighted with the little girl, though Imelda wrote jokingly that she thought her sisters were more than enough girls for one household.

Mary had a separate drawer for all of Imelda's letters. They started with the little note she had recieved the day after the plane had left. Mary had cried when she read the childish scrawl on the torn scrap of paper. Imelda's letters had improved in leaps and bounds over the years. Now she wrote reams with a tight clean fist.

Mary had worried about Imelda every day, hoping everything would turn out right, until she received a letter saying that Imelda had booked a passage for herself and the girls to America and would probably be gone by the time Mary read it.

Only then had Imelda told her of what had become of Tommy. Mary read with amazement about how Matt and Les had smuggled Tommy into the plane, right under the noses of the Irish army. How Tommy had hung around the base in England learning to be a mechanic, while Les flew bombing missions over Germany.

Then the wonderful news had come that they had all been reunited in Wisconsin and that Les and Imelda had married, with Tommy giving her away and all the little girls as flower girls.

And now they had a baby girl. Mary smiled as she tucked the sheets of paper back into the envelope.

Mary picked up the second envelope.

She knew what the letter would say. She felt she knew Beau as if she'd made him. He would be writing to tell her that he was getting married, or at least engaged. In his last letter he had hinted that he was seeing someone. A young girl he'd met at a ball in New York. Mary hoped he'd chosen her. She sounded pretty and smart, and she shared Beau's passion for music. Most of all, she sounded kind.

Mary opened the letter. It was only three thin pieces of paper that rustled softly and smelled of violets. Mary skipped to the last page. She knew what she was looking for.

. . . If ever you need me, you must write. I know you'll shake your head and flash your eyes, but if you need money just send a note and I'll cable it through. I don't want to think of you ever doing without, or suffering in any way.

Remember, my darling, that you will stay in my heart forever. Have a thought for us when the moon is full. I do.

I will love you always. With all my love and affection,

Beau.

She did not read the rest of it.

She had read all she needed to know.

Mary tucked the letter back in the envelope and placed it on the top of the little bundles tied up with ribbon. In her heart she felt the love she had for Beau burning brightly, filling her with a sense of calm. Mary kissed the tips of her fingers and touched the envelope before closing the box.

Mary always wrote back to Imelda immediately and she sat down to that now. Over the years she had told Imelda all about her life on Inchydoney Island.

She'd told her about the farm and how well it was doing. She told her about the new calves, and when the potatoes were in bloom. She wrote to Imelda about the trouble she had with the farm-hands, and about the gales that ripped the roofs off the sheds and brought down the big pine at the top of the hill.

She wrote to Imelda about the changing seasons on the Island and the changes in town.

Imelda had been sad to hear that Dr Moloney had passed on and delighted that Tony was saving money to go and visit the Chief in Oklahoma. Mary even wrote to her when Con O'Leary, who had been calling out to visit quite often, had felt obliged to ask for Mary's hand in marriage and about how delighted he'd seemed when she had refused. They now shared an easy friendship that did not need to include any romance.

Mary wrote to Imelda about this and that, the great and the small. She'd told her practically everything about her life as the years went by.

Except one thing.

She never told her about the boy born just under a year after they had all left. The wonderful boy who lay sleeping in his bed, his dark black curls spread out on the pillow, whose wicked grin and quick wit were her pride and her joy and who had, along with his father's love, made her life more complete and fulfilled than she had ever dreamed it could be.

The fire cackled merrily in the grate. The kitchen was filled with smell of freshly baked bread and the salty sea breeze coming in off the estuary. It was going to be glorious day.

Mary hurried to get her letter finished before the boy woke up. After their chores were done she would dress and go into town with him to post it.

Author's note:

At around one o'clock in the afternoon of April 7th, 1943, a B-17 Flying Fortress bomber, christened *T'Ain't a Bird* landed in White's Marsh, Clonakilty, with only three minutes of fuel left. On board were a crew of ten men, one passenger, a monkey and 36 bottles of rum. They had taken off that morning from Marrakesh en route to join the 8th Airforce at a base in England. A storm and a misleading radio report threw them off-course (there was no radar on the plane).

The crew stayed in O'Donovan's Hotel for about four days before being taken by lorry up to the border and handed over to the RAF. Over a month later a portable runway was brought down to Clonakilty and the plane was flown out to join its crew in England. *T'Ain't a Bird* flew its first, and last, mission in June 1943.

Miraculously the entire crew, along with the passenger, all survived the war after flying many combat missions. The monkey, alas, did not fare so well. Tojo died during the crew's stay in Clonakilty and was given a funeral, with full military honours in the back of O'Donovan's Hotel.

Most people who know Clonakilty have heard about the landing. Photographs of the B-17 still hang on walls. Everyone knows that Eddie Collins was the first man to greet the crew. Tojo, the monkey, is still remembered. Stories and rumours abound (the thirty-six bottles of rum have grown to thirty-six cases in local legend). I listened to them all. Some I used, others I didn't, mostly I just made it up. I hope I will be excused when I bent the facts to suit the fiction (yes, I know they couldn't have built a runway in just one day, so don't bother to write and tell me!).

Three of *T'Ain't a Bird*'s crew still survive: Jim Stapleton, the co-pilot; Arlie Arneson, the waist-gunner, and Guy Tice, the top-turret gunner on whom the character of Les Wagner is loosely based.

The characters and events described in *Only a Paper Moon* are entirely ficticious. I have borrowed a lot of local names to amuse myself. I thank those who gave me permission to do so, and hope that those I didn't ask will not feel offended.

Guy Tice visited Clonakilty again in 1997, fifty-four years after *T'Ain't a Bird* landed. He stayed at O'Donovan's Hotel.